"YOU DID WHAT!" CAROL EXPLODED

Ethan's tone was gloating. "I simply informed your employer that you wouldn't be returning and ordered your belongings shipped home. All I didn't do was kiss lover boy goodbye for you."

"You couldn't have! What gives you the right—I" Tears of angry frustration suddenly flooded her eyes.

"Don't tempt me to tell you," Ethan warned, pulling her close. But he didn't kiss her and she wasn't prepared for the jolting surge of longing that echoed in the wild beating of her heart. "You don't have forever to come to terms with what's between us," Ethan added. "In fact, you haven't much time at all."

Carol turned her panic-filled face away from him, to hide the rawness of her feelings. Something in her wanted him to claim her—now.

AND NOW...

SUPERROMANCES

Worldwide Library is proud to present a
sensational new series of modern love stories —
SUPERROMANCES

Written by masters of the genre, these longer,
sensuous and dramatic novels are truly in keeping
with today's changing life-styles. Full of intriguing
conflicts, the heartaches and delights of true love,
SUPERROMANCES are absorbing stories —
satisfying and sophisticated reading that lovers
of romance fiction have long been waiting for.

SUPERROMANCES
Contemporary love stories for the woman of today!

JEAN DeCoto
HEART'S AWAKENING

A SUPERROMANCE FROM
WORLDWIDE
TORONTO · LONDON · NEW YORK · SYDNEY

Published August 1982

First printing June 1982

ISBN 0-373-70029-6

Copyright © 1982 by Jean DeCoto. All rights reserved.
Philippine copyright 1982. Australian copyright 1982.
Except for use in any review, the reproduction or utilization of
this work in whole or in part in any form by any electronic,
mechanical or other means, now known or hereafter invented,
including xerography, photocopying and recording, or in any
information storage or retrieval system, is forbidden without
the permission of the publisher, Worldwide Library,
225 Duncan Mill Road, Don Mills, Ontario, Canada M3B 3K9.

All the characters in this book have no existence outside the
imagination of the author and have no relation whatsoever to
anyone bearing the same name or names. They are not even
distantly inspired by any individual known or unknown to the
author, and all the incidents are pure invention.

The Superromance trademark, consisting of the word
SUPERROMANCE, and the Worldwide trademark, consisting of
a globe and the word WORLDWIDE in which the letter "o" is
represented by a depiction of a globe, are trademarks of
Worldwide Library.

Printed in U.S.A.

CHAPTER ONE

Outside, the icy wind peppered the windows of the luxury apartment high above a fashionable Chicago street. Festive sounds swirled about Carol Charbonnet as she sat contemplating another bleak, cold season. Curled in the corner of the softly yielding sofa, Jim's rich brown hair gleaming in the lamplight where his head rested on the cushion near her knee, she thought how different these last two winters were from all her winters past.

Her jewel-green eyes focused on the fireplace festooned in boughs of fall foliage, the oranges and reds and varying browns in competition with colorful ears of partially shucked Indian corn. Her thoughts moved from the future season to the unknown person who had wandered the autumnal woodlands gathering branches that had ultimately made their way to this particular setting, doubtlessly passing through the hands of some very artistic florist before they came to rest on this ornate mantelpiece. Her gaze dropped to the hearth and the startlingly bright pumpkin nestled in a sheaf of cornstalks. She knew that pumpkin would never reach the dinner table, just as no glowing oak limbs would ever smoke the elegant marble facade from which electric logs sent simulated fire shadows against gleaming brass andirons.

Although Thanksgiving was still a few weeks away, the apartment was filled with touches and splashes of the upcoming holiday. Slim orange tapers vainly attempted to reproduce the intensity of the color of the pumpkin as they flickered on the highly polished cocktail table where her host, Maxwell Thompson, pondered his next move.

The touch of Jim's hand on her trim ankle brought her back to the men seated on the floor, chessboard on the table between them. Like two children they had slipped away from the party to take a stolen moment in preferred company, and she had followed. She, too, enjoyed the sanctuary of Maxwell's study, a quiet isle in the din of preseasonal activities.

"Come on, Carol. Leave the whiz kids to their game and join the real party," a slightly inebriated guest hailed her from the partially opened doorway. She gave a lazy smile of denial, making no move toward the more boisterous enclaves of the Thompsons' guests.

What good friends she had made—Maxwell Thompson, his wife, Helen, and Jim...dear, dear Jim. She knew they were all curious, but no one pressed. They simply accepted what she had to give and allowed her to accept in return. Carol leaned deeper into the soft sofa, her eyes fluttering closed against nagging fatigue. It was a good tired.

During the past two years she had proven her worth over and over to Maxwell, head of the Thompson Construction Company. It had not taken Maxwell long to realize the expertise of the attractive young woman who had answered his advertisement for a trainee in drafting, just as it had taken only a few minutes for his personnel director to realize that this particular draftsman needed no training.

From the first it had been a steady climb upward, and soon Carol's name had reached the main office. Maxwell had asked only once where she had gained so much knowledge about a traditionally male-oriented business, and why she had not proclaimed her skills. She didn't answer. Thereafter he unquestioningly acknowledged what she offered his business, rewarded her accordingly and still wondered at her background. It had come as a surprise when, after months of employment, he discovered his pretty draftsman had a degree in structural engineering from the prestigious Tulane University in New Orleans. That was the way it had been with her; the only information known had accidentally worked its way to the surface through an expression, a word, a mannerism as she climbed the company ladder.

Nothing had pleased Maxwell more than her becoming involved with Jim Harding, his personal lawyer and friend. Carol and Jim were his kind of people, a matched pair. They were both intelligent, well schooled in the social arts and quietly aggressive. He especially liked Carol's serene beauty, the soft honey-colored hair that swept her shoulders in heavy silken swaths, the contrast of her startlingly green eyes beneath dark lashes.

Never had he seen her full mouth in a petulant pout. Most frequently she presented a glimpse of even white teeth in a quiet smile, and many a lingering masculine glance noticed. Helen, his wife of almost twenty years, called Carol a long-legged thoroughbred, but then buxom Helen was envious of the trim waist and slim hips of the younger woman. Sometimes when Helen was feeling a little jaded, she criticized the soft Southern accent, saying Carol Charbonnet should not be wearing a hard hat and carrying a calculator but sheltering beneath a fringed parasol while sipping mint juleps.

The neat line of silk-clad leg distracted Maxwell only momentarily, but it was long enough for him to make a foolish move, and his queen now sat in check. Since Jim obviously had him beaten, he lifted from the floor cushion, bowed to Jim's rising form and growled a conceding, "Uncle."

His glance flowed tellingly over Carol. "We both know you used unsportsmanlike weapons," he taunted Jim in mock anger as Carol veiled her eyes in equally mock modesty at his teasing implication.

He stretched his long arms over his head. "Oh, well, it's time I rejoined my own party, anyway. Come on, you two, put in your appearance at the watering hole before Helen sends out a search crew." Straightening his tie, he ambled toward the other room, pulling the door closed behind him.

In one graceful motion Carol rose, standing only a few inches shorter than Jim. She reached for the scattered chessmen, replacing them in readiness for the next match, but Jim stilled the hand that sought an elusive pawn that had rolled beneath the dried leaves and pinecones of the seasonal centerpiece.

"Sometimes in your life you just have to walk away from a mess—especially one created by other people," he lightly chided. Often he called her "Tilly Tidy" because of her habit of never leaving anything out of place.

Sometimes... you just have to walk away.... Carol shook her head as a memory came stalking through the back of her mind. Her long honeyed tresses swayed against her cheek at the movement of denial against that intruding thought.

"What's wrong, darling?" Jim placed a caressing hand against her pale cheek, searching her eyes for some explanation for the pained expression that fled across her brow. "Are you tired? We can leave now if you like." He placed the other hand beneath her hair and began gently massaging the nape of her neck. Automatically she leaned into the relaxing knead, closing her eyes against his penetrating look.

It wasn't fair to him, she knew that. But she didn't want to talk about the ghosts, not tonight, perhaps not ever. Neither did she want Jim to get the wrong idea about other things. She needed his closeness, his friendship and warmth; she didn't want the other emotions she had begun to notice developing in him. Sometimes she wondered if she would ever be ready to make another permanent emotional commitment to anyone.

Jim repeated his quiet question. "Do you want me to take you home?" Carol effectively disentangled herself from the touch of the tall muscular man by reaching down to brush imaginary creases from her cocoa-brown suede skirt.

"No, I think we should join the others for a while, anyway. I could use a drink to warm me." Her eyes sought the darkened window. "This howling wind makes me feel the cold more deeply. Maybe a nice drink would help." She smiled warmly and began moving toward the door.

The difference in the den they had just vacated and the long living room they now entered was amazing. Just as the other chamber with its quiet colors, large softly upholstered furniture and expanses of mellow wood was pure Maxwell, this showplace was totally vivacious Helen Thompson. It was all glass and polished chrome. What wasn't white was silver, punctuated by startling accents of black or solid red, and Carol hated the room. The angular lines offended her, and the brittleness of the silver and coolness of the white echoed the colors of the northern climate so alien to her blood, which had been sun bred and sun nurtured.

She led the way to the bar, a metallic study of geometric design. Carol recognized the bartender as a young man who worked part-time for the firm, a struggling student taking work wherever he could find it, and she admired his spirit and especially his industry. A familiar type to her, he was just the kind of temporary help Claud would have hired during the summer and the long semester breaks.

Again the memory strutted into forbidden recollection. She paused mid stride, nearly causing Jim to bump into her. This time she schooled her features in time to ward off further inquiry, quickly stepping forward as if nothing had happened.

She smiled and greeted the youth by name. "Good evening, Joel. How is the fall term developing? Were you pleased with your mid-semester grades?"

She was rewarded by his big grin. "Fantastic, Miss Charbonnet, the best yet. Thanks to that tutoring from you, I really blew their minds in design class with my project. I wish there was some way to repay you." Admiration emanated from him.

She sensed Jim's immediate and unfounded jealousy as his grip on her elbow tensed. She experienced an unwarranted guilt at offending him in any way, but habit was hard to break. Claud had always run his company on a first-name basis. Of course, he had always been Mr. Guerard, but he knew the name of every employee and most of their family members. The firm and all its men stood together. Even when....

The smile froze on her face.

Why did everything keep surfacing tonight? Tonight wasn't a special night. It wasn't a birthday, a feast day or even an anniversary of some family or business accomplishment. Those were the times when she usually had to fight the memories the hardest.

"You can repay me with a glass of champagne." She watched the youth's work-marked hands as he handled the delicate crystal and unconsciously compared them to the well-tended hands of Jim as he reached for the sparkling wine and the Manhattan cocktail he had requested.

She allowed Jim to move her away from the bar and into a circle where the latest theatrical hit was being discussed. Drifting along with the conversation, she laughed at the amusing anecdotes an effeminate man told of mix-ups in tickets and dates, all the while trying to ignore the plaintive cry of the prewinter gale blowing across Lake Michigan as it battered the thin shield of glass separating her from the bitter cold.

It seemed as if a never ending flow of guests moved in and out of the Thompsons' apartment. Even though it was after midnight, people were still arriving as others left. During a lull in the conversation around her, Carol whispered to Jim her desire to leave, and he promptly gathered their outdoor garb from the heap piled in the guest room.

Together they bade Helen and Maxwell goodnight, Jim's proprietary hand on her elbow. She accepted Helen's gregarious and totally sincere kiss on her cheek and Maxwell's equally sincere brush of lips across her forehead. She had not failed to note the way the Thompsons were pairing her and Jim. But how could she discourage it without hurting anyone? She valued their friendship, and she could never intentionally hurt Jim. During the past weeks it had been a problem about which she had spent increasingly more time thinking.

In the hall Jim held the heavy woolen coat for her to slip her arms into. "You always suffer from the cold so much, Carol. You should get a fur for this kind of weather. Maxwell pays you well enough, and you would be especially glamorous in a pastel mink." It was a statement, neither prying nor reproachful, not even meant to be flattering.

"I already have one." It slipped out before she knew what she was saying.

"What?" Immediately a closed expression replaced her usually open honest features, an expression he had encountered before. "You should wear it, Carol. It would be warmer than this."

She fixed her eyes on a spot over his shoulder as he shrugged into his own fleece-lined overcoat. "Yes, I guess I really should."

She turned toward the elevator, the set of her shoulders denying further conversation, and Jim had known her long enough to realize the futility of trying to get her to talk about anything she considered private.

Their cab struggled against the wind. "You're pretty lucky, you know," the driver injected into their silence. "There's been some talk of calling the cab fleet in. If the street conditions worsen at all, we'll be shut down. Nothing more dangerous than ice on the pavement." He paused for some response before adding, "Already closed the airport. It's not a fit night for anything but crawling under an electric blanket."

Both passengers ignored his attempt at friendliness as each contemplated problems far more personal than the weather. Jim would never understand her reticence to discuss her life before she had come to Maxwell's firm. Many times he had led her to the edge of disclosure only to have her effectively steer him away. He sensed there must be some man in her background, yet she spurned his romantic overtures with virginal denial. That alone made him believe that man never to have been her lover.

Though it had not been totally ethical, when Maxwell mentioned her degree, Jim had personally typed a request on his firm's stationery and sent for her university records. To his dismay, much of the ordinary information, information that he particularly wanted, was blacked out. With all the laws of privacy in disclosure, he needed her written consent to release the background information she had supplied the university during her attendance there.

What he had received from Tulane University had been her date of birth, grades, minor health records, three letters of recommendation from professors and deans, and a copy of her diploma. There had been no indication that she had been on scholarship, so someone in her past must have had a fat wallet to afford the tuition to the private institution. Who had paid that tuition? There was no employment record, so he didn't think she had worked her way through. Besides, students who had to work usually went to one of the state-subsidized colleges, not the more expensive and exclusive private university.

And there was the scene tonight about the coat. Anyone who could possibly afford it had furs to fight the biting cold of the Chicago winter. Carol professed to have a fur but didn't wear it. Why? That did not make sense to him. She was always commenting on the cold, always anxious for warm days, obviously longing for a milder climate. Could she have received the coat from a lover, and now it brought too many unhappy memories? He just could not believe that. She might send out an aura of social graces, but her demeanor bespoke sexual inexperience. Men did not lay out that kind of money for sweet kisses. Whoever or whatever else she was, she certainly was a lady of mystery, and that mystery gnawed at him.

In the darkness of the cab he felt her reach out and give his hand a gentle squeeze. He slipped his arm around her shoulders, drawing her slim form against him. Her reaching out had been a wordless plea for patience, and she was well worth waiting for.

The cab crunched to a stop on the frosty pavement. In the lobby Jim briefly kissed her lips, promising to call the next day, then hurried out to the waiting cab.

Carol watched until the taxi pulled away before turning to the row of brass-plated mailboxes. From the one marked with her first initial and last name, she removed the day's accumulation. As she stood waiting for the elevator, she glanced through the stack—a circular from an American Indian charity, an advertisement from an insurance company, a bill from her dentist, the utility bill, a journal and a cream-colored envelope that stopped the breath in her throat. Great curled capital letters began each word, creeping in a spindly black scrawl across the rich vellum. There was no need to turn to the engraved return address on the back flap. She knew the street address on historic St. Charles Avenue only too well.

Shuffling the ominous letter into the stack, she entered the now waiting elevator. There she leaned against the back wall, her knees too weak to hold her. So now they knew where she was. She tried to steel herself with the idea that she had been self-sufficient for two years; they could not get her back now. She had proved herself. Claud had said they didn't need her then, now she could return the insult. She did not need them anymore. She would begin by not reading the letter. She could and would ignore whatever was inside.

With these positive thoughts she opened the door to her apartment, her hands still unsteady. The blast of warmed air from the central unit reminded her of the extreme cold outside. After placing the letters and her handbag on the bar separating her tiny but thoroughly efficient kitchen from her only slightly larger living area, she began peeling off the layers of clothing—lined gloves, knit hat, scarf, lined overshoes, the great woolen coat. She opened the small closet in the living room. It was here she kept her coats and other heavy outdoor clothes. As she hung the garments she had worn tonight, her hand brushed the furred softness of an elegant sable hanging against the back wall of the cubicle. The reminder caused her to flinch as if something dreadful had touched her, something yet alive that she had thought dead. She drew back her hand quickly, determined to control the emotional turmoil building inside her soul.

In the pink-and-white bedroom she began removing her other garments. In her meticulous way she placed each item where it belonged before turning to another task. She slipped on a warm velour robe of deep rose, girding it tightly around her slim waist before reaching for the brush on the dressing table. With long deliberate strokes she pulled the silver-backed bristles through the gilded flax of her hair.

She creamed the light makeup from her face before applying a moisturizer. How she hated what the harsh winter did to her skin!

It was no use. Bedtime routines would not make her forget the letter in the other room. Stiltedly she walked back to the counter and stood for some extended moments staring at the familiar handwriting. She turned to the refrigerator and removed a quart of milk. From the cupboard she took instant chocolate and a mug. Soon the steaming hot chocolate rested on the small coffee table before the green velvet sofa, and in her hand she held the letter.

It read more like a telegram, containing no salutation or signature on the single sheet. Nor was there need of either.

"Claud has had a stroke, and hopes of recovery are dim. Come home."

Her thoughts careered through her brain. Questions without answers flowed with lightning swiftness. How could this happen to Claud, the oak of the family forest? To the others, who were slash pine, it was conceivable, but not to strong, indomitable, wind-resistant Claud. Who was tending the firm? Definitely not Claud's sister Antoinette, called Tante Nan by the three grandchildren left in Claud's care when both his son and daughter and their spouses had been killed in a private-plane crash. Tante Nan was a crippled old lady who might know the intricacies of organizing a debut and all the protocol of a Mardi Gras ball, but cement and blueprints were outside her concept of reality. Nan could line up seventeen pieces of sterling flatware without consulting an etiquette book but had not once thought of the placement of an iron girder.

Carol's cousin, René? Impossible. Spineless René was only happy at his drawing board, creating the fantasy floats for the endless Mardi Gras parades. When Claud had finally accepted that the least significant of his hourly workers had more concern for Guerard Construction than had his grandson, he had arranged for the last of the Guerard line to work for the biggest float company in the city, and there René had flourished. Claud had tried convincing himself that the designing and building of parade floats was equal to the building of hospitals, office buildings, grand hotels. He hadn't succeeded.

That left René's sister, Eva. Eva Guerard was "La Belle Dame Sans Merci" in the flesh, an elfin child as evil as she was beautiful. She was Tante Nan's social heir, a Guerard to inflame the society pages of the great Southern newspapers. Never would Eva do anything so mundane as work, even if she knew how. The only time she had ever appeared at the Poydras Street offices was to ask for and to receive additions to her already generous allowance. Eva had been Claud's blue-eyed china doll, pampered and shown off.

It had been Carol who had followed in the big footsteps of Claud Guerard. And it would be Carol to come to the call now.

Solemnly she folded the letter and replaced it in the envelope. How much it must have cost Tante Nan to summon her home, to ask anything of her after Carol's fall from grace. And that was what the letter was—a summons, an edict. It was a proclamation having the force of law, and to deny that force was impossible. The tie to her family had not been broken, merely stretched tautly.

With calm deliberation she reached for the phone. If she were lucky, she could be on her way in the afternoon. The Amtrak train would have her in New Orleans by midmorning. She would not risk being weatherbound at O'Hare. After making reservations through a sleepy night clerk, she reached into the closet and extracted two lightweight suitcases. With great selectivity she began to fill them, taking the lighter fall clothing, for there would be no need for all the insulation so necessary in Chicago. Working through the dawn and into the morning, her list of things to do shortened until only two phone calls remained. She had to let them know she was leaving.

Although she didn't want to call Jim or Maxwell, either, her sense of propriety would not allow her simply to walk out. It took Jim several minutes to understand the implications of her call. For a while all she heard was the electronic pulsations of the telephone. Then came one quiet word. "Why?"

She could tell the emotionless question was the result of a great effort on his part, and she had to respond.

"My grandfather is seriously ill. His sister has asked me to come home." In a smaller voice she added, "I have to go." The last was an entreaty for understanding. She had made that same silent appeal so frequently in the past that she knew Jim would not be satisfied this time.

"Carol, when was the last time you communicated with your family?" She guessed the pieces were beginning to fall into place for him. "What happened that drove you here?" Before she could reply, he continued in a stronger tone. "And don't deny your being driven here. God knows, as much as I've tried to warm you, you've been only half a person since I met you."

He had truly deserved more, and now it was probable that she was saying goodbye forever to this man. "A lot of misunderstandings, Jim, a lot of horrible misunderstandings," she responded, in an attempt to skirt the directness of his questions.

"And have these misunderstandings been resolved? Are you returning to have yourself hurt again and maybe this time so much that you can't flee to some strange environment to put the pieces together again?" He had cut to the heart of the thing that had nagged her for the past few hours, and she gave him the same answers she had given herself.

"No, but it doesn't matter anymore. I can't let it matter." If he had been there, he would have seen the determined tilt of her finely shaped chin.

"Will you be back?" This question had an edge of thinly concealed desperation. He was losing her and he knew it, just as he had always known that she would never be completely his.

"I . . . I don't know."

"Carol I—"

She sensed he was about to make a declaration that would only deepen the pain of separation, and to prevent it, she cut into his words. "Let's wait and see what happens. There are so many things I have to do and to think about." She paused before making a pledge she didn't want to make. A clean break would be best, but he had been such a good friend when she had needed someone to lean on. How much more simple it would have been if he had not hoped for more, or if she had been able to give more.

"I'll call you as soon as I'm settled," she promised against her better judgment. Quickly she broke the connection. She couldn't deal with him anymore.

Next she dialed the Thompson apartment, and to Maxwell, who had not yet slept off the result of too many cups of cheer shared with his guests, she made a brief explanation of why she would be away for a few weeks. She told him only that she had a family emergency, then asked him to tell Helen goodbye for her. She deliberately allowed no time for him to ask details before she replaced the receiver, assured that he was back to sleep before she had completed her farewell. She only hoped that he would remember the conversation later.

Now there was only one more problem facing her. Would she find transportation to the train terminal? Last night the driver had sounded grim about the possibilities of the taxis running much longer, and the weather had not improved throughout the day. But a call assured her that she would make her connections. And with that assurance she removed the luxurious sable coat from the closet and closed its dark warmth about her.

WITH MIXED FEELINGS Carol boarded the train, appropriately named "The City of New Orleans." She settled into the coach seat, ignoring the interested looks of the other southbound passengers as she draped the magnificent coat over her like a protective blanket and awaited the train's departure. Absently she stroked the fur's softness.

With no activity to occupy her, it was impossible to keep unwanted thoughts at bay, and her assumed calmness turned to grim dread. On first reading the letter, all she had responded to was a memory of the closeness, the unity, the pride in being a member of the Guerard family. She had forgotten the reason for her leaving.

At dusk, before the settling of the bleak and starless November night, it all came back. The mental image of Claud in a blaze of fury superimposed itself over the sights around her; the memory of his angry voice raised against her covered the sound of a fretful child. Claud had railed with a vehemence she had not known him to possess, his temper soaring to great abusive heights.

"My father and I between us amassed seventy-five years of maintaining a profitable business, with integrity, with total honesty," he shouted. "The people trusted us. And all for some stupid, selfish vanity, some idiotic desire for sables, no less, in a climate that makes the wearing of them ridiculous, everything that I have worked for and everything my father worked for has been destroyed. Destroyed for absolutely nothing." She had cringed as he sent a chair tumbling across the room.

"Has there ever been one thing that any one of you needed that I have not provided for you? Haven't I always seen to the needs of my whole family? To think that my own flesh and blood would betray, cheat, lie—" He had stopped his tirade in mid sentence, as if noticing for the first time that she still stood there. His voice dropped to an acid hiss. "Get out of here, Carol. Get out of my sight this very instant. I don't need you here. I'm not sure I want to see any of you ever again."

That had been the last time she had seen him, even though she had waited at home for nearly a week, finally concluding that he would not return as long as she was there. All her attempts to reach him, to convince him that she was not the one who had betrayed his trust, the Guerard integrity, that she was innocent of the charges leveled against her, had been in vain.

With a little whimper Carol forced the images down, but as always when she did manage to confine the memories, there was one elusive thought that trailed behind like the innocuous tail of a kite. What had been Eva's role in the events of two years ago? And then she had safely boxed everything up again—until the next time. Periodically, like the release of a time lock, every word, every look, every action would parade once more before her.

She turned briefly to the window, but there was little she wished to see, and she allowed the passing towns to flash by her, taking no interest in the sights. She had worked hard the day before, gone straight from the office to the party, and from there she had spent the remainder of her time making her trip preparations. Now the conscious effort of keeping her mind blank along with the rhythmic motion of the train pushed her into the healing sleep she so badly needed.

When she awoke, it was past the conventional dinner hour. The party snack she had nibbled at had long been consumed, and she hoped she was not too late for the dining car. Gathering her coat and handbag, she made her way to the rest room. There she washed her face and applied fresh lip gloss and eye shadow, masking the outward signs of her increasing inner stress.

In the dining car she smiled at the choices on the menu: chicken Louisiane, seafood crepes Louisiane, Creole omelet. It was like the first taste of home. After her meal she moved to the lounge car, which featured a piano bar. There, to the sounds of Southern-flavored music, she indulged in café Mardi Gras, a potent concoction of a half cup of black coffee, a shot of rum and a shot of vodka, topped by a dollop of whipped cream. The taste was very interesting but far too strong for her.

Forcing herself to relax to the music, Carol stayed with the odd collection of insomniacs as the train sped through night-shaded mid-America. By dawn the view was familiar, but when they crossed the Bonnet Carré Spillway, her heart began to thud painfully as she caught glimpses of Lake Pontchartrain through the moss-clad cypress trees. She clasped the arms of her chair in a white-knuckled grip until the sight of the great Superdome glowing in the rays of the morning sun announced the culmination of the trip. Slowly the train crept into Union Passenger Terminal to the accompanying call of the conductor, "New Aah-leens, New Aah-leens."

Her first step down was hesitant. There was only a hint of coolness in the air, not nearly enough to warrant the coat, but she was not the only debarking passenger overdressed for the subtropical climate. She paused before the entrance to the terminal building, allowing the other passengers to surge around her. It was the air that stopped her, air you could feel, smell and almost touch. The humidity wrapped around her with old familiarity, the heaviness of the atmosphere effortlessly bearing with it the smell of the city—the fumes from the cars on the adjacent interstate highway, diesel from trains, the water smells of the surrounding swamplands, lakes, canals, rivers. It also bore a pleasant wholesome yeasty smell of freshly baked bread, an aroma that wafted from a nearby bakery across and under the elevated highway. Taking another deep breath and giving a whispered one-word sigh, "Home," she moved forward, her heels clicking sharply across the station floor as she headed for the row of public phones, effectively spurning the porters' attempts to assist her with her luggage.

Her first call was to Touro Infirmary, to confirm the whereabouts of Claud. That was the closest major medical facility to his home, and she felt certain he would have been taken there.

"Yes, ma'am, we have a patient Claud Guerard in Intensive Care. Who is calling, please?"

The Irish Channel accent of the switchboard operator, which sounds so like the New York Bronx speech pattern, reaffirmed her sense of homecoming. The Irish Channel was a district upriver from Canal Street. The standing joke was that if you were arrested, the journalists said you came from the Irish Channel, but if you committed a deed of heroism, automatically your home was in the Garden District. The people of the Irish Channel laughed loudest.

"My name is Carol Charbonnet. I am Mr. Guerard's granddaughter." There was a pause, as if the operator had been forewarned of her impending arrival, but Carol knew this to be her imagination. But then again, maybe it wasn't. Perhaps there was a list of people to whom they dispensed information. Oh, God, surely her name had not been left from the list!

Before the panic could settle into cold fear, she was connected with an intensive-care unit's floor nurse. "I'm sorry, but there are no more visitors allowed in Intensive Care this morning. There are two periods this afternoon. If you wish to see your grandfather, you may do so at those times, though I must prepare you." The cold efficiency of her voice droned on. "Mr. Guerard has not responded to any visitors, and there is really no need for you to come until he is conscious. We are attending to his every need."

Carol stated her intention of seeing her grandfather at the first available visiting time and replaced the phone. The next call she placed to Patricia Trehan, who had owned an apartment in the French Quarter. She crossed her fingers as she waited for an answer.

Patricia was a fashion buyer for one of the big department stores fronting Canal Street. She had loved her job too much to have moved elsewhere. But she could be out of town on a buying trip. The phone rang several times, and Carol was just at the point of breaking the connection when a breathless voice answered.

"Patti? It's Carol...Carol Charbonnet." There was a long pause, and Carol could almost picture Patti's surprise at realizing her caller's identity.

Patti's response was quick. "Where are you?"

"At the train station."

"Do you know Miss Nan has been searching high and low for you? Where have you been?"

"Tante Nan found me." Carol ignored the second question. "Patti, can you give me a place to sleep for a short while?"

"You want to stay here when there's that fabulous house waiting for you?"

"Please, Patti. Can I stay there, just for a week or two?" There was an urgency in her appeal that was not lost on her friend.

"You can stay as long as you like. You know that. In fact, if you stay long enough, you will have the place to yourself. But we can talk about that later. Do you want me to pick you up?"

"No, you just get the coffee on. I'll take a cab. Expect me as soon as I can get there."

Carol sighed with relief at Patti's kindness. They had been best friends since grade school. It must have been a case of attracting opposites; they had always been foils for one another. Dark-haired Patti had dressed her dolls in her own creations while Carol had stuck hers in a toy truck and had them haul loads of gravel to imaginary construction sites.

Nonetheless, the relationship had thrived through grade school, high school and into university. They had belonged to the same sorority and had had their debuts at the same time. It had been a warm and wonderful growing up together. And now Patti had remembered the depth of their friendship and had welcomed Carol without reservation. At least that had not changed.

To reach the St. Ann Street apartment, the cab traveled down Decatur, providing Carol with glimpses of great warehouses fronting the Mississippi, the father of rivers. The familiar smells assaulted her. As they neared the French market, Carol inhaled the aroma of frying *beignets* and the chicory-laced coffee of the Café du Monde, blending with the river scents of fuel oil from powerful ship engines and the aroma of the tropical cargoes of bananas, papayas and pineapples.

She wanted desperately to stop and sit at the open-air café. She wanted to watch the people go by as she ate her fill of the holeless square doughnuts that always sprinkled her clothes with the powdered sugar in which they were covered. She wanted to drink the rich coffee blend and watch the tourists as they in turn watched the painters around Jackson Square.

But time was passing, and she had told Patti that she would go directly there. The cab driver yelled a greeting in the patois of Cajun French to the driver of a flower-bedecked horse-drawn carriage transporting visitors through the late-morning traffic of the Vieux Carré, the French Quarter. She was home.

Turning left, away from the river, then circling back, the driver soon stopped in front of the numbered building Carol had requested. After paying her fare and adding a tip, she stood for a moment renewing herself in the city like no other city in the world, "the city that Care forgot."

The lacy ironwork of the overhanging balconies cast shadows of filigree onto the shutters flanking the French doors. At street level everything was closed to the passerby, but inside were some of the most elegant abodes in the South.

Carol rang the bell beneath the single name Trehan and promptly heard the electronic click as Patti released the lock. The only light in the tunnellike hall connecting the street to the courtyard streamed from the archway at the far end. At the other end of this passage another world awaited.

It was a typical New Orleans patio, resplendent with ferns, banana trees, weeping figs and goldenrain trees. Philodendrons gleamed from beneath the stairs leading to the gallery on which Patti's apartment opened. Nothing here had changed very much, not in more than a hundred years.

Patti waited in the open doorway, dressed in jeans and a sweater. For a moment the two women stood looking at each other. Not sure of the expression on Patti's face, Carol slowly climbed the stairs. When she reached the landing, Patti took her cases and set them inside the apartment, but when she turned back to Carol, her expression was certain. She was smiling with open warmth, and she immediately clasped Carol to her with a quick hard hug of welcome. Link-ing her arm through Carol's, Patti led her friend directly to the heart of her home—her kitchen.

"I don't suppose you will tell me what's been going on for the past couple of years," Patti stated as she poured the coffee into modish cups of yellow porcelain.

"Not yet. But I promise soon...." Carol rose to stand at the long window overlooking the courtyard while taking a tentative sip of the potent beverage smoothed with a generous portion of heated milk. She relished the bite of the chicory blend.

A downdraft caught at a few dried leaves below and rescattered them along the flagstones. She longed to stand down there and let the sun beat on her face and warm her.

Sighing, she turned to ask her friend, "What do you know of my family? Can you tell me anything about what happened to Claud or about Tante Nan?" Carol noticed how Patti was studying her.

"You haven't said anything about Eva. Is that an oversight, or is it deliberate?"

Carol reached slender fingers beneath the shining mane of her hair to massage the tense muscles. "I didn't ask about René, either. All right, what about Claud, Nan, Eva, René, Gracie the cook—and lest I forget, old Judson, the handyman?" She turned reproachful eyes toward her friend. "You know how I feel about Eva. For Claud's sake, I left her alone, and for his sake I shall continue to leave her alone, but I don't know if I really care what happens to her. Although there's no proof, I know that what happened two years ago was at her instigation."

"Carol!" Patti was obviously shocked at the accusation and at the venom in Carol's voice. "How can you think that? I know you two have had your differences over the years, but she's your cousin, part of your family. There was usually little harm in her juvenile pranks, her hateful attempts of humor at your expense. I know how she embarrassed you, but even your grandfather dismissed her jokes as silly parlor games, unkind as they were. The worst Eva ever did was to charge things on your accounts, and Miss Nan always made that up to you." Then her voice became calm. "Do you have something concrete on which to base your opinion? Do you have something other than her mean little tricks and her cruel teasing?"

It took Carol a few seconds to answer. "You seem to have forgotten the successful play she made for Jack, how she made the initial move by imitating me on the phone."

Patti's opinion of that was expressed in one rude word. "You can never make me believe that had any effect on you at all," she derided. "You never cared for Jack that way in the first place. And in the second place, we both know you were tired of him long before Eva ever decided to make her move. As I remember it, you heartily welcomed her intervention. Try again, Carol."

Carol clenched her fists against the surging of unwanted emotions. She had been back only hours, and already feelings she thought dead were awakening.

"You said that I would have this place to myself. Where are you going?" She forced the black feelings down with an icy determination to keep them there.

"Are you trying to change the conversation?"

"No, my dearest and best friend, I *am* changing the conversation. When are you leaving, where are you going, and is there anyone interesting going with you or meeting you there?" She returned to the round oak table and sat in a pressed-back chair. This was the kind of room she liked, old and lived in. She stirred more warmed milk into her coffee.

"I'll be in and out until Thanksgiving. Then I'll be away for six weeks. I didn't get a vacation this summer, so if I intend to take one this year, it has to be soon. First there's business in New York—all business, I'm sad to say. But when I'm finished there, it's the Bahamas before joining my parents and the rest of the family in Miami for Christmas and the New Year."

She paused before responding to Carol's last question. "And yes, he's very interesting...maybe interesting enough to take home with me at Christmas."

There was a romantic gleam in the dark eyes, and Carol's heart swelled to see her friend's happiness.

"From the dreamy expression that's come over your face, it must be pretty serious."

They continued chatting, with Patti doing most of the talking and Carol asking questions intended to keep the conversation away from her problems. The time passed in comfortable companionship, but the later it became, the more restless Carol became to go to visit Claud.

After showering and dressing in brown tweed

slacks and coordinating dark brown blazer over a cream silk shirt, she was still ready too early. With the time to spare she searched the business section of the newspaper for any mention of her grandfather's firm and searched the society section for any mention of her cousins. There was nothing. She didn't know whether to be relieved or concerned.

Patti gave her apartment keys and urged Carol to use her Mazda that afternoon. Carol hadn't forgotten how difficult it was to find parking space and chose instead to walk the few blocks for a bus to Canal, where she could transfer to the rumbling and swaying old St. Charles Avenue streetcar.

It was the city's quietest time, and she almost had the streetcar to herself. As it crossed Poydras, she strained to see the building that housed Guerard Construction. The familiar dry scorched smell of the electric transport cut her throat, and she automatically braced herself for the swing around Lee Circle. It wasn't far until her stop.

She walked the two blocks from the tree-lined avenue to the infirmary and made her way to the wing where her grandfather lay.

She was early and spent fifteen minutes thumbing through outdated magazines and pacing the floor. At exactly two, a nurse whose very posture stated no nonsense led her into what was little more than a cubicle. There amid tubes and wires was Claud.

The once lustrous steel-colored locks lay limply across his forehead, and the cheeks once tan from the many hours in the sun as he watched his buildings rise were now gray and slack. Carol's breath caught in painful constriction.

"Is he being mechanically sustained? Is he alive? Really alive?"

Hearing the pain and fear in Carol's voice, the older woman came to place a comforting arm around her. "We are not mechanically sustaining any of his vital functions. Mr. Guerard had the foresight to have expressed to his physician and his lawyer his wish that he should never be kept alive artificially. He's getting oxygen, glucose, medication. The other paraphernalia is for monitoring only. It's not nearly as dreadful as it appears."

As Carol stiffened, the nurse withdrew her supporting arm. "There's really no reason for you to stay. He doesn't know anything."

"I'll stay, anyway. I still have a few minutes."

The nurse walked away with a shrug.

Carol made her way past the equipment and stood over her grandfather. She placed a hand over his and gently caressed the chilled fingers.

"Oh, Claud, what has happened to you?" she whispered. "Why didn't you back down? Why wouldn't you let me explain? Just look where our pride has led us." Tears began spilling down her cheeks. She lifted her hand to wipe them as she turned away.

"It's time for you to leave, Miss Charbonnet," the nurse called in her efficient tone.

"When may I see him again?" Carol needed more time with Claud, though just seeing her grandfather like this was a form of punishment.

"There's another five minutes at four. Mr. Greenlaw usually looks in then, but he called earlier. He won't be in today." The nurse busied herself among the computers that helped her to watch the four patients in her charge.

"Mr. Greenlaw?" Carol could not place the name.

"Yes, he's the one who brought Mr. Guerard in." That information told Carol exactly nothing.

"Who is my grandfather's doctor?"

The nurse supplied the name and the location of his office, which Carol wrote in a notebook she carried in her leather shoulder bag.

"Can't I see him again before four?"

"We have our rules. I can't let you see him until the assigned hour." Carol knew she couldn't but felt she had to try.

Leaving the hospital, she walked back toward St. Charles. If she rode the streetcar, she wasn't far from the house. On the other hand, it was a rather long walk, but what else did she have to do between now and the next visiting hour?

She brushed back a stray lock and turned upriver. St. Charles Street held a mixture of old Victorian mansions and modern apartment complexes. Juxtaposed among them were derelict boardinghouses and thriving businesses. Thankfully, in the past years more and more of the shabby structures had been bought from negligent owners and were being restored. Carol paused before a remembered shop. How many times, she wondered, had she traveled this street to and from school, university and Claud's firm? Moving on, Carol began to pass familiar houses to which Tante Nan had once taken her to visit.

And then there it was across the street. Heavy wrought-iron gates opened to an empty circular driveway. Her first impression was that guests were expected, for it had been ingrained in them never to leave the gates open unless someone was coming to visit. Standing for a long time, she studied the imposing red-brick structure set back from the avenue amid ancient oaks and magnolia trees. White Doric columns rose tall and trim to support the balcony and the heavy slate roof that extended over the balcony and verandas. She shifted her eyes to the second-story French doors that opened onto the left side of the balcony. The heavy draperies were drawn against the afternoon sun in what had been her room since childhood and had been her mother's room before her.

Then she dropped her gaze to the impressive front door. The leaded glass effectively hid the hall's interior from the view of passersby, but the blaze of the crystal chandelier splintered against the design of the panels, making a brilliant pattern of refracted light.

This was her home, stately and elegant as it had always been, but something was wrong, something missing, something not as it should be. She could not determine what was disturbing her, and time permitted no more contemplation. As it was, she would have to catch the streetcar back to the infirmary instead of making a return walk.

As she started toward the streetcar stop, her motion was frozen by a dark-colored sports car pulling into the short driveway. The passenger door flew open, and she immediately recognized the alighting woman. Looking at Eva was so nearly like looking at herself, Carol thought, especially from this distance.

She could not pull her sight from her cousin and thus did not notice the whipcord-lean man who climbed out of the driver's side of the sleek-lined Ferrari. It was finally the rumbling of the approaching streetcar that roused her, and she fumbled for coins. When she looked up again, the driveway was empty except for the sassy car.

When the streetcar stopped, she clasped the brass pole and pulled herself aboard. The return trip was brief, and soon Carol was again beside her grandfather's bed. It seemed to her that Claud was not so gray, and that his breathing was more natural. She spent in quiet talk the scant five minutes the hospital allowed her. She told Claud's inert form about her work in Chicago, the new engineering techniques she had learned, and about Maxwell, Helen, Jim. When she left, she was convinced that the crease between the great bushy brows had smoothed a bit, and made a silent promise to come again tomorrow.

Tomorrow, tomorrow.... The word kept echoing in her head as she made her way to the streetcar. When it crossed Poydras, she pulled the cord to alert the driver that she wanted to get off. As she walked toward the river, her pace slowed when she neared the towering structure that housed Guerard Construction. Carol lifted her face skyward, counting the levels as her gaze moved up, up to the seventeenth floor. That was where she was really needed. It would be a difficult step, but it had been much more difficult to return to New Orleans. But she felt she really hadn't any choice. Someone had to be the family representative at the firm, someone with authority and the ability to make decisions. Tomorrow would make a week since there had been a Guerard in those offices. She was overdue. But tomorrow would begin the work week, and she, too, would begin tomorrow.

PATTI WAS WAITING for her when she reached the Quarter apartment, and the look on Carol's face told her that Carol didn't want to talk about her afternoon. Carol flopped onto the richly upholstered sofa, and Patti waited until she chose to break the silence.

"It's rather late. Shouldn't you be getting ready to go out? It's not like you to be staying in, even if there is someone 'interesting' meeting you in the Bahamas." Carol's tone was peevish.

"It's not every night that you return after being God only knows where, either. I can stand being in if you can," Patti protested.

"But I don't think I can," Carol lied. "If you did what I think and canceled your date for the evening, can I make it up to you by treating you to dinner?"

"I accept, but it's my treat. Earlier I made reservations at both Antoine's and Brennan's. Or we can stand in line at Galatoire's. Which will it be?"

"Well, you've named the three most prestigious restaurants in the French Quarter.... Front room or back at Antoine's?" Carol asked.

"Back room, of course," Patti retorted in mock anger. "What do you think I am, a tourist in my own city?"

It was to the back rooms that the regular patrons, after being met by their "own" waiters, were taken. This custom of making reservations through a favorite waiter made Antoine's not just a historical restaurant for the out-of-towners to enjoy, but a special place for the local clientele who relished the extra attention, although the food was the same wherever the table.

"The back room, huh?" Carol cocked her head at Patti, a mischievous grin playing around her mouth. "Race you for the bath!"

STEERING CLEAR of raucous Bourbon Street, they made their way down the more sedate Royal, stopping to admire the antiques and rare furniture displayed in the exclusive shops. They were eventually seated in the dimly lighted back room and faced the task of deciding on their menu. There were so many regional foods that Carol had longed for in her absence. They ultimately settled for a meal of the oysters, tournedos *marchand de vin*, soufflé potatoes—another creation that came to Louisiana with the original Antoine in 1840—and *salade Antoine*. With the extra treat of generous portions of Montrachet and Château Haut-Brion, they had absolutely no room for dessert.

"Let's walk to the market for coffee and doughnuts. By the time we get there, I will have found room," Patti suggested in a whisper, not daring to offend "her" waiter. A fine light reflected in Carol's eyes at the mention of the French Market; being away had cost more emotionally than Carol could openly admit.

At St. Ann Street they turned toward the river again. The street formed one side of Jackson Square and led directly to the market and the Café du Monde. Carol's steps began to lag when they came into full view of the lighted facade of St. Louis Cathedral. It reflected a soft glow on lovers sitting on benches and provided a picturesque background for the street musicians who played a haunting fugue behind opened instrument cases baited suggestively with paper currency and coin. A father and his two small children zipped by on roller skates while a young crowd obviously out for a good time argued the merits of various night spots.

Carol stood looking across the square at the statue of Andrew Jackson astride his horse, at the fountain splashing and gurgling in the darkness, at the lush tropical vegetation, at the intricate design of the ironwork of the Pontalba Apartments.

"Many songs have been written about missing this city. I always thought they were just sentimental tunes to which we danced away an evening or two. But not anymore. I know what it means to want to walk these narrow streets, to want desperately to stand on a balcony decorated in metal lace and look out over the city, to feel the antiquity of it all. There is no place like this in God's universe, and at times, Patti, I thought I would die with the need to be here."

She reached up to brush the tears away and gave a nervous laugh. "I'm becoming maudlin, aren't I?"

"Yes, you are... and I want my dessert now. How about crying over fingers burnt by *beignets*?" Patti's reply set the right tone, and by the time they had crossed Decatur to the outdoor café, Carol's mood had been effectively restored.

Aggressively and quickly they secured a table. With her first bite of the blistering hot fried pastry, Carol's skirt was afloat in powdered sugar.

"One time I saw someone eat here without spilling one speck of sugar, and she was dressed all in black. Got right up from the table and didn't even have to check her dress," Patti teased.

"I don't believe you," Carol denied as she dampened a paper napkin in her water glass to remove the powder.

"Sister Mary Agnes in her full habit, wimple and all."

Their combined laughter at the private joke drew admiring male glances to them, and the attention dwelled long after the music of their gaiety faded.

CHAPTER TWO

CAROL FITTED A LONG-IDLE KEY into the door marked Guerard Construction hours before the office staff would leave their beds. By the time everyone else was stepping into morning showers, she had files spread across her old desk. Some were projects that had been in the works before she had left two years ago.

She picked up the folder containing information about a ferry-landing structure. It had been one of her grandfather's dreams to have a part in revamping the old landing upriver from the city. Hesitating before she opened the folder, she weighed it on the palm of her hand. The file was unusually light and very thin. Warily she reviewed the preliminary work, some of which she had done herself—estimates on labor costs, yards of cement required, steel reinforcements—all the things one calculated prior to placing the competitive bid. She remembered Claud shaving percentages off the company profit. He really had wanted this particular job.

But there on the last page was the outcome stamped in large red letters: BID WITHDRAWN.

Why, Carol wondered. Claud had been so proud when she had presented her figures for verification. With the ball of her thumb she rubbed the bold initials he had placed at the bottom of each page and quickly reviewed the estimates to see if there had been some wild miscalculation that would have made their bid unacceptable. Seeing nothing, she returned to the last page. Peering closely at the red message, she saw the date of the withdrawal had been only two weeks after she had left.

Quickly she thumbed through several more folders. Many of them ended in the same jarring red stamp. After replacing the inactive folders, she moved to the active-files section. She knew without hesitation where to find the most recent projects. Soundlessly the drawer slid effortlessly forward.

But the drawer was only a third filled. In the past there had barely been room to add a thin sheet of onionskin. Now there were perhaps twenty folders in neat alphabetical order, nothing that would raise the ire of Mrs. McLin, the office manager. Claud had always been digging in the drawers and stuffing back the files after he had finished. This was the first time Carol had ever found the drawer in order, and it seemed ominous.

At random she selected five projects. The first contained a preliminary job description that had come through an architect for whom they had worked frequently in the past. This was for a fourplex apartment in Jefferson Parish. There was no notation about who was working on the project, and none of the research had been started. She discovered another of the five to be in the same state. But at least it had a later due date for the bid.

The third folder held her interest. It was for a

branch bank. Most of the estimates were complete, but the authorization initials were not familiar to her. Strange letters—E.L.G.—marched across the foot of each page. She stretched her memory but could find no name to fit the initials.

After she had been there nearly three hours, and the only progress she had made was to completely baffle herself, a key turning in the outer-office door lock interrupted her. Carol rose to greet the first of the office staff, and she was glad to see the face of Mrs. McLin. Surely, Carol thought, her grandfather's personal secretary and office manager would be able to explain why so many of the bids had been withdrawn, and why the active files were so few in number.

Carol could see the middle-aged lady's expression of puzzlement as she removed her coat and noted the lights on in the file room. Then her glance moved down the hall to the doorway in which Carol stood.

Mrs. McLin's first reaction was the old smile of welcome, but it quickly changed to surprise. "How long have you been here?" she queried.

"I've been in the office for a few hours, in the city since yesterday morning."

With uncharacteristic stiltedness the older woman walked to her desk and opened the bottom drawer. There she placed her small handbag and knit gloves. "It seems strange that Miss Nan didn't let me know you were coming in. She should have informed me so that I could have had your old office made ready."

"Tante Nan doesn't know I'm here, Mrs. McLin. In fact, you're the only one who does...other than Claud."

Carol saw the hope rise in her eyes. "Your grandfather had regained consciousness! Thank God!"

But that hope died with Carol's next words. "No, he's not conscious, but he knows I'm here. I know he does." Her determined features brooked no further discussion of Claud, and she quickly asked about the other subjects she wanted settled.

"Mrs. McLin, what's going on here? As best I can tell from the files, the company is functioning at a mere fraction of its capacity. What's happened?"

Mrs. McLin hesitated, then chose her words carefully. "As difficult as this is for me to say to you, that dreadful man's accusations lost us many accounts. We never fully recovered from that bad publicity." The secretary sat at her desk, her face averted.

That answer was like a knife in Carol's back, and the pain made her angry. "Those were all lies! Every word from that man's mouth was a lie. Maybe I couldn't prove it, and maybe I'm the only one who believes in my innocence, but this company never took or made a kickback—never. Not me, not Claud—not even a field supervisor. Claud should have stood up to the charges. He should have let me get to the bottom of all those lies, and I would have cleared the Guerard name once and for all! Oh, what's the use. None of you would listen to me then, and it seems you aren't prepared to listen now." She took a deep breath and consciously tried to relax before continuing.

"But that was two years ago. Even if the charges had been true, there has been ample time to rebuild any losses incurred as a result of—as you put it—'bad publicity.' What else happened?"

Again Mrs. McLin hesitated, unable to face Carol. She fidgeted with the things on her desk, moving the stapler from the right corner to the left, checking pencil points.

Carol refused to allow her voice to rise to match the level of her frustration. "Mrs. McLin, I fully intend finding out one way or another. What else?" She leaned over the desk, resting her weight on her knuckles in a most unfeminine, completely aggressive position.

Mrs. McLin ventured a glance upward before she answered. "The whole thing must have taken the wind out of your grandfather's sails, so to speak. He just didn't go out after the jobs after you left. We finished the projects we were absolutely committed to, then he began cutting back on the staff here in the offices and on the sites as he began to withdraw bids. He gave early retirement to some, and others he just laid off with good recommendations. He was beginning to negotiate the liquidation of some equipment when he had the stroke. And that's how things stand now."

"What about those new jobs in the file, those estimates verified by the initials E.L.G.?"

There was an instant softening of Mrs. McLin's face, and a flickering aura of optimism entered the room. "That's Mr. Greenlaw. He was working with Mr. Guerard on the selling of some equipment. Before any of us knew what had happened, he had persuaded Mr. Guerard to take a few small jobs, then a few larger projects. Mr. Greenlaw did all the work; your grandfather sat back and watched him work. After your grandfather had his stroke, Mr. Greenlaw showed up with power of attorney, and he's been coming in for a while each day. I just don't know what we would have done without him."

Carol stood up, feeling even more confused. "Power of attorney? How did he get that?"

"I couldn't say. René and Eva came in with him and explained it to me, but I was very upset at the time, and there wasn't much I understood. I was too grateful to have someone assume responsibility. Bids and buildings I know, but not legal terminology."

Her reply amazed Carol. How could a woman so competent in the construction field be so incompetent when it came to the rest of life? Claud had admired that in the woman, swearing it made for loyalty, but right now Carol felt it made for frustration, primarily her own.

"Can you tell me who this Mr. Greenlaw is?" she asked impatiently.

"There isn't much to tell. He hasn't been around very long. I do know he worked for various big construction companies for short periods before he and Mr. Guerard came together. He's not from around here. If you ask me, I believe he's from up north. He doesn't talk like a Southern boy."

Carol repressed a smile at Mrs. McLin's description. To her anyone under forty was still a boy. "What time will Mr. Greenlaw be in today?"

"He doesn't come in at any regular time. Sometimes he works here at night and just leaves things on the Dictaphone. Most of the time he's out on the sites, just like your grandfather always was.''

Realizing she was not to learn anything more about the mysterious Mr. Greenlaw, Carol asked about other aspects of the business. She was told which of the office employees had remained, and what their assignments were. She could now hear the offices coming to life and knew it was time to greet the staff. She didn't know what kind of reception to expect from them, but she hoped for the best. First, however, she wanted to check on Claud.

Mrs. McLin made a call to the hospital, and Carol talked to the person in charge of the morning shift. Her grandfather was the same. While Carol talked with the nurse, Mrs. McLin arranged for Carol a conference with Claud's doctor for later that afternoon. After her phone call Carol made rounds and spoke to staff members individually. All of them pretended not to remember the circumstances under which she had left. These were Guerard Construction employees, the men whom Claud had never hesitated to let Carol accompany when they went out to survey a job site, or when they supervised actual construction. They were the main reason she knew her job better than many who were twice her twenty-four years. Since she had been ten, she had spent her summers and holidays tagging along behind the men of Guerard Construction. She had owned a hard hat when most young girls were having their ears pierced.

After an early lunch Carol spent the afternoon with the accountant, who painted a grim picture of where the company stood. Debts and expenses were being met, but income projected would have to increase if Guerard Construction was to regain its standing in the business community. At present the company did not have the financial resources necessary to meet assurity bonding for any large project. Carol had no doubts that it would be a slow climb upward if Guerard Construction was to regain its position.

At four she was back at the hospital. She talked in a low tone to Claud, trying to will him back to consciousness. Sometimes the words spoken softly were violent, but always the tone expressed love and need. When the nurse touched her shoulder, she departed without urging.

She hurried to keep the appointment with Dr. Frahm and stoically listened to his blunt prognosis. It was just as Tante Nan had written. Hopes of recovery dim.

Numbly she returned to the office just as most of the staff was leaving. She pulled open the active-files drawer and removed the folder containing the information on the branch bank and placed it atop the cabinet. Quickly she thumbed the rest of the files, finding three more projects for which no bids had been prepared.

She gathered the four files to her bosom, clutching them there as she returned to her old desk. It would be a hard task to restore the company to its former position but not impossible. If Claud had given up because of what had happened two years ago, it was her chore, even her responsibility, to pull it all back together. Somebody had to support the family. One could live on accumulated capital only so long. Nan was a crippled old woman, René was useless, Claud fallen, and Eva... Eva was Eva, willful, beautiful, decorous, sensuous Eva.

She studied the folder completed by the unknown Mr. Greenlaw. It was meticulously executed. Not in the flamboyant style of Claud, but it was every bit as precise.

Reaching inside her desk for the small calculator she had kept there, Carol encountered nothing but dusty emptiness. For the first time she noticed just how vacant her old office was. Gone were the mementos and photographs that had once covered the walls. The only supplies left were the sparse furniture; not even a pencil lay in the drawer. Someone had tried to erase her personality from the room and succeeded.

Carol decided to use Claud's office until the proper equipment and supplies could be restored to her former work area. Deftly she shuffled the papers into proper order and transported everything to the big office that overlooked the foot of Poydras Street.

Darkness came early in the Southern November night, and she stood looking out toward the river, watching the streetlights blink on. The atmosphere of the room made it difficult for her to settle directly into her work. There were too many memories in this room, too many associations. She could almost smell the fat cigars Claud had carried in his shirt pocket, had puffed on when he leaned back in the chair to mentally organize, assess, think. She knew that her sitting in that seat was an act of presumption; she was not ready to replace Claud as head of the firm, but she was the best substitute the family had to offer.

Carol had many doubts that she would be able to accomplish any of her goals. First, she would have to rouse Claud from his dreamless sleep and then resolve the business of a stranger having control of their company. To Carol, Ethan Greenlaw owed his position in the firm to an arrangement typical of Eva. If through him Eva could control the company, Carol didn't doubt Eva would liquidate everything, claim her share of the cash and chase off to wherever her crowd was chasing this season.

As Carol worried about how she could stop Eva if her assessment were correct, the last rays of the setting sun cast a glow at the window but left the rest of the room in semidarkness, broken only by Carol's trim silhouette standing in relief against the blue and purple of the evening. A contemplative stillness settled about her as the building vacated, and then the streets below her emptied.

Claud must get better, Carol prayed. He was the rock in her life, the supportive shoulder upon which she had always leaned, even during their separation, just as she had lived by the code he had taught her. How many times had he placed one hand on her shoulder, the other beneath her chin to tilt her head and point her vision toward a specific sight. She could never find the elusive object without his physical direction, not until he placed a hand under her chin and said, "There, just at the end of your silly nose." Then he would place a kiss on that silly appendage.

Carol had been four when her parents were killed. Claud had been the only one who had attempted to replace the affection she had lost with their death, and she missed him desperately. It had been a long two years without him, but here in his office she could feel his presence, his physical warmth, even relive the touch of his hand on her shoulder. She leaned into that memory, against his tall frame. She felt his hand beneath her chin, turning her face for the fatherly salute. She closed her eyes against reality and tilted her head into the fantasy.

This dream did not end in a kiss on her silly nose. Two demanding lips closed over her mouth, and the hand that held her poised against that searching probe gripped her with the firmness of physical urgency, not fatherly love.

The shock of realizing that the presence in the room, the commanding hand on her shoulder, the fingers holding her chin firm against a demanding kiss were not Claud's phantom, immobilized her as muscular arms turned her against a rocklike torso. It was the movement of a masculine thigh brushing intimately against hers and a hand sliding down her shoulder to caress her throat before moving downward to cup her breast that jarred her into action.

As she tried to wrench her mouth from the sensual onslaught, Carol's thoughts moved in disjointed sequence. Who was this man? How did he get into the locked office? Was this her fate—to return only to be attacked by some stranger?

The adrenaline pounded through her body, preparing her for the struggle ahead, but her heightened senses became aware of a barely perceptible change in the body thrust so intimately against hers. There was a different tautness in the way the lean man stood over her, his legs slightly apart. The crushing grip relaxed slightly as his mouth lifted slowly from hers to allow Carol a first encounter with eyes the gray of a fog-shrouded morning. Grooves on each side of his sensuous mouth deepened as he allowed her to push another scant inch between them.

In the fading light her impression of a deeper darkness was accentuated—night-shaded hair brushed across a tanned forehead above heavy brows of the same blackness. His smoothly shaved cheeks, only hinting at the heavy black beard so recently shorn, betrayed his wariness by the flicker of a rippling muscle beneath their angular surface. The subtle sign that betrayed his attempts to control himself brought her eyes past the slight flaring of his narrow nose back to mist-colored eyes that effectively cloaked the thoughts behind them.

Silently her captor slid those ice-chip eyes over her hair, discernibly narrowing at the green of her own, then down over the contour of her lips and chin. Then a deep voice wrapped in sarcasm broke the silence. "You may be a prodigal returned but definitely not the son." His words and the suggestion behind them brought her into action. She called on all her energy and in one movement pulled away from him, but before her palm made contact with his arrogant cheek, a viselike grip on her wrist stopped her hand in midair.

"This first mistake was mine, Miss Charbonnet,

and I assure you that I do not make a habit of embracing strange women. You were about to make a mistake of your own, an even graver mistake, for which my response would have been very swift and very deliberate."

From her first impression she had no doubt that if her blow had landed, his response would have been in kind. He had an aura that bespoke biblical justice. She could easily imagine his carrying out an old-country vendetta of an eye for an eye, but with him, it seemed more probable to expect two eyes for one.

In the semidarkness the masculine voice continued, "When females cease acting like ladies, I cease treating them as such." He paused to measure her reaction. "If I release your hand, will I have loosed a lady or some scratching, clawing hellcat?" He stood a good half foot over her, his strong body telling her that he was more than capable of carrying out his threat.

She did not dignify his question with an answer, but he slowly released her hand. With the completion of that release, he was the first to move out of the close confines of the window embrasure. She watched the lithe movements of his body as he reached beneath the shade to click on a table lamp sitting on the credenza that served as storage area for Claud's daily ration of Scotch whiskey.

Carol finally managed to find her voice. "And am I to assume your attack was the action of a gentleman?" So many conflicting emotions were racing through her she didn't know how to approach this dark stranger.

Once more the steel gray eyes narrowed. "I told you I had made a mistake. I thought you were—" he paused over a name, then continued "—someone who would have welcomed my...attack, as you called it."

She clenched her hands in anger. She was sure that Eva was the name that he had omitted.

"I'm not like her at all." Her chin quivered in denial.

Completely at ease and unheedful of the spotless elegance of his dove gray suit, the stranger knelt on one knee and removed two glasses and a half-filled bottle of amber liquid from the carved cabinet. Without looking at her, he questioned quietly, "Like who?"

She turned once more to the window. So far she had not moved from the position in which he had found her. The street below was lighted with the flow of traffic and the glow of the globed streetlights. Over the levee she could see the river traffic moving slowly.

"I'm not at all like my cousin Eva. That's who you thought I was when you came in, didn't you?" This time he chose not to answer.

An arm reached around her and proffered a glass of Scotch. Automatically she accepted, took a small sip, then turned to face the stranger.

"Who are you? You know my name, but I don't know you."

"I was beginning to wonder when you would get around to asking." His eyes locked with hers. "I'm Ethan Greenlaw. I believe that you and I are—" he searched for a term "—associates in this firm. At least until Claud recovers." Then he added in an undertone, "If he recovers."

Her gulp was audible. "Of course he will recover!" Then the meaning of his other words registered. "Associates? That, Mr. Greenlaw, absolutely cannot be! This is a family firm. There is no way you can have a share in this business unless... unless...."

"No, Miss Charbonnet. I haven't married your beautiful cousin. Even if I had, power over her portion of the company wouldn't be enough to give me control of anything. I'd be just as powerless as you are with your little share." He paused to sip his drink before continuing. "As you know, your grandfather divided the firm into six equal parts and gave one part to each member of his family—Miss Nan, René, Eva and yourself. The remaining two he kept. I now have control of all those shares except yours." Again he paused, this time to watch her. "I can see the wheels in your brain turning, but it won't work. If by some fluke you could manage to control Claud's portion, it wouldn't do you any good since I have the other three positively locked up. You would only reach a stalemate in any action against me. That is, if you are against me."

Quickly she tried to remember what Mrs. McLin had said about power of attorney. But there was no help there. He held control of all shares save hers. And he was right about the other: if she did wrest control of Claud's portion, it would do little good unless she could persuade one of the others to her side. Claud had miscalculated when he had divided the company long years ago.

She could not prevent the tears from flooding her eyes. "Then with Claud's power of attorney you... you have everything."

He watched dispassionately as the tears gathered. "Right now that may be the case. But since the prodigal *child* has returned—" he deliberately paused at the word as his eyes drifted slowly to the shadow showing at the neckline of her blouse "—I'm sure you'll set about trying to have that changed in your favor. I advise you not to waste your time."

It was as if, having sensed her hopes rising, he quickly moved to slash them with the cleanliness of surgical steel. "Don't count on anything, not even Miss Nan's proxy. Something tells me I have them all firmly in my camp. So, as I said before, it looks like you against me."

He finished his drink in one last gulp and placed the empty glass on the cabinet. She glanced at the file lying on the desk corner. Desperately she clutched at one last hope and referred to what he had said earlier.

"Maybe we won't be against one another," she pleaded. "Maybe we both want the same thing."

Ethan walked to the desk and casually rummaged through the papers in the center drawer. "That sounds encouraging. It's too bad I can't stay tonight to talk about the things I want for Guerard Construction, but I have an appointment for which I'm already late. I just came by for these papers." He tapped his hand against the envelope he now held.

"An appointment with Eva?" Carol could have bitten her tongue the minute she spoke the name. What business was it of hers with whom he had an appointment?

Ethan turned toward her, a derisive twinkle in his eyes. "Now that would be telling, wouldn't it? Nobody likes a fellow to kiss and tell, no matter how interesting the kiss or how wild the tale." His implication was not lost on her, but before Carol could reply, he had crossed the office and was closing the door behind him.

Carol stood for a long time, staring at the door. Tomorrow would be another day, she told herself encouragingly, and with luck she could find out what Mr. Ethan Greenlaw's plans were for the company. If they could work together, Carol mused, then maybe she could protect what Claud had spent such a long time building. But if Ethan intended to liquidate the company's assets—the trucks, the stockpiles of lumber, brick, iron and steel, the warehouse inventory, the great machines that moved the earth and drove the pilings—just to provide Eva with what she considered the "necessities" of life, then Mr. Greenlaw would have a fight on his hands, Carol vowed. He might think he had Nan in his camp, but Nan could be persuaded. Carol had spent her youth convincing Nan to do things she didn't want to do. She was better prepared than Mr. Greenlaw could possibly surmise when it came to dealing with her great-aunt.

Then Carol remembered. Even before the problem of two years ago, Nan had never approved of Carol's role in business. Scarcely a day went by that Nan hadn't urged Carol to be more socially active. She constantly upheld Eva as the ideal for Carol to emulate. But when Nan heard of the accusations, she had scathingly denounced Carol, decrying the shame she had brought to them all. Nan told Carol repeatedly that she didn't deserve a place in their home. It had been a week of recriminations, not because of what Carol had supposedly done, but because she had brought the Guerard name into scandal. How many times had she heard that she didn't belong there? And she had come to believe it. She couldn't go home as long as she bore dishonor—as long as Nan was ashamed of her.

She thought about Nan's health. Carol remembered how painful Nan's rheumatoid arthritis was, so debilitating that some days Nan hadn't been able to rise from her bed until noon and even then could barely get to the dinner table. She had no longer visited the upper floors of the house and had left their upkeep to others. She had given in to her illness and refused to go out. What life or activity she had was got vicariously through Eva's social activities.

Praying the progress of the disease had taken no further toll, Carol shook her head to dismiss the image of the regal white-haired woman, bejeweled fingers beautifully tended though the joints were gnarled, leaning on her ebony cane as she scolded Carol for her unfeminine ways, particularly for a female with Guerard blood. No, Carol thought, Nan had not meant for her to return to the house on St. Charles Avenue. She had meant for Carol to return to these offices, and that's exactly what Carol had done.

Forcing herself to return to matters before her, Carol seated herself at the great walnut desk and spread the folders. As she leaned forward in the padded swivel chair, she could not prevent her mind from picturing a dark-haired man sitting in the same chair, bent over similar work, if not these same folders. She gritted her teeth to destroy the image and reminded herself that this was Claud's office; she had more right to the seat than Ethan Greenlaw. As far as she was concerned, he suited Nan's term of "upstart" more aptly than any person she had ever encountered.

For several hours she studied projects let for bid. Time after time she returned to the files, searching out those projects she believed they stood the best chance of earning. By nine o'clock she had selected four. Glancing at her watch, she decided that tomorrow would be time enough to begin the actual compilations. Right now she was ready for a bath and a good supper.

WHEN SHE ARRIVED at the French Quarter apartment, she gave up all thoughts of an early night; Patti's friends had gathered for an impromptu party.

She cautiously waded through the collection of people, mostly strangers to her, and for that she was thankful. The fewer people who knew her, the fewer would remember the scandals associated with her and Guerard Construction. Those whom she did know obviously had been warned by Patti not to speak of it or chose to ignore what they remembered. She didn't believe for one second that they had forgotten.

It seemed to Carol as if people were standing or sitting everywhere. With only a furtive, longing glance at the candlelit table of cheeses, breads and wines, she eventually finished the round of introductions and managed a quick shower, though not without teasing knocks on the door accompanied by offers for back scrubs, all delivered in deep laughing masculine voices.

When she rejoined the party, she felt that the soft cashmere sweater and pleated slacks she had changed into were more in keeping with the others' dress. Someone had placed a jazz recording on the stereo, and a friendly argument about favorite musicians rose above the smooth glidings of a trombone. With the shower, fresh clothes and a glass of claret, Carol allowed the mood of the party to dissolve her fatigue. When someone suggested that they all go to a jazz club, she enthusiastically agreed.

On the way along famed Bourbon Street several people drifted off to various clubs, but others joined them, so that the group's size remained fairly constant. As they neared their destination, there were still more than a dozen people in their party. They all walked down the center of the narrow street, now a pedestrian thoroughfare that marketed everything from T-shirts, to oriental food, to fine art, to bawdy entertainment. People of all ages and classes walked in the street, stopping to ogle the views of exotic dancers with which the barkers at club doorways teased potential customers.

Carol had always found the strip shows embarrassing, as well as degrading. When their little caravan stopped to whoop and holler at one particularly revealing sight, she automatically turned to face the opposite side of the street. They were across from a celebrated hotel, and there entering the door was Ethan Greenlaw, one hand beneath the elbow of a very familiar figure. She didn't have to see the face of the woman to know who it was. Carol's hand reached up to touch her own hair, styled almost like her cousin's. In the past Carol had made it a point to wear her hair short when Eva's was long and to allow hers to grow when Eva's was short. It seemed ironic that their hair was now styled the same even though they hadn't seen each other for nearly two years. No wonder Ethan Greenlaw had mistaken her for Eva; people who had known them all their lives had frequently done so.

A painful knot developed in her stomach when she remembered the passion in that early-evening kiss from a man who now was smiling so intimately at her lifelong rival. Carol winced at the familiar way in which those lean fingers that had sought the rounded contour of her breast now grasped another's arm. Everything suddenly became clear—much clearer than she wanted. Ethan Greenlaw, the most physically devastating man Carol had ever met, was Eva's lover.

Eric, one of the young men she had met for the first time at Patti's apartment, slipped an arm around her shoulders. "Come along, Carol. Let's start walking toward the club, and the others will follow. They're probably as ready for a drink as I am."

She forced a gay laugh from her constricted throat and reached her arm out to slip around the waist of Frederic, who had joined them on her other side, so that she stood between the two men. Just as she stepped forward, she felt an emanation of disapproval, and her glance slipped past Frederic in time to see the flash of condemning eyes before Ethan turned back to Eva.

That look sent a surge of indignation through her. He had no right to make judgments about her social life. His relationship with Eva gave him no authority over her whatsoever.

All the way to the club Carol tried hard to recapture her earlier good spirits. All she accomplished was a burning memory of Eva and Ethan as they stood in the doorway, posed and poised like a slick magazine layout. Eva, as always, had been dressed to perfection. Carol could not erase the image of the soft chamois gown clinging to the svelte figure, the way Eva had carried the fox stole with studied casualness. She had been dressed in ice blue, a color deliberately chosen to match her eyes. Eye color was the one startling physical difference between Carol and Eva. They were genetic freaks, nearly identical in looks even though they shared no parent.

Once inside the club and with great effort, Carol finally shook her mood and joined the others in enjoying the jazz performance. They had pushed the handkerchief-sized tables together and rearranged the chairs so they could be seated together. Since most of the group were native New Orleanians, they were very knowledgeable about jazz, and all of them agreed that the group featured at this club was playing their kind of music. After a while the joking and casual conversation had subsided as the icy-hot syncopation filled their thoughts. It was here in the Vieux Carré bars and nightclubs that Dixieland jazz was still the king. If one wanted modern jazz, one went to Seattle or San Francisco or even St. Louis. One came to New Orleans and the French Quarter for Dixieland.

Customers came and left, but their little group stayed, awash in the seemingly effortless melding of rhythmic improvisation. As a waitress was clearing the empty glasses and dumping the overflowing ashtrays, Carol asked the location of the rest room. No one paid attention to her leaving, except for Patti and Eric, both of whom acknowledged her request to be excused with perfunctory nods as they applauded a particularly exciting bridge by the clarinet.

She made her way through the crowded tables to the patio and then to the rest room. Because the light was so dim she didn't notice the dark-haired man who was watching her with tight-lipped intensity from a table set well to the edge of the patio, nestled among tropical plants. When she emerged from the small lavatory, those same eyes were waiting. As Carol came adjacent to his sheltered table, the man rose.

The tall figure looming before her without warning startled her, but Carol quickly realized who the man was and immediately turned to rejoin her friends. Before she could step away, his hand whipped out to grasp her arm.

"Don't go," he requested in the tone of someone used to having all his requests fulfilled.

She looked down at the flickering candle on his table and saw illumined there only one glass. Nor were there cigarette butts in the ashtray, which would have indicated that her cousin Eva had been at the table recently. As she glanced at the nearby tables, he said, anticipating her thoughts, "I'm alone."

Ethan had chosen to be obvious, and she reciprocated. "Where is Eva?" Carol queried. His only response was a noncommittal shrug. A noisy outburst of appreciation from her group of friends called her attention back to the enclave of aficionados in the main room. His eyes followed the same path.

"Who are those people?" he questioned.

Carol turned to observe a mysterious narrowing of his eyes and a tightening of his facial features as he watched the friendly camaraderie among the crew. "Friends," she answered quietly, not at all comprehending the reason for his attentiveness. "Just friends. One I've known forever; the others are a mixture of old and new."

Ethan's gray eyes flashed in the dim gaslight of the wall-mounted coach lanterns. "And the man sitting next to you? Is he the one you have known forever?"

"The man next to me?" Carol honestly couldn't remember who besides Patti had been next to her and had to look back to identify the man of whom he spoke.

"You must mean Eric—" she began in a surprised tone.

Ethan cut her off sharply. "Don't speak his name as if it's news to you that he's even in the same room. Every chance he gets, he's leaning over you, brushing his hand across your shoulder, whispering to you. What does this Eric mean to you?"

This whole confrontation had been too queer for Carol to be startled by his question. She was finding the sudden encounter with a man whom she had seen for only a brief minute a few hours earlier and who now was treating her as his exclusive possession nothing less than unbelievable. She was beyond being shocked.

"Mr. Greenlaw—" Carol began.

"Ethan," he corrected.

Carol eyed him warily. "Ethan," she amended. Then she paused to look once more at the group, thinking that surely Patti would realize she had been away from the table for quite some time and would somehow afford her a chance to escape this uncomfortable encounter. But Patti was deep in conversation and seemingly oblivious to Carol's prolonged absence.

"Ethan," she began again, "I don't know what you're thinking, but I find it strange that you should just turn up at this particular club, alone, to interrogate me about the company I'm keeping."

He did not answer any of her implied accusations. "It doesn't matter why I'm here other than my feeling a degree of responsibility for you."

"Your control of Guerard Construction does not extend to me personally," she proclaimed.

His only response to that statement was an odd

brief smile, then his features hardened again. "I didn't like the looks of the crowd you were with and the scene some of your 'friends' created earlier in front of that striptease place."

"I think I understand your concern, and I suppose I should thank you, but they didn't mean anything by their actions. Their loudness was a natural response to cover embarrassment, and those places *are* embarrassing."

"If that's the way you want to interpret the lewd remarks being made.... Still, it's late, and I think you should be home by now. Miss Nan will undoubtedly be worried about you. If you will say good-night to your friends, I'll take you home now."

His dictatorial invitation revealed more information than he realized. If Eva had seen Carol, or if Ethan had mentioned meeting Carol in the offices, Eva would have quickly informed him that Carol had not been to the impressive house on St. Charles Avenue.

"I don't think that is necessary, Mr. Greenlaw."

"Ethan," he corrected again, this time with greater emphasis.

"Ethan," she parroted. By now, Patti, Eric, as well as several others, had begun looking around the room for her, and Carol was becoming uneasy. "I'll rejoin my friends. They seem ready to leave, and I'll make my way home with them. Thank you again for your concern." She tugged against the grip he had maintained on her forearm. When she had secured her freedom, she knew it had been because he decided that she go free.

Carol looked back at him only when she was safely settled between Eric and Patti, and after she had taken a tentative sip of the fresh drink before her. Ethan still stood in the shadowed courtyard, his hands thrust into the rear pockets of his suit trousers, a casual posture at odds with his formal dress. For a moment she watched the play of the flickering light along the planed surface of his face, but she could not maintain her bold perusal as his eyes returned the detailed examination. She turned to the band on stage. When she chanced another glance toward the patio, he was gone.

IT WAS well into the early morning before Carol and Patti were settled into the twin beds. In frustration Carol punched the pillow in the darkness, attempting to destroy the image of those eyes that had been so accusing when suggesting that she should leave the club.

"Just who the hell does he think he is?" she muttered into her pillow. She wasn't so settled in her ways that she couldn't stay out past ten o'clock and still function the next day. Again she flipped over in the narrow bed.

"Want to talk about it?" Patti asked quietly, awakened by Carol's restlessness.

"I'm sorry, Patti." Carol rose and stood beside the bed. "I'll take my pillow and sleep on the sofa. The way I feel now, I won't be settling down for a while. There's no point in both of us missing our sleep."

Patti clicked on the light and smoothed her dark

hair with the back of her hand. Carol deliberately kept her face averted. She didn't want her friend seeing her disturbance, something she didn't understand herself. But it was too late.

"I think it's not an *it*, but a *him*. My God, Carol!" she exclaimed, upon seeing the expression on her friend's face. "How did this happen?"

"Nothing has happened," Carol denied.

"Not yet, but it's brewing," Patti corrected. "I saw you on the patio. You thought I was oblivious to that little tête-à-tête. That was Ethan Greenlaw, wasn't it? In the construction business, frequently seen with cousin Eva. What kind of fool are you, Carol? You aren't about to tangle with that witch over a man, are you?" Again she watched Carol closely, then reached back and pulled the pillows up against the headboard. "I think we do need to talk."

Carol confronted her friend. "Are he and Eva deeply involved?"

"If you mean have they been pictured together in the society section, the answer is no. She hasn't got him that far." Patti's tone softened. "On the other hand, since your grandfather's illness there hasn't been much social publicity about the Guerards at all."

"That's good." Carol couldn't keep the bitterness from her voice. "It's too bad it couldn't have been that way before I left."

"You'll have to get over that some day," Patti advised.

"It's easy for you to say that," Carol retorted. "You weren't the one accused of accepting kickbacks to insure subcontracts got to the right firms, of leaking bids. If only Claud had let me defend myself!"

"Was that the reason for the estrangement between you and your grandfather?" Patti asked, incredulous. This was the first time Carol had let any conversation of her family shame reach this open level of discussion.

"Yes... that and a lot of words that neither of us meant." Carol sat on the edge of the bed, her head bowed. "What was worst was him believing I was guilty. If he had believed in my innocence, trusted my integrity, then he would have let me defend myself." Her hands fiddled unconsciously with the ties of the lacy sleeping gown of casaba yellow. "I never took one red cent from that contractor. He did *not* give me that sable coat. I don't care what he said, or how many receipts he had. I bought that fur with my own money."

She stopped to control her rising voice. When she had control, she continued, "For once I felt I could outdo Eva. She had asked Claud for a fur, and he'd refused. He denied Eva something that I could get without help. So I moonlighted and earned extra money by selling a house design. Oh, I could have gone to my trust fund and just taken the money, but it was important to me that I earn it." She gave a mocking laugh. "The irony of it all is that I earned the money by designing a house that I hated. It was everything that I never want in a home of my own."

Then her voice became husky as she remembered the ignominy of her past. "And I sold that design to a name recognized all over the city. He took it, boldly slashed his famous signature across the bottom and resold it at a most extravagant price. Those people paid dearly for an original by the city's most fashionable architect. They got a good copy of his style and are probably still singing the praises of that name and spreading his fame even farther." She raked graceful fingers through her hair.

"I couldn't make public the fact that my friend had not personally created those plans and leave him open to lawsuits and the possible destruction of his career. What I did was dishonest, but no one was hurt by it. My friend was happy; he had an acceptable design that he hadn't had the time to create. His influential clients were happy. Everybody was happy." Bitterness filled her words. "That's how I paid for that coat initially, but I don't think I'll ever finish paying the debt."

For a long time she sat silently, her index finger sliding up and down the ribbon of her nightie as tears streaked her cheeks. "Do you know how many times I've worn that coat? Twice. The first time I wore it, the man who had accused me of selling him false information for which he had paid with the coat just happened to be in Claud's office when I came parading in with all my smugness at having finally outdone Eva. God, how I hate that coat!"

Now her wound was fully open, and Carol wanted to let the pain ebb completely away. "I just wanted to have something that Eva didn't have. Claud always treated her like a prized and priceless piece of art; Tante Nan gloried in her; and René idolized his beautiful sister. I was so jealous—absolutely consumed with it. When Claud refused to buy her the fur, I saw my chance. How that one-upmanship cost me! Will I never finish paying?"

She lifted her shoulders in a shrug of bitter acceptance as her friend remained silent to allow Carol to exorcise the pain. "And look where we all are today. I've got a coat I don't need or want; Claud's in the hospital, maybe dying; and Eva...Eva's snug in the folds of the family, being squired about town by Ethan Greenlaw while I impose on you for bed and board."

Patti lay mutely on the other bed, then she snapped from her semireclining position and onto the floor. "You're not imposing on me. But since you're here, and you know how much I care about you, I think I have the right to say a thing or two." Patti awkwardly began to smooth the linen of her bed. Having accomplished that, she settled beside a very dejected Carol, throwing a comforting arm about her slumped shoulders.

She began quietly, "We didn't get around to discussing Ethan Greenlaw, and we both think he is influencing your mood, but we'll save that topic for another time. Right now I'm concerned about you and your home. Don't deny yourself the right to go home. Don't let anyone or anything stop you. It's your home now as much as it was three years ago or ten years ago or when you first went there to live." She watched Carol closely, but there was nothing to indicate what Carol was thinking.

"I like having you here, and nothing would please me more than your staying here permanently, but if you need to go home, if you want to go home, you just march right up to the front door, stick your key in the lock and yell out that you're there. Don't be afraid. Will you think about that?"

At Carol's nod Patti changed to a lighter tone. "Hop up, and I'll help you smooth these sheets. And since it's almost time to get up, we'll have to sleep fast."

Carol's responding smile was weak, but a smile nonetheless; she felt that at least she had made a crack in the shell Carol had constructed around herself and had allowed to harden during the period of estrangement from her family.

There was so little of the night remaining that Carol had no inclination to reflect on the happenings of that day or the conversation with Patti during the night. All too soon the morning would interrupt what little sleep she would manage.

CHAPTER THREE

CAROL AWOKE to find Patti standing over her with a steaming cup of coffee. "Up, up," Patti urged. "Unexpected business, and I have to be at the airport by nine. I'm taking a shuttle flight to Houston. You slept through the alarm and the phone. We'll be late. Get moving!"

Patti insisted that Carol make use of the car after taking her to the airport. The drive to Moisant International took more time than Carol had anticipated. As Patti entered the terminal, Carol waved a hurried goodbye and immediately headed the bright yellow car back toward the heart of the city. Lost time or not, she still wanted to stop at the hospital and spend the allotted few minutes talking to Claud.

The morning traffic was relatively light, and she quickly reached her destination. As she mounted the steps of the hospital, her spirits slowly sank. What did she hope to accomplish? Reaching his room, Carol stood in the doorway. The gaunt lines of his shrunken figure outlined beneath the sheet tore at her heart. She went to his bedside and leaned over his inert form. She urged his spirit to fight, to return to consciousness, but she knew she was not reaching that part of him with which she had always been in union.

Even though they had been separated for long years, Carol had always felt her grandfather still loved her. Why couldn't she reach that love now? A living and vital thing, it had existed independently of their moods and disappointments, independent of the others.

At the end of the session, she felt no nearer to bringing him back to her than she had on the first day. Even that little ray of hope she had first possessed was dimming.

Dejectedly she turned away, this time not waiting for the dismissing hand of the nurse. With one backward glance at the wall of monitoring machinery, she left.

Arriving at the office later than she had intended, she found Mrs. McLin in the process of preparing a coffee tray. Carol didn't have to ask for whom. Nor did she linger over her good-mornings to the secretary or the other staff who were visible through open doors. She reached her own office in time to answer the grating buzz of the interoffice phone. Mrs. McLin had wasted no time in heralding her arrival.

Out of sheer perversity she waited until an impatient second buzz sounded, and when she did answer, she assumed a quiet tone. "Miss Charbonnet."

She was surprised at the strange sensation she felt on hearing his voice again.

"Miss Charbonnet," he mocked, "would you please come to my office."

"Do you mean my grandfather's office?" Her voice was sweet, but she didn't feel sweet. She could not adjust to him being there. If anyone other than

Claud belonged in that office, it was she, power of attorney or not.

He had no intention of being drawn into a discussion of office ownership over the office communication system. Her question was answered by the blankness of a dead line. He had hung up on her.

"Two can play the game," Carol muttered. "First, it's what time I should be home, and now he hangs up on me." She removed the khaki-colored jacket she had worn with a matching slim skirt. She checked the garment to make sure it wrapped discreetly at her trim thigh as it had been designed and had not slipped as it tended to and exposed more of her leg than she felt comfortable with. After applying a fresh coat of lip gloss over her full lips and running a comb through her hair, she deliberately took her time in walking across the suite to the big windowed office.

Opening the door without knocking, she steeled herself for the encounter, hoping it would not be as devastating as the first or as confusing as the second. Ethan, however, was yet again a step ahead of her. It was not the penetrating gaze of his eyes that greeted her. Instead, he had swiveled the upholstered chair to face the expanse of glass overlooking the skyline of the sprawling city; presented to her was the back of his finely shaped head.

Without turning, he spoke in a tone of authority, "Pour yourself a cup of coffee and sit down." Carol couldn't help wondering if he used this tone with Eva, but she doubted it. Eva wouldn't stand for anyone telling her what to do, no matter how handsome he was.

She wanted to disobey his command but decided not to waste her energy. Instead, she poured her coffee and added a drop of milk to cut the chicory tang, since she was still in the process of reacclimatizing her palate to the New Orleans blend.

From where she settled into a chair, she could see the swirl of steam from the cup held in his strong hand. Still he did not face her as he began his inquisition. "Have you seen Claud?" At her affirmative answer he continued, "Have you spoken to his doctor?" Again she answered simply. "And what do you think? Do you really believe he will recover?"

The directness of his question startled her. It was the same question she had mentally asked herself a thousand times since she had come home, but it still hurt to verbalize an answer.

She stared into the brown liquid, wrapping her hands about the container to stop the chill that the thought brought. When she lifted her head, that riveting granite glance met her eyes.

Her answer was little more than a whisper. "I don't know. There doesn't seem to be much hope." What more could she say?

His manner changed abruptly with his next question. "Where have you been?" he demanded, his voice brittle.

Misunderstanding him completely, Carol's anger rose and she snapped, "I took my friend Patricia Trehan to the airport, and then I stopped by to see Claud." Ethan's questioning completely offended her, yet he managed to bait her into answering him—and that riled her even more.

"Don't be obtuse, Carol. Where have you been for the last two years?"

"Oh...." Carol's eyes opened wide, as she realized her error, which exaggerated their river greenness. Then Ethan, always aware of her, slid his glance from her face down her body to the neatly crossed legs and up again to where the unmanageable wrap skirt had opened to expose a generous expanse of shapely leg. His intense examination flustered her so that she couldn't answer.

What was it about him, Carol wondered. She had been perused in a sexual manner before. How and why was Ethan's study of her body any different?

"You were right," he said, an odd huskiness in his voice. Noticing Carol's look of puzzlement, he continued in the same tone, "You aren't like your cousin at all." His eyes moved upward to where a single pearl on a fragile gold chain rested in the hollow of her throat, then up to her lips and once more to lock with the green of her eyes. Suddenly the huskiness vanished as quickly as it had come. "I can't imagine Eva stumbling over a simple question like that."

She felt the flash of her indignation rising to the surface of her skin in two red flags on her cheeks. Before she knew what she was doing, she found herself accepting the lure.

Angrily she answered, "For your information, Mr. Greenlaw, I have been employed for the last two years by Maxwell Thompson Construction, home offices, Chicago. When I took leave of absence from that firm, I was in charge of federal bids. You needn't look at me as if I had spent the last two years under a rock or being kept by some man. There isn't a man alive who can keep me better than I can keep myself."

That he found her tirade amusing annoyed her even more. "Really, Miss Charbonnet?" He mocked her, formalizing her name. "Then you've not been kept by the right man." The lines around his mouth deepened with humor.

"You don't know who's kept me, and who hasn't. And if you think the right man is patterned after you, then just think again." Carol rose with the final word, slamming the delicate china cup and saucer against the tray. "If that's what you have to say, then you can say the rest of it to the wall!" She almost made an effective exit, but the iron bar of his arm was at the door before her.

"I'm not finished, Carol." His gentle use of her first name stifled whatever she had intended to say next. "This isn't turning out the way I meant it." He softened his tone but still held the door closed. "I think we both need to relax and get back to the business of Guerard Construction."

She reached up with a not-too-calm hand to brush a lock of heavy hair from her cheek. As she did, he took the lock from her and pulled it between his fingers. They stood motionless in their closeness, he intent on his examination of the hair and she intent on the quelling of her pulse, which raced with anger and something else, something new to her.

"Yesterday was such a long difficult day. I was so tired when I came here, and I still had more to do. I'm not usually so unobservant, but I wasn't expecting to find anyone here. And you had your back to me. It was your hair.... It's so much like Eva's."

It was as close to an apology as she was to get, and she knew it. She pushed the strand back into place, deftly removing it from between his thumb and forefinger. She kept her vision on the door, determined not to look at him.

"Mr. Greenlaw, I want nothing more than to restore this company to its former position among the greats in this city, and if you can help achieve this, then I am willing to work with you. But my personal life, including the last two years, has no bearing on anything that has to do with you."

He moved away from the door. From the corner of her eye Carol could see him standing at the window, his jacket thrown open and his hands at his narrow waist.

There was a heavy silence until he said blandly, "The question was not totally frivolous, nor did I mean to pry. If you had been uninvolved in this kind of business for two years, then you might have needed a period of orientation. Prices are still skyrocketing. Every company is economizing in areas where there was no previous thought of economy. Corners are being cut, and we have to make sure they are safe corners. I hope you see my point."

Ethan looked over his shoulder at her as she walked back to her chair and resumed her position. Then she calmly replied, "I think, Mr. Greenlaw, that you will find me a fairly reasonable person of fairly good intelligence. I could have understood your need to know about my background if you had approached it this way from the beginning."

He now stood with both hands leaning on the back of his chair. "Point taken. Pax, Carol?"

She looked fleetingly at the steel gray eyes before replying, "Pax, Mr. Greenlaw."

His face was expressionless; only his eyes narrowed to acknowledge her acceptance of peace between them. "It's Ethan," he corrected in a tone reminiscent of the night before. Then he became the professional. "Let's get on with the business of Guerard Construction."

He peeled off his coat and turned to the computer terminal adjacent to his desk. "First things first. Let me show you what we're into at the moment. There's nothing nearly so big or impressive as the projects Claud carried on in the past, but I think you'll find that we're involved in interesting construction, buildings that the right people are watching." His enthusiasm erased the earlier animosity and misunderstandings between them and made her feel that they were starting over on a new level.

Her full attention moved to the screen where the plans for a series of waterfront buildings were projected. Stepping around the desk, Carol came to stop directly behind Ethan's shoulder. As he slowly moved from diagram to diagram, a little grin flickered around her mouth. No, the finished product wouldn't look like much on the outside, she thought, just a series of decorated boxes stacked atop each other. But the structural design held implications of a possible change in the way all buildings, depending on pile foundations, might be constructed in the future.

The three-level buildings, consisting of an open parking level beneath the two stories of office suites, had exteriors expressing Brutalist detailing. Carol unconsciously signaled her impatience each time Ethan returned to an exterior view. She simply didn't like the style. To her the hoodlike projections over the windows and doors were awkward and made the openings look like vacant eye sockets. But these architectural features were unimportant. It was the supportive design that she wanted to study.

Unthinkingly her hand moved to Ethan's shoulder as she leaned forward to get a closer look at the skeletal outline, and she indicated the time she needed to examine each view by the pressure of her touch.

"Let me see the construction schedule," she asked, her interest evident in her tone. The schedule would tell her what should be happening on the site at any given time. She was startled at how brief it was start to finish; the plan called for only six weeks' worth of work.

At her intake of breath Ethan chuckled, "Shocking, isn't it?" He got up and urged her to take his chair, quickly reciting the computer formula so that she could call up the designs she wanted to review, then went to pull up another chair for himself.

Carol looked up from the screen to ask, "When can I visit the site?"

"Today, if you brought a change of clothes with you. There's no way you can go climbing over a construction site in an outfit like that. Even if you could, it would mean an absolute work stoppage with every man on the site watching you." He flashed a wicked grin at the dark color rising in her cheeks. Slowly the grin faded as he realized that Carol had heard none of his teasing banter. Her attention was riveted to the screen.

Carefully he set the chair beside her and stood for a while, also caught up in the lines and numbers on the screen. Carol was the first to break the silence. "Show me the rest of this."

He placed a firm hand under her elbow and pulled her from the seat and into the other chair. "You weren't supposed to see any of this," he responded tightly.

"Why not?" she asked as she watched the hard lines settle on his face as he resumed control of the machine.

"Primarily because I don't think I'm supposed to have the job plans and maybe not even supposed to know about the project."

"And is that all you're going to tell me?"

His face softened a little. "Almost. But I didn't get these plans and specifications by nefarious methods. I asked an old friend what he had that was interesting, and he sent me these." Ethan changed the image. "See the architectural firm?"

As she read the impressive legend, he explained, "Simon was my closest friend at university. Maybe he knew he was giving me an edge on the competition, and maybe he didn't. But I'm taking advantage of a gift from the Fates and doing everything in my power to win this contract."

There was such hard determination in his tone,

threaded like steel through concrete, that she had no doubts Guerard Construction would get the job. Then her misgivings surfaced. "Are we ready?"

"We?" He turned from the screen to her and repeated the word as if he was testing it for taste and texture. "We? Yes, we'll be ready." This was a new Ethan Greenlaw, one who upset her more than the other; then just as quickly as this facet of his personality had emerged, it was gone.

He changed the slides. "Now that you've seen this much, you might as well see everything I have." He started at the beginning and the identification—Taalot Shipping Lines. That was as impressive as the proposed structure itself.

Together they viewed angle after angle, design after design, of the office building that would someday rise five hundred feet and cover a ground mass equal to an entire city block.

From time to time Carol would watch Ethan's face instead of the screen, and she saw eyes that contained a possessive cast. He wanted that building. Her question was barely a whisper as she absorbed the implications of winning this contract. "How long do we have?"

"If everything works the way I have it planned, long enough." It was an elusive answer, but Ethan offered no other as he moved to the foundation plan. She kept with him as he slowly reviewed the foundation, the framework, the electrical outlay, the plumbing, straight through to the sheathing of Italianate travertine and tinted glass.

"Do you know the limitation the builder has set on

the extent of work done by subcontractors?" It was general practice that the owner determine the amount of subcontracting to insure the general contractor retained control. With limitations on subcontractors, the general contractor would supervise all work to insure the operation would develop on schedule.

Ethan leaned over to examine a detail. "We would handle the usual—the concrete, masonry, carpentry." He flicked back to the foundations. "Look at this, Carol."

Under normal conditions, the kind of building she was studying now would require forty-ton bedrock to support it. There was no bedrock beneath New Orleans, hence the elaborate system of pilings and mats. They would drive the piles down until they hit shale and then sink them deeper and deeper into the shale until they were assured of a stable foundation. The reports accompanying these plans indicated there would be shale at ninety feet, and they would drive through that for an additional one hundred and ten feet.

Ethan asked her to study those figures and named a structural engineering firm. "Are you familiar with them?" At her nod he continued, "That's where these numbers and stress factors came from. But that happens to be the same firm that did the factors for the Sibley complex, and you know what happened there." She remembered irreparable fissures running up exterior walls.

"I'm hesitant to trust these figures. I want you to make tests and see if you derive the same information." As a structural engineer, she would use her mathematical skills and determine the soil conditions deep beneath the surface. She would take borings at several depths at the proposed site and compare her findings with the figures that had been provided with the foundation specifications and pray that everything agreed.

"I'll get permission for you to work the property." Ethan let the screen go dark and rubbed his hand over his brow. "That is the one thing I find difficult to deal with here, never knowing what's underneath us. Do you suppose it's true that they never found a stratum of shale beneath the Superdome? I was told they drove the pile to two hundred feet and quit without ever hitting shale."

"Who knows? The rumors that came out during the construction of the dome were so wild you had to search for the truth," she answered seriously, then smiled at a memory, which she shared with him. "I like the one about the operation engineer who dug up a buried treasure, and the last that was ever seen of him was the glint of the knife he held in one hand to fend off his fellow workers and the bag of gold in the other." They both laughed. "But it is true that the closer you are to the river, the deeper you have to drive for shale."

He flicked on the screen for one last exterior view of the mighty building he wanted with tangible desire. Then he expelled a long breath. "I think that's enough of this for today. Let's get our heads out of the clouds and back to the projects at hand." Ethan summoned another program on the computer, and they continued to study the working projects. He was correct in that none of the projects was as grandiose as those of the past, but the company was at least busy. In fact, she was very surprised at the diversity of jobs that he presented to her.

From the working projects, they discussed jobs on which the company should bid and debated the merits of each. Unknowingly they worked through the lunch hour. Finally Ethan glanced at his watch, then leaned back in his chair. "Let's see what we get done on this," he indicated the folders before them that they had agreed merited their attention. "We'll give ourselves time to get most of this under way before we brainstorm again." He divided the lot between them. "Tomorrow have other clothes with you, and I'll take you *site-seeing*," he teased.

She liked him in this light mood, but it added to her worry of what the man was really like because in the next breath he was all business again.

"I think that's enough for today."

Accepting the dismissal, she nodded and rose to go, gathering the notes she had taken and her share of the folders. When she reached the door, he added, "Don't think we can do it all overnight, Carol. Competition is stiff—stiffer than it's ever been."

She paused long enough to see him reach for the phone. When she heard him ask Mrs. McLin to return Miss Eva Guerard's call, she didn't even bother to agree with his assessment of the business scene. Several times during their conversation Mrs. McLin had buzzed his office, and each time Ethan had answered with a terse no or equally terse yes. Now he was making amends to those callers.

Carol opened and closed the door to his office quietly, wondering why Ethan's relationship with Eva bothered her. She had just demanded her private life be kept independent of the office, and he should be able to expect the same privilege. His affair with Eva was none of Carol's business, but as she thought of how interesting she found Ethan, she added another item to the list of things for which she envied Eva.

After a late lunch in a downtown café, she allowed herself a few minutes in a large chain store. There she purchased a few items to restore her office to some of its former attractiveness. The dark green blotter and matching accessories would help. Later, she decided, she would find a better lamp. She wondered what had happened to the photographs that had been on the walls, photos of her cutting ribbons at opening ceremonies, of her with rolls of blueprints under her arm conferring with a supervisor. She wanted to find them and made a mental note to ask Mrs. McLin.

Back at the office she spent four hours doing the computations Ethan had requested. Twice Mrs. McLin interrupted to place steaming cups of coffee at her elbow but did not stop to chat. Once a call came from Patti to say she would be out of town until the weekend, and that Carol wouldn't need to meet her flight.

When Carol finally looked up from her work, the sky had already begun to darken. She felt resentment at herself for having worked through the last visiting hour at the hospital. Her shoulders slumped with the dejection she felt whenever she thought of her grandfather.

Another thought cut through her personal anguish. Why hadn't she seen any of the family during her visits? There weren't many times available; it stood to reason that she should have encountered someone. Involuntarily she twirled a pencil in her hand, leaning her head against the back of the chair.

Unconsciously she rose from her chair and crossed the suite. Without realizing it, she now stood in the window of Claud's office. It wasn't Claud's closeness she was seeking. It was the haunting figure of a much younger man.

When her subconscious thoughts became conscious, she pressed a hand in painful acceptance against the fast beating of her heart. Patti was right. Something was going on. She was compelled to acknowledge that she was becoming far too interested in her cousin's lover.

Quickly she gathered her jacket and handbag. She locked the office suite behind her and collected Patti's car from the underground garage of the complex. Her first thought was to return to the Quarter, but instinctively and for reasons she couldn't quite grasp she turned the small car upriver instead.

The traffic flowed smoothly, and she had no trouble finding a place across the avenue from the impressive residence that had been her home, and to which she knew she would have to return, and soon. But not just yet. She wasn't ready.

She sat watching the house. From her position she had a view of both the front and the side. There was something about her home that bothered her, had bothered her on the first afternoon, something elusive, elusive and frightening. She examined the exterior details and found nothing changed. The lawns were still as meticulously tended, the front columns shown in pristine whiteness, illuminated by the great hanging veranda lights. But still there was something cold, something foreboding.

She shrugged in an attempt to shake the eerie feeling, then started the car, pulled into the flow of traffic and turned once more downriver.

She didn't want to go back to the Quarter just yet. For one thing, she didn't like being alone, not now. She had spent enough time alone in the past, and already she was missing Patti's company. Secondly, once she got there, she knew she had to deal with Jim, and she still didn't know how to handle that situation. She also doubted that time would provide her with an answer, so she reluctantly headed back to the apartment.

After preparing a light supper of canned soup and a grilled-cheese sandwich, she finally drew the phone onto her lap and dialed the series of numbers.

As the rings sounded, she couldn't help wishing he would be out. When Jim finally answered, she didn't know what to say. For the first minute they exchanged banalities, then Jim took control of the conversation.

"Carol, how is your grandfather?" There was genuine solicitude in his tone.

"He's not well." Tears shook her voice. "I think he may be dying."

For a moment Jim said nothing. Then in a quiet voice he asked, "Do you want me to come to you?"

No, no, she silently shouted. That was the last thing she wanted. Her life was complicated enough without having to cope with keeping him as a friend when he wanted to be much more.

"Not now. So far I'm managing well. Will you call Maxwell and let him know that I'm not sure when I'll get back?"

Again Jim answered in protective tones. "You know I will, and if you decide you want me—"

Carol interrupted, knowing the rest of his sentence. "If I need you, I won't hesitate to send for you."

She gave him her address and phone number, and again reassured him that everything was under control. When she broke the connection, she hoped he wouldn't read more into her call than she meant. She could already feel the break in her ties with Jim and with the life she had lived in her self-imposed exile. There was no way she could ever go away again, come what may. And she had Guerard Construction to work for. Within the next week she would compose a letter of resignation so that Maxwell could find a replacement for her.

WHEN SHE ARRIVED at the office the next morning, Ethan was not in. She wondered at his whereabouts, but when she questioned Mrs. McLin, the secretary only knew that he had checked in with the office by phone. He had his pocket pager and could be reached if any emergency arose. He did not put in an appearance all morning.

Carol wryly acknowledged the way Ethan Greenlaw was influencing her life. In the closet hung jeans and shirt, and on the floor was a pair of safety boots stuffed with a thick pair of socks. She had come prepared, and he hadn't come at all.

She took time from her heavy work load to see Claud, but it only depressed her. On the way she stopped by the florist to buy a pot of forced-bloomed tulips of vibrant red. Even if he didn't know they were there, she felt as if she was doing something about such a hopeless situation. Maybe this feeling of utter uselessness was the cause for none of the family coming to see him.

Returning to the office, she reached for the phone to call the doctor. What could he say that he hadn't said Monday afternoon? She replaced the instrument and buried her fears in the problems of Guerard Construction.

When she reached the apartment, the phone was ringing. She almost didn't answer because she thought it would be Jim. After the eighth impatient trill she lifted the receiver.

It was one of the men who had been at Patti's fete the other night; he asked if she wanted to join a few people for another evening of jazz. She felt that Patti had probably asked him to include her in their plans, but since she didn't want to sit around feeling sorry for herself and worrying about Claud, she joined them. Again she had a late evening, but it made sleep so much easier.

THE NEXT MORNING had a sameness to it, but in midafternoon Ethan came in, strode across the office without greeting her, pulled open the narrow closet

He sat without moving. Around them the garage began to empty as the building vacated at the end of another business day. "Where have you been staying?"

"In the Quarter." Though her face was still averted, she felt him tensing, then a firm hand lifted her head and directed her face toward him. It was like looking into an Aztec mask as the reflected glow of the yellow headlights bronzed his skin. His words bit into her as much as the grip of his fingers on her chin.

"With whom?"

As she explained her relationship with Patti, Ethan relaxed but did not release his grip. "You have to go home sometime."

Carol shook her head.

"Miss Nan needs you."

"She never needed me," she insisted. "She has and always did have Eva." Again the grip on her chin tightened.

"She needs *you*," he disputed. "I suggest that you go upstairs, change your clothes, and I'll take you there now."

"No!" Her denial was so pain filled, and the haunted look on her face so pronounced that he couldn't fight her; he couldn't force her.

"All right, Carol. Not tonight. But I want you to decide when and how you are going home, and if it isn't soon, I'll drag you there screaming and kicking if I have to. You may be surprised at what you find when you get there." He released her chin and at the same time glanced at the clock over the elevator door. "You might as well call it a day. I'll read over the field supervisors' reports, and if there isn't anything demanding my immediate attention, I'm finishing for the day, too." He looked down at her heavy boots with the steel-reinforced toes that offered some protection from dropped building supplies and the like. "Are you coming up to change, or are you returning to the Quarter like that?"

"I'll change."

Once inside the suite, he bade her good-night, then he closed himself in his office, leaving her to change her clothes and make her way back alone to the French Quarter apartment.

PATTI HAD RETURNED from Houston when Carol finally made it back to the Quarter. Having arrived that morning and spent the rest of the day at her office, Patti was ready to go out with her friends. She urged Carol to join them, but Carol was in no mood for boisterous company.

Instead, she wanted a quiet evening to mull over the things Ethan had suggested about her going home. And ponder them she did, but eventually the quietness of the apartment and her inability to reach a conclusion began pressing in on her, and she had to get out.

Automatically her feet led her to Jackson Square, and she settled on a bench to watch the passersby. For an hour or more she was content, then again her restlessness betrayed her, and she had to move. This time she went down to the market and into the produce stalls, where she watched the regular customers haggle with the vendors. Eventually she bought a few pieces of fruit and a stalk of sugarcane, which the friendly vendor peeled and cut into bite-sized portions for her. With her little bag of mixed fruit tucked under her arm, she walked back up the market, indulging in the time-honored feminine pastime of window-shopping.

Back at the square she crossed over the market wall, the railroad tracks, and climbed the ramp of the Moon Walk, an observation platform that afforded an unobstructed view of the river. Rejecting the benches for the walk itself, Carol descended the steps of the mock boat landing to sit at the water's edge. She chewed the sweet nectar from the sugarcane. When only the stringy fibrous residue was left, she tossed the remains into the river and popped another section into her mouth. The forlorn wail of a tugboat's horn echoed her own despair.

She decided that she must do something and soon. She had to make that first contact with the rest of her family but was no closer to determining how than she had been earlier. She liked the freedom from stress in not having to deal with Eva on a daily basis, but she was also tormented with guilt at not attending to Nan. That sense of family was part of her cultural heritage. Maybe she could deny the strength of the ties to René and Eva, but she could never forget her responsibility to Claud and Nan. She had tried—she saw how far she got with that. One little note from Nan and she had come running, and her guilt at not coming all the way was eating her alive.

THE NEXT DAY Ethan kept her busy reviewing building sites, but after she returned from visiting Claud, while they were having coffee, he broached the subject again. "Have you thought about going home, Carol?" At the shake of her head he changed the topic. "When is your friend leaving?"

Patti would leave Thursday morning, she told him, and Carol had already thought of the emptiness without her. Carol had purposefully avoided most of her other friends and all of her family. She knew Ethan had guessed as much when he raked a lean hand over his face in exasperation.

"Carol, Carol, what am I to do with you? You cannot continue this solitary existence, and now that your friend is leaving, you need more than ever to renew some of your old ties. You cannot remain this isolated forever."

Carol rose from the straight-backed chair to replenish her coffee, ignoring his opening for her to talk to him.

"This friend, Patti, seems to have accepted your return without any recriminations or putting any restrictions on you. Doesn't it seem likely, then, that others, especially your family, will welcome you in the same manner?"

"Patti is special." Carol couldn't tell him how deep her trauma ran, and how brave it had been of her to turn to that one friend. Nor did she relate her suspicion that Patti screened the small circle of acquaintances Carol had seen.

Ethan had been leaning back against the wall in his chair, balancing on two legs. Now he plopped his cup down on the small table and in the same motion snapped the front legs of the chair down to meet the tiled floor, both staccato sounds accenting his impatience with her.

"Since we seem to be at a deadlock, I have one more solution to offer. Let me introduce you to some people who have never heard of Guerard Construction except through me, and if they have heard it elsewhere, they will never associate your name with the company."

His suggestion stung her, and she whirled around defensively. "I don't need your charity. I have friends both old and new. I don't sit around bemoaning my state, thank you. I go out, have dates. There's Eric and—" But her litany didn't pass the first name.

"You keep away from him!" Ethan, too, was on his feet now, his face dark with barely suppressed thunder.

"And what's wrong with Eric?" she demanded but took a defensive step back, flinching at his vehemence.

"What's wrong with Eric?" he mimicked. "I'll tell you what's wrong with him. He wants you. It's written all over his face."

His words shocked her to the core. "How dare you sit in judgment of a man you have seen only once, and then across a street and in a darkened room. You know nothing, absolutely nothing, about his feelings for me." Her sense of injustice at his manner and accusation rose to match the anger within him.

"You think it takes more than one look at you, do you? Your naiveté surpasses belief. I recognize what's in him even if you don't, and you are to keep away from him. Do I make myself clear?"

"You most certainly do. You make yourself loud and clear." She raised the volume of her voice to a level that nearly matched his as she continued, "So loud and clear that I'm sure half the central business district, as well as every single person in these offices, knows that you want me to keep away from the man and exactly why."

A dark flush stained Ethan's neck and face. Both of them were aware of an unnatural stillness in the offices that usually hummed with the sounds of telephones, typewriters, human voices, the sounds of productivity. It was as if all Guerard Construction held its collective breath.

He turned to the doorway and realized that the door hadn't been closed. "My God, Carol, I apologize, I sincerely apologize." He spoke in a softly modulated tone. "If you want me to, I will apologize at the top of my voice so that all the ears out there can hear that part, too." He lowered his voice even more so that she would be the only one to hear. "But I apologize only for shouting at you. I do not apologize for what I said."

"Oh, Ethan...." She turned to the counter top and rested her weight on her hands, her back to him.

She knew he would come to touch her, and he did, drawing her back against him. "I am sorry, Carol. I don't know what made me rage at you like that. You didn't deserve it." He loosened his grip on her shoulders, but he did not release her. "Let's restore some of our amicability, and you hear me through this time with no interruptions from you and no lectures from me. Forget about my introducing you to people, forget everything. Just come out with me this weekend, and let's relax together. We could go to a football game or boating, or to dinner and dancing. Will you come with me?"

She was tempted to turn his caring embrace into something more powerful, and that same urge decided her answer. "No," she stated clearly.

He dropped his touch from her. "No? Why? Do you think my instincts are as base as those of which I accused Eric? Is that why?"

"I don't know why." She turned to face him, hoping he couldn't read the lie in her face. It wasn't Ethan's instincts she feared. They were obvious, and things in the open could be dealt with. It was her own muddled feelings that alarmed her. "I can't," she said numbly. Then she went to her office, seeking the sanctuary of work and left him standing alone.

CHAPTER FOUR

WHEN CAROL ARRIVED at work Monday morning, Mrs. McLin greeted her with the message that Ethan was out of town. She didn't know exactly when he would return, maybe Tuesday or Wednesday afternoon. He hadn't said where he was or how he could be reached; all he had left were instructions that Carol was to take over while he was away and to recheck the deep strata of earth beneath the location of the proposed Taalot building.

Carol decided to get that under way first. With the help of one of the men in the office, she loaded her equipment onto a Guerard truck. Other much heavier equipment was to be brought to the site directly from the warehouse. After so much emotionalism in the past week Carol looked forward to taking samples, running tests on them, doing the necessary calculations.

By afternoon she had showered away the dirt of the field and replaced the jeans and gingham shirt for more businesslike dress. Seated before the console, she began to program the computer and spent that afternoon analyzing the data and arranging the printouts for comparison with the competing firm's information. It was absorbing work; she had little time to think about the vacant office on the other side of the suite. The only break she took was to visit the hospital, then she was back again with the objectivity of mathematics.

She did stay late to review the daily reports of the field supervisors, but Guerard men were well trained, and except in the most extreme circumstances, they handled the fieldwork without aid from the construction engineer. Part of their great sense of responsibility might have come from their knowing that Ethan—and before him, Claud—would be in and out and on top of everything, which didn't afford them too much opportunity to be slack. Their dedication gave the company the distinct advantage of few delays on projects and few labor difficulties. The hourly worker knew he would be treated fairly and justly, but in return he was expected to perform his job competently.

THE NEXT DAY Carol did manage to get out into the field, but she kept a low profile. When she had been out with Ethan the previous week, she had noted the raised eyebrows of a few of the employees, those who had known her for many years. She could guess at their thoughts, and those imagined thoughts made her uneasy.

The afternoon was spent with her data and with setting up the background for bidding on upcoming projects. She did pause to think about Ethan's words concerning her returning home. She knew it had to come sometime. Either she would go home or return to Chicago or someplace like it, and she knew she never wanted to do that again.

For Carol the third day was much like the second. All afternoon she listened for the arrival of Ethan. When she returned from seeing Claud, she felt sure he would be there. The door to his office was ajar, but no dark head was bent over the desk.

Forcefully she immersed herself in work, not even looking up when she bade Mrs. McLin good-night. If she finished this section, tomorrow she could get a rough estimate of the bid they could present in the time-honored sealed envelope. On she worked, ignoring the passing of time until the feeling of being watched caused her to raise her eyes from the column of figures.

"Do you always concentrate with the tip of your tongue between your teeth?" a low voice asked. Ethan stood there grinning, a lined overcoat slung over one shoulder, his tie loosened, and a heavy shadow of blue black stubble darkening his chin. In his hand he held an attaché case.

She peered over the bright desk lamp to where he stood in the shadows. All she could manage was a breathy "You're late."

The pleasant half smile faded. "Don't nag, Carol. That's not what I need from you." Ethan's good mood vanished. "Bring in what you've done, and let's get to work. But first call that corner restaurant, and tell Nick to send up a couple of po'boys. Roast beef and whatever you want." The last was called down the hall as he made for the big office.

At Ethan's mention of food, Carol remembered that she had not eaten, and she was hungry for a po'boy, a sandwich made on narrow French bread, crackly crusted on the outside and light on the inside. Her hunger increased as she tried to decide what filling she wanted—soft-shelled crab, Italian sausage, fried trout.

She had the phone directory open and half the number dialed before she realized how arrogant he had been to assume that she would do his bidding without a please or thank-you. How dare he! She had been working hard since early morning and had no intention of spending half the night at the office because he hadn't bothered to show up during the day. He could damn well send out for his own food. Slamming the phone down, she started to rise from her chair, then had second thoughts....

He was probably trying to rile her. He had likely spent some of the past five days—or *nights*—with Eva, listening to some wild tale about Carol and now had decided that having her back in the company would be no benefit to him. If that were his purpose—if he was trying to get rid of her—then she could thwart him more effectively by feigning indifference rather than by openly rebelling. Carefully she redialed the number and placed the order. Schooling her features to a studied casualness, she made her way down the hall.

He stood, stripped to the waist, at the hand basin in the washroom adjoining the executive office. He had already scraped half his face clean of the icy-smelling shaving cream. The sight of his naked torso tightened the muscles in her lower stomach as she watched taut sinew ripple across his shoulders when he reached down to rinse the soapy razor. She stood entranced at his performing that totally masculine act.

Without moving from his reflected image in the mirror above the basin, he addressed her. "Did you get the food?" He didn't miss a swipe even as he talked; he was quite comfortable in front of a female audience.

Turning away from the tantalizing scene, Carol reached out to touch a paperweight on the desk. She had given the glass reproduction of Excalibur to Claud, paid for with money she had earned when she was only eight years old by helping a neighbor repave his patio. Even then she had loved building. The rough edges of the brick had made her hands bleed, but how proud she had been! Even Nan's scolding about how a lady should protect her hands didn't remove the glow. These memories and the polished-glass memento helped to calm her now.

"The food is on its way, Ethan." In the glass of the window she could still see him as he wiped the last traces of lather from his face. Covertly she watched him put on the pale blue shirt, button it halfway up his broad chest and roll the sleeves back, exposing strong wrists. Standing transfixed by his intimate movements, she watched as he unbuckled his belt, then unzipped his trousers to tuck in the long tails of his shirt.

She saw him reach up to extinguish the washroom light. They stood now in semidarkness. "Carol," Ethan began in husky tones that stopped her breath. Though she could no longer see him, she heard him take the long strides that brought him to her side.

This time she was prepared for the hand that turned her to him, but she could not have been prepared for the jolting surge of longing that echoed in the wild beating of her heart. But he didn't kiss her, and she simply could not breathe. She felt as if the thumping of her struggling heart was audible to him. Every cell in her body screamed for relief, for the touch of his mouth on hers.

Finally she forced her lungs to take in air, but that only served to increase her torture, for now she could smell the soap with which he had washed his hands, the hands that now held her face scant inches from his mouth. She thought her knees would buckle beneath her, and the thudding of her heart resumed. He was marking her. She was now within his domain, a territory in which his desires knew no restrictions.

What was he waiting for? Surely he knew her torment. She was in his arms, but he just held her, branding her with his all-seeing eyes. His breath mingled with hers, and she waited.

Suddenly the strident summons of the entrance bell shattered the anticipation, destroyed the moment like the first streak of heat lightning cracks through the oppressive heaviness that presages a summer storm. His hands pressed painfully against her cheeks as if to deny the intrusion. He took one slow step away from her, took a deep breath, then went to answer the summons. She knew the moment was irrevocably lost, and she didn't know whether to rejoice or to lament its passing.

She heard Ethan engaged in friendly banter with someone and realized that the delivery boy had arrived. Judging from their tone, the two were acquainted with each other. Obviously this was not the first time Ethan had called for supper to be sent up to the Guerard offices. Unbidden, thoughts of Eva sharing a repast here came to Carol's mind.

When Ethan returned, he was carrying a bag containing the sandwiches. Without looking at her, he ripped the bag down the side to form a protective covering for the desk top. Then he opened the first of the crusty loaves.

"Oyster, must be yours." He handed her the loaf, his manner casual and his glance revealing nothing of his thoughts. While she arranged her sandwich on the small table before the office sofa, he searched the liquor cabinet.

With a grunt of satisfaction he said, "I knew I had seen one here." He held for her inspection a bottle of rosé. She nodded in approval, and he deftly uncorked the flagon to pour them each a glass. He placed hers on the table beside her food, then eased himself into the chair behind the desk.

Carol bit into the po'boy, remembering the countless times she had tried to make the local specialty while she had been away, and how often she had failed. The secret had to be the French bread, she thought.

Ethan sipped from the glass, neither touching the sandwich nor looking at her. Finally he gave a sigh, "Carol Charbonnet, you are the least curious lady I've ever met." He turned the chair around to face her directly.

She brushed the crumbs from her fingers onto the wrapper. "Why do you say that?"

"Don't you want to know where I've been?" he asked with growing irritation.

"Only if it concerns me, and it concerns me only if it has something to do with Guerard Construction. Did your whereabouts concern the company?" She managed a tone that sounded as disinterested as her words.

"Only part of it concerns the company, but all of it does concern you." He rose and leaned against the desk, looking at her intently. "I've been to Chicago."

Carol immediately was wary. "Why? We haven't involvements in Chicago."

"Ah, now you are curious," he mocked. His sarcasm angered her because he had deliberately whetted her curiosity, then ridiculed it.

"Ethan, will you stop the cruel taunts and tell me what you've been up to?" Her temper was rising. She had spent little more than a week with this man and in that time had experienced the whole spectrum of emotions.

He deliberately took a slow sip of wine before continuing. When he spoke, it was not in answer to her original question.

"Do you really think I'm cruel?" Curiosity mixed with puzzlement was evident in his tone.

Carol flung at him, "I honestly don't know what to think about you. You are a stranger to me, someone who has made his way into the affairs of my family, into this company." With a quick jerk she wadded the half-eaten meal and flung it into the trash basket, all delight in it gone.

"Look, Ethan, I'm tired. I've been here all day,

it's late, and I'm going home." She got to her feet. "I don't know what you have planned, but it can just wait until another day."

He didn't move, but his next words stopped her. "The crates and trunks from your apartment will arrive by airfreight Friday morning."

Carol stared at him, disbelieving. "What did you say?" Surely, she thought, she couldn't have heard him correctly.

"You heard me," he snapped. "I informed Maxwell Thompson that you would not be returning, packed up your belongings and had them shipped home. All I didn't do was kiss lover-boy lawyer goodbye for you."

She whirled to face him. "You couldn't have! You had no right to touch one item of my personal property. You are the most insufferable human I have ever encountered. What gave you the right...?" The tears of frustration floated to the surface, making her eyes even greener.

His expression had not changed, and the mask he wore angered her more. Then something drained from him, and for a second his shoulders were not so straight. "Don't tempt me to tell you what gave me the right," he said wearily, a flatness in his voice. "I think we've said enough tonight. You were correct. It can wait. Go home."

She stood staring at him in openmouthed amazement.

"Don't say anything more tonight, Carol. I've changed my mind. Now is not the time to talk about any of this. It's way too soon."

If only Ethan realized that she had nothing more to say, nor did she understand what he meant by his last remark. His arrogance left her wordless. Carol turned and went out, leaving Ethan to contemplate the contents of his wineglass.

All the way to the apartment and even as she prepared for bed, Carol sought a way to avoid the situation Ethan's presumptuous action had created. Ultimately she accepted the only solution: she would see Nan the following day.

THE NEXT MORNING, as soon as she awoke, Carol remembered it was Thanksgiving, and she remembered the three things she had to do. She had to take Patti to the airport, visit Claud and—go home.

Seeing Patti off was more emotionally draining than Carol had anticipated, for this time her friend would be away for weeks instead of a few days. They hadn't had much time together, and within the recess of her heart Carol knew that in the weeks to come she would have need of her friend. Refusing the fear of loneliness permission to surface, Carol had cheerfully waved goodbye as Patti's plane taxied away. From across the river the early-morning mist floated and seeped out of the surrounding peat-bog swamps that were prevented from reclaiming the land only by a small dike.

From the airport Carol went directly to the hospital. After her visit to Claud she continued up St. Charles Avenue, the whole time repeating to herself that she had to do this. She had to visit Nan. Ethan had made sure of that. Besides, it was time. There would not be a better one. Nothing would change the past.

Finally she reached the familiar house. The wrought-iron gates were closed and still locked, so she made her way to the side entrance, where she fitted a key she had carried for so many years into the old but well-tended lock of the pedestrian gate opening to the side street.

Once inside the yard, she was overwhelmed with misgivings. Perhaps she should have called Nan and let her know she was coming. Perhaps a holiday wasn't the best time to put in a surprise appearance. It was too late to be thinking like this; there was absolutely no way for her to back down now. She had set her course and compelled herself to follow it.

The back door was unlocked, and she tapped lightly against it as she pushed it open. Gracie, the old black woman who had been cook and companion to Nan for so many years, sat at the kitchen table, a portable television tuned to a soap opera in front of her. She looked up at her entrance and made no mistake at who stood in the doorway.

"Oh, my sweet honey! You've finally come home." Huge tears began to trail down her shiny face of polished ebony. Before Carol could take a deep breath, she was clasped against Gracie's fat bosom and thoroughly hugged. Each squeeze was accompanied by a soft croon of joy.

"Honey, is Miss Nan going to be happy to see you!" Finally she released Carol. "Just let me look at you a little while, and then I'll go tell her you're here." She pushed Carol back and stood inspecting her from head to toe. A frown marred Gracie's soft features, and she shook her head.

Carol laughed. Gracie had always found some fault in every member of the family. She felt the whole lot was too skinny, and evidently she hadn't changed her mind about proper proportions. "Where have you been that you didn't get very much to eat? You're skinny as a rail." Then the gentle brown eyes moved to her hair. "I don't like that hairdo, me. I don't like it one bit. No, ma'am, not one bit." Then she broke into another gold-toothed grin. "But I'm sure glad to see you, even if you are just a bag of bones." Once more she embraced Carol before leaving to prepare Carol's great-aunt, her departure accompanied by dark mutterings about her baby coming home on Thanksgiving, and there not being a thing in the house fit to eat.

It was Nan's pride and joy, her grand salon in which she reigned over the silver teapot and fragile La Courtille cups. Here a protective film applied to the windowpanes filtered the sunlight to protect ancient and costly fabrics—the muted green silk covering the walls and draping the tall windows, the red damask of the serpentine-backed sofas, the pale creams and darker greens of the Savonnerie carpet that spread thickly under fragile chairs and graceful tables. On an elaborately carved cabinet between two side windows sat a tall vase filled with long-stemmed roses of the same vibrant red as the damask. Their beauty was reflected in the ornate mirrors.

Carol took a deep breath of the perfumed air and let the serene beauty of the room wash over her like a healing balm. It was beautiful but too formal to suit the upcoming reunion.

They had always gathered in the smaller family room, a refuge from the splendor of the rest of the ground-floor rooms. It was to this den that she now moved.

Looking at the familiar family pictures mounted on the wall, she felt her spirits lift. They couldn't be called portraits in the strictest sense; some were snapshots, others newspaper clippings or school photos. Included were drawings done in childish crayons. It was a wall of mementos, a scrapbook on permanent display.

She trailed her hand over the big reclining chair near the fireplace. It was Claud's chair. He had sat there every Sunday morning, first reading the New Orleans papers, then the one from Baton Rouge. He preferred the news in the *Times-Picayune*, but when it came to sports, he relied on the paper from the state capital.

Her eyes lingered over the contemporary leather sofas, easy chairs, the tables with marproof tops. She walked to the piano that was seldom played and ran her fingers through a quick scale, then closed the cover.

She loved this room, and this love for her home and family must have been showing in her face, for the elderly lady's mouth softened as she watched her niece fondle the lamp shade, the curtains, the porcelain dog by the fireplace.

"Well, young lady, it's about time you got back where you belong." The interrupting voice startled Carol almost as much as the sight.

Changes had taken place in Nan, too—not just physical changes. There was a new gentleness about her that Carol had never seen before. Gone was the hauteur, the social arrogance, which Nan had worn like a badge against not only those she felt to be socially inferior, but also against anyone she felt was getting too close. And that had frequently included Carol.

She had never seen the shield go up against Eva or René. Perhaps because they had never tried to elicit warmth from Nan, she had never had to shut them out. It was only Carol who had craved a maternal touch that never came. But something was different now.

Carol took in the physical alterations. The most obvious was the absence of the silver-topped ebony cane. In its place was a three-sided walker upon which her aging relative rested both hands. Carol watched as she took a pain-filled step, then dragged the walker forward before taking another awkward step. Each movement tugged at Carol's heart. As many times as her overtures of love had been rejected, she couldn't keep aloof from the woman now.

Especially not now. They were a family, a Creole family only slightly tainted by the lighter strains of some German interloper in years too far back to remember. And family was everything. It had taken Carol two years of loneliness to remember that code bred into them, but her being back was proof that she had remembered.

"Tante," Carol addressed Nan as she gently helped her to the small wing chair that was her chair

much as the recliner belonged to Claud. After she had settled her aunt, Carol pulled a stool in front of the woman, then waited. After a while Nan spoke, and it was much what Carol had expected.

"We Guerards have never fled in the face of adversity, Carol, and your choosing to do so was a deep disappointment to both Claud and myself. It showed what little faith you had in us to weather the *scandale*," Nan whispered the dreaded word. "You should have known that Claud would protect you."

"But I did nothing wrong. I tried to tell you all that I had done nothing." Her shoulders slumped, and the finely shaped head bowed as she repeated, "I didn't do it."

The gnarled hand reached out to stroke the golden hair of the younger woman, the touch of comfort a new sensation for both. "So Claud said—and would have said to you if you had waited, and if he had not been so violent during those first days. Now it is finished. We will go on."

Carol's head came up at those words. "He knew that I didn't do it?" she questioned as her hope flickered, then died. Claud would have been able to convince Nan that everything had been a mistake; Nan would never question what Claud had decreed. If he had proclaimed Carol innocent over breakfast one morning, then for Nan it would have been fact, a fact forever unless Claud would announce a new truth. The matter had been settled to Nan's satisfaction. She believed Carol to be innocent of wrongdoing concerning the business because Claud had said so, and Carol was forgiven for running away. It was obvious to Carol that Nan had said all she meant to say about the subject and wanted to turn to another topic.

Carol knew instinctively what that topic would be and listened patiently as Nan recounted Eva's social accomplishments. Eva was as always the darling one; that much had not changed, but it didn't hurt Carol as much anymore.

"Won't René and Eva be happy to have you back," Nan stated joyfully as she thought of the impending reunion. Once more Nan reached out with unaccustomed familiarity to touch Carol.

"Where are they?" Carol questioned. "The house is too quiet for them to be in. Have they gone for the tree?"

It had been a family tradition to get their Christmas tree on Thanksgiving morning. While Nan saw to the holiday meal, Claud and the three grandchildren would drive across Lake Pontchartrain to wooded land that Claud owned. Once across the lake, they would mount horses and ride to the boundary of the property, where the land gradually merged with the swamp. With the tree secured on a truck brought home from the company pool, they would return to the city in time to bathe, change their clothes and sit down to the long table filled with the foods traditional for a Creole feast day.

The meal always centered on the *cochon de lait*, a milk-fed suckling pig roasted to a golden hue; the *vol-au-vent*, a baked shell filled with oyster stew; and a turtle shell stuffed with richly seasoned turtle meat. And present on the holiday table, as it was at every

Sunday dinner, was "dirty" rice, a local specialty made with chicken livers and gizzards, plus a potpourri of herbs and other seasonings. The wonderful meal would be served late, and guests would be plenty.

The company always included godparents, distant cousins only seen on high holidays, and anyone Claud thought needed the warmth his family could offer on that day. It had not been unknown for him to bring in a laborer or two who had ventured far from home in search of work and had no family to share the holiday.

Carol should have known that there would be no feast today, for the kitchen had been empty of simmering pots and the tangy aromas associated with the big meal. Nan's eyes shifted to the fireplace as she answered Carol's question.

"I don't know where René is..." she began sadly, but the gleam was restored to the faded blue of her eyes when she mentioned Eva. "Eva is in New York right now. She did call earlier to say where she would be having dinner, but I can't remember. She sounded so excited. She's been there a little over a week, and every time she calls home, she seems pleased with her success there."

"Whatever is she doing in New York?" Even as she asked the question, Carol's quick mind was thinking of other things. Now Carol knew why Ethan had had so much time to spend with her—Eva had been out of town. Carol was not foolish enough to think Ethan would prefer her company over that of her much more glamorous cousin; there had to be some other reason. Eva knew and was accepted by every important and influential person in New Orleans social circles, by people who could help Ethan to restore Guerard Construction to its former prominence. And Eva's life was decidedly more exciting than Carol's; she lived in and thrived on the limelight. Carol had always known these things, but it didn't make her feel better to have it verified that she had been only a substitute.

"She's a maid in the Court of Hebe and couldn't find a thing in New Orleans she wanted to wear. You know how particular she is. Of course, her ball gown is being designed and made right here. We have so many fashion experts who have devoted all their talents exclusively to creating gowns for the Mardi Gras balls it would be an absolute waste of time to think you could find something better elsewhere. What she has gone after are the little dresses and gowns for the teas, suppers and soirees."

Carol was dumbfounded at Nan's statement. Here the family was in a time of crisis, and Eva had left on a shopping spree to New York. "How nice," was the only comment she could manage. She knew how much Nan relished the old New Orleans traditions. "I know just how proud that makes you."

As Nan went on to identify the other maids and the queen of the court, Carol let her thoughts drift. Mardi Gras...the Carnival. She hadn't heard the words in two years, not in the same connotation. To the rest of the world, the word carnival brought images of popcorn, beer, booths of chance, midways. In New Orleans the word was capitalized and treated with a respect bordering on awe. In New

Orleans, Carnival was an entire season officially beginning on Twelfth Night and continuing until midnight of Shrove Tuesday—Mardi Gras. It was a season of debuts, elaborate tableau balls and of parades. It was a season of krewes, private clubs with strange names like Okeanos, Pegasus, Nemesis, Daughters of Eve. And those krewes existed solely to stage the balls and parades, to become reigning royalty in the mythical lands depicted in their balls. To be invited to reign beside a krewe member was the highest of all social honors.

The Krewe of Vili, of which Claud had been a member, was honoring Eva. But with that honor came tremendous financial responsibilities. It was true that money alone could not buy a position in court, that family remained the most important consideration, but someone must be able to pay the expenses that reigning in a Mardis Gras court entailed. Even when the krewe presented the queen and maids with their jewel-encrusted trains, crowns and scepters, there were still the ball gowns to be purchased, and many were known to cost thousands of dollars. In addition to that special gown, there was the rest of the wardrobe to be paid for—gowns for teas, receptions, dances, parties, breakfasts, luncheons, and ball after ball after ball.

While keeping half a mind on Nan's account of last year's Carnival and her expectations for the upcoming season, Carol wondered how Eva was affording all the trimmings that came with her position. Eva's income came solely from her share in the company, and from Carol's understanding, there hadn't been much income from the firm. She concluded Claud had provided for Eva before his illness.

"I suppose René is running around in circles with the Mardi Gras season not very far away." Carol deliberately shifted the topic from Eva.

"My, yes. He doesn't even get home for dinner very often." The old eyes saddened. "Without your grandfather here and with Eva out of town, it's been very lonely. So many of my friends have passed on. Yes, it's very lonely."

Her facial features softened as she looked up from her twisted hands. "But that will all change now that you're here. The first thing I have to do is get on the phone and assure myself that you won't be left out of the Carnival season. It's too late to expect a position at court, but I just know you will receive call outs to all the really important balls. Soon, with Eva back and you here, this house won't be so still anymore."

This was proof positive that Nan didn't know she had been in the city for nearly two weeks. But Carol wasn't ready to return to the house, not until she came to terms with herself about the painful events of two years ago. And right now, playing the part of a socialite didn't fit into her plans.

Gently Carol covered her great-aunt's hands with her own. *"Tante,"* she began in a small voice, "I'm not coming directly back here. I'm going to stay for a while in the Quarter. You remember Patricia Trehan. Patti has loaned me her apartment."

At the authoritative look on Nan's face, Carol began to waver. "You have no business staying down there among all those *hippies*, those bohemians,"

Nan charged. "It's not the proper place for a young lady to live alone. I cannot understand what has come over the Trehans. I know that Patricia's parents have left the city, but she still has enough family remaining here to see after her well-being."

"Antoinette," Carol chided affectionately, "I don't think there are any hippies nowadays, and many and 'proper' young ladies are living in the Quarter."

"Well, that certainly wasn't true in my day nor in your mother's. I think your place is here in your own home, sleeping in your own room. Your staying in a friend's apartment—why, the very idea!"

Carol knew she would be in for the same lecture she had been hearing since she was three years old if she didn't change the topic immediately. "Do you think Gracie could use my help in the kitchen? There didn't seem to be much going on in there when I came in, and it's getting late."

"Probably. She—like the rest of us—is getting on in years and doesn't move nearly so nimbly. We do have another maid who comes in three days a week. Gracie says she has always taken care of this house and always will; that she spends as much time checking behind the maid as she would have spent in doing it herself. But it has eased a great burden from her."

Carol found the kitchen a much busier place when she returned there. "You should have let me know you were coming," the black woman fussed. "Miss Nan won't eat no matter what I fix for her, and Miss Eva is always on a diet. And lately Mr. René would rather drink his meals here. With you home this kitchen will be a place where something happens other than making coffee and toast."

Judging by the ingredients spread over the counter tops, Carol didn't doubt the prophecy. "What are you making?" she ventured as she filched a stalk of celery from the freshly washed pile near the sink.

"The best I can do today is a chicken gumbo. It won't be anything like Thanksgiving is supposed to be around here, but you just wait until tomorrow night, and I'll make up for serving nothing but a common old gumbo."

To Carol, nothing that had ever come out of Gracie's kitchen was common, and this gumbo wouldn't be, either.

The house was oddly quiet for a holiday, with just the two of them, Nan and Carol, at home for the meal. It was not at all like any Thanksgiving of the past. Nan insisted that Carol remain at the house, and Carol was equally adamant that she should not. By late afternoon she could take no more.

"Sweetheart, I'm returning to the Quarter now. You're not to worry. It's just for a couple of weeks until I have a few more things sorted out. But I'll see you every day, I promise. I'll come for dinner and let Gracie fatten me. But I must go now." Carol planted a kiss on the still-smooth brow and left before Nan could convince her to stay.

She went out the front, opening the big gates electronically. When they closed behind her, they would automatically relock. Standing on the street, she looked back at the house. Now she knew what it lacked—life; it needed an injection of vitality. Carol had no idea how to make things livelier, but she would start by getting a Christmas tree. In the old days, she mused, it would have been on the veranda by now, waiting for Judson to help Claud move it into the parlor early in the morning.

The thought hurt her. Just as today there was no cypress for the house, tomorrow there would be no Claud, robust and active, to bring it inside.

BY THE TIME she got back to the office the next day, it was nearly noon. On her desk was a message from Ethan, ordering her to report to him immediately. There was no avoiding another confrontation with him, but that was all right. She had a few questions to ask about his having been to her apartment in Chicago.

With determination she entered his office, and for some time now she had thought of it as his. The traumas to which he had subjected her there had effectively superimposed his personality over Claud's.

Today Carol knew instantly that he was not prepared to make this encounter any easier than the preceding ones. His first action was to glance pointedly at the watch strapped to his wrist. "We don't keep bankers' hours here, Carol. I know Claud trained you better, but heaven only knows what bad habits you picked up at Thompson's."

It was a totally unfair accusation. Carol had been in the room less than thirty seconds, and already he had her on the defensive. "Don't you tell me what hours to keep in my own offices," she said angrily.

"*Our* offices," Ethan amended. "You seem to

forget that I am controlling this business." He stressed the word controlling in a strange manner as he leaned back in the chair, eyeing her appraisingly.

He noted with approval her designer suit of brick red worn over a black silk blouse that matched the decorative braiding on the jacket. The slight gathering of the skirt accented the curve of her hips, which he marked with his perusal before his glance moved down and stopped at the trim legs clad in sheer silk. His frank assessment embarrassed her; as she remembered the last time they had been in this room, she could feel the heat rise in her cheeks.

"Well, where have you been? Visiting time for Claud is well over." His demeanor had shifted back to the old familiar attack, and not a shadow remained of his earlier approval of her, sensual or otherwise.

"I've been out selecting a Christmas tree for Tante Nan." Carol made the statement sound as matter-of-fact as she could, hoping that if Ethan thought she didn't mind his questioning, he might stop.

She got an entirely different reaction, however. "Is that where you were yesterday—with Miss Nan? I tried several times to reach you. I'm glad you finally went to see her. It's been long overdue."

She maintained her nonchalant attitude as she walked to the coffee service, replying casually, "I don't see that you left me much choice. You said you went to Chicago to send home my belongings. I didn't want them to arrive before Tante Nan knew I had come back to the city." She poured herself a cup of coffee.

"I guess I do owe you an apology for that, Carol. I

also want you to know that I did have other business in Chicago—that I didn't just strike out of here with the intention of pirating your property. I went to get financial backing for the Taalot building."

At that moment she didn't give a hang about the Taalot building. "Why did you do it, Ethan?" Although her back was to him, she knew he hadn't looked away from her for one second.

"Because Claud told me to get you home. I did. And you are going to stay," he stated positively.

She wanted to wring the self-assurance out of him. "*You* didn't bring me home. *Tante*'s letter did."

"And who the hell do you think found you? Who stood over Miss Nan while she wrote the letter, dictated every word to her? Who licked the stamp and dropped the envelope in the mail?" His voice rose with each question, then dropped to a pain-filled whisper. "If I had found you sooner, I might have got you home in time to patch things up with Claud and in time to settle this unfinished business about the firm."

What did he mean, Carol wondered. She would never be able to understand this man. "If you knew where I had been during the past two years, why did you ask me where I'd been?"

"All I had was an address. I didn't know who else lived there. The phone was unlisted, and I didn't even know where you worked. For all I knew, you were married and someone's glamorous housewife. Time was too pressing for a proper investigation."

"How long were you looking?" It was important for Carol to know when Claud had begun to look for her. She took her coffee and sat in a chair as far removed from Ethan as she could.

"I began making inquiries toward the end of October. I can't remember exactly when." He emitted a sneering sound. "You know what finally led to you? An inquiry to the Tulane registrar's office. Your lover-boy lawyer sent out a call for information about you—checking your pedigree, I guess. I simply reversed the trail and it led to his office, where a not too bright secretary gave me your address."

Carol wanted to wipe the self-satisfied smirk from his face. At the same time she resented Jim's role in spying on her. On the other hand, she was finally getting some answers. "Did Claud have a specific reason for wanting me home at that particular time?" She kept her control even though Ethan waited a long time without answering, nonchalantly twirling a gold pen between his fingers until she thought she would snatch it from his hands.

"Well, did he?" she pressed.

Finally he tossed the pen onto the desk and answered, but she felt he had been deciding how to answer. "Yes, Carol, he had a very valid reason for wanting you home—a reason other than that he loved you very much and regretted the things that drove you two apart. But his reason is no longer important. I don't think it would serve any practical purpose for you to know why he wanted you back here—not right now, anyway."

"Are you ever going to tell me?" Carol asked quietly. The effort to mask her frustration was draining her energy.

"Maybe," Ethan replied in a tone that meant the discussion was over. "We haven't finished going over the projects, but I think we can get them done this afternoon. Right now I'm meeting someone for lunch, then I have to check a site. I'll be back at two, so we'll be able to get to them then." Now he was dismissing not only the earlier topic, but her, as well.

Carol returned to her office and thought about the things Ethan had said to her. He might criticize her absence, but he hadn't been around when her world came tumbling down. If he'd been in Carol's place, he might have handled things differently. With that hard shell around him, if that emotional chaos had happened to him, he probably would have blocked out the pain and kept going. Maybe that's what they had thought she would do—block out the hurt and keep going; she had always been the strong one. How often she had borne her suffering silently!

But that time two years ago had been especially difficult for Carol. It was true that nothing had been accomplished by her flight; for all intents and purposes, Claud had believed to the end that she had taken a kickback and was responsible for bringing shame to his name. Probably everyone else still believed it, too. Although their opinion mattered, what she cared about more was Claud knowing the truth.

Carol had pondered the situation for two years. How could she have told Claud the truth when she had the chance if she didn't know what had gone wrong, either. She felt in her heart that Eva was at the root of everything, but all Carol knew for a fact was that she herself had not sold any information about Guerard Construction to anyone. Running away had probably been the worst thing she could have done, but regardless of what had been expected of her two years ago, she couldn't have kept her sanity and faced daily all the reproving eyes. But most devastating of all had been Claud's disapproval and censure.

Shaking the thought from her, she set about the tasks before her. There was not to be one thing about her work for her "partner" to criticize. He had made it clear that her previous actions had been wrong in his view. She would make sure that her present deeds left nothing over which he might raise a dark brow.

She left word with Mrs. McLin not to be disturbed and worked diligently through the remainder of the morning and into the early afternoon. During her brief break for a sandwich, she returned her calls. She smiled pleasantly when she recognized Eric's name on the short list. She had enjoyed his company even if Ethan had voiced such resolute disapproval. She returned the call.

Eric asked her out to dinner, but she had promised to dine with Nan. Instead, she agreed to early cocktails at the nearby Hyatt Regency.

It was nearly three-thirty before Ethan returned to the suite. Carol had been in the file room, which afforded her a good view of his office. Covertly she watched the lean figure place his hard hat on the top shelf of the small closet. She remembered distinctly how Claud had always left his hat on a chair on the sofa, and whenever he had a client in his office, he always had to move the bright yellow hat, sometimes placing it on his desk and rubbing his rough index finger over the embossing of the company logo. His pride was an open thing.

Ethan had not been wearing a Guerard hat, and something about the green hat he had worn almost surfaced. Before she could bring the thought into focus, Ethan turned and noticed her presence.

Without commenting on his lateness, he came bluntly to the business at hand. "Bring in your data, Carol. We're running behind schedule."

She didn't mention that had he returned when planned, they wouldn't be pressed for time now. Determined to maintain a professional atmosphere between them, she kept that observation to herself.

They worked steadily for almost two hours. Not once did he place the sanctioning initials at the end of the pages. Carol refused to get her hopes up that he was to allow her to work under her own authority. Something held back that anticipation.

No changes were required in her estimations as each item met with his approval. Carol had just relaxed when he leaned back in the swivel chair and viewed her fully. His eyes were shot with the glint of polished steel, as if daring her to dispute his next statement. Steadily he leaned forward again. "I want all the figures reworked using this list for leasing the equipment with operators. I've marked the machines we're interested in."

The lean-fingered hand placed a printed flyer on the desk corner near her arm. Quickly her glance registered the lists—bulldozer, backhoe, crane, earthmover, pile driver. "But why? We still have this equipment. There's no need to lease any of it."

He leaned back again, still keeping a firm eye on her. "We won't have after next week. I'm selling it all to Randle Equipment."

Her eyes flew back to the paper she now gripped in her hand. "The same company from whom you intend renting?" Her question was barely audible.

"The same," he carelessly dropped his answer.

It cost a great effort for her to keep her tone level when she wanted to scream at him that he was destroying Guerard Construction. If they rid themselves of the machinery, they would be no better than a second-rate company. They would be waiting in line for the equipment and getting behind in their construction schedule. These things she vocalized as calmly as she could.

Ethan let her finish before he began a refutation of each point. "I have interviewed many of Randle's clients, and the longest wait has been sixteen hours. A little planning on the part of that client and even that wait wouldn't have been necessary. As to this change in procedure making Guerard's second-rate, I think our structures will speak for themselves. If we build superior buildings, no one will ever accuse this firm of being other than the best."

"Carol," he continued on a softer note, "we have had a major repair on over a third of our machines in the last year, and another third needs overhauling. One dozer was stolen, and a backhoe was set afire at a job site by vandals. Do you realize just how much our insurance premiums are on that equipment? Add to that the area used to store the machinery when it's not in use, land that could be put to better use. So far we haven't talked about taxes, operating expenses and the cost of keeping operators on standby." He paused to allow her time to absorb the impact of the data he had presented before continuing.

"With Randle we'll be saving a great deal of money, money that needs plowing back into the firm. Whatever else you may think, I'm not trying to destroy the company. You must believe that I want this firm to be what you want it to be. Can you take just this little bit on faith?"

Intellectually she couldn't deny the points he had made, for he had thoroughly covered all avenues of rebuttal. He seemed so compassionate in his plea that she had no emotional choice, either. She believed him. Sensing her acquiescence, he moved from the desk to stand behind her chair. He placed one hand on her shoulder, the other he used to pull her head against his flat firm torso. It was a filial motion designed to erase any last doubts.

"We've all put you through a lot over the last years. I guess he knew that, but it doesn't make my role any easier." He spoke as if to himself. She wanted to ask what he meant, but he eased her away and gave her shoulder a brotherly pat. "Go paint your face, or whatever it is you women do in powder rooms, and let's go. I promised we would meet Steve Randle at the Hilton. He thought you might have some questions before we finalize the deal."

She rose to do his bidding and then remembered. "I can't go. I have a date for cocktails already, and following that I promised Tante Nan I would be home for dinner."

That hand on her shoulder tightened. "Break your date." It was a harsh command.

"I can't. Eric's already waiting for me at the Hyatt Regency." She sounded as adamant as he, but she had spoken the forbidden name.

She watched as he reached for the phone, not heeding his purpose until he was speaking to the bartender in the lounge. "Mike, this is Ethan Greenlaw. Do you have a customer Eric, obviously waiting for a date?" Then his purpose sank into Carol's bemused brain.

Carol reached across for the phone, but Ethan effectively prevented her access by hauling her against him and pinning her there with his free arm. "He's there? Good. Tell him that Miss Charbonnet regrets she will be unable to join him, that a business complication has arisen. No, I don't care if you do tell him I delivered the message. Just give him another drink on my tab. And thanks, Mike. I'll remember this next time I'm in."

He replaced the receiver none too gently. "It's too late. I'm sure the bartender has already delivered the message and a fresh drink. Eric is probably scouting around for someone else to share his evening." The way he said Eric was a cutting edge.

"You had no right to do that." She was now trying to pull away from him instead of trying to plow over him as she had done in her attempt to wrest the phone from his grip.

"I'm getting damn tired of your defining my rights! Before this year is over, you will find I have more rights than you ever dreamed possible." The punctuation for his angry words was an overpowering possession of her mouth. It was not like the frankly sensual kiss of the first night when he mistook her for Eva. It was a branding, hot and searing. As much as she fought against it, it was permanent.

Struggling against him was useless. All she could deny was the response she longed to make by repeating to herself, *He's Eva's lover...Eva's lover....* Yet she was forced to acknowledge the swirling counterthought. *I want him for myself.*

The idea of her cousin was enough to keep her from yielding to the now pliant urging of his mouth. Very slowly he lifted from her lips to place a different kind of kiss on each of her closed eyelids.

"Open your eyes," he directed caressingly.

When she obeyed, it was to meet the narrowed gaze of molten steel. "You were away too long. I was tired of waiting." He spoke the mysterious words huskily as he smoothed her hair away from her face. Then he pushed her away from him, flicked off the lights and led her to the elevators. No thought was given to the forgotten trip to the powder room.

CHAPTER FIVE

THEY WALKED THE FEW BLOCKS to the New Orleans Hilton. The stiff breeze blowing from the river carried a chilling dampness that penetrated her light coat. Ethan glanced at her when she turned up the collar without breaking the straining stride she had maintained to keep up with his pace.

"Cold?" he questioned as he paused at the curb to obey the traffic signal. He made a slight motion toward her as if to shield her body from the wind with his own, but the light blinked a green "Walk," and taking her elbow, he steered her across the street. "It's only a block more," he commented unsympathetically.

Once in the lobby, he turned directly toward the elevator that rode the exterior of the building, and soon the glass cage had whisked them to the top of the structure. There he urged her into an indoor rain forest, complete with simulated rainfall and the eerie night sounds of jungle creatures calling to pagan gods.

Either Ethan's eyes had adjusted quickly to the dimness of the darkened cocktail lounge, or he had prior knowledge of where Steve Randle would be sitting. Deftly he maneuvered Carol across the dance floor to a corner table at the end of the sheet of falling water. There a man sat before a steaming cup of coffee. As he rose from his seat and extended a hand to Ethan, Carol's eyes fastened on that hand with its crossing of scars and enlarged knuckles. It had the markings of the fist of a bare-handed fighter. Slowly her gaze lifted to the face of the man Ethan was introducing. She encountered a hard countenance now marked by cynical amusement. It was the most unrevealing face she had ever seen.

Steve Randle raised an eyebrow toward the two chairs on the opposite side of the minuscule table. Ethan seated her against the wall before settling into the chair close beside her. She tried concentrating on the warm conversation between the two, but she was pulled into speculation about the stranger. Compared to him, Ethan seemed a gentle lamb, and her attempt to arrest a shudder was futile.

Ethan glanced her way. "You can't still be cold." He allowed his eyes to move over the crowded room in search of their waitress. "Maybe I should get the drinks myself. It may be a fairly long wait before our turn comes up."

Without excusing himself to either of them, he made his way toward the bar and a relatively available bartender. Carol followed his departure until a gravelly voice took her attention.

"Your grandfather had a great deal of confidence in your ability in construction. He was very proud of you."

She turned a surprised expression toward the man seated across from her. "Did you know Claud?" She could not imagine the Guerard circle merging with the man before her, not even in business. He seemed positively sinister. The harshness of his face, the decisive movements of not only his hands but his entire body filled her with foreboding.

"This deal we've come to finalize tonight was originally the plan of Mr. Guerard. Ethan was just a go-between until this thing between them developed. For a while I thought...." Immediately his features froze into an even deeper stage of impenetrability as he noted the rapt attention of the woman before him.

"You thought what, Mr. Randle?" she urged demandingly.

"I thought many things, Miss Charbonnet. Many things."

It was useless to press him. This was a man who gave nothing away unless it was his decision. She knew intuitively that no persuasion available to her could sway him. Turning her head, she gained sight of Ethan as he wended his way toward the table, two drinks in his hand. Her eyes shifted to the still-full cup in front of Steve Randle.

"Anyone who knows me at all knows that I do not drink alcoholic beverages. They don't bother asking after the first time." Again there was that streak of cynical humor that quickly washed across his face, then disappeared almost as quickly as it had come.

Ethan set the tall frosted glass in front of her and the shorter glass before himself. He hadn't asked her what she wanted, and she was surprised to taste the mild vodka collins, one of her favorite drinks. Immediately the conversation turned to the equipment.

Carol now had less trepidation since learning the plan originated with Claud, but she still found the idea distasteful.

There wasn't much the owner of Randle Equipment could add that Ethan hadn't already told her in his office. There was but one new item.

"Miss Charbonnet," the swarthy-skinned man began while facing her fully, "I make it a policy to let all my clients know exactly with whom they are dealing." There was a dramatic pause. Carol had no idea where the conversation was leading.

"When I was nineteen years old, I was convicted of hit-and-run driving while under the influence of alcohol. The result was a seven-year sentence in prison. I will not go into the story of whether I was guilty or innocent, but I do want you to know that Randle Equipment hires as many ex-convicts as it can possibly find room for. A great many of those, without the slightest doubt and frequently by their own admissions, were justly convicted. Some people are hesitant to have that many former criminals around their construction sites. If you have any doubts, I want to hear them now."

The obsidian eyes bore into her. "Not one of my employees has had an accusation leveled against him while working for me, and no one has ever accused me of any unfairness in my business dealings. Not many people can make that boast." Carol was in no doubt as to the allusion of his last statement.

"Do you feel you can cope with a company of ex-criminals?" He did not rush her for an answer but turned to watch the boisterous crowd around them, took a sip of the now cold coffee, then returned his glance to her.

During his impassive account Ethan's eyes had watched her closely, as if waiting for a facial expression to betray her thoughts. She turned from Steve Randle to look at Ethan briefly before answering in a cool tone.

"Some people are lucky, Mr. Randle. They serve their sentences, and it's all over and done with. Others pay and keep paying, and sometimes the price goes up without there being a thing they can do about it. Your personnel will receive no unfair criticism from Guerard Construction."

She thought she saw a glimmer of gentle sympathy in Steve, but before she could confirm her suspicion, he stood to extend a hand to Ethan in departure.

"Our lawyers should get this settled soon," Ethan commented as he stood, effectively keeping Carol pinned in her place. Without pushing Ethan aside, there was no way to rise with the men. She returned the usual parting pleasantries from her seat. She watched as Steve moved out of the lounge before turning to Ethan who stood looking down at her.

"Do you want another drink?" He glanced at his watch. "We have enough time for one more."

It had been a long day, and she accepted his offer. This time a waitress took their order. She had fully expected Ethan to reseat himself beside her, but he had taken the place vacated by Steve. It made her uneasy to have him directly in front of her, watching her so intently. She didn't want him beside her, either. Where did that leave, other than the next table? A smile lifted her mouth at the ridiculousness of her own thoughts.

The sound of a coin hitting the table startled her. There next to her empty glass a nickel spun a lopsided orbit before coming to rest beside her hand.

"What is that for?" she asked in her confusion.

"Your thoughts. With inflation, they must be worth more than the traditional penny?" He reached up to loosen his tie and unbutton his collar. "I've been in this suit since seven-thirty this morning." It wasn't an apology, just an explanation. "Okay, give me my money's worth. What were you thinking that brought the little grin?"

She placed the tip of her right index finger over the coin and slid it back across the table. "They are not for sale."

"Everything has a price, even you, Miss Charbonnet." He reached into the inner pocket of his coat and withdrew his wallet. Carol's eyes darkened to a mud green in the dim light. Surely he wasn't about to...?

"Will that be all, sir?" the waitress asked as she placed a small round tray containing their drinks on the table. Ethan extracted a bill from his wallet and placed it atop the check. A derisive glimmer filled his eyes, and the grooves on either side of his mouth deepened. As soon as the waitress had placed their drinks before them, thanked Ethan for the generous tip and departed, Ethan picked up the nickel from the table, rubbing the surface between his forefinger and thumb. There was a subtle sensuality in the movement that sent a flicker of awareness through her.

"Sometimes there is something for nothing, after all. Your last thoughts were freely readable." He pocketed the coin before taking a sip of his Scotch and water. "Drink up, Carol. The good *tante* waits."

She knew he was making fun of her misunderstanding of his earlier actions. To cover this embarrassment, she removed the speared fruit from her glass, laid it on the cocktail napkin prior to taking a sip from the fresh drink. She tried to think of a topic of conversation to no avail.

There had been no need to make the effort, for Ethan began explaining some of the problems he had encountered on the job site and asked her opinion about their resolutions. He had the problems already solved, but she was grateful that he had the courtesy to attempt an appeasement for his earlier teasing.

The conversation flowed smoothly. They both had little left other than melting ice cubes when Carol picked up the plastic spear containing two cherries and a wedge of orange. Before she could move the miniature lance to her mouth, Ethan's strong hand wrapped around her wrist to deftly move her hand to his mouth. He picked off the first cherry with his teeth, then pushed her hand to her own mouth, holding it here until she bit into the second red berry.

There was overwhelming intimacy about the presumptuous act. And once again he had unsettled her, a frequently recurring event. When he released his hold, she proffered the orange wedge. "Do you want this, too?"

His reply was flat as he removed the spear from her fingers and dropped it, with the orange, into her glass. "No, and I'm not making any comment about what I do want, or you'll jump to conclusions the way you do every time I come near you. Let's get out of here." He got to his feet and waited for her to gather her bag and coat.

She was surprised when he led her to the hotel car park. He answered her silent question. "When I went for the first round of drinks, I called to have it delivered here. It's too damp for you to walk back to the office building."

After escorting her to the passenger seat, he settled his frame into the other soft leather seat separated from her by the console, then started the powerful engine to move effortlessly out of the lot and onto the busy street.

Ethan handled the car with aggressive surety. He maneuvered through the narrow side streets and quickly had them onto the avenue and soon parked in the circular driveway. The gates had been left open, and the hanging lanterns blazed across the great expanse of the lower gallery. Nan had been waiting.

Something else caught her attention. There at the far end of the porch lay a huge evergreen tree. A coiled garden hose gave evidence that Judson had remembered the safety procedure of soaking the live tree thoroughly before it could be brought inside.

She hopped from the car before Ethan had time to open the door for her. She hurried to the tree, which had to be twelve or more feet. With the stand it would just fit beneath the sixteen-foot ceiling in the front room.

"Your purchase?" an amused voice behind her reminded Carol that her escort was still there.

"Oh, yes. Isn't it magnificent?" She leaned over and tried lifting the tree in order to get an idea of its symmetry, but it was far too massive for her to upright. Anxiety crept into her posture. "How am I ever to manage this thing alone?" It was directed to herself and unconsciously vocalized.

"After dinner we'll get it up and inside together." At her puzzled expression he explained, "I wheedled an invitation to dinner. After we've eaten, we'll tackle the tree. Right now we need to let them know we've arrived." He steered her toward the front doors.

There was no questioning Ethan's methods in getting the invitation. He and her aunt were more than polite acquaintances. There was a gentle camaraderie between the two that bespoke many evenings of quiet dinners. The thought of those dinners cast a shadow; they would have been at Eva's invitation.

The meal itself overwhelmed Carol. The old cook evidently had spent the day in the kitchen, for on the Adams sideboard was exhibited a festival of Creole dishes. Ethan surveyed the offering, which displayed no thought of menu balance. Gracie had cared only that she welcome home her pet with samplings of all Carol's favorite foods: *manquechou*—a dish of corn and smothered onion; *jambalaya au congri*—kidney beans and rice cooked with ham; and *daube glacée*. By the deepening of the grooves of either side of his mouth and the flicker of a twitch in the lean cheeks, she knew he had something to say about the selection.

"Go on and get it out so you can eat without choking," she urged under her breath.

The humor moved to his eyes, giving them a soft smoky hue. "I was just thinking that all you lack is the fatted calf to complete the feast of the return of the prodigal. But I'm sure it's here, probably camouflaged in an *étouffée*."

Carol shook her hand in refusal of the dish of crayfish stew that would be served with yet more rice, the main staple of Louisiana meals.

"It is here." She pointed to the *daube glacée*. "That's jellied veal."

It would have taken a far larger number of diners to do justice to the culinary efforts of Gracie. She had spared nothing in the preparation of the food. Several times Carol observed Ethan's hand move quickly to either his wine or water glass after an initial sampling.

"Creole cooking combines the French love of delicacies with the Spanish taste for poignant seasonings. Sometimes Gracie lets the Spanish taste overwhelm the French love," she teased as he once more reached for his water goblet.

"And to think I believed she was doing this to honor your return. She must be punishing your absence," he as quickly retorted.

Though Nan didn't partake of most of the highly seasoned dishes, she did join in the discussion, telling them of the old Creole foods that were almost impossible to find: *bière douce*, a combination of pineapple peelings, brown sugar, cloves and rice; *calas tout chaud*, rice cakes fried in deep fat, liberally sprinkled with sugar and always served hot.

She told them of the youthful summers she and

Claud had spent in the romantic bayou country, of the *gumbo ya-ya*, a social gathering where people came together to talk. She told of the *fais-dodo*, a community dance given on Saturday night either in a private home or in the town's dance pavilion. In glowing memory she told of how at sundown everyone gathered at the dance, whole families from grandparents on down to newborn babes. The little ones were put to sleep in the *parc aux petits*, a room set aside just for a nursery. If there was no special room, the babies were lined against the walls of the dance hall itself. During the evening's entertainment, if a child whimpered, the couple dancing nearest offered comfort by replacing a lost bottle or dropped dolly. At times, a couple would take a restless child into their arms and dance it around the floor.

Although some of the older people danced, others played cards or joined in the ever present *gumbo ya-ya* held in corners or on the porches. They talked and laughed around the tables laden with wine, beer, lemonade and *café noir* or *café au lait*.

The dancing stopped at midnight, but only long enough for supper. Then the dancing continued until the musicians declared they had made music long enough. And those musicians were never subtle. They simply abandoned their instruments, went into the yard and fired several pistol shots into the air, proclaiming loudly, *"Le bal est fini."*

The old blue eyes misted as she recounted a youth past. "You people today don't know what a real party is. You go to midnight Mass on Christmas and come home to tiny glasses of champagne and scrambled eggs masquerading as an omelet. *The réveillon* of the bayous was a great Christmas breakfast, which lasted until it was time to go to another Mass. When Claud and Monet first married...." The regal head bent as the gnarled hand reached to a wineglass as a covering motion against too many memories.

"*Tante*, would you like to visit the hospital?" Carol asked quietly. "I'm sure Ethan will help me to get you there. He and I can get you into the car, and there'll be a wheelchair once we arrive. Would you like that, *tante*?"

Grateful eyes met those of the two younger people. "Yes," she whispered, "yes, tomorrow, please." She reached to their hands, giving each a pat to signal the regaining of her control.

"Now if you will help me up and fetch Gracie from the television, I'll retire. You have your dessert in the parlor while you plan the erecting of that hunk of forest that's on the veranda posing as a Christmas tree. You're so like Claud. Christmas trees only come in one size as far as the two of you are concerned, and that is gigantic."

They helped her into the walker as Gracie answered Carol's call. "Now I don't need help with Miss Nan. She and I have this routine worked out, and you'll just get in our way. Right, Miss Nan."

"Correct. Good night Ethan...Carol." Slowly she made her way with the help of the loving black woman.

Ethan's eyes were not on the retreating figures, but on Carol as she watched the painful exit. He placed a comforting hand on her shoulder. "Stop whipping yourself. There's nothing you can do for her." Turning her toward the table, he added on a whimsical note, "We could show our appreciation to the cook by clearing up."

Carol brushed a tear from her cheek before beginning to place the soiled dishes on a nearby tray. Quickly they worked together and within a few minutes had the dishes in the dishwasher, the food in the refrigerator and a fresh tray set with coffee and slices of cake rich with fruits and nuts.

Instead of taking the tray to the parlor, Ethan led Carol to the more intimate family room. There a small fire lay ready in the fireplace. After placing the tray on a table, he set match to the kindling. It seemed natural when he eased his lean frame into the big reclining chair, Claud's chair. He ate the sweet confection slowly, savoring the subtle spices. "This is almost familiar to my singed taste buds. What is it?"

"Gracie calls it hummingbird cake," she answered, licking a morsel of the cream-cheese icing from her lip.

"Without the fruit it would be like the Italian cheesecake back home." It was his first mention of anything other than Guerard Construction and her own life that he had ever made to her.

"Where's home?" She watched as his face assumed a shuttered look before he answered.

"Philadelphia." Immediately he changed the topic. "I should have thought to take Miss Nan to the hospital myself. She shouldn't have had to wait this long."

"Then, you don't mind my volunteering your

help? I should have asked first, I know." She stirred the coffee absently.

"No, I don't mind. I owe Claud far more than that." He folded his napkin and dropped it on the tray. "Let's see to the tree before I get too comfortable and fall asleep here. I have jeans in the trunk of the car. See if you can find something more practical, and let's get busy."

She climbed the stairs to what had been her room. As she opened the door, she expected to find some startling change, but it was as if she had vacated her quarters only an hour ago. An unfinished novel lay on the bedside table, a miniature flagon of perfume blended just for her by the small company in the Quarter still rested on her dressing table. There wasn't a sense of a preserved shrine, but Carol knew that it was with deliberation that the room had remained as she left it, and she wondered at whose orders.

All the racks of clothes she had abandoned in her flight still hung in order in the wall of closets. She selected a pair of dark green corduroy slacks and a soft cotton flannel shirt. There was nothing glamorous about the outfit, but it was practical for working with the tree. Quickly she stripped down to her briefs and slipped into the comfortable old clothes. She neatly laid the discarded garments across the peach silk covering of the bed before finding topsiders to complete the outfit.

She gave the room one final glance, her eyes catching the glimmer from the hand-decorated perfume bottle. She couldn't resist just a tiny sampling of the essence, and she moistened her fingertip in the fragrant liquid to apply it to her pulse points and one daring drop between her breasts.

Then she turned out the light and joined Ethan on the veranda. He had found a place to change and had obviously located the specially constructed stand that Judson had brought out of storage.

After much swearing on Ethan's part and giggling from Carol, they wrested the tree upright and into the front room. Taking a break to sip a snifter of brandy, Ethan watched her turn the tree first one way and then another before she finally settled on the side to face the room.

"Miss Nan was right. It is a piece of forest and a sizable piece at that," he teased from his position on the roll-armed sofa. She refused his offer of a drink as the antique clock in the hall chimed the lateness of the hour.

"I'll help you get the lights on, and then we call it a night," he suggested. "Tomorrow you can decorate and trim to your heart's delight."

They worked steadily at stringing the tiny golden lights over the tree. As they worked and planned the trip to the infirmary for Nan, the task went briskly. At last the chore was complete, and Carol knelt to plug the extension cord into an outlet. Sitting back on her heels, she watched the hundreds of twinkling lights bathe the room in a dim glow as Ethan extinguished the overhead light.

"You look like a little girl, lights sparkling in your eyes," he mused, coming to stand behind her. "Christmas must be very special for you."

The glow of her animation put even more sparkles in her eyes. "Yes... most definitely, yes. I have never seen an ugly Christmas tree, but this one is perfect, don't you think?" She looked up at him and discovered a familiar expression on his face as he knelt beside her. It was back, that look was back on his face, the look that stated ownership, staked possession, the look of a man desiring a woman.

"Please, Ethan... don't."

But his hands reached for her while his intoxicating voice flowed over her. "It's just a little Christmas kiss. Payment for all the work I did moving the tree inside, for withstanding the allure of your perfume and for not staring even though I know you're not wearing anything underneath that soft shirt."

She knew it wouldn't end with a little kiss even before his firm lips met hers. Futilely she tried to resist her overwhelming response.

He did not block her self-denial with force. He simply took his Christmas kiss, a sweet and gentle honeyed salute on her mouth. If only he had stopped with one, but he kissed her again with the same tenderness and yet again. Not once did he try bringing her closer; the only inducement he offered was the tantalizing sweetness of his mouth. It was she who made the tentative move toward greater fulfillment by lifting her trembling arms to his shoulders, by drawing slowly nearer until the throbbing fullness of her breasts touched him. And that touch released the primitive passion he had held dammed since the first day they had met. It came bursting through every cell in her body, washing over her, sweeping her up in the overflow.

"My God, what are you doing to me?" he cried against her throat. The other words were lost against her mouth. One hand reached into her hair, tangling the spun-gold strands as he wrapped their silken texture around his fist, entrapping her, binding her to him, though she harbored no thought of denial now. Not now—when he was making her feel things she had never felt before.

The fastenings of her shirt gave to his agile fingers, and his whispered words were now breathed against the darkened rise of her swollen breast. Ethan whispered, "I knew you would look like this, feel like this...." A sense of pride pervaded the other primeval emotions. She was beautiful to him, and that moved her to greater elation. But that thought was lost in electrifying sensations when he circled her breasts with his tongue. "And I knew you would respond to me like this," he groaned before bringing his mouth back to hers.

With the firm edge of his tongue he searched for and found her flowing sweetness, and he kissed her deeper and deeper until she was crazed by the hungry urgency of his mouth devouring hers. It was a swirling passion that filled her with torturous pleasure, that brought them both to lie on the softness of the thickly carpeted floor.

She fitted against him, his manly desire burning against her as his searing touch brought her to greater heights of sensation. "What do you feel...want? Talk to me, Carol."

"I can't." Carol's words came as jerkily as her breath when his fingers drew erotic patterns over her exposed stomach and then moved to sketch the low line of her panties.

"Tell me," he repeated moistly against her breast.

"Inside, inside I'm melting...." She reached to open his shirt so that she could caress him.

"I can feel my heart...." She brought her mouth to his furred chest and touched her tongue delicately to his sensitive skin. His response was a dark moan and the pressured flattening of his hand against her stomach. The sensation was awesome, and it frightened her.

"Just stay like this and stay with me. Don't let me leave you behind," he whispered before his mouth left a trail of burning kisses over her body.

Time was suspended as they touched and caressed, savoring the discoveries until his voice roused them to consciousness. "Come home with me, to my apartment," he whispered against her ear. At first she refused to acknowledge the verbal intrusion into the tactile world they had created with their desires.

He softly repeated his instructions. "Come home with me. If we continue here..." he hesitated, then continued in a husky voice, "When we make love, I don't want to have to hold anything back, nor you to hold back." His words burned against her as he rested his forehead against hers. "I want you in my arms all night. Our first time has to be perfect...all my needs and all your needs fulfilled. It can't be that way here in the middle of the Guerard's grand salon. I can't take you the way I want to here."

With the mention of the Guerard name, reality washed over her. She reached to gather her clothes and cover her nakedness. If he hadn't spoken, he could have taken her without any protest. The thought stung how he must be crowing! He had taken control of the company, of Eva, and now almost her. That was the operative word, *almost*. Thank God he had been greedy and had demanded that she spend the whole night. That had been her salvation. As she fumbled with zipper and buttons, he suddenly clamped his hands over her wrists.

"What are you doing?" He had been instantly alert to the change in her mood, but his puzzlement at why she had changed was evident in his voice.

"I'm trying to get my clothes back on, and I wish you would do the same. Then I'm leaving but not to go home with you. Now turn me loose."

She twisted against his grip, but it was unrelenting. A new quality pervaded his tone, his angular features becoming rigid, the softness in his gaze now completely gone. "What the hell has got into you? One minute you're mine, mine to do with as I wish, and now you're like some insane creature." He held her pinned beneath him, with his chest pressing firmly against hers, his hands firmly clasping her arms over her head.

"Yes, insane. I must be insane to have allowed this, this—" She broke off, unable to speak of their earlier intimacy.

His expression set in a frozen facade, but she could feel every muscle in his body harden. "I should take off your clothes right here and now. I should...."

He stifled his own words against her mouth, and there was nothing in his kiss that was like the others they had shared. Nor was there a sharing in any of his demands as he took without giving until she felt dizzy. Then he moved to her breast, planting urgent kisses and leaving marks where his lips had pressed too firmly against her vulnerable skin.

"No," he said, denying the change in her. "I want you the way you were."

Carol didn't know if he spoke to her or to himself, but she knew her only defense against his anger-coated frustration was to lie passively beneath him. She could fight him no other way; he had seen to that with the use of his pinioning bulk. So she lay rigid while with his kiss, his touch, his whole body, he demanded and asked and begged for the return of the willing woman he had held just minutes before. He tried to revive the flame of their previous passion, but it was too late. He stoked a dying ember.

Gradually his breathing slowed, and his heat burned away. His head bowed, then buried against the perfection of her bosom. He lay without moving, heavy on her, until without a word he got up and stood over her. His eyes moved to the glimmering tree as he pulled on his shirt and tucked the tails into his jeans. She knew when he looked down at her even though her eyes were shut.

"Get up." There was nothing readable in his voice as he grasped her hand and pulled her to her feet. Ignoring the tears streaming down her face, he roughly straightened her clothes and smoothed her hair. In the same brusque manner he asked, "Do you want to stay here tonight?"

She could only shake her head.

"Then let's go. You can leave all this for tomorrow."

"I'm not going anywhere with you." She had found her voice and tried to give it a strength she didn't have.

"Don't be stupid." He took a slow step toward her. "I'll take you to the Quarter."

She wanted to scream at him, scream her hurt, wanted him to get out of her sight, but she hadn't any reserves left to argue with him. She knew it would be useless, anyway.

In the car his only word was "Address?" to which she responded mechanically. As soon as they reached Patti's apartment, she started to open the door, but a firm hand prevented her.

"I want to know what you're feeling about tonight." His question, as well as the concern in his voice, surprised her. "Is it anger, fear, disappointment? I have to know." When she didn't answer, he caught her chin in his hand and forcefully turned her head. "Look at me when I'm talking to you."

She raised her eyes, now a deep-water green from her emotional turmoil, but she defiantly pushed his hand away.

"Yes," she answered with total disdain, "it is everything you mentioned: disappointment that you would take advantage of the situation; anger at your abusive manner; and fear that I might some day get caught alone with you again and suffer more of your degrading attention. You have no right to...to...." She faltered, at a loss to describe what he had done to her, to associate his actions with the word love.

"There you go with my rights." He expelled a breath of exasperation. "Good God, Carol, you're old enough to understand what happened tonight. You don't just bring a man to the absolute edge like that and then turn him off." He gripped the steering wheel in a white-knuckled grasp. "What exactly do you think it was that I did to you, anyway? I kissed you, and for a while you returned my kisses." The timbre of his voice deepened with remembered passion. "I touched you and you touched me." Then a grating quality entered his tone. "As to my right to do so, I had the right of our mutual desire, and protest as much as you like, until you went through that sudden metamorphosis, the desire *was* mutual. I don't know what made you change. I only know it's useless to ask for an explanation. I also know that what we shared until that point is nothing compared to what we will share. The things I want to do to you and with you, and the things I want you to do to me and with me *will* be done. My right is preestablished. It was established with your permission tonight, not too very long ago. And I don't give a damn what you say to the contrary."

He didn't pause to watch the effect of his words but slid around to open his door. He rounded the front of the car and held her door for her. Gripping her elbow, he pushed her across the street ahead of him. At the courtyard doorway he extended his palm for the keys, which she nervelessly placed in his hand.

He marched her up the stairs, their steps ringing across the patio. She waited beside the door to the apartment as he opened it. He entered first, flicking on lights as he made his way through the small flat, checking each room, even the bathroom, closets and the locks on the windows.

Satisfied that the apartment was secure, he placed the keys on the table by the front door, then turned to where she had remained, motionlessly leaning against the wall. Her hands hung limply at her sides, her head thrust back and eyes closed.

She knew he was standing in front of her, but she couldn't bring herself to look at him, not until she felt his fingers opening her shirt to expose the roundness of her breasts. She gasped at the gentleness of his touch as he brushed caressing fingertips over sensitive skin, then placed a tender kiss on each rosy peak before gathering her unresisting body against him, to hold her in tender solemnity. His silent action was like an apology, an apology that she did not fully understand. Then he was gone.

She stood transfixed as his steps sounded across the courtyard. But when the shock of what she had done set in, she was barely able to make it to the sofa before the last horror tore through her. In the moment that he had held her, *she had forgiven him*. Like the Pied Piper, he had called the tune and she had danced. But she couldn't dance again. She must in some way master the physical control he held over her—she had to.

CHAPTER SIX

CAROL WAS GRATEFUL that the weekend had arrived so that she wouldn't have to put her vows to the test by being near Ethan for the entire day. She was also thankful that their next meeting would involve taking Nan to the infirmary to see Claud; without knowing it, Nan would be her protector.

Carol wished she had the courage to call Ethan and refuse his help, but then she would have to make explanations to Nan, and that she couldn't bring herself to do. She did go so far as to attempt to contact René, but there was no answer at his studio or at any of the places he frequented. René would have been worse than useless, anyway. He had always been given to panic and wasn't a physically strong person. Carol doubted whether he would be able to prevent Nan from falling if the occasion should arise.

What baffled her more than not being able to find René was that no one seemed to care what was happening to their aunt or to Claud. At the hospital there had been a stack of cards that had not been opened until Carol took it upon herself to attend to them. Many were from people she had known since childhood, and each morning she spent a few minutes in writing brief notes, thanking her grandfather's friends and business associates for their concern, always signing them with the family name, never her own. That morning she had arrived at the house as the mail was being delivered and knew Nan must be writing thank-yous even though taking a pen into those crippled hands must have been very difficult.

Mentally she made note to see that when Eva returned and when she finally located René, the three of them could at least share in this chore. She knew, too, that she had to find out how the household expenses were being met. None of them had ever contributed to the maintenance of the house, and if the company had been going downhill since she left, there was no way of knowing the state of Claud's personal finances. No doubt the cost of his medical care would be enormous, regardless of how much insurance he had—that was something else Carol would have to look into.

Another unsettling thought hit her. If Ethan had power of attorney for Claud in dealing with the firm, did he also have control over his personal wealth? Would the domino effect of the complications arising from Claud's disability ever cease? The only way Carol felt she could cope was to take things one step at a time. When Ethan arrived, she would find the answer to at least one of her questions, and that would be the first step.

At noon Carol had Judson bring Claud's Lincoln to the front door, since there was no way to seat Nan in Ethan's low-slung sports car.

She was still lingering over her lunch when the sound of voices in the hall interrupted her depressing thoughts. Now that Ethan had arrived, how would she face him after the previous evening?

Before Carol could move from the dining-room table, Ethan entered, utterly without self-consciousness, as if he belonged there and she were the visitor. His first action was to lightly brush her mouth, then he closely examined her face, trying to read her expression. Carol didn't know how to react.

"Are you all right?" His question, seemingly full of genuine concern, left her speechless. Gracie's entrance with more coffee and a generous portion of the rich cake she had served the night before allowed Carol to conceal her confusion.

Ethan pulled out a chair, seating himself across from Carol, and let the beaming cook cater to him. "You and Miss Carol are doing something nice for Miss Nan. A body sure would think that some other folks around here could stop pleasuring themselves and pitch in now and then," Gracie said, her delight at Ethan's presence so evident.

Gracie's reference to Eva and René wasn't meant to be obscure, so Carol quickly changed the subject, telling Gracie how much she had enjoyed the dessert, and if there were just one thin slice more, she would like to have it. Carol hoped she could get the plainspoken woman to leave the room before she offended Ethan with her complaints about Eva. Then the two of them were left alone, and Carol inwardly breathed a sigh of relief when Ethan chose to discuss a troublesome project he had inspected that morning rather than mentioning the previous evening.

Over their cake and coffee they talked business until Ethan suggested they get under way. Carol then told Gracie, who went to aid her beloved employer.

Nan made it to the front door unassisted, except for her walker. At the first step down onto the veranda, Ethan positioned himself in front of her, ready to prevent her from falling. Carol stood behind, one hand on Nan's arm. The procedure was repeated down the three steps leading from the veranda to the pavement. Each step made Carol wince; she knew how much pain the movements caused her aunt.

In an attempt to spare the elderly woman from further effort, Ethan asked quietly, "Miss Nan, don't you want me to carry you?"

Carol couldn't hear Nan's response, but she saw the determined tilt of her head. As soon as time permitted, Carol silently pledged to have a ramp constructed, regardless of any complaints about how it would look.

Once they reached the hospital it was much easier to get Nan inside since the entrance was constructed for disabled persons. But there was nothing Carol could do to make Nan's first glimpse of Claud any easier. Then Ethan fetched a wheelchair, brought Nan to Claud's bedside and left the three of them alone. For long minutes Nan said nothing, and her silence broke Carol's heart.

"He's getting the best of care, *tante*. There's nothing more that anyone can do, sweetheart, and the doctor assures me he's in no pain."

Carol moved closer to Nan and placed a comforting hand on her drooping shoulders.

Very slowly Nan laid her cheek against the young

woman's hand. "We can go now, Carol. Get your young man back in here. I've seen Claud now." She reached out a crippled hand and tenderly straightened Claud's bed covers.

Carol could see Ethan waiting in the corridor, both hands thrust in the back pockets of his navy cords. When he saw Carol motion to him, he came quickly to her. His searching glance moved over her face and posture before asking the oft-repeated question, "Are you all right?"

She only nodded, for if she said one word, the tears would fall. Without speaking to each other, they got Nan back into the car. As they pulled away from the hospital, it was Nan who finally broke the silence. "I would like to go to church. You may have to carry me inside, but I would like to go."

Carol saw Ethan reach over to place one hand on Nan's. At the corner he turned to Carol, who was sitting in the back seat and asked, "Where's the closest church?"

She read the unspoken message in his eyes that this was something positive they could do. From that message she took the strength she needed and replied, "St. Stephen's. Is that all right with you, *tante*?" With Nan in agreement, Carol directed him to the ancient church. This time he didn't even bother getting the walker from the trunk.

Effortlessly he lifted the frail woman and carried her inside the church and set her down before the altar, anticipating her every wish as he brought tapers so that she might light the vigil candles. He stood supporting her, one arm around her bony waist. As

Carol knelt before the altar and lighted another candle, she felt his free arm rest on her shoulder.

THE AFTERNOON had taken its toll on Carol, and she could imagine the strain it had caused her aunt. When they returned home, Carol helped Gracie get Nan ready for bed.

After she delivered a cup of tea to Nan's bedside, she found Ethan at the piano, picking out simple tunes with one hand, holding a glass of Scotch whiskey in the other. He stopped playing as soon as she entered and watched her make her way to the fireplace, where she stretched out her hands to the warmth of the open fire.

"Do you want a drink?" he asked, his voice quiet and gentle. "You probably could use one."

After she accepted the glass he brought her, she was able to speak. "I don't think she'll go back to see Claud."

Ethan stood very still. "Do you really feel there's any need?"

"Not for Claud and I hope not for herself." Then neither of them said anything more for a while.

Now, Carol felt, in the stillness of the early evening was the time for her to discover what other role Ethan Greenlaw was playing in the family.

She turned around, her back to the fire, to find him settling on the sofa, his long legs stretched before him, his head resting on the cushions. For once he was not looking at her as his long lashes lay against his tanned cheeks. It was the first time she had been allowed the chance to observe him without him knowing it. She took the stolen moment to admire the masterpiece of his body; every line of his hard physique from the broad chest to the flat stomach down the long length of his slim yet muscular legs. He was a beautiful creation, and she remembered his beauty when he had not been so completely clothed.

Suddenly Ethan spoke up. "Stop procrastinating, Carol, and tell me whatever has been plaguing you this afternoon."

Her cheeks colored at having been caught in the act of enjoying this view of him. She tried to cover her embarrassment by fiddling with her drink, but Ethan was not to be put off. He patted the seat next to him and said gently, "You haven't anything to gain by waiting. Sit over here and tell me what's bothering you."

Slowly she walked to the couch and sat down to begin explaining her fears and worries, especially her concern about the family's finances. Ethan assuaged her fears by promising to set up an appointment with the trust manager of her grandfather's bank, who was also in charge of Claud's personal funds. Every two weeks his agent took care of the household accounts. As far as Ethan knew, there was nothing for her to do for the care of the house or Nan. Claud had amply provided for them.

"On the other hand, I have no idea about the provisions for you and your cousins. You will have to find out for yourself exactly what Claud arranged for you."

That last remark offended her; she didn't care about Claud's money and never had. "I don't care about myself," Carol rejoined, her hurt evident in her tone, "I only wanted to know if I needed to transfer money from the trust fund left me by my father to see Nan through. I'm not the mercenary you imagine. You're judging me unfairly."

Nor did he like her words. Decisively he moved closer, and his hand threaded into her hair to draw her inexorably to him. "How can you possibly make such accusations about me? God only knows what suspicious thoughts go through your mind every time I try to get close to you. You completely misunderstand me. I certainly didn't mean to imply you are money hungry. This hasn't exactly been a picnic for me, either. Now apologize for making those unpleasant remarks."

Resignedly Carol apologized. "I'm sorry, Ethan, you're right. It's been a difficult day, and I'm tired."

His entrapping touch changed to a caress. "Too tired to go out to dinner with me?" he asked as his thumb made a lazy circle beneath her ear. As much as Carol wanted to be with him and to allow that stroking hand to evoke even deeper emotions from her, she remembered the resolution of last night and withdrew from his reach.

"I think I should stay here with Nan a while longer to make sure there are no ill effects from her outing today. I'll probably finish decorating the tree," Carol answered distantly as she watched the flames leap upward in the fireplace.

"All right, I'll tell Gracie to fix us some sandwiches, and I'll stay and help you."

That was the last thing she wanted. The thought of

him remaining any longer in the same room made Carol panic. "No—that isn't necessary."

"I know it isn't necessary. I want to stay."

"But I don't want you here." She turned toward him, exposing the rawness of her feelings.

Ethan tried to control his impatience before he spoke. "You have no idea what you want, but I'm giving you more time. Just don't think you have forever to come to terms with what's between us." He touched her mouth gently with his fingertips. "You feel it flowing between us, even now—at this very minute when you are saying with these lips that you don't want me with you. I won't let you deny your feelings for me. A little more time—that's all you have."

He studied her for a moment, then rose. "You needn't see me out." He bent to brush a light kiss on her cheek before turning to leave the room.

Once more Carol was assailed by doubts. Would she have the strength to resist him? It was clear that he would come to claim what he called his right to her, a right he said she had yielded on the evening before. She sat without moving, trying to force her mind to go blank to avoid having to face the truth, only to be pulled back to earth by Gracie's entrance.

"Did Mr. Ethan leave?" The kindly old woman bustled about the room, smoothing imaginary creases out of pillows. Carol watched her, observing the weariness in the housekeeper's movements. Even though another maid came every day, Gracie, too, had had a great burden on her since Claud's illness.

"When's the last time you had a day away from

this house?" Carol inquired sternly. Gracie's answer was a noncommittal shrug.

"Tomorrow morning, as soon as I can get here after the early church service, you can take the rest of the day off. Tante Nan can be here alone long enough for me to dash over to see Claud. Other than that, I'll be here the whole time. How would you like that?"

"Well, that would be a fine treat. It's been a long time since I spent a day with my family. We talk on the phone every day, but that's not the same as seeing them." She paused to run her apron over an already dust-free surface. "I'll go call my nephew to pick me up. It'll do his lazy bones good to get up early. Yes, I think I'll take tomorrow off."

To Gracie's retreating back, Carol said, "I'm glad. You've been working too hard." Inwardly she blamed René and Eva for allowing another injustice.

Then she looked about the room, and in the gathering darkness the remembrance of every caress, every kiss, every passion-filled breath touched her so that, after once more checking Nan and conferring with Gracie, she returned to Patti's apartment, there to take a long soak in the old-fashioned claw-footed tub and to have what she hoped would be an early night.

But sleep eluded her. After thumbing through several fashion magazines and attempting to cheer her spirits by watching a comedy show on television, she finally allowed herself to face the subject she had been trying to avoid, and that subject was Ethan Greenlaw. Try as she might, she couldn't forget the responses he had evoked from her as they had lain before the towering Christmas tree. Wrapping the satin comforter more tightly over her, she curled her body around the pillows and yielded to the sensual memories.

GRACIE'S NEPHEW came for her a scant ten minutes after Carol arrived at the house. Left alone, she enjoyed a cup of rich coffee, then began a breakfast tray for Nan. Tucking the heavy Sunday papers beneath her arm, she balanced the meticulously arranged tray and made her way to Nan's room.

For the rest of the morning she catered to the old woman's needs, reading aloud the social events from the newspaper, helping her dress, making her bed, administering her medication.

It had been quite some time since Nan had had any visitors other than the family, so Carol suggested that she invite a few of her friends to brunch. Nan seemed to Carol more vulnerable and frail since her visit with Claud, but Carol felt it was important that Nan have some activity. As much as Carol loved the family home, she feared it would become little more than a tomb for Nan if her great-aunt had no contact with the outside world.

She bought Nan's favorite chair from her bedroom into the kitchen, where Nan could supervise the preparation of the light but tasty meal Carol planned for the two *grandes dames* who had accepted the invitation to the impromptu meal.

It didn't take Carol long to prepare rich crescent-shaped rolls and set them aside, ready to pop into the oven. Next she scooped succulent balls of melon into thin crystal dishes and placed them in the refrigerator. She cut mushrooms into thin slices, measured the herbs and spices, and set the table with cheerful flowers and crisp linen. After the guests arrived, she would need only fifteen minutes to make the omelet and brown the croissants.

Promptly at noon the doorbell rang, and Carol ushered in the elderly women for a few hours of gossip and a tantalizing luncheon. Both guests were aware of the physical strain Nan had been under and were careful not to prolong their visit. By two o'clock Carol had Nan resting, and the table was cleared.

Carol went to change her clothes and returned to the parlor, where she rummaged through the boxes containing ornaments, searching for the fragile trinkets to hang by golden threads onto the branches of the fragrant evergreen. Each ornament brought tender memories, and the impatient ringing of the door chimes rudely interrupted her sentimental reveries.

Carol hurried to the door, hoping that the urgent pealing would stop before Nan was disturbed. In her haste she forgot to put her shoes back on, which put her at a distinct disadvantage when she opened the door to find her cousin looking down at her.

Eva obviously had spent her time in New York well, Carol thought, for she had the East Coast look about her, from the jaunty angle of the mink beret to the slim heels of her snakeskin shoes. In her hand she carried a hatbox bearing the name of a Fifth Avenue shop, and over her arm a dress bag boasted a designer logo. None of that bothered Carol as much as the man laden with more garment bags and a suitcase who stood behind Eva.

Making no attempt to conceal her displeasure at Carol's presence, Eva was the first to break the silence. "Don't just stand there, Carol. Get out of my way." The tone of cold hauteur changed to syrup when she called over her shoulder to Ethan. "Darling, just place everything by the stairs. Gracie can take them up."

Carol stood holding the door while Eva and Ethan came in, bringing the crisp air with them. Deliberately she avoided Ethan's prolonged look as she responded to Eva's last remark. "Gracie isn't here. I've given her the day off." She reached for the garment bag Eva had already draped over the banister. "I'll take this up for you, Eva," Carol said evenly, but before she could pick up the bag, Ethan stepped in front of her.

"There's no need, Carol. I can manage one more bag, and Eva can take the box up when she goes." His look silenced any protest she might have made, but Eva's reaction took an even deeper toll on her shattered composure.

"Why, thank you, darling. You know my room." Carol knew the added sentence was intentional—Eva's way of staking her claim to Ethan. If there had been any doubt in Carol's mind about the relationship between Ethan and her cousin, Eva was making sure to set the record straight.

She refused to watch as Ethan effortlessly carried Eva's possessions up the curving staircase. Instead, she turned to Eva who stood before the hall mirror, applying a shiny lip gloss. Carol took the gesture as another broad hint, that Ethan had kissed those lips bare when Eva had arrived. Carol was sure Ethan wouldn't have any use for her now—not when he had Eva to attend his needs.

She blushed when she thought how strong those needs had been, then caught Eva watching her through the mirror and tried to cover her thoughts.

"I'm glad you're home, Eva," Carol managed. To her amazement she sounded sincere, and she hoped Eva thought so too.

But Eva was not to be placated. She turned on Carol and hissed, "Why? I'm certainly not glad that you're home. We were doing just fine without you."

Carol caught her breath sharply. There had been no mellowing of her cousin's feelings, nor in the manner in which those feelings were expressed. Though Carol had always tried to hide her dislike, Eva had never held her true feelings in check when the two of them were alone. It was only in front of others that Eva barely managed to tolerate her.

Carol stood speechless for a moment, then turned to the parlor and the task she had abandoned upon their arrival. Picking up a small box, she removed a carefully wrapped glass ball and held it before the night. Viewed through the fragile globe, the whole room assumed a rosy glow. It reminded her of something Claud had said about holding onto the rosy hue of dreams as long as possible.

What dreams did she have? Could she dream that Ethan preferred her to Eva? It wasn't a thought she chose to linger over, so she stretched forward to place the ball on a high limb so that it caught the afternoon sunlight. She worked nimbly, contentedly putting up the delicate ornaments, until she sensed she was being watched.

Ethan was leaning negligently against the doorway, his hands thrust in his hip pockets. "I thought you would have finished by now. You didn't work on it last night, after all, did you?" He spoke reproachfully, without moving from the door. "If you had let me stay, it would have been done by now."

What was he trying to tell her, Carol wondered. It sounded as if he was speaking about the tree, but her heart was hearing other words. If she had let him stay, she felt that something besides the tree decorating would have taken place; she would have capitulated to his overwhelming physicality.

Her alarming thoughts were interrupted by Eva's entrance. Wrapping her arm around Ethan in a possessive gesture, she murmured sweetly, "Come along, or we'll miss the kickoff."

Ethan straightened and started to turn away, then he stopped and looked back at Carol. "We're going to the Superdome for a play-off game. Do you want to come? We're sitting in a private box, so getting a ticket is no problem."

Eva's brittle laughter cut through his invitation. "Don't be foolish. Carol would never leave her Christmas tree. As it is, she's left it longer than Claud would have liked, and whatever Claud would have wanted, Carol will deliver."

A strange cynicism marked Ethan's next reply.

"So I've been told." He looked at Carol again. "We wouldn't have time for you to dress, anyway. Maybe next time."

Carol looked down at her bare feet, her faded jeans and loose cotton shirt. The clothes were fine for tree trimming but definitely not for joining people in one of the exclusive boxes at the Superdome. When she looked up again, the doorway was empty, and Carol resumed hanging the ornaments.

WHEN NAN AWOKE later that afternoon, she was disappointed to learn that Eva had come and gone, but just knowing that her favorite had returned cheered her markedly. They had their coffee in the parlor, with Nan making a few suggestions for moving an ornament or two. They were still discussing the plans for decorating the hall and dining room when the front door opened again, but this time the cousin who greeted Carol was far warmer. René hugged her demonstratively, kissed Nan resoundingly and flopped on the elegant sofa across from them.

"Fantastic tree, Carol. As soon as I've caught my breath, I'll help you stow these boxes." He was the same as always, the shadow of handsomeness lurking behind his dissipated features. Five more years and he would be fat and nearly bald.

At least René had never been jealous of Carol's relationship with Claud, in fact, quite the opposite. The more attention Claud had given to Carol's achievements, the less notice and pressure he had placed on René. Nor did René now have any recriminations about Carol's self-imposed exile, either. Just as he had sought refuge from Claud's disapproval in the fantasy world of Mardi Gras parade-float design, he could understand her flight to Chicago.

They talked at length about his work as together they restored order to the room. He even offered to drape the greenery and tie the red velvet bows on the curving banister of the graceful main staircase. So, while Carol prepared their supper, he applied all his impressive artistic ability to decorating the entrance hall.

After supper, once Nan had been ensconced before the television, they stood back to survey his work. René shook his head, muttering sadly, "It's a waste, a real waste. The tree, the decorations...and for whom? Nobody ever comes here anymore; this is a dead house."

Carol quickly made an adamant denial. "None of this is a waste, and this house is not dead. How can you say such things about your own home? And people do come here, but even if they didn't, we deserve all this for ourselves—me, you, Eva, Tante Nan... perhaps her more than anyone else. And speaking of no one ever coming here, where have you been? I've tried repeatedly to find you."

He laughed at her frustration. "That's exactly how I wanted it. I had to finish some designs, and I kept being interrupted, so I stayed at a friend's. What did you want me for?"

"Isn't it obvious? With Claud ill, Tante Nan needs you more than ever, and I need you, too—" Carol broke off as she tried to choke back a sob.

René's rounded face went slack, and his expression

reminded Carol of the kind of people he associated with. They were the sort of people Claud couldn't or wouldn't tolerate, people he had forbidden René to bring home. Now René, too, had begun to take on some of their debauched physical characteristics.

"I really think you should make it your business to visit Tante Nan daily, no matter how inconvenient it may be. I also think you should make sure that your sister does the same. I'm not asking you to stay here day and night; I'm not willing to make that sacrifice myself, and I won't ask more of you than I ask of myself. Just spend some time each day with her."

Carol waited for his response. When nothing but a chilled silence was forthcoming, she continued, "Neither of you has been to see Claud. I want to know why. Another thing I want to know is why I had to rely upon a stranger to help me get Tante Nan over there."

He sank onto a stair, his hands clasped between his knees, his head hanging low. "Every point you're making is valid, Carol, but only to a degree. You can't imagine what life in this family has been like lately. Not just since Claud had his stroke, or since you left, but even before then."

He pressed the heels of his hands against his eyes. With a mirthless laugh, he raised malice-filled eyes to Carol, who stood looking down at him. "He turned us out—the great god Guerard turned us little Guerards out."

At her sound of disbelief, he reached up and pulled her onto her knees in front of him. This close she could see the fine lines around his eyes, the sallowness of his complexion.

"He said we could either begin pulling our own weight or get out. It didn't matter to him. All he was willing to provide was a place for us to sleep and three meals a day, with the condition that we were here to eat them," he snorted derisively.

"That wouldn't have bothered you one iota, would it, dear productive cousin. In fact, it couldn't. He didn't even feel the need to deliver that message to you. You were already pulling your load, weren't you, dogging his every step, lapping up every word." His face hardened. "And now you're thinking that it shouldn't have made much financial difference to us. After all, we each have a share in the company."

The grip on her hand tightened. "This was before the company began to founder. At first it didn't matter too much to me; I had my job, and I was doing what I wanted. Then all of a sudden I began to get bills for things I had always taken for granted. Do you realize just how much it costs to keep a boat at the yacht club? Green fees and dues for the country club? I hadn't always used all the yearly income from my share, but one year's dues in my Carnival krewe wiped out all the surplus in my account—that and wrecking my car. I had forgotten to pay the insurance premiums. Claud had always taken care of that, too. What babes he loosed in the world!"

Finally René released his hold. "I tried borrowing, but it doesn't take long for word to spread—another side effect of Claud's withdrawal. And just as he had predicted, I discovered who my real friends were.

You can guess the number wasn't nearly so large as I thought. Are you beginning to get the picture?"

The blue eyes—so like his sister's—gave Carol a searching look, then closed. He took a deep breath and leaned back against the step, his confession still incomplete.

"And how do you suppose it was for Eva? You sit there in those clothes feeling like a million dollars, and it doesn't matter that the shirt is cotton instead of silk or that the jeans aren't designer made. It's not that way for Eva.

"And we can't blame either of us. The only person we can blame is Claud. He molded her, and with help from Tante Nan he created the most beautiful cold-hearted and useless woman who ever lived." He opened his eyes to focus on the great chandelier above them.

"The cruelest part was Claud's letting us find out for ourselves just what he had created. It's not very pleasant to see yourself for the first time and not like what you see, not very pleasant at all."

He stood up and looked at Carol's bowed head as she absorbed this new picture of Claud. "I cannot say I'm glad that Claud has fallen, but you can't lay a guilt trip on me because I don't visit his sickbed or hang around his house. I came tonight to see my sister. And believe it or not, I stayed because you were here. You and I have nothing but watered-down blood in common. If Claud had left us alone, we might have been friends, as well as relatives. It's probably too late now."

He reached for the coat he had carelessly thrown

across the chair. "I'll be in and out, but don't expect me to take up permanent residence. It's all I can manage. Say good-night to Nan for me."

Before she could rise, he had slipped into his coat and left the house.

After René had left, Carol prepared Nan for bed, tidied the house and had a little time to reflect upon René's words as she waited for Gracie's return. It was with her return that Carol knew *something* good had happened that day, for Gracie was full of smiles and happy news of her family. It comforted Carol to know she was leaving the house on a happy note, even if it was from Gracie's tune.

CHAPTER SEVEN

IT WAS A NIGHT of unrelenting agony for Carol. Previously, when she had thought of Ethan and Eva together—a thought upon which she acknowledged over and over that she already had spent too much time—it had never been with the same shattering, totally debilitating sense of reality. Seeing them together added a new dimension to her confusion, and she despised the way her imagination conjured up pictures of the manner in which they had spent the rest of the evening, the way they might still be together while she writhed in emotional misery. Having tasted the power of Ethan's appeal and knowing that Eva never denied herself anything she wanted, she was torn by vivid images of the two of them with each other.

Along with all the other pressures, this mental anguish was too much for Carol. She didn't know how to deal with this new view of Claud, his weariness and disgust with René and Eva and their parasitic existences. She was alarmed at René's attitude, at Eva's selfishness. And to let herself think of Ethan being ultimately involved with Eva was an excessive cruelty to inflict upon herself; such thoughts dangerously tipped the balance of her stability. She couldn't live this way, she couldn't. There were too many pieces that had to be kept in their places, in rational perspective. Carol felt she was being attacked from all sides—Claud, Nan, René, Eva and...Ethan— and she had to devise a way of protecting herself. If she didn't take better care of herself, she didn't believe she would survive.

And what did she have to use in her self-defense? There was only one thing that she could control; everything else was beyond her influence, except for that one thing: her own relationship with Ethan. She could erase from her mind what those times with him had meant to her. She could and would control her feelings about him. The others were not within her power, but she would make herself forget the night in front of the tree, the events leading up to that night.

These thoughts were only night ramblings, Carol knew. She could no more deny her feelings for Ethan than she could cease to breathe. She was in love with him. It would take forever to deny that love, and she only had a few hours to do it before she would see him that day. Good Lord, what was she to do?

Nothing—nothing at all but keep her torment to herself. Carol felt powerless to fight her feelings, but she couldn't let him know. With the power he held over her, he must not know.

With abject determination Carol faced the working day, in an office in which Ethan was conspicuously present. Each time the office intercom buzzed, she held her breath and waited. As a result she accomplished nothing in her work and was a screaming bundle of nerves by midmorning. When the tension finally became intolerable, she was forced to act.

"Mrs. McLin," she addressed the secretary, "I'm taking a company car down to the market to pick up some wreaths." Like decorating the big tree at the house, there were traditions that she intended to maintain in the offices. Claud had loved the holiday season and had always insisted that at work the rooms be decorated, too.

"Mr. Greenlaw said he wanted to see you whenever you were free. Why don't you check with him before you leave?" Mrs. McLin suggested.

"That won't be necessary, Mrs. McLin. I think I'll just tag along with Carol, and we can settle our business on the way," rang out a familiar voice, making Carol cringe and grit her teeth at Ethan's unexpected appearance. This was the last thing she wanted or needed. She really did want to get the Christmas wreaths, but her main purpose in the trip was to avoid any possibility of a confrontation with Ethan at a time when her nerves were raw. There was no escaping him now, so Carol numbly let him escort her to the parking garage.

Once they were seated in the car, Ethan promptly let Carol know that he knew she was trying to avoid him. "You've sequestered yourself with Miss Nan for the whole weekend and pretended to be busy with work all morning. Now it's just the two of us." He turned to glance at her profile. "We've had a couple of days to think things over, and obviously you've come to some decision that you should share with me, but you don't intend to, do you?" He paused for verification that didn't come. "Well, you're not the only one who's reached some conclusions, and since you won't talk to me, I'll talk to you." Still he got no reaction, and her closed expression annoyed him. "Damn it, Carol, what do you want me to do? If I could control what's between us, don't you think I would?" Then his voice lowered. "But I can't, and although I believe that was your decision—to control it—you can't, either, can you?"

Carol sat, still mute, but her mind was awhirl with the implications of his words. Then suddenly, in frustration he took her by the shoulders and swung her around to face him. "Answer me, Carol. Can you truthfully say that you want the feelings between us to be dead forever, that you honestly don't want me to be with you again, that you really don't want me to kiss you, to touch you, to want you?" His voice was laced with remembered passion.

Now he did get a reaction and watched in shock as the panic surged over her. "My God, Carol," Ethan gasped, "I won't make demands of you that you aren't ready to meet. I thought I had made that clear. I won't hurt you, not ever again in any way, I swear. Now that we both know how far we can go with one another, together we can give what's between us time to develop, to grow into whatever it is meant to become."

She closed her eyes in an attempt to shut out his honeyed words. Ethan was saying everything she wanted to hear, and she didn't know if she should trust those words. But she wanted to—oh, how she desperately wanted to! She had to have more from him than the passion that was between them, and the only way she would ever have more was if they gave it time to blossom apart from their physical desire for one another. Now he was holding out hope to her that they could make things work. Perhaps she could even survive his relationship with Eva if she knew there was some chance that she would be the ultimate winner, that one day she could have Ethan love her.

Then Carol answered him, carefully choosing her words; she knew she must not reveal too much. "I can't say I can stop my feelings, either. But we have to slow down, we have to be careful." This was her way of agreeing to his proposal; she meant to say no more, but her next words came of their own volition. The husky little whisper communicated all the fear she had fought so valiantly for the past weeks and especially last night. "You can destroy me, you know that, don't you?"

He lifted his hands from her shoulders and placed them on either side of her face with tenderness. "I'll take care of you, not destroy you," he pledged with a sweet passionless kiss to her mouth. "We'll slow it down, give it time, but don't shut me out," he said, pleading for confirmation. With Carol's positive response the atmosphere between them lightened.

"Now that you have a chauffeur, where do you want to go?"

"To the French Market—the vegetable stalls."

Now there was a comfortable easiness between them as Ethan drove through the morning traffic, and Carol relaxed. It would work out, she knew it would. The sunlight streaming down held warmth—a good omen. It would work.

Ethan interrupted her musings with a muttered imprecation. "Whatever is the holdup?" he grumbled impatiently. "That looks like a parade, it sounds like a parade, but I could swear I saw a hearse."

Carol slid nearer to him to have a better view of the cause of the traffic tie-up. "It's not exactly a parade; it's a jazz funeral. Haven't you seen one before?"

His expression was one of utter disbelief.

"Let's find a parking place and walk over to have a look," she suggested.

They quickly caught up with the funeral entourage, led by a brass band playing a mournful dirge. In front walked the parade marshal, his umbrella furled, his hat over his heart and a pathetically sad expression on his face. Directly behind the band came the long line of black vehicles carrying the deceased and the immediate members of the dead man's family.

"If you like, we can join the second line," Carol informed Ethan, who with great fascination was taking in every detail of the colorful spectacle.

"Just join in? And what's the second line?"

"That's the group of people who follow the parade band, mainly friends and acquaintances of the person who died. It's usually not minded if others participate, but you might be a little more comfortable if we lag a little behind."

Ethan was too flabbergasted to ask more, and he let Carol lead him. At the cemetery the band ceased its playing, and a low drumroll began to reverberate.

Slowly the hearse passed through the parted ranks of the musicians.

"They've turned him loose," Carol whispered to Ethan as around them expressions of grief became more and more vocal. The casket was moved into the tomb, and the whole atmosphere changed from weeping and wailing to a cheerful dancing celebration of life after death. As the band struck up a lively tune, the gaily decorated umbrellas streaming with ribbons and feathers were unfurled, and the second line began to dance and clap hands to "When the Saints Go Marching In."

The unusual display left Ethan speechless. "It's an old New Orleans tradition," Carol interjected into his silence. "Does it offend you?"

He thought for a moment. "No, I don't think it does, but it amazes me. I suppose this kind of funeral is a particularly healthy way to release tensions, to pick up the pieces and go on living," he reasoned.

They continued to follow the second line, retracing their earlier route, and reached the street where they had first joined the procession. Many of the onlookers were as amazed as Ethan.

"Who was he?" he questioned when they were back at the car.

"I'm not sure, but I do know that jazz funerals are usually held for three kinds of people: members of an order who are pledged to that kind of farewell; black musicians—noteworthy or not; and devoted jazz fans regardless of color, who have requested and in their own way earned the right to be 'turned loose' by a brass band."

"Do these funeral happen often?"

"Well, they aren't rare, but often they don't attract much attention."

"Just a local custom," he teased.

"Yes, a New Orleans tradition."

The streets cleared rapidly, and Ethan drove on to the French Market, where Carol quickly located the object of the trip. Just where she knew they would be, in back behind the melons and citrus fruit, were the rustic wreaths made by the concession's owner when business was slack. Made of things available at the stand, these wreaths had always been her favorites. There were wreaths with nuts of all kinds, ears of dried corn and bright kumquats. With their great burlap bows, they were perfect for the main entrance to Guerard Construction.

Ethan carried the awkward bundles to the car and once back at the offices saw to hanging them up. As Carol watched, a soft light came to her eyes at the fulfilling of a time-honored Guerard tradition.

That day seemed to establish a good mood between them that lasted for the rest of the week. There was a gentle awareness, but neither spoke of it as they worked together, sometimes having lunch with each other. Carol went to work early, visited Claud and stopped by the house at every opportunity, but still she refused to move out of Patti's apartment in the Quarter. She had dinner with the family on most evenings, but those dinners usually included only her and Nan.

She hadn't heard from Eric in some time and assumed Ethan's message had killed his interest in her.

She did receive a scathing call from Jim, which made it clear that Ethan had effectively destroyed forever that friendship, also. Carol was not unaware of the irony of her situation: on most evenings, after she had carried out her self-assigned obligations to others, she was even more lonely than she had been in the alien North.

But that loneliness also brought time to think. She wished a thousand times there wasn't any because far too many of her questions had no answers. One matter that particularly bothered her was how Eva had been able to afford the shopping spree in New York and the expenses that went with being a Carnival maid in the Mardi Gras celebrations. Gracie had been keeping Carol well informed of Eva's many purchases, expressing her disapproval in unveiled terms.

"Poor Mr. Claud lying on his deathbed, and there she goes traipsing all around, buying party dresses, going out every night, strolling in here at all hours like she doesn't have a care in this world with her 'Gracie do this and Gracie do that.' As if I don't have a thing to do in this big old house but wait on her hand and foot. It's a crying shame. Poor Mr. Claud."

Gracie would shake her head and grumblingly make her way back to her domain, the kitchen. Carol couldn't bring herself to ask with whom Eva spent those late nights. Ethan wasn't showing signs of late evenings, but she couldn't very well ask how he occupied his time.

On the rare occasions that Eva was home for the evening meal, Carol was willing to sacrifice almost anything for a tranquil visit. At first there were Eva's innuendos and subtle snipes, which seemed to go by Nan but were always on target with Carol. Then finally came an evening when the elderly woman could no longer remain oblivious to the conflict between her two grandnieces.

It had all begun on a rather festive note. René had unexpectedly arrived during predinner drinks. Carol found the fireside scene pathetic. It hurt her to know how little it took to please Nan, and how seldom that little was available to one who seemed to have so much. But Nan's possessions were not the kind that gave comfort, Carol thought, as she watched the great dinner rings capture the light and fling it back in unstructured rainbows.

Carol stopped counting the trips René made to the Waterford decanter of blended whiskey. Now she understood Gracie's allusion to René's drinking the few meals he took at home. By the time Nan painfully rose to lead them in to dinner, René had a glazed look in his eyes, and his speech came slowly, precisely enunciated, as if he carefully weighed each word to make sure it left his mouth the same way his brain ordered it to.

At the table he barely touched the scant food he dished onto his plate, but Carol noticed Gracie, with a telling roll of her brown eyes, replace the wine bottle.

"Carol," Eva began innocently, turning her attention from René, "where is the emerald?"

"What?" It was so bald a question that for a moment Carol didn't know what Eva was talking about.

Then she recalled the snatches of conversation she had overheard between Eva and Nan, remembering their discussions about fashion, clothes and accessories.

"The little emerald drop your mother wore—where is it?"

"It's in my safe-deposit box at the bank, Eva. Why?"

"I want you to get it out. I need it." Eva spoke in the same way she would ask for a tissue.

"I'm sorry, I don't understand. Do you mean you want to borrow it?" Carol didn't think that was what Eva meant at all.

"No," she replied, her blue eyes blazing with a possessive flame, "I want it for myself, and I want you to give it to me."

"But it was left to me by my mother—it's mine," Carol protested.

"That was some kind of mistake. The pendant is a Guerard heirloom and should have been kept in the family."

"Eva," Carol protested in shock, "I *am* in the family."

"But you don't bear our name. In that way, you aren't a Guerard. That pendant should be worn by Guerards, isn't that right, *tante*?" She made her appeal to Nan, who for the first time Carol could remember, seemed disconcerted by one of Eva's demands.

"Eva... I'm not sure that...."

Eva immediately sensed Nan's hesitation and knew it would be better if she herself continued the argument. "You lose the rights to that stone because you do not bear our name, Carol," she reiterated.

"If that's the case, when you marry and your name is no longer Guerard, you won't have a claim, either."

Undaunted, Eva still pressured Carol. "That is correct," she said in a brittle precise voice as she turned to her brother. "It shall then become the property of René's wife or daughter."

Carol ventured a glance at René, who flushed at the attention directed at him. "Isn't that correct, René?" Eva asked relentlessly.

"I think there should be a duel fought beneath the City Park oaks or behind the cathedral. I think that would settle this issue much better than all this wrangling at the dinner table." René reached to refill his wineglass, spilling a puddle of the blood-colored nectar onto the fine old lace of the tablecloth.

"And I think that you are drunk," Eva accused. Because René hadn't supported Eva, she struck at him with the sharp edge of her scathing tongue. It was another first for Carol to witness.

"And you are a selfish, greedy two-faced bitch," René retaliated smoothly, lifting the glass to his lips in a mocking salute.

All three turned at the sound of Nan's sharp intake of shocked breath. Carol quickly apologized on behalf of the others, then turned to Eva.

"The jewel is mine to do with as I see proper. If you would listen a little more and talk a little less, Eva, you would know the history behind the rather insignificant emerald you covet. It is not now nor has it ever been Guerard property. It came to my mother through my grandmother, who received it from her mother and on back. You have no claim to it—especially because of your name."

"Bravo, Carol, bravo. I'll drink to that." René raised a markedly unsteady glass to his lips.

"Tante," Eva wailed, turning as always to Nan for the magic solution that would give her what she wanted, but tonight there was no way Nan would ask Carol to give in to Eva. It seemed that she saw, as did the others, that Carol would no longer automatically accede to Eva's requests.

In a conciliatory tone Nan said to Eva, "You may have my sapphires, my darling. They suit you so much better—the blue for your eyes. Tomorrow I will have them brought to you. They really are much more impressive than the small emerald." She placed her hand on Eva's, and Carol felt her heart lurch. In a way Eva had won again, and knowing Eva as she did, she couldn't help wondering if getting the sapphires hadn't been her original goal.

Then René lumbered to his feet. "If you two aren't going to at least pull hair and scratch, I might as well seek livelier entertainment elsewhere."

Carol caught her breath as he stumbled near the glass-fronted cabinet of priceless china and crystal, but he managed to brace himself against a chair. Rising from her own seat, Carol followed him out.

"You aren't driving tonight, are you?"

"I surely am. Riding a broom like the rest of the harpies in this mausoleum is not exactly my style."

"René," Carol appealed, "let me drive you wherever you're going."

For a moment he seemed almost sober as he straightened his tie and pulled his coat more neatly onto his shoulders. "Oh, little cousin, you can't go with me. You wouldn't want to be where I'm going tonight." He went out the door and left her standing alone beneath the blazing chandelier.

After a moment Carol turned and wearily climbed the stairs, feeling how badly she needed respite from all the turmoil she'd been through lately. The ugly scene at dinner upset her terribly, and as she got ready for bed, she realized that she knew true solace only in her work. The precision and rationality of applied mathematics were strangely comforting, but even stranger was the solace she found in a quiet word of encouragement from Ethan. That, along with the office staff's requests for assistance, carried her through. They were responsible for checking and rechecking that everything depicted on the architects' plans and specification sheets was available when it was needed. With the use of the computer their jobs were much easier, but it was still necessary to make personal contact with delinquent shippers when the great mechanical brain determined that certain supplies were not where they were supposed to be, when they were supposed to be, as they were supposed to be.

If a shipment of materials arrived that seemed defective, the staff sought out Carol, asking for verification or analysis to determine whether all was in order. Could the subcontractor substitute this carpeting for that carpeting? Carol was grateful for their conscientiousness; nothing was too mundane for their attention, from three-quarter-inch nuts to great slabs of precast concrete.

Each morning when she arrived at work, she went immediately to the new computer that had been installed in her office and punched in the codes to examine the calculations Ethan had done the previous day. Seeing for herself the enormous amount of work he'd been doing, Carol felt her anxiety about his relationship with Eva subside. He couldn't possibly get so much done on the bid for the Taalot building, carry on the day-to-day business of the company and give Eva as much time as a torrid affair with her would require. Carol held fast to that thought as she drifted off to sleep.

THE NEXT MORNING Ethan called her into his office to discuss the specifications for the Taalot building. "I need some help." He nodded to the glowing image on the computer screen. "Can you figure out how much time we'll need to drive the piles after we have the preliminary work done?"

Carol sat at an adjacent desk and worked for a while with the figures he gave her. "What do you have?" Ethan demanded impatiently.

"I have this." She moved closer to him and flinched as he bit out a harsh word.

"That's it?" His face fell.

Not to be bullied, Carol responded in kind. "With what I have to go on, yes. If you want a more accurate estimate, you'll have to give me better information.

I'm an engineer making mathematical computations. I'm not a sorceress conjuring up figures in the dark of the night."

Ethan muttered a rude reply, then barked, "Get Randle on the phone and tell him to come over here right away."

"Will you stop it," Carol scolded. "Mr. Randle cannot abandon his own business and come running over here to worry with these numbers."

Ethan abruptly stood up and began pacing with frustration. "Are you calling him?"

"You're becoming impossible over the Taalot bid, Ethan."

"If I can't get the estimates down, we won't be able to finance a bid." His anxiety was palpable. "Every thousand dollars I can shave off brings us that much closer to getting the financial backing we need. You know that the construction industry depends more on borrowed capital than most other businesses, and right now our financial status is getting stronger daily, but I don't think it will right itself in time." In a gesture of despair he raked his hands through his hair, then continued.

"Every day I spend hours wooing the money men, and when I'm not out there with my hat in my hand, I'm thinking about it. If we had more time, I know we could manage it. Carol, I don't want to make this a joint venture with another company, but if we can't get the backing and resources to undertake the work, that may be our only option." He suddenly stopped pacing and in a firm voice said to Carol, "I'll call Randle myself."

In what seemed to Carol like minutes, Steve Randle arrived at the office. Ethan asked her to leave so that the two men could discuss the matter in private. As he had the last time they met, Steve Randle frightened Carol. She had got only a glimpse of the tall man, but that was enough to reaffirm her previous impression, that within him were rivers of rage held in check with great effort; should his control ever snap, she felt that the torrent of his anger would destroy everything around him.

Carol had just settled back into her work when the buzz of the intercom interrupted. "I need your help again," Ethan commanded.

Carol wondered at Ethan's anxiety about the project; she had worked with him too often to doubt his competence. On the way to his office she decided to discuss it when Steve left.

She had just joined the men and was working on the data Ethan had given her when Mrs. McLin entered in near panic. "There's been an accident at the Jefferson Parish site!"

Ethan got up immediately and reached for his hard hat and safety vest. "I'll go there right now. Any injuries?"

"Two, but the project supervisor didn't say how serious they were."

Carol started toward the door, intending to leave with Ethan, but he declined her help. "If I need you, I'll be in touch. In the meantime stay with Steve and finish up," he instructed tightly as he slammed the door.

Carol stared at the door for a moment, then looked

warily at the husky man seated across the desk from her. Steve had removed his coat and tie and rolled back the sleeves of the neatly tailored shirt, exposing strong wrists burnished with gold-tipped hair. Her eyes were riveted on the slightly deformed and scarred right hand. Then she looked up at the night black eyes set in the chiseled face that betrayed nothing beneath the stony surface.

When he stood up to get a cup of coffee, his towering height intimidated Carol even more. On that powerful frame was the musculature of a young stevedore, but Carol guessed his age to be near forty. He moved softly, like someone who had carefully studied the efficiency of walking and found the way to navigate between two points with the least expenditure of energy. At the coffee service he poured two cups and with that same disturbing economy of motion, placed one in front of her, switched off the computer's power supply and resumed his seat.

In the ensuing stillness it seemed to Carol that Steve weighed a decision, and when he spoke, it seemed, too, that he weighed each word. "Miss Charbonnet, how do you see the future for us?"

Puzzled, she repeated, "For us?"

"Yes, you as Guerard's representative and me as Randle Equipment's. Do you see repeated business encounters, or do you think we will work very infrequently?" He waited for her answer.

"You know Guerard's no longer has the equipment that you supply, that we are dependent on your firm or a firm like it," Carol responded.

Steve added, "And Ethan has been rebuilding

Guerard's at an amazing rate, so that means even more transactions in the future. Correct?"

"Yes," Carol answered, still not sure of his point.

"And don't you think that you will handle many of these transactions, deal directly with me?" he questioned.

"Yes," Carol acknowledged.

"Because we *will* be working together, I've decided to share something with you, something that I don't share normally. It is the reason I am as I am." He settled deeper into his chair and began in his usual dispassionate manner. "When I was nineteen, life was wonderful. I had the world by the tail and had every intention of 'passing a good time.' I firmly believed I was obligated to 'let the good times roll.' *Laissez les bons temps rouler*, the motto of South Louisiana, was my personal code."

Steve's tonal inflection marked his Acadian heritage. She had never dreamed he was a native, but with that one expression he had revealed his roots. "There were only my mother and I, but we had a fierce *joie de vivre*. What a special gift for life she had!" Carol sensed his defenses were about to break.

Steve took a sip of the coffee. "Then her zest began to fade, but I didn't notice, not right away. She worked in the office of an oil refinery; I worked for the landed gentry." Now Carol clearly understood what lay behind his defenses because for a brief moment the mask did slip, and what was exposed was raw and ugly. "The judge..." he snarled. "At night the judge's son and I ran wild. Books are written about the kind of youths we were." Again the icy reserve was back.

"One afternoon my mother didn't come home from work. She had collapsed and been taken to the hospital. The doctors told me she was dying of acute leukemia and had been ill for nearly a year; she hadn't told me and I hadn't seen it. Youthfully, foolishly, I celebrated that news with a spree to end all sprees. We took the fastest of the judge's cars, and we ran the strip between Opelousas and Lafayette. It was nearly dawn when the accident occurred. In my drunken stupor I got out of the passenger seat and looked down at the crumpled mess of humanity on that deserted back road and knew the old man was dead. Somehow we made it back to the judge, and I told our story. His son had passed out on the lawn.

"The judge poured me a great glass of smooth expensive whiskey, with a taste I had only read about, and over that whiskey he put his proposition to me. If I would assume responsibility for the accident, he would take care of my mother. He would pay the hospital bills, the nursing care, and when the time came, see that she had a proper burial. He had political plans for his son; once the details of the accident were known, his plans would be destroyed.

"So I agreed. But when I had paid his son's debt to society with five years of the seven-year sentence, I found that the judge had not kept his word. My mother had died in a charity-hospital ward and was buried in a pauper's grave with only a five-by-seven metal disk marking her place."

Carol was amazed at how he recounted the story

like a journalist reading the six-o'clock news. "What did you do?" she asked timidly. "Did you rescind your confession?"

He gave a mirthless laugh that made Carol shiver inwardly. "What for? My mother was dead. Naturally I thought about it, but when I went to see the judge, to confront him, to make my feeble demand of restitution, his son was there, fresh out of the best school in the East. And it took only a word for me to know that he honestly didn't know that he had been the driver while I was only the semiconscious passenger."

"What did you do?" Carol prompted. She was fascinated by his tragic story.

"I made lots and lots of money. I think I have more capital at my command now than the judge ever had, ever will have, or can call to back him up. And that's where it stands now. When I started this business, I bought a broken-down backhoe with money I saved working double shifts on the offshore rigs. Instead of working fourteen days on and fourteen days off, I worked twenty-eight on and twenty-eight off. Do you realize how much money you can save when all you have to buy is work clothes?" He looked down at the handmade shoes and the tailored pants and shirt that he now wore, and she knew he compared them to the rough garments he had worn on the rigs.

"One night when I was on shore and finding work with my secondhand backhoe, I ran into a former prison mate who was having trouble finding work. We teamed up, and then the process repeated itself.

Sometimes our struggling company would be so strapped for cash that I would go back to working the rigs; sometimes several of us would go back out there, but we finally started paying our way with the secondhand equipment. Then there was new equipment and new ex-cons needing work."

"Your rehabilitation program is very noble."

"No ma'am, it's not noble; it's not intended to be noble. It's profitable. I have no insurance against theft or vandalism other than a little sign on the fence of any site using my equipment. There's no need. There isn't a criminal ring or group of thieves other than the Mafia who would confront the men of my company, and I'm not sure if they would try."

Carol thought of the types she had seen manning Randle equipment and shuddered at the image of what might happen should they get angry. "I can see now why you can manage the machinery better than we can. At first I thought that Ethan had other reasons for liquidating our equipment."

Steve stood up to take his cup back to the service tray. "Every year American contractors spend millions to replace obsolete construction machinery. Add to that sum great losses inflicted by vandalism and theft, and you see the implications of my being able to supply equipment. As soon as a unit becomes obsolete, I can immediately afford to replace it with something larger, more powerful, something that might give the builder a better product because he has a better performance from my operating engineer."

Carol turned to face Steve. "Why did you tell me all this?" she asked softly.

The unusual eyes that seemed to see more than was meant to be seen moved over her from top to toe in a disquieting assessment. "Because you needed to know. *I didn't need* to tell you. I don't have some ancient-mariner's obsession to tell my tale. But you needed to know, so that every time our paths cross you won't cringe inwardly while you effectively hide all outward signs of your distaste for me."

"Mr. Randle..." she began humbly.

"No, Miss Charbonnet. We came from two different worlds and have two different sets of motivations. You are frightened by my world, and therefore you are frightened of me. I don't know if you have just cause or not. You may find this hard to believe, but I am terrified of your world, and you can see that I do have just cause." He resettled in his chair.

"Now that we have removed some of the tension between us, maybe we can come up with some of the figures Ethan asked for," he said with a disarming smile. Briefly Carol had a glimpse of the man he could have been, and her fear dissipated.

After Steve Randle left, Carol returned to her own office to anxiously await Ethan's report. Twice she decided to go to the site, but each time she talked herself into being more patient. As the daily exodus from the building began, Ethan came in, the lines of strain around his eyes and mouth more pronounced. Without stopping, he went straight to his desk and slumped into the chair, not even turning on the lights. Carol stood in the doorway, not knowing if she dared to intrude.

"Would you pour me a drink, please?" he asked,

sensing her presence without opening his eyes. She did his bidding and silently proffered him the drink. Tiredly he reached up both hands, one to accept the drink, the other to restrain her hand. His lips went first to the palm of her hand. After that gentle salute he placed her hand on his shoulder and held it there while he lifted the drink—as if he needed that physical link with her.

"Two men were injured. One has a broken leg, the other has undetermined internal injuries, but the doctor seems to think he isn't in danger. We may have union trouble...I don't know."

"Why union trouble? What happened?" Her hand on his shoulder tensed. Ethan rubbed his thumb over her fingers, easing out the stress.

"I fired three workers on the spot—I didn't do it tactfully, not diplomatically at all."

Carol placed her other hand on his shoulder and began a gentle massage. "There shouldn't be any union repercussions," she encouraged. "The firings were justifiable."

"I have no definite proof that those particular workers were responsible, Carol...no proof. And you know how things like this often go. The firings could have a negative effect on the other workers, and their output may nose-dive. We're in enough trouble now, with worker productivity lagging behind wage inflation. I don't need to battle a deliberate slowdown."

"Maybe enough of the crew will know the truth and prevent trouble."

"I hope so—God, how I hope so." She could hear

the fatigue in his voice. "Do you have any *good* news for me?" He lifted her hands from his shoulders, placed a kiss in each palm and rose from the chair to turn on the overhead lights.

As the room brightened, Carol suddenly thought of the quality of their relationship. Recently there had been no tension between them, no heavy sexual overtones to overwhelm her, just a quiet togetherness that had been comfortable for both of them. It was what she had hoped would happen—that the flaming passion between them would be moderated for a while but not quenched. It was there, of course, just below the surface, but getting stronger daily was their love and compassion for each other. The little seed of hope that he might love her sent up another shoot that she nurtured with a flicker of internal sunshine.

"Why the secret light in your eyes, Carol?" Ethan stood watching her, intently measuring, judging, analyzing the little ray of life-giving sunshine reflected in her eyes.

The color rose to her cheeks only slightly as she turned to the data she and Steve had compiled for him. "Just good news. Here." She held out the papers to him.

Ethan reached for the material but kept looking at Carol. "What are you doing for dinner tonight?"

"I'm having it with Tante Nan." Carol was spending as much time as possible with Nan, especially when she knew Eva would be out. René had been to the house only once more since the incident over the jewelry, and again he had overindulged in drink.

"Wouldn't she understand if you had a change in

plans?" He watched her closely. "Have dinner with me instead."

"I can't do that, Ethan. She needs me." Carol turned to leave. She wasn't sure if she actually heard his last remark, or if she only imagined the words that her heart wanted to hear. Had Ethan whispered, "I need you, too"?

He slid the unread papers onto his desk and walked over to where she stood. "Are you going now?" he asked quietly.

"Yes, I have to see Claud. I didn't go this afternoon for fear I would be needed if the accident at the site had been worse."

Ethan reached up to trace her eyebrow with his finger. "You're taking on too much, Carol. Let the others carry some of the load. Claud and Nan aren't entirely your responsibility, you know."

"I know." And that she did know, but she also knew that neither Eva nor René would assume any responsibility, that she would be the one to ease Nan's loneliness, make the daily visits to the hospital, keep the household running smoothly, help manage the company. "I know," Carol repeated with a sigh.

The tracing movement stopped when Ethan shifted to cup her chin in his palm before placing a tender kiss on her mouth. "Take care, darling." He gave her a little nudge through the doorway before turning back to his desk.

CHAPTER EIGHT

ETHAN HAD SPOKEN of restaffing some of the empty offices, and from the work load Carol was facing, she knew the time was at hand when they would have no choice. He had been extremely aggressive in pursuing clients for Guerard Construction—exhausting every lead, even settling for smaller profits to reaffirm their position in the building trades. Determined to be ready for the Taalot building, he spent long hours searching out new sources of supplies and whetting the appetites of subcontractors, new and old. For that reason more and more of the day-to-day office management was hers.

The day had been unusual, with Ethan in his office more than had become customary. Now in the late afternoon when she needed his opinion, he was out again. Equally as frustrating was a missing file. Her first thought was to have Mrs. McLin search for it, but she, as well as the other office staff, had sensibly left. Rising from her desk at which she had been sitting too long, Carol decided that the only place the file could be was on Ethan's desk.

But when she went into his office, the file was not in sight. Feeling like a thief in the night, she began to rifle through the contents of the drawers. It was in the second drawer that the elusive information rested, but the discovery of that file was not what held her attention. Beneath it was a small topless box containing half a dozen tapes, each dated more than two years previous, and each labeled with her name and the name she had hoped never to see again.

Lifting the box from the drawer, she placed it on the desk top. For a long time she simply stared at the little cassettes, then she reached for the machine Ethan used to dictate his work for Mrs. McLin. Gingerly she snapped the first reel in place. It began with a voice unfamiliar to her, a man's voice steeped in the accent of southern Louisiana. It was the accompanying female voice in the recorded telephone conversations that held her spellbound from the beginning.

Low and rich, just a trifle husky, the tones spilled into the room. It was she, Carol herself—almost. Had Carol not been teased and taunted a thousand times in her life by the almost faultless imitation of her voice, she would have believed she had actually spoken the incriminating words. But there was one flaw in the performance, a flaw that the years of practice could not remove. Carol only laughed when she was sincerely amused, and Eva could never emulate the honesty in Carol's laugh. It was the falseness, the insincerity that identified Eva as the true possessor of those soft melodious tones.

For an hour she listened to the horror unfold on the tapes. Then she started the series over, to let every word burn into her memory. No wonder Claud had been so adamant in not listening to her and not wanting her to bring legal suit against the man who had accused her. The voice was so undeniably believable. How could he not believe this to be irrefutable evidence against her? The voice, as well as the exorbitantly expensive fur mentioned again and again in the tapes, had effectively made her guilty in Claud's eyes.

While the tapes were playing for a second time, Carol searched the entire contents of the desk and every other available space in the office, but there was nothing to accompany the little box. Dejectedly she slumped once more in the large chair and placed her head on her crossed arms in utter despair as the nearly perfect impersonation continued in the stillness of the room.

She lifted her head only when the voice suddenly stopped in the middle of a word. A lean hand ejected the cassette from the machine, tossed it negligently into the box with the others, then slid the drawer containing the machine silently yet emphatically shut.

Carol turned away from the searching countenance. She didn't speak, nor did Ethan until she found the courage to face him. Then Ethan spoke first and asked, "Do you know who that is?" His nod toward the box of tapes was barely discernible.

"Yes...do you?" It was important to her. So many things depended on whether he knew that the voice was Eva's.

"I only know whose voice it isn't. Do you want to tell me who it is?" He was watching her intently, too intently.

"I...I can't...not yet." No, she had to have time to think about an answer. There was no definite proof it was Eva except for her own knowledge and experience at Eva's hands. Should Eva ever learn of Carol's accusation, she would certainly find a way to turn it into a weapon against Carol. What if Ethan did believe Carol's accusation and stopped seeing Eva? Would she feel victorious? Even worse was the possibility that Ethan would realize Carol spoke the truth and still continue his relationship with Eva. With so much at stake Carol refused to give a definite answer.

"How do you know that I didn't make those calls, that the voice isn't mine?"

Ethan shrugged. "I know. I don't know how; it's mostly a feeling because neither of us can deny it sounds like you." He turned to the window. "I suppose it would be simple enough for an expert in voiceprints to prove that it isn't you, but it might serve to stir up dead embers rather than to bury forever the question."

"Oh, Ethan, those embers aren't dead. You seem to forget where we are and who I am. 'Interesting' things are never forgotten here, especially when they concern the older families." She rose from the chair in frustration just as he moved back to the desk and lifted the box of tapes. "What will you do with those?"

He stood with the box poised over the trash basket. "I really don't know what to do with them. I should dump them right now, and then both of us should forget them." He hesitated, then reached down to replace the box in its original location. "For some reason Claud kept them. We'll keep them a while longer, though I see no reason why we should.

"Why are you here so late? I don't like your staying after the others have left." He turned to the closet and removed his briefcase. "I came back to get this. I have work that must be finished tonight."

Carol indicated the folder she had come in search of. "I wanted to finish the calculations for that warehouse extension, but you had the folder."

"It can wait until tomorrow." He tugged at his tie, then loosened the collar button beneath. "If you'll name a quiet restaurant where it isn't essential that we have reservations, and where we don't have to wait so long for a table that I get sloshed on the predinner drinks, I'll treat you to supper." He looked exhausted, and Carol regretted that the kind of restaurant he described was so rare as to be nonexistent.

"I know just the place. It's in the French Quarter, not too far from the supposed residence of the notorious voodoo queen Marie Laveau," she responded with all sincerity.

"Sounds fine. I could use a little black magic to get rid of this headache." Then it dawned on him. "You'll fix dinner? You've put in a day as long as mine. I can't let you do that."

"Don't worry. Half of what you get will come from the freezer, compliments of Gracie," she explained. "Every time I leave the house, she sends a little something along in case I don't get there for her to feed me the next meal. And her little something is usually enough for four. It will be primarily a case of thaw and warm. Fair enough?"

Ethan gratefully accepted and then drove Carol to the apartment building so that she could start the meal while he went to park the car. There was an oppressive heaviness in the air, and black clouds hung low in the sky. When she let him in the building, his hair glistened with beaded moisture as did his coat and the briefcase he brought for safekeeping.

Carol handed him a towel and pointed him toward the bathroom just as the first vicious clap of thunder rumbled and reverberated through the narrow and ancient streets. Returning to the kitchen where a pot of rice simmered on the back burner and a dish of chicken in *sauce piquante* thawed in a microwave, she busied herself with domestic chores.

"Whatever is in that pot has begun to bubble around the edges," Ethan proclaimed as he settled at the oaken table.

"That's chicken in *sauce piquante*. It's a...." Carol tried to think of a way around the word, but there was none. "It's a *peppery* mixture of thick tomato gravy in which the chicken has been slowly cooked. It has a characteristic Cajun flavor, very spicy." At the rising of the dark brow, she laughed the husky melodic trill that could not be duplicated.

Carol placed a bowl of freshly washed salad greens before Ethan. "I forgot to tell you that part of the price for this supper is your help." At his mock grimace she laughed again but saw that he tore the greens with a practiced touch.

He brought the broken greens back to the sink, where she was just removing salad dressing from the blender.

He rested his hip against the counter top while she checked the rice for tenderness. "Do you want a drink while I set the table, and we give this a few minutes more?"

"No, I don't think so." He rubbed a hand across his forehead.

"Headache worse?" she asked solicitously.

"No, just no better. I think that after we eat, it will ease. I was busy with an electrical-supplies dealer and missed lunch." Just then the timer for the oven buzzed, and Carol reached in for the oysters *en brochette*.

"Why don't you start on these. Maybe it will help." She indicated the skewered appetizers.

"I can wait for you," he protested. "The headache isn't fatal."

"But you are uncomfortable."

"Yes, I am. So why don't we compromise: I'll set the table while you dish up. Then we can get to the food quicker and together."

The matter settled, they worked together in a serene companionableness that was at odds with the amassing turbulence outside. Ethan expressed his pleasure at the rich chicken dish but refused wine with his meal. At the little flicker of disappointment in her face, Ethan looked puzzled.

"There's a liqueur in the dessert, just a tablespoon or so."

"I think I can handle that," he promised.

"And I have a special after-dinner treat, especially for you."

"Okay, okay," he conceded. "The headache is nearly gone, anyway. Bring on your spirits," he laughed. "Better the devil I know in here than the one that is raging outside," he said, alluding to the windswept rain that now washed the windows.

When they finished the dessert cup, a concoction of mixed fruits, ice cream and Cointreau, Carol dragged Ethan into the living room with a childlike urgency. And he indulged her, though he did protest at not being allowed to help clean up.

She quickly stacked the soiled dishes in the dishwasher, disposed of the leftovers and then arranged the special silver service.

When Carol entered the living room and found Ethan reclining on the sofa, his eyes closed, she felt a surge of disappointment. "I can see that you aren't ready for this. I'll make regular coffee."

But Ethan reached out to place a restraining hand on her arm. "No, honestly the headache is gone. I was just thinking, that's all. No headache, I swear." He smiled at her so convincingly that she believed him, and the playful look about her eyes and mouth returned. He eyed the equipment with trepidation. The chafing dish, ladle and the coffee cups all had a devil motif as decoration. "What kind of witches' brew are you serving?"

"*Café brûlot*," Carol announced proudly. Ethan watched in fascination as she gracefully flamed the mixture of brandy, sugar and cinnamon in which floated an artfully curved ribbon of clove-studded orange peel. Then she added the strong coffee. The aromatic perfume of the beverage hung on the humid air as she ladled the fragrant brew into the special cups. And Carol's eyes sparkled at her success in fulfilling to perfection another old New Orleans tradition.

"Well, how do you like it?" she asked before Ethan had time for little more than a tentative sniff of the blended aromas.

"Are you sure this is safe to drink?" he teased with a grinning countenance. At her moue, he yielded and took another sip. Carol could tell he liked the taste as much as he had enjoyed watching her make it.

"But why devils?" he asked, referring to the unusual design of the implements and cups used to serve the beverage.

"Sometimes it's called *café brûlot diabolique* because the coffee is 'black as the devil and hot as hell.' That's why there are devils on the cups and on the feet of the *brûlot* bowl." She watched him closely as he drank again.

"Headache still gone?" Carol asked anxiously. A flicker of concern was evident in her eyes, but again Ethan reassured her that he was all right.

"If the *brûlot* hadn't cured you completely, I had alternative treatments in mind to make you well."

With a sigh of contentment Ethan settled deeper into the sofa cushions and placed a throw pillow behind his head. "Just what else have you dreamed up, short of burning the house, which I thought you intended to do when you set fire to the devil's brew." He watched the dim lamplight play in the burnished gold of Carol's hair.

"Do you remember I mentioned that Marie Laveau lived near here?"

"Yes, you said she was the notorious voodoo queen."

"Well, she had some cures for headaches we can test if you'll cooperate by getting your headache back." Ethan quirked his brow at Carol's unusual suggestion before she continued, "All we need is a long cord in which I'll tie nine knots while I say little secret things handed down to me. We drape that around your neck, and then *voilà*, no headache."

"Why do we put the cord around my neck? Are you going to hang me?" he countered mockingly.

Carol pointedly ignored his joke. "There's also the banana-leaf treatment, which some say is even more effective. We just place one on your forehead. There are leaves on the patio, freshly washed by a thunder-driven rain." Her voice changed to a whisper as she pretended to be imparting a dark secret. "The thunder is the sound of the devil driving his black horses and chariot across the sky."

"I think being around you and your magic could possibly lead to worse things," Ethan teased.

"If you're suggesting that I'm being a pain in the neck, I even have a cure for that. Find a disgustingly dirty dishrag, the dirtier the better, and drape it around your neck. Works every time." Carol fought to keep a straight face at Ethan's surprised expression.

"How do you know it works?" he asked skeptically.

"I know it does. Whenever I recommended it in the past, the sufferers' symptoms just disappeared, and they never had the ailment around me again." Carol couldn't pretend to be serious any longer, and they both broke into hearty laughter.

"I guess not if you threatened to put that filthy rag on them," Ethan rejoined. "Where did you learn about all this nonsense?"

"You shouldn't scoff," Carol protested as she feigned wide-eyed horror at his irreverence.

"All right, I'll rephrase my question. Where did you learn this marvelous folk medicine?"

"Here and there. Some come from old-timers living in the bayou country, and a lot comes from Gracie."

"Well, my pretty voodoo queen, what else can you suggest?"

Carol kicked off her shoes and nestled into the sofa beside him. "If your headache were actually the beginning of a cold, I could break it by sticking to your temples squares of yellow paper smeared with rendered animal fat." When Ethan made a derisive sound, Carol retorted, "And just what has modern medicine to offer for the curing of a cold? Aspirin and orange juice—not at all interesting and very common!"

"That's why they call it the common cold," he joked.

She sat up and placed her hands on her hips in mock indignation. "It's obvious you don't appreciate this invaluable information I'm sharing with you."

Ethan threw his hands up in a prayerful attitude. "Please don't make me sit in the corner. I'll be serious from now on," he teased.

"I'll give you one more chance. Since you don't seem receptive to lessons in first aid, I'll just have to save you from other things." She leaned back and placed her finger against her cheek as if in deep thought, but the sparkles in her eyes betrayed her when she expounded her first lesson in Creole superstition. "If you cross your eyes, they'll stick and stay that way forever." Ethan promptly crossed and uncrossed his eyes twice.

"Idiot," she laughed before she resumed her pretended seriousness and delivered a Cajun warning. "If you don't stop making fun of me, the *cauchemar* will get you. He's the night spirit."

Ethan looked around the room as if seeking the phantom. "Is it bigger than a bread box? Should I be frightened?" He imitated her earlier expression of wide-eyed fear.

"You most definitely should. He can do awful things to you." Carol was becoming more beautiful as she shed the dross of family troubles and continued to entertain him with the folklore of her heritage.

"If I say I believe you, will you tell me how to keep the *cauchemar* away? I'm sure you must know a way."

"I know several. And as a Southerner, I'm just too, too hospitable to let a Yankee boy be carried away in the dark of the night—even if he does deserve it," she interjected in an undertone.

"The first thing you should know is that the *cauchemar* has two weaknesses: he can't stand the daylight, and he can't count well." Ethan smothered a laugh. "You must keep him busy until daylight drives him away, which you do by sprinkling grains such as rice or cornmeal on the floor or by placing the broom behind the door. He feels compelled to count the grains or the broom straws, but remember, he can't count well. He keeps losing his place and has to start over. This way he's kept busy all night and can't harm you."

"You just made that up," Ethan accused.

"I most certainly did not," Carol denied vehemently. "Ask any self-respecting Creole or Cajun if you doubt me. And the *cauchemar* is going to get you," she dramatically prophesied.

"He probably will because you'll stay up late, and little mathematician that you are, you'll help him count the straws in my broom."

"Do you even have a broom?" she queried.

"If I don't, I'll buy one. Anything to keep your Cajun demon away."

"You should have a broom, Ethan. Brooms have very powerful magic. If someone sweeps under your feet, you'll never marry."

"Do vacuum cleaners count?" Ethan countered.

Carol ignored him and continued, "If you sleep in the moonlight, you'll go crazy." She waited for his repartee, but when Ethan did respond, it was in a voice tight with seriousness.

"If I don't let me hold you soon in the moonlight, sunlight, no light—I'll go crazy, anyway." Then in a more tender tone he went on, "Just let me hold you. We know our limits. Just to hold you," he entreated.

Carol made no move to deny him as he lifted her toward him slowly, ever so slowly, until the length of her body rested on him. He held her, then turned so that they lay side by side. His head rested against hers as he gently caressed her cheek, waiting for her resistance to wane, for her moment of panic to recede.

"Ethan?" Carol said timidly. But he would not let her speak as he placed a finger against her lips.

"Shh, my darling, just lie still, just for a while." The wind washed the rain in rhythmic waves against the windows as peals of thunder echoed the thudding beat of Carol's heart.

Finally Ethan broke the forced silence. "It's not enough," he whispered in her mouth, and she reeled at the force of his desire. He deepened the intimacy with his mouth, with his hands at her waist, on her hips, at her breast, but she knew he would keep his pledge even though he kissed her passionately. His hold tightened, but still he held back.

His words burned into her. "I'll never hurt you again, Carol. I can wait, and I *am* waiting for the morning, the afternoon, the night that you can say yes and look at me and have no doubts, not one moment of denial. Then you will be mine. But if I ever discover what holds you back, I will smash it and scatter the fragments to hell and back." There was urgency in his voice, but his hand moved gently, resting against the softness of her lower stomach. "You do care for me, don't you? I can feel that you do when I touch you like this." Carol tried to restrain the sound that caught in her throat in response to the sensations he was arousing with his touch. "When you want me as much here and here," he said, placing a finger on her forehead before moving to a tender spot above her heart, "then there will be no more denials. Not from your mouth—" he kissed her gently on the lips, followed by a feathering brush of his mouth against her temple "—nor from your head and definitely not from here." He placed the last kiss against the spot he had so tenderly tormented. Then he stood up and went to the window to draw open the draperies and stare out at the torrents of water falling relentlessly from the sky.

After what seemed to Carol like an eternity, Ethan spoke. "I've got to go." He nudged his briefcase with his foot. "There's a lot of work in here that needs my attention." Again he rubbed his forehead, and with that gesture another streak of lightning split the dark sky.

"You can't go out in this storm," Carol protested. "Your headache is back, and you don't know how bad it is outside. By the time you get to the car, you'll be soaked, which will only make matters worse. All I can offer you is an umbrella, and that's useless in a downpour like this."

"And what do you suggest? Neither of us can take any more of what happened on the sofa without waking up to regret it tomorrow, and you know it, as well as I," he stated baldly. Carol knew he was right, but she couldn't prevent the blush that was staining her cheeks.

"Besides," he added, "you need your rest. Because of this—" he gestured toward the rain "—every site will have to be double-checked, and extra pumps brought from the warehouse to help drain open foundation excavations. And I have bank appointments tomorrow."

"Just stay here until there's a break in the rain," she insisted as she got up from the sofa with determination.

"That could be hours, judging by the way the weather has been so far, and I have to prepare for those appointments, I'll go now." He picked up the briefcase and his jacket.

"No," Carol said firmly as she pulled the briefcase from his hand. "I'll make Yankee coffee—no chicory—and you can work at the kitchen table." His briefcase in hand, Carol headed for the kitchen.

"And what will you do?" he questioned, looking at the determined set of her as she measured the coffee.

"You said I needed my rest. I'm going to bed, and you can let yourself out as soon as you're sure you can make it to the car without getting completely drenched." She plugged in the coffeepot and with not even a glance at Ethan went to the bedroom and left him leaning against the doorjamb, his hands thrust deep into his back pockets while the rain and lightning lashed angrily around the city.

CAROL DIDN'T KNOW how long she had been sleeping when she felt a light hand on her shoulder gently awakening her. She propped herself up onto her elbows, still sluggish from her deep slumber.

"The storm is moving toward the lake, and the rain has settled to a steady drizzle," Ethan said softly. "If you tell me where I can find that umbrella, I'll be on my way." Carol flung the bed covers back and started to get up.

"No, just tell me where it is, and I'll get it. You stay here." As he reached to place a restraining hand on her shoulder, his hand encountered the warm soft contour of her full breast that was shielded only by a gossamer layer of sheerest white silk. The shock of that unexpected encounter froze them, each unable to pull away from the touch, each unwilling to deepen the intimacy. The unnatural stillness stretched across the minutes, the unbearable strain becoming tauter and tauter until it snapped, and she was in his arms, smothered by his hungry mouth that was communicating his need for her.

When he ceased the plunder of her mouth, it was to rain hot hard kisses over her body through the thin silk of the brief nightshirt she wore, and then even that no longer separated her from him as he forcefully removed it.

"You are the stuff of which men's dreams are made," he whispered against her throat, against her naked nipple, against her navel. "A man dreams of working late, returning home tired, drained, wanting only to go to his bed." He pushed her back against the sheets still warm from her interrupted sleep.

"And then he finds a love goddess waiting in that bed, love warm and love willing, smelling of jasmine and Southern nights." He traced his tongue around the throbbing thimble of her breast, an action that brought her surging against him, but still he tormented her with his words. "And she takes away the tired and heals the hurt, makes him whole again with her woman's way." He was drowning her will with his words, with his touch, and Carol could resist him no longer as he pressed his body full length over her, making her doubly aware that his needs were as great as the ones he was so ably arousing in her.

"God, how I need you," Ethan moaned, and Carol ached at hearing the pain in his voice. "I'm hurting, Carol.... You've torn me into a thousand pieces. Please put me back together," he begged. "You know how." He slipped his hands beneath the hip band of the delicate briefs she wore and slid them down her thighs. He was giving her no time to deny him, and Carol was both terrified and sensuously overwhelmed at the white heat of his hunger. His kisses and his touch were everywhere, and she felt herself slipping away, floating in a liquid flame, being consumed by him. She didn't know how a thought of rejection survived the sizzling around them; she didn't know how she reached down to still the hand that touched, that tested her intimately. And the sound was only a little sound.... She wasn't even sure she had made it, wasn't even sure she meant it. But as always, as if he lived partially inside her head, he heard it, and the seeking hand stilled and his breathing stilled. Again they waited. Then his weight lifted from her as he shifted to kneel over her, straddling her legs.

She could not see his face, for the only light in the room spilled through the doorway behind his back, bathing her but leaving his dark features in shadow. Slowly, inch by measured inch, he brought her toward him. She didn't know how long he held her like that, how long he watched her as she in turn tried to penetrate the shadows of his face, to read his thoughts. For a time that hold tightened, and she was lifted another measure closer. Then in the same precise manner, she was returned to the pillows, and in a liquid movement he raised himself from her. Only the sound of his labored breathing told her that he stood in the darkest corner, away from the bed and as far away from her as he could be and still remain within the confines of the room.

When he finally spoke, he articulated each syllable carefully. "If you say one word, move one fraction of an inch, I will forget the promises, the pledges and convince you that you want me to take you... now...tonight...in ways you never thought possible." A lingering flash of lightning momentarily illumined the angles of his face, and in the briefness of that revelation she saw the pain of his self-denial.

In the same clipped manner, he continued, "And we will not accuse one another about this night, not now, not tomorrow, not ever. You will not use what happened and what *nearly* happened on that bed against me or against us."

She thought he stood for a while watching her, she wasn't sure. Nor could she bear to watch his leaving, but she knew he went out into the quietly falling rain, leaving the residue of his unfulfilled desire, the residue of her unfulfilled desire to smolder deep inside her, where only he could fan it back to all-consuming flame or extinguish it forever.

CHAPTER NINE

THE GATHERING DUSK of the December evening brought with it a deeper chill. At this time of year the sun was no longer strong enough to keep at bay the dampness left by the storm of the previous evening. Carol rubbed an oil-streaked hand across her cheek and listened to the steady hum of the water pump. It had been one hell of a day from dawn onward. She was upset at not having seen Ethan, although she knew he had been keeping a pace as killing as hers. Even so, she needed to see him. Then she had got a call summoning her to a construction site to have a look at a faulty pump.

As Carol sat back on the heels of her muddy boots, she thought that at least she now had this problem settled, though at no small cost. The hourly workers had left at three o'clock, and for the rest of the afternoon she and the field supervisor had tried to fix the damn pump, which had been functioning only intermittently. Finally they got it working, and Carol decided she could now leave it running while she went home to shed her mud-caked clothes. She would check it once more on her way to Nan's house, where, she hoped, Gracie would have a pot of thick seafood gumbo waiting.

It was strictly against company policy for her to be alone at a site, not just because she was a female, but also in case of accident; there would be no one to administer first aid or to summon help. Carol knew she should have left earlier, after she had dispatched the field supervisor to the emergency room to have his hand stitched where he had cut it while working on the pump. Carol had promised to leave as soon as she had gathered her tools, and if she didn't do it soon, she reminded herself, in a few more minutes it would be too dark to see anything.

At the very moment when she snapped the lid closed on the toolbox, the portable engine gave a loud explosive pop. As she instinctively recoiled, she banged her head against a sharp protruding piece of iron, knocking her toolbox and her hard hat into the excavation hole that was filled with more than a foot of mud and water. She peered into the pit, trying to see where her equipment had landed. The hat wasn't important, but if she didn't retrieve the tools, they would be ruined. Carol sighed. She had no choice but to climb down and fetch everything up.

Steeling her courage, she carefully descended the extension ladder into the wet hole. Within the pit the black mud slid and oozed beneath her boots, but she managed to reach her hat and the metal box of tools without mishap. It was when she placed her second muddy boot onto the ladder that she fell flat on her backside in the mire. From her long experience around construction workers, she unleashed a string of epithets that would have done justice to any seasoned sailor. If Miss Nan could have heard the invectives Carol called forth upon the rain, upon excavations, upon one pump in particular and the whole of life in general, she would have disavowed association with her niece forever.

Once more Carol removed the hard hat from the slime, unthinkingly slammed it back in place, only to empty over her own head a deluge of muddy water. Now there wasn't a clean spot on her, and she was too mad to cry. Taking a deep breath of determination, she approached the ladder once more and slowly, carefully, cautiously navigated through the only exit from the hole.

When she finally reached the high ground, she flopped gracelessly onto the relatively dry soil and leaned back against the idle pile driver. Then suddenly a rumbling voice almost sent her back into the watery pit. "What are you doing here, boy?" Carol looked up at the figure of a construction worker whose hostile tone scared her as much as did his overbearing physique.

Carol stood up, every muscle alert now as the adrenaline surged through what had been a very tired body. She eyed the man warily, assessing her chances of escape. Trying to sound fearless, she answered with great bravado, "Working on a pump. And who are you, and what are you doing on this property? Obviously you didn't notice the sign that clearly states No Trespassing."

She was taken aback when a wide grin flashed in the light of the security lamp. "Well, I'll be damned! It's a woman," he repeated over and over disbelievingly. "Well, little woman, I'm a Randle man, and I came to check this piece of equipment. The gate was opened when it should have been closed and locked. I thought someone might have forgotten just who owns this machine." He touched the pile driver with a hand that almost caressed.

"Well, Mr. Randle Man, if you have the keys to that monster, you can take it and drive that pump straight to China." Carol's temper replaced her fear. The mud began to dry and cake in the breeze, and she examined her sleeve for a clean spot to wipe her mouth, but there was none.

"You can't do any more tonight, miss, so you might as well leave it for tomorrow," he advised with the words she had already told herself. Together they walked toward the Guerard truck parked in the shadows, the worker carrying her dripping toolbox.

"What's the trouble, here," a gravelly voice halted them. "My God, Carol Charbonnet! What happened to you?" When Steve Randle saw she was unhurt, merriment invaded his usually grim features.

"You laugh, Mr. Randle, and I'll...I'll...." At the moment she could think of no punishment to fit the insult of his laughing at her.

"She might put you under the pile driver and send you to China with a pump for company," the other man warned. At the same time he, too, struggled to hide his amusement at her appearance.

"I'm not going to laugh," Steve promised as he produced a handkerchief and attempted to clean some of the grime from her face. As he gently blotted and wiped, he questioned his employee.

"I called in before I left my vehicle, Steve. I swear."

"I know you did. That's why I came by. When you didn't report back quickly, we were afraid you might have found something here and needed help. You did everything the way you were supposed to. No problem." Randle gave his employee a look of reassurance and then turned his attention back to Carol.

"I think I've done as much for you as I can, Carol. Why don't you get in your truck and go home to a hot bath. You're wet through and through, and you're so cold that you're—" He was interrupted by a beeping sound.

Carol reached to the waistband of her soaking jeans and turned off the pocket paging device that had miraculously survived the mud bath. "I have to make a call. Do either of you know where the nearest phone is?"

"In my car," offered Steve, and he promptly steered her toward an opulent silver vehicle shining in splendor beneath the street lamp. "You check in at the office, then go home. I'll take care of Miss Charbonnet," he called to the worker as he started to remove the casual lined Windbreaker he wore. When he tried to drape it over Carol's shivering shoulders, she protested. "You're freezing, Carol, so no more arguments." He tried to usher her into his car, joking that if he couldn't afford to have the vehicle cleaned, then he couldn't afford to own it. But Carol obstinately refused and insisted that he call her answering service to check if there were any messages for her.

"Claud is the same, Miss Nan is fine, but get to the house immediately," Steve reported.

Carol chewed at a none-too-clean underlip. "Who called?"

"Gracie. I'll drive you there," he offered.

"No, I'm not getting into your car and making a mess. I can drive home myself." She dug a dirty hand into her jeans and produced the truck keys. "But if you'll lock the gate behind me, that would help."

During the entire drive home Carol's mind played a medley of possible events leading to Gracie's asking her to come to the house, but nothing could have prepared her for what she found.

Carol approached the house from a side street instead of the avenue and as she parked the truck was startled at the sight of the two police cars in the driveway, their blue lights flickering beneath the crossed limbs of the ancient oaks and sending eerie shadows onto the lawn of the old house. For a moment her heart beat faster, and when she ran up the back steps and tried the door, the earsplitting sound of security alarms cut the air. Once inside the entryway, she nearly collided with a policeman who was trying to determine which lever would shut off the alarm system.

At Carol's appearance he made a barely perceptible move toward his weapon. "Carol Charbonnet," she answered, then scurried off to Claud's study, jerked open a drawer in his desk, removed a key, and returned to the policeman who was still studying the control panel. Carol inserted the key into a barely visible plate on the opposite wall, and then both of them relaxed in the ensuing silence.

Now Carol had time to notice the door behind her, which had been broken from the inside, as if an object had fallen against it. Turning away, she began to retrace her steps.

She realized she had passed through the kitchen and the other rooms so quickly that she had not seen the damage nor a snarling violent René pinned against the foyer wall by two burly policemen, while a third held a makeshift ice pack against his own chin.

The smell of alcohol brought Carol's stomach into a surge she fought hard to control. "René?" His answering curse told Carol all she needed to know. "Get him out of here," she ordered. She felt violently ill, and it was all she could do to keep upright.

"You want to press charges, ma'am?" the injured officer asked as he took in her appearance and seemed to doubt that she belonged in such elegant surroundings.

"Just get him the hell out of here, and I don't care what you do with him. You can arrest him, drop him in the river or the lake, or put him on a Lebanese freighter. Just get him out of my sight before you have to charge me with murder."

"What about his friend?" he asked with a nod of a grinning idiot of a man who sat cuffed to the graceful newel post, babbling about what a great party it all was.

"The same goes for him, whoever he is." Carol watched blankly as her cousin and his companion were led through the great double doors of the main entrance.

"We have to make out a report. Will you get the others from that room for me?" requested the officer who had unsuccessfully tried to stop the alarms.

Then utter exhaustion overwhelmed her. Was this what the family had come to? Her aunt and Gracie cowering somewhere while René, in a drunken rage, wrecked the house as an alcohol-soaked friend cheered him on. And what about her? She, a structural engineer, had spent the afternoon wallowing in mud to do her share to hold together...what? A crumbling has-been first family of the South. Carol had been maintaining a grueling pace for a month now and not a thank-you from any of them. Nan blithely assumed that was Carol's role in life, and according to her code, one did not receive a reward, be it so modest as a thank-you, for doing what one was supposed to do. Eva openly declared she wanted Carol anywhere other than in the family, preferably in the netherworld. And René scoffed at her attempts at tending the Guerard flock. Was she some kind of masochist? Whatever she was doing was of no benefit to anyone or anything—least of all to her own self-esteem.

"Ma'am," the man tried again, "the other car has taken the men to headquarters. I need to make my report. Could you please get the others out here?"

Carol focused on the shiny badge pinned to the dark blue jacket he wore. "Where are they?" Carol asked wearily.

He nodded toward the door that led to the downstairs bedroom suite, and she turned to do his bidding. The drying mud from her clothes and boots left a trail of flaked dirt with each of her clumping steps.

Carol rapped impatiently at the solid oak door. "*Tante*, Gracie," she called. "You can come out now. René is gone." She heard a grumbled "thank the Lord" from Gracie and the scraping of heavy furniture across the highly polished floor, then the grating of a key turning in a seldom used lock.

It was Gracie who came out first, her hands flying to her cheeks in dismay at the wreckage around them. "He was crazy drunk, that fool René. He acted like a wild man. Why would he want to do this, Miss Carol, why? He didn't have any call to do that. He was crazy. Just look at this mess. Whatever are we going to do?"

"Will you shut up and stop your infernal babbling! It's enough to drive anyone mad." Eva's high brittle voice overrode the frustrated words of Gracie.

Then Eva turned to Carol, and her delicate nose wrinkled in distaste at Carol's bedraggled appearance. "And you, my dear, are absolutely disgusting." She drew the elegant dressing gown closer around her all-too obviously naked body.

"Where is *tante*?" Carol asked, ignoring the insults, tacit and expressed.

"She's lying down," Eva answered.

"She hurt her arm when René pushed her," Gracie added. "I gave her a pill to calm her down and to soothe the ache."

"René did what?" Carol asked in disbelief.

"Don't panic, Carol. She's not hurt." Eva applied a flame to a stylishly long cigarette and exhaled a blue plume of smoke.

"Why didn't you stop all this?" Carol gestured wildly at the upheaval of furniture around them. "You let him physically abuse an old woman, and what did you do to stop him?" Her anger rose to match the volume of her voice.

"He might have attacked me if I tried to stop him. Just how would I explain a battering to my friends? I have my appearance to keep up for the Mardi Gras balls. I couldn't go out with bruises and cuts and no acceptable explanation."

That was all Carol could take, and she turned from Eva to watch Gracie straightening overturned chairs and moaning over the shattered bric-a-brac that had adorned the gleaming entryway table. Then her eyes moved to the officer who stood like a silent sentinel, storing the scene in glowing detail so that he might entertain his wife and sisters with another tale of the shallow existence of people who lived in elegant houses. She wanted to wipe that satisfied smirk from his face, to scream at him for judging them by what he had seen tonight, and she opened her mouth to alleviate some of her bottled rage when the entrance of another visitor arrested her words.

Ethan stood in the doorway, his jaw clenched in anger at the sight that met him. He was in formal evening wear, the white of his silk shirt enhancing the dark complexion now flushed an even deeper hue. He brought with him a new tension that permeated the room, a tension that in itself wiped the ridicule from the policeman's face, stopped Gracie's ineffectual attempts at restoring order and widened Eva's blue eyes.

It was only Carol who stood unaffected by his presence while his gray eyes glanced about the room and at each person there before finally settling on the policeman. "What happened?"

Briefly and simply the officer gave a colorless account of the events that resulted in the chaos around them. "And if I can get this report filled out, I'll be on my way, sir," he concluded.

Carol watched dispassionately the way Eva moved toward Ethan and pressed her thinly clad body against him while the tears streamed down her face. She proceeded to tell Ethan her version.

"René wanted money, and when he found we didn't have cash in the house, he went berserk. Ethan, you know I don't have cash. It was just yesterday that I came to you, and you know all that you gave me was obligated." She wept huge tears, crying prettily like a Hollywood starlet without any accompanying redness in her eyes and cheeks.

"What are we to do now? Carol has had René arrested, and I know it'll be in all the papers. What if the Mardi Gras committee asks me to resign my position in court? Ethan, darling, you must do something. Make her drop the charges," she pleaded, placing her head on the broad shoulder. As misplaced as it was, Carol knew that Eva's distress was genuine. All that mattered to Eva was her role in New Orleans social circles, and Eva would protect her place at all costs. The truth became a lie and a lie the truth until Eva could no longer tell the difference.

"You go down to the police station and do something. I know you can. You can call Judge duPlantis, and he'll take care of everything." Eva turned the big blue eyes on him. "You'll do that for me, won't you, darling? While I dress for the party, you'll take care of everything. Gracie and *tante* can help the officer with his report, and we won't be more than fashionably late. And I'll take care of an excuse for that." Eva had resolved the whole situation—and as always, to her benefit. She pressed a kiss on Ethan's mouth and gracefully glided up the stairs to prepare for the party.

Carol had no doubts that everything would work out the way Eva planned, and she realized again that she didn't stand a chance with Ethan if Eva wanted him for herself.

"And what happened to you?" Ethan asked. It was the only thing he had said since addressing the policeman who was now trying to fill in his report with Gracie's help.

"What do you care?" Carol was beyond politeness.

"I care." He spoke sincerely, but Carol wasn't swayed.

"Then you better care enough to do Eva's bidding because not even this family can withstand two scandals within one generation." She turned in the direction of the kitchen.

"Where are you going?" Ethan walked up to her, but Carol eluded his outstretched hand.

"To see about repairing the back door and getting the alarm back on. This house is too vulnerable without it."

This time he managed to stop her retreat. "Don't

you think a bath and clean clothes might first be in order?"

"Don't you think a call to the judge and a trip to rescue René are in order before you go traipsing off to hobnob with the rest of the elite?" She wrenched her shoulder from his hand and continued toward the kitchen. "Don't let me dirty your pretty outfit. Eva's counting on you for both René and for her social affair, and probably for something else," she flung at him.

"I don't like your insinuation, Carol." He glared down at her as she stopped to inspect the broken latch on the door.

"And I can't think of one thing that has happened to me since I left Chicago that I like." She ripped off the jacket that Steve had insisted she wear and draped it over a chair. Moving to the laundry-room sink just off the kitchen, she began rolling up the sleeves of her shirt as she prepared to wash the dirt from her hands and face.

Ethan watched her for a minute, then turned to the broken door. "Can you fix this?" he asked, studying the complicated lock that had to be repaired precisely if the electronic security system was to be reactivated.

"I can come nearer to repairing it than anyone else available," she answered caustically.

He reentered the kitchen and seized the back of a chair in a white-knuckled grip. "I suppose that is another dig at me." His calmness was forced, and she didn't push again when she saw the fabric of Steve's Windbreaker crinkle beneath his fingers. Ethan followed the movement of her eyes. The intricately intertwined monogram told him to whom the article of clothing belonged.

"I know he has a sordid background, but even he wouldn't find you attractive tonight." Ethan finally struck a telling blow, and it was low and dirty and brought tears to her eyes, but Carol returned to the task she knew would keep her busy for hours to come.

IT HAD BEEN VERY LATE when Carol left the house, and now back in her apartment, she sat listlessly over her breakfast. The unappetizing bowl of cold cereal became soggier as she buttered a piece of toast she didn't want, either, even though habit dictated that she start the morning with some semblance of nutrition.

How she didn't want to face this day! She didn't want to face her family, and she most definitely didn't want to face Ethan. She propped her chin on her palms and tried to analyze her position. One thing she was certain of: she was shattered over Ethan's relationship with Eva. She also knew she was tired of agonizing over her life, and she was tired of being depressed. And bemoaning her lot over her morning coffee wasn't changing anything.

Bolting up with determination, she poured the remains of the barely touched food down the sink and turned on the food disposal. The noisy sound of the mechanical teeth mirrored her own attitude. "That's what I should do with all of them, grind them up and wash them down the drain," Carol said aloud. "How could two such spoiled, selfish and rotten people have evolved from the care that always was lavished on them? They had everything—background, money, education, social position. How could they behave so badly?"

Carol had always thought them unworthy of their names and known how vindictive and cruel Eva was. But René had her completely baffled. She had oversimplified his problems. Carol knew she must do something, if not for their sakes, then for Nan's protection.

Resolutely she prepared to meet the day. She would first see Nan. Ethan Greenlaw could take care of Guerard Construction without her help for a while. Somebody had to take care of the family.

As she waited at Canal for the streetcar, she bought the morning paper. She flipped idly through the front section, reading headlines at a glance, seldom moving beyond the leads. When she reached the society section, she almost let the streetcar leave without her. There in the upper left-hand corner were pictured several couples standing behind a lavishly decorated table featuring a silver punch bowl. She scanned the caption. "The Krewe of Hebe entertained the ladies of its court with a wassail party. Pictured at the wassail bowl are...."

Carol resented the picture of Ethan and Eva. There was nothing in their faces to indicate they had any thoughts in their heads other than an enjoyable evening, while she had spent a frantic evening trying to restore order to the house and calm Gracie and Nan, who eventually needed medical attention. Eva and Ethan blithely danced the evening away as René slumbered in alcoholic unconsciousness.

Deliberately she folded the paper so that the smiling visages were buried deep within the pages. When the streetcar crossed Poydras, she didn't even venture a glance in the direction of Guerard Construction. She reached the house to find the company truck still sitting on the side street, her muddy handprints on the door and equally dirty body print on the seat, unpleasant reminders of the traumas of the previous evening.

Inside the house Gracie sat before a cup of coffee gone cold. Some attempt had been made at completing the cleanup, which had been abandoned last night when the old woman finally gave in to her emotional upheaval. Carol now placed a reassuring hand on her shoulder. "How's *tante*?"

The soulful eyes gazed at her. "The doctor came early on his way to the hospital. He told her not to get out of bed, and he left more pills. If anything happens, we're to call him."

"And Eva and René?"

"Hmph! Haven't heard a word about that worthless René. I don't know what time Miss Eva came in last night, but I do know that she hasn't stirred this morning. She seldom gets up before noon these days. I don't think she would grace us then, but she knows I can't be climbing those stairs to clean her room, and if she doesn't want to do it herself, she better get out of the way while the daily's here, or it won't get done."

Carol wasn't in the mood for another recitation of Eva's callous ways. "Let's get in there and check the damage, throw out what can't be repaired and call someone in to fix whatever can be salvaged."

There wasn't as much damage as Carol first thought. In rooms seldom used, an overturned chair received disproportionate attention. There was nothing to be done about the smashed porcelain, so Carol swept it into the dustbin. Three chairs would have to be repaired; their delicate spindle backs hung like arms akimbo. Several tables were scratched, and although those could be covered, Carol was tempted to leave them as permanent reminders of René's rampage. She called a glazier to reglass the great china cabinet that ran from floor to ceiling along one wall of the butler's pantry.

After she did as much as she could, Carol looked in on her aunt, who lay on the heavy four-poster bed, staring up at the pale blue silk canopy trimmed in ancient cream-colored lace. Carol wondered what Nan thought as she studied the ornament that gathered the costly fabric, an ornament depicting fat little cupids frolicking in the endless chase of love, bows drawn and arrows ready.

Carol came nearer and braced herself against the foot of the bed. *"Tante?"* Carol's voice pulled Nan from her daydream. "How are you feeling?" Carol thought her question was trite, but she didn't know how else to breach the awkwardness of shared shame.

"The house? How is the house?" The faded blue eyes, filled with concern, searched Carol's.

"Everything is fine. Gracie and I have taken care of it all. As soon as the doctor says you may get up, you'll see for yourself. You won't be able to tell that anything happened." That wasn't exactly the truth, but Carol thought the situation required a little lie.

"René didn't spoil Eva's evening, did he?" Nan's question jolted Carol's perspective, and she knew at that exact moment that her role in the family would never change, that only Claud had ever cared about her, and without him she would always be on the fringe, always be the one who was almost loved, the one who almost won. Nan wanted to care, but it was too late. Her concern would always be for Eva. And Carol had implicitly chosen to accept that position by returning home.

She addressed Nan's question about Eva. "I'm sure Eva's evening was a success. Here, let me get the newspaper for you. I know you'll enjoy the article about the party, and there's a picture for your scrapbook." She hoped that her smile wouldn't betray her true feelings.

Surreptitiously checking the time as Nan studied the article, Carol thought that if she could get away within the next few minutes, she might not have to see Eva, and that would be better for them all. When Gracie came in with a tray of coffee, Carol used the interruption as an excuse to leave.

From the house Carol went directly to the hospital. As she had done at least once a day for weeks, she stood looking down at Claud. Because his health was irreversibly declining, it was no longer necessary to keep him in the intensive-care unit. When Dr. Frahm had moved Claud to the private room, he had been very straightforward with Carol, telling her that he didn't know how long Claud would remain in his present condition. He cited instances of comatose patients who had lived for years but stated that he doubted such would be the case with Claud.

Claud's removal to more ordinary medical surroundings gave Carol more time to spend with him. She moved to the window and opened the slatted blind to allow the sun's rays to slant brightly across the room, bathing every corner in a cheerfulness incongruous with her own spirits. She sat in a chair in the corner of the room, which was painted the usual institutional green. *The color of peace,* she thought, *cool, relaxing, tranquil green.* Then her thoughts became cynical. Maybe she had been wrong to want Claud to recover and rejoin the family. What had they ever given him—the one who had given so much? She remembered how, in spite of the glamour, the money, the image they held up to the world, there had been many moments when Nan would hiss at them, *"On lave son linge sale en famille,"* the code of old Creole families that meant any dirty linen should be washed in private, among one's own family. Carol sneered at the memory. Who would have thought their piles of laundry would one day be so overwhelmingly high?

Had it been the series of crises that had caused Claud to give up? Had she been too involved in the Guerard world on Poydras Street to notice the burden he shouldered from the Guerard world on St. Charles Avenue? And how much of his pain was she responsible for? When did she ever say thank-you? No, she was as guilty as the others, taking for granted the ways paved for her by him, by his name—a name she didn't even bear. She thought back over her life under his tutelage and wondered how many doors he had opened for her without her being aware that there had even been doors there.

She got up from the chair and moved restlessly around the room, pinching faded blossoms from a pot of lavender chrysanthemums, checking the water level in a vase of cut flowers. She rearranged two red velvet bows she had tied to a potted plant she had brought on the first day Claud had occupied the room. Then she went to the bed. Leaning over to brush back a lock of lifeless hair, she placed a single kiss on Claud's forehead.

"I'm sorry, Claud, so very, very sorry," she whispered. She didn't look back as she closed the door behind her.

Carol's third stop was her office. Ethan was waiting for her, seated at her desk, elbows on the arms of the chair, fingertips pressed together to form a steeple upon which his chin rested. He watched her remove the jacket of the casual pantsuit she wore, followed her with his eyes when she opened the closet and hung it there and placed her purse on the shelf above. "I replaced the pump that gave you so much trouble," Ethan injected into the heavy silence.

Carol assumed a professional tone. "Good, I should have done that yesterday. By the time I decided that was the solution, it was too late." Picking up the mail that had been placed on her desk, she flipped through the envelopes.

Ethan made a derisive sound as he shoved the chair back and stood up. Still she didn't look at him. "Don't you want to talk about it?"

"The pump?" she said casually. "I'm sure you took care of everything." Carol perused a letter intently though she saw nothing on the page. His uttered obscenity brought an embarrassed tinge to her inordinately pale cheeks and her undivided attention. "All right, we'll talk if that's what you want. What happened to René?"

"I got him out without the help of your obliging Judge duPlantis, thank you," he scoffed.

"He's not *my* judge," Carol retorted.

"Whosoever." Ethan's patience was wearing thin. "I took him to my apartment and had someone come in to watch him, just in case his becalmed state wore off."

"Thank you. I suppose I acted hastily by having the police take him away."

"You should have had him committed permanently," he muttered as he eased closer to her. "How is Miss Nan?"

"Much easier now that I've assured her the fracas didn't taint the enjoyable evening had by one and all at the wassail party."

He repeated the obscene word, but this time Carol didn't betray her shock. "What's the matter? Did I misinform her? Wasn't a lovely time had by everyone?"

"You don't know the half of it." He turned his face from her, and all she could see was the working of a muscle in his jaw as he ground his teeth.

"No," she answered in a small voice, "and I don't suppose I ever shall."

But Ethan heard the remark and snatched the letter

from her hand, crumpled it into a ball and hurled it into a corner. "What the hell is that supposed to mean?" He towered over her, his breath audible. "What's wrong with you?" he demanded, examining her features minutely. "You've changed. You're different—so different that I'm not sure I like you this way."

"I wouldn't lose any sleep over it if I were you," she replied rudely and quickly. Too quickly, she realized instantly. She had pushed him too far. She took a defensive step backward, away from the vibrations her body was only too capable of reading. But with each step she took back, Ethan took one forward until that towering body was pressing hers against the wall in intimate familiarity.

"I think I distinctly hear the sounds of doors slamming. And I want them opened. You've held me to promises that were damned near impossible to keep, and I'm holding you to yours. Don't you dare shut me out."

He moved against her, reminding her that they both had pledges to keep. "And you have no concept at all of the sleep you have already cost me," he breathed into her mouth just before he closed over her. It was a searing, plundering kiss. When she thought she would die of the hotness of his hungry mouth, he moved to touch with the flickering lick all the magically sensitive places of her face, the outer corner of her eyes, the faint little cleft low in her chin, the bow of her lip. And if the trauma of the previous hours—beginning with the devastating scene in her bed, through the frustration of yesterday's work, René's drunken tantrum, Ethan's evening with Eva, the morning with Nan, with Claud, and the questions... the questions about her own role in Ethan's life, Eva's role in his life—had not pushed her over the edge of rationality, his deliberate, sensuous assault would.

Unbidden, the knowledge that he could leave her one night to spend the next with Eva, only to move against her now, like this, and to have her *want* him to touch her, to make love to her, jarred through her benumbed brain. And that jolt awakened a slumbering sense, a sense that alerted her to a strange intrusion. The intrusion began as a thin sound deep, very deep within her intellect, only a little faint wailing sound, but it was growing and growing and she recognized it. It was an internal keen, resounding so dimly, ever so faintly.

She came swirling out of the mist to fight his hands on her body, his mouth on her mouth, his absorption of her self into his. Her rejection was not a disavowal of their passion but a pleading for her survival. It said there was not enough of her left. Now she had to save something for herself, save herself. And she fought with the only weapon in her arsenal—one small low soul-stirring whimper, "You are killing me. I can take no more—no more."

The hand at her breast stilled, the weight on her body lightened, the mournful sound abated, quieted to a small reverberation inside her. In the silence he waited, did not move from her, and she did not push him away.

He had been correct in his assessment that she had

changed, and now she knew what that change was. The protective shield was gone. She had returned to her family with a fragile store of resources, and they—the Guerards and Ethan—had worn it away, eaten it up. The strength that she had gathered in the desperation of this moment was her last.

"What do you need, Carol, what?" There was only concern in his voice and only caring in his body, which still touched her, thigh against thigh, hip against hip.

"I don't know." She searched for anything to hold onto. "Maybe not to come here anymore...."

"Is that what you really want? Think!" he commanded. "What do you *need*? If you don't come here, what will you do all day? Worship at that shrine you're making of Claud's room? Play nursemaid to Miss Nan? Pick up after Eva? Patch things up after René?"

"No...no," she whispered. "I just need time. You promised—just a little time."

"Time for what?" Ethan's voice hardened.

"I don't know." And she really didn't.

"How much time do you need?"

"I don't know that, either." She searched his face for some hint that maybe he knew but wouldn't tell her. But there was nothing there, nothing but a telltale line between the dark brows. And then a new expression transformed his handsome face; and his manly shoulders drooped.

Ethan slowly stood up. "You will have, as you have always had, as much time as you need, but you will continue to work here. I need your help, and you need to be able to work here." He paused and turned his head toward the window, and she could feel the resolve hardening within him. Then he turned back to her, still holding his body within inches of hers.

"You are to leave the door open between us, Carol. Once before we had this discussion, and again I implore you, do not shut me out. Sometime, and I believe it will be soon, things will come right between us, and openly we will acknowledge that rightness. Leave the lines of communication open. Give me your word." He waited. "Give me your word," he demanded again.

Carol's affirmation was a slight nod, but Ethan acknowledged her mute promise with a lessening of the tension in his body.

"I'm going to kiss you now, Carol. And then I won't kiss you or touch you again until you let me know the time is right." And he did, with a kiss that was so incredibly sweet, tender, and caring that she felt she had been in the presence of a preternatural force that touched on the sublime.

CHAPTER TEN

CAROL STAYED AWAY from the family for several days, needing the time to recharge. On the third day René came to the office. When Mrs. McLin buzzed through, Carol was tempted to deny him entry, but she knew the confrontation had to take place. Now was as good a time as later, she rationalized.

René was even more uncomfortable than Carol as he paced restlessly in the small room, touching the objects, examining the prints on the walls. She observed him closely.

"You aren't making this easy for me, are you?" he accused bitterly.

She watched him fumble about the room a moment more, then answered with a question. "Do you think you deserve to have anything made easy?" she thrust. "My God, René, what did that old woman ever do to you that you had to use physical force against her?" The hideousness of the memory hung between them. René slumped into a chair and covered his face with his artist's hands, as if to hide from Carol.

"Why, René?" she continued relentlessly. "Tell me one reason why."

He squirmed under her prosecution. Then, with his

hands still covering his face, he answered, "It was the drink. I was drunk."

"Drunk? Drunk?" Carol was on her feet, standing over him, every line of her slim body screaming her disapproval. She stared down at him until the rage burned away her blinders, and she saw the pitiful mass huddled in the chair for what it really was, and she went on her knees before him, pulling away the shielding hands so she could look at him.

Softly Carol said, "Don't you think it's time you had help with this problem?"

The red-rimmed blue eyes filled with wariness. "What problem?" A wiry tenseness invaded his body as he moved deeper into the chair, withdrawing from her.

"René, haven't you admitted to yourself that your drinking is out of control?" Carol asked, even though she knew the answer.

"I'm not an alcoholic, if that's what you're implying." And she knew he believed his lie. "Do you really see me as one of those living horrors lying about in Lafayette Square? I live in a nice place, have friends, go out to dinner wearing nice clothes. I have a job," he recited in an attempt to counter her accusation.

"René," she reasoned, "you don't have to be a derelict to have a problem. Think about your average day. How soon do you start the cocktail hour? How many drinks do you have before dinner, with dinner, after dinner? How many days do you miss the morning's work? Think, René. Think about the destruction you brought to the house. Think about striking *tante*. Doesn't that sound like you have a problem?"

"You don't know what you're saying. I can handle it," he laughed hollowly. "You know our life-style—'a meal without wine is a day without sunshine.'" René desperately searched for justification of his behavior. "'Let the good times roll'—'pass a good time.' *Les Créoles ne meurent pas; ils se dessèchent.*"

"I don't think the expression 'Creoles don't die; they dry up' has ever been associated with drinking." Carol knew it was hopeless to reason with him, but she felt she had to try. "René, you don't have to join an association for people with drinking problems if you don't want to. See a doctor, a therapist, a counselor, but do something." The more she talked, the harder his resolution to deny the problem became, and Carol finally admitted that she was wasting her time. Rising to her feet, she returned to the other side of her desk. "Why did you come here?"

"I suppose to apologize."

"I don't need an apology, but maybe Tante Nan and Gracie do. Have you seen them?"

"Last night." René refused to look at her and stared at the opposite side of the room.

"And..." she prompted.

"And nothing. Life goes on." René stood up. "I'll see you around, Carol." He left quickly, not giving her a chance to delay his departure.

Carol tried to concentrate on her work but made more errors than progress. Slamming down the papers in disgust, she jerked up and reached for her jacket and bag.

In the hallway she would have unknowingly passed

right by Ethan had he not caught her arm. Blocking her departure, he studied her strained features. "Where are you going?"

Carol raised her chin defiantly. "I'm going to check on Claud."

He clasped her arm tightly. "You don't need to go there now. You must stop running to him every time something disturbs you. You must find some release other than these morbid conversations with a dying body."

His callous words cut her. "Ethan...I need him. And he hears me, I know it. He always listened."

"Oh, my God, Carol, what are you doing?" In his alarm he moved toward her, but she jerked away from him.

"I'm going to see Claud."

But she didn't. Instead she walked past the Whitney National Bank to the Plaza de Italia. There she sat in the sunshine and pondered Ethan's words. He was right; she was treating Claud as if he were a priest, recounting her sins and problems to him. She knew it had to stop, or she would be no good for anyone, especially herself.

A shadow fell across her. "I'm sorry, Carol. I shouldn't have come down so strong." It was Ethan, lines of strain etched around his mouth.

"No," Carol said firmly, rejecting his apology. "You're right. I must get a hold on myself, and I will do it." She could manage only a weak smile, but it was enough to make the lines of tension in his face ease.

"Lunch?" he offered, holding out his hand.

"Yes," Carol replied, accepting the offer but not his hand.

LATE ONE AFTERNOON shortly before Christmas, Ethan stopped by Carol's desk with contracts for her to read. As she bowed her head over the papers, trying to concentrate on the details, Ethan stood, hands in his back pockets, never taking his eyes from her. When she had studied the documents and expressed satisfaction with their terms, she returned the papers to him. Still he stood there.

"Miss Nan has invited me to Christmas dinner," he announced, at the same time measuring her reaction. Carol tried to show nothing. "I told her I would let her know later." Still Carol didn't comment. "I also told her not to expect you for dinner this evening, that you and I were eating out." From this remark he did get a reaction.

"You know I can't." She folded the papers she had been working on, creasing them carefully with her nails.

"There's no reason why you can't. It's no different from having lunch," Ethan insisted.

There was a difference, and there were a million reasons, each of them belonging to her sense of touch, the senses he aroused when he came near even in the starkness of these surroundings, Carol thought as she felt her heart pounding in anticipation of even an accidental touch.

"I just can't." She licked her lips. "Nan counts on my being there each evening. I have to see Claud first, and I'm tired." She rushed through the litany of reasons but not once did she state the truth.

His eyes bored into her as he calmly disqualified each excuse. "Miss Nan is happy that you'll be having a night out. She feels that you tie yourself to her and Claud too much. As for seeing Claud," he glanced at his watch, "we have time to do that yet. If you're so tired, then a change of pace and setting will do you good."

Frantically she sought a plausible reason for rejecting his invitation as again he stepped nearer. Catching her chin in his hand, he lifted her face to him. "The only excuse I'll accept is that you're afraid of me. Have I completely destroyed your faith in me? Did I do that?" His hold tightened as he searched her face. "The truth, Carol. Are you afraid to go out with me?"

Truthfully she answered him. "I'm not afraid to go out with you. Nevertheless, I'm not going." She had no fear of him.... As always, it was herself that she feared.

He expelled his breath slowly. "If I promise again not to kiss you, not to touch you, will you come then? There are things we need to talk about, and there's no reason why we can't talk over dinner."

She wrenched her chin from his grasp. "You're touching me now!"

"Stop it, Carol. You've been pushing yourself so hard you don't even know what you're saying, and I'm not taking no for an answer. Let's go."

For some inane reason she even tried the old feminine excuse of not being properly dressed, but Ethan wouldn't be swayed. "I'm not letting you out of my sight long enough for you to change, or you might change your mind, as well as your dress."

Carol found that amusing. He wouldn't allow her to have a mind, so how could she possibly change it? Besides, there was nothing wrong with the softly gathered rose-colored skirt and the silky shirt of the softest of pinks, set off by fragile gold chains looped delicately about her throat.

Ethan took the papers and signed them while she straightened her desk. As she slid a coat of gloss on her lips, she glimpsed a hungry look on his face that he masked so quickly she thought perhaps she imagined it. But that glimpse gave her an unfamiliar feeling of power. He still wanted her with pure desperation, but tonight he would keep his word—for tonight.

AS THEY DROVE from the hospital, she wondered why she kept up the pretense that anyone benefited from the visits. She could admit that not only had there never been progress in Claud's condition since her return, but also that she could actually see his decline. She wasn't helping him, and if tonight were any barometer, she was hurting herself by these daily visits.

Each time she left the hospital, a depression enveloped her that was becoming increasingly more difficult to shed. Tonight it was worse than ever. As she tried to shake the blackness of her anguish, she took no notice of the direction in which the powerful car hurled itself through the darkening afternoon. Then it registered with her that they were crossing the causeway spanning Lake Pontchartrain. She roused herself from her lethargy to ask what their destination was.

"There's a nice quiet restaurant across the lake that hasn't been 'discovered' yet. We need someplace relatively private so we can get a few things straight. This restaurant will do nicely."

Carol watched the darkness of the water broken by lighter shadings of the whitecaps. "I wasn't aware that we had anything to talk about. We're doing better than we expected with the firm."

At the exit Ethan slowed the car, then sped up until they reached the quiet town of Covington. The restaurant was located in an old restored Victorian home. The interior was a mixture of bentwood and wicker, hanging baskets of lush ferns and potted rubber plants. More than that, it had a hushed tranquil atmosphere, which was just what Carol needed.

They were seated in a small garden room dimly lighted by candles. The darkness of the interior provided them with a view of the illuminated garden, a profusion of greenery gleaming darkly beneath the slowly rising moon.

They were attended immediately by an unobtrusive waiter, who took their cocktail orders and left them to study the menu. It boasted typical southern Louisiana fare—crabs, shrimp, catfish, crawfish, trout—prepared in a variety of ways. Ethan protested her selection of salad, followed by shrimp Creole, but Carol was satisfied with ordering a light dinner. She had little appetite, though she knew she was losing weight she could ill afford to lose.

While they waited for their food, Carol thought Ethan might begin the discussion he seemed to think was so important, but before she could make that suggestion, he spoke.

"There's no dancing here, but we can take a walk in the garden while we wait. It was a long ride over, and I could use the exercise." His eyes wandered the expanse of plate glass. "The garden wall provides wind protection, so it shouldn't be cold."

He got up immediately, and like an automaton Carol followed. They passed through the French doors and followed the walkway leading past massive oak trees. Although it wasn't a large yard, it was adequate for a short stroll. His silence pressed on her, and she felt compelled to break it. "Have you been here often?" she asked, her voice reverberating in the oppressive silence.

"Not as often as I would like. It's too out of the way, but that's good, too. Sometimes after I've been to a site and have had to yell over steam hammers and rivet guns, I need the stillness of this place."

"Is that why you didn't stay inside and talk shop at the table?"

"One reason. There are others." He stopped to glance over the landscaped grounds. "It's strange to be walking here with the ferns still green even though it's late December." Ethan obviously was eager to change the subject.

"It's not always this mild in December," Carol commented. "There can be a blast of Rocky Mountain weather that's incredible. Still, it's not like the winters I experienced in Chicago." She shivered at the recollection of the wind-whipped sleet blowing off Lake Michigan for days without relenting.

The moonlight flowed over Carol, bathing her face in a soft mysterious light. For a moment he stood watching her, then his hand came up to stroke her cheek tenderly. "You're home now, where it's warm." His voice was husky, and she thought he would kiss her. Instead he tucked her hand beneath his arm and led her toward the garden room. He remembered his promise.

They were finishing dessert when Ethan brought up the topic at which he had hinted. "I want two things of you. The first is that you move back to your home. You're exhausting yourself with trying to keep up the trips to the hospital, your work at the firm, take care of Miss Nan and that house, plus your apartment—" He wasn't even finished making his request before Carol began to refuse.

"No, I can't do that," she said adamantly.

"Give me one good reason why not," Ethan countered. "You're there almost every evening, being the legs and nimble fingers for Miss Nan."

Carol tried to make Ethan understand. "I can't just let *tante* waste away or slip into some fantasy world of yesteryear. As it is, she spends too much time poring over scrapbooks and memorabilia—hers, Eva's and even my mother's."

"That's not my point, Carol. I understand how it is. And I also know you've been arranging all those luncheons and tea parties for her. Still, wouldn't it be easier if you were there all the time?"

She could give him dozens of reasons why she

couldn't stay at the house, most of them having to do with possibly interrupting a lingering good-night between him and Eva. "I just can't," Carol repeated.

She knew, too, that if she didn't have Patti's apartment to retreat to, she couldn't bear the confrontations that occurred every time she and Eva met—the cutting remarks and innuendos. If Eva should discover how she felt about Ethan, her life would become unbearable.

"Will you consider staying there during the week? You could return to the Quarter for the weekends. Will you at least make that concession?" Carol knew Ethan wouldn't understand her refusal, but she could only shake her head.

"Someday, Miss Charbonnet, you'll explain to me what's going on in that muddled brain of yours." He turned to look at the garden as he mulled over a thought. Turning back to her, he opened his mouth as if to speak again but changed his mind and signaled their waiter. Ethan ordered brandy and a packet of thin cigars for himself.

"You don't smoke," Carol protested.

"In times of stress I do many things you don't know about." The waiter returned, and without asking her permission, Ethan slipped a thin wooden-tipped cigar between his teeth and applied a match to it. Carol watched in openmouthed amazement.

"I do this quite well, don't you think?" He took a long draw of the cigar. "Oh, Carol, stop looking at me as if I just set fire to my nose." His remark so completely changed the mood of their discussion that

Carol laughed even as she wondered if it were by design.

"What's so funny?" Ethan asked.

"You. Smoking cigars is supposed to enhance the macho image, but for you it doesn't do a thing." Her eyes sparkled with humor.

"Just wait until you become used to it. You'll see what an attractive addition it is to my masculine image, and you'll find me so irresistible I'll have to lock my office door to get my work done."

"Is that before or after we call in a fumigation service?"

"Droll, Miss Charbonnet, very droll. Keep it up, and I won't show you my favorite trick." With that he folded his arms across his chest, leaned back in his chair and released a series of smoke rings that drifted across the table and hovered near the candle before dissipating.

Carol cheered him on with applause. "I'm impressed."

"Not as impressed as my parents were with what it cost to live in a fraternity house at the university, and that's all I had to show for it." He tipped the long ash into the ashtray. "But you haven't seen the coup de grace." Sitting back once more, he began to puff in quick little strokes until he filled the air with a gray pall.

"That's a great accomplishment if you don't turn green," Carol teased.

Above their laughter-filled banter, a loud "ahem" and coughing coming from a table a few feet away brought them both quickly to their feet, and they made for the cashier without waiting for the check to be delivered to their table.

They could feel the irritated stares of several patrons following them even after they reached the parking lot.

"You were ridiculous, Ethan. Those people won't even let you within shouting distance of that lovely restaurant again." Even as she scolded him, she couldn't help grinning at his refreshingly amusing antics.

He unlocked the car door for her and, as he helped her in, replied, "But you still love me, ridiculous as I am."

She couldn't see his face, but the slamming of the door echoed the jarring of her heart. It was true. It never had been just a physical attraction that she felt for him. It had always been, still was and always would be love.... And he knew it. Now what was she going to do?

He backed the powerful car onto the highway before speaking. "I never did tell you the second thing I wanted from you. Will you let me come up to your apartment where we can talk about it?"

"No," Carol answered unhesitatingly. "We can talk while you drive or wait until tomorrow."

"No seems to be the only answer you have tonight. How about a drink in the city?" he asked, trying another tactic.

"It's late already."

But Ethan wasn't about to give up. "Okay, we'll talk now. But don't say no to my next suggestion until you've given it some thought, will you?"

"That depends on what you're going to suggest."

He chuckled at her evasive response. "Couldn't even get a yes out of you by chicanery." He drove on for a while before continuing. "I want to start some concentrated public-relations work. The Taalot contract is being let right after the New Year, and I want everyone to know that we'll be contending for it. I want the whole city to know that we're ready to compete with them all."

Carol ventured a glance at him, wondering what he was aiming at. He didn't need her permission to do what he thought was necessary. She responded carefully. "There are several good public-relations firms around. You shouldn't have too much difficulty in finding one that would suit our needs and be able to put together an effective campaign."

"I don't need an outsider to identify *our* needs—either for Guerard Construction or for the two of us." His sarcasm sliced into her. To where had the gay companionship of so brief a time ago vanished?

"Ethan..." Carol began, pronouncing his name tiredly.

"I'm sorry, that wasn't called for, and I shouldn't have said it. But I meant it when I said we don't need a consulting firm. For the most part all we have to do is get to the right ears and let them know that we're back in big business and intend to stay there."

"And how do you intend to accomplish this—by more smoke signals?" Ethan's responding smile told Carol she had struck the right note to restore his mood.

He reached over, took her hand and placed it on

his thigh. "Not this time. But I must say that feat held your attention for a while." He ran his thumb across her knuckles, and this time Carol didn't pull away.

"What I had in mind," Ethan continued, "was a great big noisy cocktail party with a nice band playing in the background and the most beautiful structural engineer in the South standing in the doorway personally greeting Guerards' clients—past, present and future."

Panic ran through her like an ice spike. She couldn't face those accusing faces again, and that's where most of them had been—among their clients. She tried to pull her hand away from his clasp, but Ethan tightened his hold.

"Hold on, Carol."

She turned to look at the firmness of his jaw, illumined by the muted glow of the dashboard lights. Those were so nearly the instructions he had given her once before. She wondered if he remembered, too, for she saw the grinding of his facial muscles as he added, "Don't say no... not just yet."

"But why do *I* need to be there?" Carol asked. "You're the official head of the company now. You don't need me."

"What's a party without a pretty hostess?" He still held her hand firmly against his leg.

"Then ask Eva. She even has the right name." There was desperation in her voice. "Ethan, I can't do this. Get Eva. It's just the kind of thing she does best, but please don't ask me."

They were now entering the narrow streets of the

Quarter. He released her hand to maneuver the car through the heavier traffic. Rudely pulling into a parking place that belonged to an awaiting car, he ignored the obscene gesture of the thwarted driver and hurried around the car to assist Carol.

As they entered the building's courtyard, Ethan promised, "I'll not violate your sanctuary tonight. We can finish our talk on the patio." He urged her onto the stone bench by the fountain. At first he just stood looking down at her, then he sat close to her but without touching. "Eva has a role in my plans, but not the one I'm assigning you. She can't take your place, nor you hers. You must be there."

Unaware of the crippling effect his words were having, he continued, "Eva can flit about the room looking beautiful and making small talk with wives and sweethearts, but it's you who will have to answer the more substantial questions."

"Like how much is the going rate for selling confidential information?" Carol asked bitterly.

He angrily took her shoulders and shook her until the tumbled gold of her hair became entangled in his hands. "Do you think that for one minute I ever believed that garbage about you and the coat?" His words bit like his hands.

She lashed out at him, "Why not? I've got the 'evidence' upstairs to prove it."

She had to look away from the heat of his own glare. "Damn you. I don't know where you got that coat, but I know damn well where you didn't get it." Finally his grip eased as he breathed deeply, and when he spoke, his tone was almost normal.

"Eva said that whatever Claud wanted of you, you always tried to do. Is that true?" He watched her closely for the effect of his words.

"In a way..." Carol answered. Memories of Claud's words of praise when she had done something that he had just hinted he wanted done came forward, only to be pushed aside by the last memory of him before his illness. "I just couldn't tell him where I got that coat."

"Forget the coat. If I told you that this cocktail party was something Claud and I had planned together, would you believe me?"

"I don't know." Carol spoke truthfully. Every time she came into the presence of this man, so many conflicting sensations raged through her she didn't know what to think or feel. It would be such a glorious relief if just for one day she didn't have to feel anything. The highs and lows of the past six weeks were driving her crazy. She must have betrayed her feelings in some manner because Ethan's hold changed to a comforting stroke as he brushed the hair away, then cupped her face gently in his palms.

"I wanted you to move home because of the strain you've been under, but I'm afraid that tonight I've done more damage than good." He rubbed his thumb across her lips, parting them. He took a long deep breath, then released it slowly. "I'll keep my promise, but I'm checking upstairs before I leave. Still trust me?" The question was accompanied by a crooked grin that deepened the grooves beside his mouth.

At her nod he helped her from the bench, draped

his arm about her shoulders and walked her up the stairs. Later he bade her good-night by placing a single moist kiss in her palm.

SEVERAL TIMES the next day Ethan conferred with Carol about various projects. Each time he treated her gently but not too familiarly. Only once did he ask if she were giving thought to his plan. At her affirmative nod he dropped the topic and moved on to other business.

At noon he surprised her as she was digging her lunch from the back of the refrigerator in the lounge. "Mine's the one in the brown bag with a Santa sticker on it. Second shelf. Would you get it for me while I make fresh coffee?"

She turned in surprise, but he was already busy at the coffee table. The idea of his bringing lunch in a brown paper bag—with a Santa decal no less—certainly didn't fit her image of him, but then neither did blowing smoke rings.

She found the lunch, set it next to her own on the Formica-topped table and sat to observe him. He filled the basket of the coffee maker, rinsed the glass pot, filled it with water and emptied it into the reservoir. He replaced the pot on the warming plate before the first drop came through.

He knew she was watching him. "And I can catch toast as it pops up from my arthritic toaster with nary a slip between the crumbs and my butter knife. This gentleman is not clumsy." He was in a teasing mood, and she liked it.

He sat down across from her and opened the plastic wrap of two suspiciously familiar-looking sandwiches. "Is that peanut butter and jelly?" Carol asked. She had never known him to have lunch at the office, and now to see him eat peanut butter.... He raised a dark brow. "And what, may I ask, is wrong with peanut butter and jelly?"

"Oh, nothing," Carol answered. She watched him bite into the crusty bread with his even white teeth and then ventured one more question. "Crunchy or smooth peanut butter?" Being far too busy watching him, she had yet to think to open her bag containing a plastic box of fruit salad.

"Crunchy," he responded as he raised the sandwich to his mouth for another bite, then stopped in midair. "With apple jelly. I made them myself." He again attempted to bite but stopped to ask, "Aren't you eating?"

"Sure," she answered in a befuddled tone and lifted the lid from her salad while he watched attentively.

"Nice salad. There are white grapes and everything in there." Ethan eyed the concoction carefully.

"Bananas, oranges, apples...." Carol turned the food with her fork as she identified the ingredients. Then they spoke in near unison.

"Do you want to share?" His white teeth flashed again, and Carol felt her heart turn over. She didn't know a peanut-butter-and-jelly sandwich for lunch could be romantic, but it was.

LATER THAT DAY Carol found herself in a completely different atmosphere. The Guerard household was in an uproar, and it didn't take her long to discover the reason. Although it should have been a secret, Eva had learned the identity of her escort for the grand march of the Mardi Gras Vili Ball. He was a man who had once left Eva stranded on the dance floor after she had made a critical remark. Now Eva was to take her regal bows on the arm of "that awful man."

To Carol, the New Orleans social code was an anachronism, but Eva and Nan lived by it. When Carol failed to show proper sympathy for Eva's situation, Eva attacked.

At first Carol meekly accepted the brunt of Eva's temper tantrum by reminding herself that every blow she took was one that wouldn't land on Nan, but Eva's vitriolic tongue more than once hit a sensitive area.

When Eva accused Carol of having undermined Claud's interest in the firm by what she called Carol's selfish flight for her own self-interest, Carol decided she had had enough.

"I don't have to stay and listen to this, Eva. I came to see if Tante Nan needs anything. Since you'll be home this evening, you take care of her. I'm leaving."

"That's right. You always run when anything unpleasant comes along. It must be nice to have money enough to go where you want, when you want." Eva's voice was ugly.

"Eva, I've never noticed you being that short of ready cash." Carol didn't know why she was arguing with Eva. At a time like this it was better to leave well enough alone. She turned to pick up her bag and the suede coat she had left on the hall chair. But Eva wasn't finished.

"Well, I'm practically destitute now. And it's all your fault. You probably took company funds when you left two years ago. That's why Claud couldn't keep the company together. René and I were lucky to get out when we did with as much as we did—with no thanks to you."

Eva had Carol's attention now. "Just what are you getting at?" Her eyes narrowed as she glared at her cousin.

Eva was a master of attack and retreat, but at least she had stopped screaming. "As if you didn't know. Go on, get out of here. And don't you worry about Tante Nan. She didn't need you before, and she doesn't need you now."

With that Eva stalked out, leaving Carol to wonder what she meant. Carol suddenly had a feeling of foreboding, which she tried to brush away by reminding herself that the barb was something that came from Eva's great store of hate for her. With a shrug, she decided to forget about it. That was always the best way of dealing with Eva.

Before leaving, Carol made arrangements to give Gracie Christmas Eve and Christmas day off. Gracie assured Carol that although she would enjoy having Christmas day with her family, she wanted to be with Miss Nan on Christmas Eve. She also asked if she could use the kitchen to make cookies and candy for the small children in her family.

A fond memory erased some of the lingering storm clouds left in the wake of Eva's tirade. Carol remembered having once visited with Gracie among all the people she called family. They filled an entire block of Freret Street.

"If you promise to leave a few samples of your cooking here, I'll help. Ethan says there'll be no work on the twenty-fourth. He and Mrs. McLin posted notices everywhere. I even saw one in the ladies' room. Do you think he really believed some overindustrious soul would work right through a holiday?" Gracie chuckled and happily accepted Carol's offer.

CHAPTER ELEVEN

IT WAS THE DAY BEFORE CHRISTMAS EVE, and just at closing time Ethan wandered into Carol's office. He watched her straighten her desk. "Do you remember the promises you keep eliciting from me?"

She knew what promise he meant and said so as she slipped the cover over her calculator and slid it to the corner of her desk.

"Didn't I keep my promise?" Obviously, Carol thought, he wasn't counting the more innocent, yet extremely sensuous, moments when he had brushed gentle hands over her. "Well, didn't I?"

She raised her eyes to his. "Yes, Ethan, you kept your word."

"If I renew my promise, will you go out with me Christmas Eve? I thought we might ride upriver and watch the lighting of the way for Papa Noël. Would you like to do that?"

He was asking her out and without the pretext of business, and she wanted to go. She didn't want to be alone on Christmas Eve. It was an important night for her, a very sentimental night, and she wanted more than anything to share it with him. He had kept his promise before; why shouldn't she have the faith that he would keep it again?

She allowed herself only a brief moment of doubt over why he was asking her and not Eva. She still didn't have a clear idea of where his relationship with Eva stood. As far as Carol knew, they could have been together nearly every night since René's destructive spree. On the other hand, maybe they hadn't been together at all. It was all the thought she allowed. He was asking her, not Eva, so he must want to be with her.

"I'd like that very much, Ethan." Carol was not only excited at the thought of spending such an important evening with him, but also at the plans he was suggesting. The last time she had been to the lighting of the way for Papa Noël, she was young enough to still believe in the magical powers of Santa. Claud had taken Carol, René and Eva to see the beacons that guided Santa through the soupy fog that frequently enveloped the river front.

"Good, I'll see you tomorrow afternoon." Ethan acknowledged her acceptance, then stretched taller. "Got a working dinner appointment with Randle tonight... wish I didn't." He left as abruptly as he had appeared.

She was the last out of the office, and even the prospect of seeing Claud and possibly having another confrontation with Eva couldn't dim the glow that Ethan's invitation had lighted. After her stop at the hospital Carol went to the house and was pleased to find that Eva was out.

Tonight she had shopping that she must do, and for that she took Claud's big sedan. She parked in the lighted lot of an uptown shopping mall. There she made her way through her short list: a thin gold bracelet for Eva; an Italian sweater for René; for Nan, black pearl earrings; and for Gracie, a new raincoat and a matching umbrella of brightest scarlet. She would give Judson a check as had been Claud's habit. That left one person—Ethan.

She debated whether to buy him a present. She had spent generously on two people who admittedly cared nothing for her, and for whom she honestly felt little of the Christmas ideal of charity. Why shouldn't she buy something for the one person for whom she truly wanted to express her feelings but couldn't? But how would she present him with such a gift? She let the idea fade.

Carol was on her way out of the jewelry shop when a flash of gold caught her eye. It was a key chain from which dangled a golden candy kiss. She stood transfixed in indecision. It was stunningly expensive and stunningly appropriate. Ethan had never denied wanting her kisses; so Carol resolved to give him a kiss.

She wrote the check before she could change her mind and placed the gaily wrapped package in her purse. It would definitely not go under the tree with the other presents. She purchased the few items Nan had requested and turned the long car toward the imposing house.

CAROL AND GRACIE spent all of Christmas Eve in the kitchen, filling the house with the smells of chocolate, vanilla, lemon and other delicious aromas. They made vanilla and maple pralines, fudge, popcorn balls, cookies and more candy. By late afternoon Carol knew she would not have time to return to the Quarter apartment, bathe and dress, so she asked Gracie to call Ethan and ask him to meet her at the house.

She spent only a few of her precious minutes in a refreshing bath, for she would have to find something from her old wardrobe for the evening. When she rummaged through her closets, she found that everything was just enough out of date to displease her. Then she remembered a suitcase that still wasn't unpacked. Wrapping the bath towel more securely, she bounded down the stairs two at a time. If Ethan had stored her clothes carefully when he sent them from Chicago, the garment she wanted wouldn't be too mussed to wear.

Frantically she dug through the trunk and had just located the object of her search when the door chimes pealed, and Ethan entered without waiting for her to let him in. He was early, and Carol only half heard his explanation that he had come to sample some of the sweets she and Gracie prepared.

His eyes moved appreciatively from the golden cascade that spilled from the topknot she had hastily fashioned to keep her hair out of the bath, down to the bare shoulders, and down again to where a rounded hip peeked out of the too-short towel. When she saw where his vision paused, she clutched to her bosom the sweater she was holding so that it covered the revealing slit.

"Get up those stairs and get your clothes on while the opportunity still exists," Ethan commanded. He didn't move from the doorway until Carol's shapely legs were out of view, and her bedroom door closed.

She tried to gather her wits as she hung the outfit in the bathroom and turned the hot water on in the shower. Soon the room would fill with enough steam so that the few creases would fall from the rust-colored slacks and sweater. They would be ready to put on by the time she finished her hair and makeup.

Makeup, where was her makeup? With shaking fingers she fumbled through the vanity drawers before remembering that she had emptied those drawers two years ago. She willed herself into greater tranquillity. She had to think more clearly. She would have to make do with whatever was in her purse. Quickly she applied the available cosmetics and brushed her hair until it shone like taffy, leaving it long and loose about her shoulders, the way Ethan liked it.

She stepped into the slacks and matching sweater of soft cashmere, leaving the sweater open to expose just a shadow of her breasts. Then she buttoned one tiny button higher. After studying her reflection, she unfastened the button again. She slipped on leather demiboots, collected her leather coat and hurried downstairs.

He stood in the doorway to the formal living room, his eyes fastened on the tree. She paused midway down the stairs as she wondered what his thoughts were, if every time he glanced into the tree-lit room, he, too, felt the strange tightening of muscles in his lower stomach as she did, if his heart beat just a tiny bit faster.

Ethan turned to watch her descent, standing motionless as he clutched the small bag that contained a selection of sweets from Gracie.

Even in the car he sat coldly remote. Carol tried to think of something to say that would break the uncomfortable silence, but there was nothing.

Ethan drove aggressively, taking full advantage of the car's racing features as he maneuvered in and out of frighteningly narrow breaks in the heavy flow of holiday traffic. She tried closing her eyes but decided it was better she monitor his driving.

Noticing Carol's expression of fear, Ethan slowed down, only to speed ahead into another lane. Carol felt as if her heart leaped from her throat into her mouth.

"Are we late?" she asked quietly. Somehow she managed to keep the alarm out of her voice.

"I don't think so. Why do you ask?" The needle on the speedometer didn't drop.

"Because you're going so fast. Is it really necessary?" She clutched at his arm as he crossed into another lane.

"Am I frightening you?" He glanced at her, and she cringed at his taking his eyes from the busy highway.

"Yes." Her answer was as faint as she was feeling, and she mentally gave thanks when he slowed the car, took another long glance at her and turned his attention back to the traffic.

After a little while he spoke. "Don't you ever let me catch you dressed like that unless you mean it," he said in a gloating tone.

"Ethan, I didn't expect you to walk in when you did." She felt he was being unfair to her, and it hurt.

"If I thought you had...." The car lunged forward momentarily, then he eased the pressure on the accelerator once more. "Don't you have any idea what the sight of you like that did to me—what it's still doing?"

She didn't think he expected her to answer, and she released his arm to hold her hands in her lap. The wall he built around himself was unbreachable.

Wordlessly they moved through the night until they reached an upriver town, and Ethan turned onto a narrow winding road that led along the river. Finally he found a suitable spot from which to view the festivities and pulled to the side of the road to park.

The traffic was heavy as cars moved slowly, many of them filled with small children who pressed excited faces against the windows. They were eager to watch the giant flares being lighted so that Santa would be able to find his way to their homes.

The scene by the river was like a huge community picnic. Chests of food and drink were unloaded from car trunks and then taken to sites near stacks of wood that were guarded by teenagers. They were taking no chances that someone might light the flares before the assigned hour.

Ethan handed Carol their bag of food while he removed a folded sheet of plastic and a blanket from the trunk.

"Ethan..." Carol began. Her plea was the first word spoken between them in over a half hour.

He closed the trunk, pocketed the key and turned

to her. A thin smile played across his sensual mouth. "It's all right, Carol." With his free hand he turned her coat collar up, then tweaked her chin. "Everything's under control." Slipping his arm around her shoulder, he led her up the levee. His mood was back to normal again, and Carol felt she could finally breathe easily.

Ethan spread out the plastic ground cover and then covered it with the blanket. Carol sat beside Ethan, her legs curled beneath her. With the rest of the celebrants, they cheered boisterously the first airborne sparks and joined in the singing of whimsical Christmas songs all about the red-clad grandfatherly man for whom the pyres had been constructed.

Down the river the fires were lighted one after another until there was a steady line that bent out of sight with the curve of the levee.

Ethan soon made the acquaintance of one of the builders of the fire nearest them. He told Ethan of how the custom had first been a way for the communities across the river to send seasonal greetings. He complained about the restrictions placed on the ceremony now, how not too long ago fires were lighted that burned all night and far into Christmas day. He told them that now the Environmental Protection Agency checked the preparations for the bonfires and made sure everything was in order, and that the Army Corps of Engineers monitored everything they did.

The young man, holding a chubby child on each knee, spoke with the thick accent of the Cajun people who resided along the area known as the German

Coast. With that speech pattern the "th" sound was lost or blended, and almost every sentence ended in the affirmative "yea" or the negative "no."

"It was diff'rent in de old day, yea. Back den we could really pass a good time. It was somet'ing else, yea," he enthused.

Carol couldn't hold back a smile at his words. He was but two or three years older than she and not nearly so old as Ethan, and here he was talking about the old days.

Ethan shared their sandwiches with him, and Carol gave the children big crunchy pralines from the bag Gracie had provided. In return, he offered to watch their things if they wanted to walk down the levee to view some of the other fires. Gratefully accepting his offer, Ethan and Carol walked hand in hand, enjoying the different scenes at the various fires. Some were built by families, and all the onlookers, from grandmothers to infants in strollers, chatted, laughed and sang. Other fires were tended by lively young people who shouted and laughed joyfully.

Everywhere they were greeted with friendly calls of "Merry Christmas" and *"Joyeux Noël,"* and were frequently offered generous amounts of a potent local drink called "cherry bounce." Once Ethan surprised her by accepting a plastic cup filled with the beverage. With the first sip, he raised a dark eyebrow.

In answer to his implied question, Carol said, "It's made with wild cherries soaked for weeks in sweetened whiskey and port wine. Then the mixture is strained and set in a darkened cabinet until Christmas."

Ethan looked down at the contents of the cup and returned in an undertone for her ears alone, "This batch was aged too long. It should have been served at Halloween. It's a real witches' brew." But he took another sip.

Carol tried not to laugh aloud and managed the muffled reply, "Only to the unaccustomed palate."

Ethan prudently took a long time to finish the drink and unhesitatingly turned down offers to refill his cup.

At one fire they listened to a rendition of "Cajun Night Before Christmas," a regional favorite that recounted how Santa would arrive in a sleigh pulled by alligators with such Cajun names as Alcée, Ninette, Tilboy and Gaston. Carol never tired of the story, but Ethan's pleasure was even greater at hearing the delightful tale for the first time.

They leisurely made their way back, collected their belongings and bid their new friend a good-night. As Ethan led her to the car, she couldn't resist teasing, "Well, ma frain, did you pass a good time, yea?"

Ethan's answering grin was accompanied by an equally authentic imitation, "Mahn, I did pass a good time, yea!" Then he hugged her to him quickly and hard.

They slowly traversed the winding road that followed the course of the river. In Destrehan they stopped at the historical landmark where St. Charles Borromeo Church now sits to attend midnight services. The church had replaced another whose sighting many years ago had been the signal for riverboat captains that New Orleans was near, and that they could now pay the boatmen their wages, since they no longer had to fear that the boatmen would abandon ship so close to their destination.

During their drive home Carol decided to stay overnight at the house. There was too much to do the following day, and she wanted to be there early to make sure that Gracie could leave on time; she certainly couldn't count on Eva. When she and Ethan had left earlier in the evening, Eva still hadn't returned. If Carol's prayers were answered, then the relationship between Ethan and Eva was dead, and perhaps Eva wouldn't return for several days.

Their trip back to the city was filled with comfortable conversation about the traditions they participated in that evening. As they passed the big houses on St. Charles Avenue, they noticed that many were ablaze with lights, and that cars crowded the driveways and the streets.

"What are so many people doing out so late? Almost every house on the street seems to have guests," Ethan remarked.

"Most probably they're hosting the *réveillon*, the meal after midnight Mass. You remember Tante Nan telling us about *réveillons* that lasted all night. In many families it's the time when gifts are exchanged, and for others it's just a giant party for all."

Ethan drove for another block before asking, "When does your family exchange gifts?"

"Until a few years ago it was after church, but then René and Eva decided they wanted to have time to attend their friends' breakfasts. Some people move from house to house until nearly dawn, and

Eva and René wanted to do that, too. After a while presents were exchanged only among Claud, Tante Nan and myself, so Claud began placing our gifts in our rooms early in the afternoon. Since his gift to Eva was usually something that she'd want to show off, he saw to it that she got it in time to wear on her rounds."

He stopped for a traffic light, and while they were stopped, he looked at her and asked, "Were there any gifts left in your room today?"

"No." Carol left it at that one word. Nan did leave a package for her at the foot of the stairs, but Carol placed it under the tree. Gifts in her room should come only from Claud.

When they arrived home, the gates were opened, indicating that Eva was probably still out. Carol had noticed that ever since Claud fell ill and wasn't there to admonish them about keeping the gates closed, Eva tended to leave them open until she returned home for the night.

"Which do you prefer?" Ethan asked as he pulled the car onto the circular driveway.

Too involved with her own thoughts of Eva, Carol didn't at first understand his question. "Which *what* do I prefer?"

"Gift-giving time. Do you like finding gifts in your room, or do you like to get them at the breakfast?" He turned to watch her as she searched through her bag for the keys to the front door.

"I like it best at the *réveillon*." Her fingers brushed against the foil-wrapped package still resting in her purse; remembering how all day she chided herself for foolishly making the purchase. Finally she found her keys.

"What are we having?" Ethan asked, and again she didn't understand. "I'm starved. I think that cherry bounce neutralized the nutritive value of any food I consumed today. What are we having to eat?"

She looked at him across the darkened car. "Are you serious? You want a Christmas breakfast?"

"*Sacré!* You t'ink I made de joke, yea? Me, I wan' some aggs, toas' brad with stromberry jelly and grits," he said, mimicking the Cajun speech.

Carol's laughter floated through the dark night. "What do you know about grits, Yankee boy? Oh, come on in. What's Christmas without the *réveillon*, even if it's just the two of us?"

They made their way to the darkened kitchen, where Ethan helped her get the repast started, then excused himself to go and build a fire in the den. He returned just as she finished making a light omelet.

"Well, Pierre, there's no *stromberry* jelly. I hope peach marmalade will do," Carol teased as they both carried their trays into the den and settled on chairs before the crackling fire.

"When did you used to open the presents? Before the meal or after?"

Ethan's curiosity about the details of the nearly forgotten family tradition amused her, although she couldn't understand his interest. "When we were children and impatient to receive our gifts, Claud would give them to us as soon as we walked in the door after church. It saved a lot of spilled orange juice and Tante Nan's nerves. As we learned to have more self-restraint, Claud gave us the presents after breakfast." With her explanation, Ethan seemed satisfied and settled into enjoying his food.

They chatted companionably during the meal, and Ethan helped her clean up. As the last dish was placed in the dishwasher, he said, "You were properly restrained tonight." At Carol's puzzled look, he continued, "You haven't exhibited too much anxiousness to open your present. You didn't spill one drop of juice all evening, nor did you bolt down your food."

It took Carol several seconds, but then the meaning of his remark, as well as the reasons for all the questions, finally registered. "You didn't!"

"Yes, I did. Will you come to the tree and accept your Christmas gift?" Turning out the kitchen light before she could utter a word, he left her standing in the dark while he made his way to the front door. Carol felt compelled to follow, and as she passed her purse on the hall table, she reached in for the little package.

The only light in the room was from the tree, but she refused to think of the last time they had been in the room together. New dimensions had developed in their relationship, and she had to trust those depths to protect her.

Ethan indicated a place on the damask sofa before he turned to the tree. Carol saw that several packages had been added to the collection. The one he picked up was large and elaborately wrapped.

He came and sat on the rosewood table directly in front of her so that their knees almost touched. If Nan could see him perched on her priceless antique, she would faint, but at this moment Carol wouldn't have cared if he carved his initials on the curved legs and covered the mirrored surface with graffiti. He kept his head lowered as he stroked the oversized red bow on the package he held on his knees.

Without looking up he began, "I think you know that on more than one occasion, I've had the distinct urge to kiss you." A cloud crossed Carol's heart before he continued serenely, "But you wouldn't let me kiss you because you were afraid—rightly so—of what might have followed. Sometimes I thought you were right, but there wasn't a time I didn't want to kiss you. Perhaps that's what prompted me to get you this gift."

As tenderly as he had spoken he removed the package from his knees and placed it on hers. Carol wanted him to look at her, to know what he was thinking, but when she knew he wouldn't raise his glance, she fumblingly opened the gift.

The reflection of the Christmas-tree lights glinted from hundreds of silver foil-wrapped chocolate kisses. Ethan still wouldn't let her see his face, only the dark gleam of his hair, but his words so softly spoken came distinctly to her. "I estimate the ratio of these chocolate kisses to the kisses I wanted to give you to be one to a hundred." Then in a barely audible tone he directed, "Open the other box."

Carol's hands shook so much that he laid a stilling hand over hers until his calmness flowed into her. Then she was able to remove the gilt covering of a package that had lain nestled among the chocolates, to expose a hinged box of black silk. She opened the box gingerly, only to quickly click the lid shut.

At the sound Ethan looked up at her, confusion printed in every feature. "I knew it was faddish and gaudy, not at all the kind of thing you would ever wear. I'll take it back and get you something in better taste. I'm sorry." He reached for the jeweler's box.

Deftly Carol moved the box out of his reach and placed it behind her as she simultaneously brought out the little gift she had hidden from him. "Before you say anything more, you should open this."

She placed the object in his hand. While he opened her gift, she began removing the thin gold chain she usually wore and dropped it into the box of candy.

When she looked at Ethan, he gave a boyish grin and exclaimed, "I don't believe this." He looked from the chain to her and back again at the chain before he slipped it into its box, placed the box on the table and followed it with the candy from her lap. Then he moved closer to her.

Taking the black box from her fingers, he removed the contents as she lifted her heavy hair so that he could fasten the necklace around her neck. The heavy ornament suspended from it rested on top of her sweater until he slipped a tiny button from its loop to allow his gift to rest in the shadowed cleft between her warm breasts. His finger sensuously traced the path of the golden links until it stopped at the ornament—another golden kiss.

"There have been an awful lot of kisses exchanged tonight." Carol swallowed the lump in her throat. "Would it seem too greedy of me to beg one more?"

His answer was whispered against her parted lips.

"You have no need to beg. I'll give it to you freely." For the second time he claimed a Christmas kiss, ten thousand times more sweet than the forgotten box of chocolates. When he raised his mouth from hers, he traced with his index finger the territory he had just explored. "Merry Christmas, my love."

Carol thought the heat generated by the beating of her heart would surely melt the golden kiss resting so intimately between her throbbing breasts. "Merry Christmas," she whispered.

If he had asked for the moon, that very night she would have fetched it for him, but instead he asked, "Walk me to the door." There in the moonlight shining across the veranda, he claimed one more tender kiss and was gone.

As soon as Ethan's car left the driveway, Carol hurried upstairs to kneel in that same moonlight and pray, first as always for Claud, then that she might be Ethan Greenlaw's real love, that he had not just used it as a term of endearment. Wrapped in the fullness of the evening's memories, she finally drifted to sleep, a golden kiss gleaming in the moonlight against the rosy pink of her breast.

CAROL GOT UP EARLY on Christmas morning, so that she would have plenty of time to prepare Nan's breakfast, help Gracie load her treats into her nephew's ancient car, and to get the formal dining room ready for the holiday meal. There would be no lunch served because Eva wouldn't get up until late morning, if she came home last night at all, and René would be even later arriving. Tonight the elegant dining room would be filled with many invited guests, although it was only one guest whom Carol was thinking of as she brought out the old silver.

"You think all this loving care at the homestead undoes two years of neglect, don't you?" Carol turned to see Eva standing in the doorway, with a glass of tomato juice in one hand and a cigarette in the other, watching but making no offer to help. Carol bit her lower lip and tried to think of a way to avoid another argument. She wanted nothing to spoil the glow that still remained from the previous evening. She was saved the effort by the chiming of the doorbell. Then the sound of René's voice drifted toward her—along with that of Ethan.

Carol flushed. What was Ethan doing here at this hour? He wasn't expected until six that evening. Why did he have to catch her like this, wearing jeans again and an awful sweat shirt? The only touch of elegance about her was the pendant swinging heavily against her bare breasts as it lay hidden beneath the unflattering shirt. Why hadn't she put on something glamorous like the clinging silk lounging pajamas that Eva was wearing?

She felt even frumpier when she finally steeled her nerves enough to join the others now collected in the den and saw Ethan's urbanely elegant dark suit and blindingly white shirt. He was passing out gifts; Nan was happily admiring the lace of handmade handkerchiefs, René had already lighted one of the Havana cigars, and Eva was draped around Ethan, planting a lingering thank-you kiss against his mouth with heart-stopping familiarity. That Carol couldn't bear to watch.

She retreated to the kitchen and prepared a tray of coffee, which gave her time to control herself. She blamed herself for raising her hopes too soon. Obviously nothing had changed between Ethan and Eva. That much was apparent by the way his hand had been so caressingly intimate against Eva's waist, and right there in front of Nan.

Carol looked down at her clothes. There was no reason to change now. He wouldn't care what she wore.

When she reentered the room, there was little to betray her stress other than a pallor to her complexion. Everyone had settled into familiar and favorite chairs. Ethan stood up to take the tray from her. She hadn't spoken a word since he arrived, and avoided touching him as she handed him the tray. She served the coffee, still avoiding contact with Ethan, then seated herself away from the others, taking a position on the piano stool.

Eva's taunts began as if on cue. "You were right to refuse to attend that dinner party last night, Ethan. It was the dullest thing I have had to endure in centuries, and the breakfast at Elyse Bergeron's was even worse. I wish I'd listened to you and stayed home for a quiet evening in front of the tree. We would have had a much better time."

Carol picked at her nail polish as the color drained from her face. Now she knew why Ethan took her out last night. He obviously had wanted to spend the time alone with Eva, but she insisted on going to the party with or without him. The only unanswered question was why he had staged the romantic interlude in front of the tree? She ventured a covert look at Ethan only to find him staring at her. Eva, too, noticed and quickly intervened.

"Look, Carol. Ethan has just about drowned me in my favorite perfume." Carol noted the expensive label on the crystal bottle Eva displayed as she nervously stirred her coffee. "I suppose your present came in a bonus check at that dreary office."

Once more Carol braved a glance at Ethan, who still watched her unwaveringly. "Tell Eva what your present was, Carol," he directed with authority. Carol looked pleadingly at him, at Nan, then she focused on Eva.

She simply couldn't leave herself open to another caustic comment from Eva, so she answered, "Candy—a huge box of candy."

Nan smiled gently. "Of course. Ethan is a well brought-up young man. He wouldn't do anything so crass as to give Carol cash. He's like one of the family. All his gifts are in perfect taste."

Carol couldn't bring herself to glance again at Ethan, even though she knew he was studying her.

When he spoke, his voice betrayed none of his feelings. "About the office, Carol—I have some business to discuss with you." He placed his cup on the tray and withdrew papers from the inner pocket of his coat. "When I called my family to wish them a Merry Christmas, I was informed of business complications that I must deal with immediately. I'm flying to Philadelphia this afternoon. I won't be having dinner with you, after all." He turned to Nan. "I hope this doesn't cause me to fall too far from grace, but I must get there as soon as possible. Besides, it will make my mother very happy if I'm able to have Christmas dinner with her." He flashed his most winning smile. "Am I forgiven?"

Nan was won over, but there never really was any doubt about that. "I think we Guerards have lived with business emergencies enough to have learned tolerance, haven't we?" No one answered her.

Ethan turned to Carol, and for her there was none of the practiced charm. "You're to turn over most of your work to one of the staffers and take the more urgent things I have under way. I have a list of the most important items here." He tapped a thick wad of papers against his thigh. "Isn't there someplace we can discuss this without boring the others?"

Nan was ready with a suggestion. "Why don't you use Claud's study? Or you can use the parlor."

Carol quickly voiced her preference. She didn't want to be in that tree-filled room with Ethan if she could possibly help it, so she led him into the cypress-paneled room. "How long will you be gone?" she asked in a tone that betrayed her disappointment.

Ethan closed the door, turned the key in the lock and walked toward her.

"Anywhere from three days to a week and a half." He paused in front of her. "Are you planning to tell me what's bothering you? You're like an ice maiden this morning."

Carol ignored his question. "What do you have scheduled for me?" Surely he couldn't be that dim-witted to think she would allow him to go from her arms straight to Eva's and then pretend everything was fine between them. He couldn't do that to her again.

Ethan made a visible effort to restrain his impatience with her. "All right, we'll take care of business first." He proceeded to outline the responsibilities, which included doing some on-site engineering for an employee on emergency leave. "You won't be able to avoid getting your clothes muddied, so dress accordingly."

"I think I know what a construction site is like in Louisiana weather," Carol retorted.

"I'm sure you do." His eyes narrowed. "As touchy as you are this morning, I don't know if I'm taking my own life in my hands when I bring up this next item. The public-relations party is planned for two weeks from today. I've already contracted for rooms and caterers at the Hyatt and arranged for musicians. Mrs. McLin has a guest list, and the invitations will go out soon. If by some chance I don't get back on time, I'm counting on you to carry on with the preparations. Can I depend on you to do what needs to be done?"

Carol swung away from him to face the French doors leading to the back patio, then answered solemnly, "I never promised you I'd have anything to do with the arrangements."

"I know, but you won't let me down, will you?"

The quietness of his voice made her ache. Why should she do his bidding? He let her build up hope that he cared for her, only to cruelly let her down by accepting Eva's willing embrace. But she couldn't refuse him now. "I won't let you down," she whispered. She heard the exhalation of a breath long held. So he hadn't been as sure of her as she believed. Still, it gave her little satisfaction.

"That was the last thing on my list, but there is one other item. Will you stay here while I'm gone?" At her instant tensing, he amended his request. "If you won't stay here, why don't you move into my apartment. It's only five or six blocks away."

Stay in his apartment! She had been wrong. He was more sure of himself than even she had imagined. How convenient to use the excuse that she's been working too hard, to get her into his apartment, get her comfortably settled, and then for him to return and join her.

Ethan seemed to have read her thoughts. "I'd prefer having you here at the house because I don't want you spending any time on domestic chores. I don't have daily help like you have here. With Gracie feeding you, and the maids taking care of your room and your bath and even your clothes, there'd be so much less for you to contend with."

There was an unfamiliar huskiness in his voice. "As much as I like the idea of your being safe in my apartment, my first choice is that you stay here—at least while I'm away. Will you do that?"

Carol searched Ethan's face, trying to see if his expression held what she wanted to see there. Then she remembered Eva. "I don't think I can stand being around Eva that long."

"You're to ignore her. When I get back, we'll deal with Eva together. Carol...." Futility choked his words. "This thing has me going in circles. I don't need extra worry about you."

"What thing?" she asked, puzzled. There was so

much she didn't know about him! She felt she knew absolutely nothing, except that she was desperately, drowningly in love with him, so much in love that she would wait for him to resolve the issue of Eva whenever he chose.

When he didn't answer, she pressed, "At least tell me why you have to go away." Carol felt she deserved to know that much.

"You know how I've been battling to improve the company's financial state so that we can bid on the Taalot building. Carol, I should have had the required backing with the first contract, but I didn't get it, and there has to be some reason for that. Actually *I* have the necessary collateral beyond what Guerard's can supply, and I should never have needed to seek it elsewhere. But the same force that here is blocking my efforts to get the capital we need is preventing me from using what is rightfully mine. And that reason is my brother.

"I have to go to Philadelphia to work things out before he pulls even more strings, and everything we've already accomplished is destroyed." He clasped her shoulders urgently, "God, how I wish there was more time to explain everything, but I can't miss that flight. Damn it, I need more time!" Then his voice gentled. "That's what you've been saying all along...that we need more time. It's something else we now share." Ethan looked at her pleadingly. "Carol, will you stay here?"

When he looked at her like that, her defenses melted away. At her whispered agreement his expression softened even more. One finger traced the structure of her face as he continued in a tender voice, "What was that talk earlier? Have you changed your mind about my present?"

She stopped his finger with her mouth as it brushed across her lips. Against it she whispered, "I don't want you to go."

"Nor do I want to leave you. We're just getting to where we need to be. I want to be here to help you fight the mercurial moments, and the Fates who have dealt you such unfairnesses." His eyes were changing with each softening word until they were the color of wintry mist. "Are you wearing my golden kiss now?"

All she could manage was a nod and a hope that her heart would not burst from its too rapid pounding as he slipped a warm hand beneath her shirt to brush a tantalizing palm over her breast, seeking the pendant.

Sensing her mounting desire, he slowly adjusted the chain so that the ornament rested against her breast. His breath came shallowly and irregularly. Then he lowered his head and kissed the place he so tenderly touched.

She closed her eyes to savor the exquisite longing that was surging through her, but she heard distinctly his parting whisper.

"Wear my kiss just there when you think of me."

Her other senses slowly resumed functioning only when the warmth of his closeness evaporated.

CHAPTER TWELVE

TIME SOARED, crawled, stood still. It flew in four-hour days when Carol needed forty. She would barely finish dealing with problems at one site when something cropped up at another site or at the office. How had Claud managed? And Ethan? Responsibility... did she want this much responsibility?

She laughed at the person she had been on the train from Chicago, charging south to take over the reins of a flourishing building firm. Now she could hardly cope with the day-to-day business of a company only a fraction of the size she thought it was. Yet she managed. When it was a matter of sink or swim, she swam, learning to delegate and to wait. Ethan would be back, and some things were better left undone. That was a decision arrived at after the fourth day of his absence.

Time crept as she waited for his return. Each day was a hundred hours without him and the nights even longer.

Time stopped when Claud's doctor called her to his office. "Miss Charbonnet, it seems that you're the one I should talk to. I called Mr. Guerard's other grandchildren, but they both deferred to you." He paused to gauge her reaction, not knowing that she had come to expect that the unpleasant things in her family would fall to her.

"I think you should be warned that your grandfather cannot last much longer. If he hadn't been such a physically vital man, he wouldn't have lasted this long. As it is, he has amazed me, but—" again he closely monitored her response "—he has used up that store of reserves."

Carol revealed nothing of what she felt. She was becoming a master at hiding her hurt. "How much longer does he have to live?"

"No more than a few weeks, probably less. There are arrangements you might want to make so that when the time does come, there won't be as much pressure. I think you understand what I'm saying. If the entire responsibility is yours, as I've begun to believe it might be, I think you should begin the initial steps.

"I don't mean to sound callous, Miss Charbonnet, but before this stroke silenced him, your grandfather talked to me a great deal when he became my patient. I believe that he would want me to have this conversation with you. If you do things as I have suggested, it will be easier on you, and I know Mr. Guerard would want that above anything else."

Her responsibility? How could it all be her responsibility? But she hid these questions as she responded, "I don't think you're callous, Dr. Frahm. It's just that I've tried not to think about it, and now you're telling me I must." She rose and extended her hand. "Thank you for caring enough to tell me what you believe he would want."

Carol returned to her office and spent the rest of the day like an automaton, doing what had to be done, refusing to let her brain do anything else besides focusing on her work. Somehow she made it through the afternoon.

For the first time she couldn't make her daily visit to the hospital; that filled her with greater guilt. Nor could she return to the house. She would go to the Quarter apartment or rent a hotel room. Anything. She just couldn't take any more.

Carol chose to go back to the apartment, and for hours she lay staring at the shadows cast on the ceiling by the courtyard lanterns. The lump of gold weighed heavily on her chest, cold comfort against an overload of pain. Who could she turn to? Even Patti hadn't returned.

Time after time she ignored the insistent clamoring of the cream-colored phone, though she could reach it without changing position. Then it rang a full two minutes. There was a brief silence before it sounded again. On the fifteenth ring she turned her head to look at it. If it rang five more times, she would answer. At the beginning of the twenty-first peal, she lifted the receiver and placed it wordlessly against her ear.

"Miss Trehan, I'm trying to locate Carol Charbonnet. Do you have any idea—"

"Ethan?" Her pain-filled cry for him cut across his question.

"My God, Carol, where the hell have you been? Do you have any idea of the sheer torture I've been through not knowing what happened to you. You promised to stay—"

Until then she had been able to hold back all but a silent trickle of tears, but now a deluge of great racking sobs tore at her until she could no longer hold the receiver. Through her uncontrollable grief, she could hear his panic-filled call for her.

"Carol? Please stop crying and tell me what's wrong.... Answer me! Are you hurt? Plese don't do this to me! Don't, please don't do this when I can't get to you. Is it Claud?"

The sobs finally subsided to sniffles as she managed to retrieve the phone from the pillow.

"That's better, my love. Just calm down now, just a little more." His voice strained over the miles to console her. When he felt she could speak, he repeated his questions.

No, she wasn't hurt, she didn't need the police or a doctor or anyone else. *Just him. Didn't he know that? Just him to hold her and keep away the pain....* The tears started again.

"Carol, don't, my love. Don't do this. I'll charter a flight out of here tonight."

For the first time she heard a background voice. What was the female voice talking about?

Ethan's next words were muffled as if he was pressing the receiver against his chest. "Do you think I give a damn? He can have it all!"

"Carol—" once more his words were directed to her "—will you go home and wait for me there? I'll call you as soon as I make arrangements for a flight out of here."

Again in the background, was the pleading voice. Something of great importance was happening there, and she knew that Ethan must stay until it was resolved. "Ethan... I'll be fine, honestly. I just needed this one time of weakness. It won't happen again. You don't have to leave."

He responded authoritatively, "Do you think any of this means anything to me if it makes you as upset as you were just a few minutes ago? I'll be there as soon as I can get out of here." He sighed, "I should never have left you with so much responsibility. Carol, did you hear me? I should be there by early morning."

"No, I won't let you do this. I don't know what's going on, but I know you're needed there more than here. I'll manage. You won't be gone forever."

For the first time ever, she heard indecision in his voice. "I don't know what to do. I can't think." She could hear his breathing. "Leave everything, Carol, and come here. To hell with the firm. We can straighten things out later. And the rest of the family can take care of themselves for a while. Just get on a plane and come to me."

It was so tempting, so very tempting, but she couldn't. "I can do that no more than you can abandon your responsibilities there. Besides, things are on a different level now." She told him of her conference with the doctor.

"Is he the one who did this to you?"

"No, he did the right thing. I needed to know. Maybe I won't be able to act on his advice, but eventually these things must be taken care of."

"But you're not to do it alone. If Eva and René won't help you, then you must wait until I get back."

"If it's possible." That was something else she had to confront. Claud might die before Ethan returned. She didn't know how she would survive that.

"Don't think about that." He shifted the conversation to talk about her work, and she heard the relief in his tone when he said, "You're sounding better. You had me worried." His voice was now gentle.

"I'm sorry. I don't know what got into me." She reached for the golden kiss and rubbed it against her lip.

Ethan's voice dropped lower. "I know what's got into me. I want you... want you!"

She clasped the ornament tightly in her palm. "And I want you."

"If you were here now, I don't know if I could wait." His sigh sounded tired, as tired as she felt. "You must return to Miss Nan's tonight; she's worried. I called there and a hundred other places tonight, trying to find you."

"I will," she promised.

"And will you be as sweetly yielding when I get back?" She could barely hear his last husky message. "Think about me."

"Good night, Ethan. Take care of yourself. I—" But he had broken the connection before she could finish. "I just wanted to tell you that I love you," she said to the dead line.

She rode the nearly empty streetcar, shielding herself with the memory of Ethan's words expressing his need of her. It supported her through the tirade waiting for her.

"I hope you're satisfied," Eva charged, the minute Carol opened the door. "I had to stay here and cope with Nan's hysterics caused by your inconsiderateness. The least you could have done is to have left a message with the servants or on that fancy answering service at the place where you work. I don't appreciate being used by you. If you and Ethan Greenlaw can't keep your business dealings straight, then hire another secretary. Don't involve me or *tante*."

Eva had always hated Carol's involvement with the company, and she was reaffirming that feeling now. Carol took the easiest way out as she had done in the past. "I'm sorry Eva, and you're right. It was thoughtless of me."

Eva's rage was almost matched by her curiosity. "What was so all-consumingly important that your *boss* couldn't wait until conventional business hours?"

Carol used the first excuse that came to her. "He discovered a mistake I made in calculating the stress factors for the construction of a new office complex."

"What's the matter? Have you lost the magic touch since you don't have Claud leading you by the hand? That kind of error would never have happened when you were under his thumb." Her sneering contempt marred the cold beauty of her face.

Carol just wanted to get to her room to savor the little glow that remained from her contact with Ethan. "We all make mistakes" was her only reply as she moved toward Nan's room.

"There's no point in going in there. She finally took a sedative and is sleeping. Don't you wake her."

She would have felt easier if she could just look in on Nan, but it wasn't worth thwarting Eva. "I'll check with her first thing tomorrow morning. Goodnight, Eva."

THE NEXT DAY was New Year's Eve. Although the rest of the employees were allowed to go home at noon, Carol worked on through the afternoon, not leaving the office building until a dusky twilight had settled over the city. A chilling wind blew across the river, and rain clouds gathered threateningly. Carol raised her eyes skyward. There would be even more accidents if the streets became rain slicked on a night that usually claimed a disproportionate number of traffic fatalities. Still measuring the threat in the sky rather than watching where she stepped, she walked directly into the path of another pedestrian, sending her umbrella, purse and briefcase skittering along the sidewalk.

There was something familiar about the figure who gathered her property so agilely, but it wasn't until she saw the scarred hand that scooped up her possessions that she identified the man. "Mr. Randle, I do apologize for not watching where I was going. Thank you for picking up my things."

"Miss Charbonnet—" the black eyes warmed "—is this the same kind of trouble you created that sent a certain Yankee engineer into such a tailspin that he even had me checking hospitals?"

Carol's cheeks paled. Had Ethan really been so upset?

"I don't think he suffered any permanent damage," he commented.

"I hope not. I'm just sorry that my foolishness caused you so much trouble. Again I thank you." Once more she held out her hand for her things.

"Have a drink with me."

For all his closed countenance, there was a loneliness and vulnerability about him that made Carol want to take the time to spend with him. "As much as I would like that, Mr. Randle, I can't. If I don't visit my grandfather within the next hour, I won't be able to see him until tomorrow. I make it a rule to see him every day. Yesterday I didn't go, and I can't let that happen again." She held out her hand. This time he yielded her property.

"I understand. Good night, Miss Charbonnet." He was the first to walk away. Carol stood watching as he reached his nearby car.

"Mr. Randle." For some inexplicable reason, she called to him. "If you have no other plans, I could have that drink with you later, after I've seen my grandfather and taken care of a few things at home."

Without turning to her, he replied, "I have no plans, Miss Charbonnet, no plans at all. Where shall I meet you?"

She gave the address of the family home. "About eight-thirty, Mr. Randle?"

"My name is Steve. The time is fine, but are you sure about the place?"

"As sure as my name is Carol. See you later,

Steve." Carol turned and walked quickly away, refusing to question her motives.

AFTER VISITING CLAUD, she hurried home, had dinner, bathed and had just slipped into her clothes when she heard the door chimes. She knew it was Steve, and she quickened her pace. She was adjusting Ethan's kiss so that it rested just beneath the draped neckline of the clinging mauve cocktail dress she had selected when her bedroom door flew open to a wild-eyed Eva.

"What in heaven's name is that convict doing downstairs? How dare you invite that...that criminal into this house. If *tante* had any idea who he is, it would be her death!"

Carol reached around her to close the door, hoping Eva's shouting hadn't been heard downstairs.

"I don't think anything will rub off on the furniture, or that any of us will catch anything from him." Carol turned her back to Eva and began putting her makeup into an evening bag.

"You haven't answered my question." Eva wrung her hands dramatically. "What is he doing here?"

From the wardrobe Carol selected a coat that was more decorative than warm, then answered calmly, "He's taking me out for a drink. I have a date with him."

"You can't be serious," she glared at Carol with blue-eyed wonder. "You *are* serious. All right, you just make sure he's out of the house in the next five minutes, because if he's still here when *my* date arrives, and word gets out that my cousin is seeing a convict while living in *this* house, you'll wish you had stayed in Chicago forever. You won't spoil things for me—not now. I got rid of you once, and I can do it again!" She whirled away in a cloud of exotic perfume that Carol remembered from Christmas day.

Downstairs she found Steve being guided on a tour of the house. In the den with him was Nan, who stood regally in the walker as she proudly told him of the family's accomplishments, which were displayed in the pictures, plaques and clippings adorning the walls. It was obvious that she had no idea that the man she was so charmingly entertaining was a former convict.

Just for a moment Carol hesitated to interrupt, then said quietly, "I'm ready, Steve." She held out the coat to him so that he could help her into it.

With a gracious bow he turned to Nan. "It has been a great pleasure to meet you and learn so much about your most interesting family, ma'am." He spoke like a true Southern gentleman, and Nan looked delighted. Taking Carol's arm, he escorted her out of the house and to the car. Once they were seated inside, he reached for her hand, turned it palm up and examined it intently.

"What are you doing?" she protested as she tried to pull her slim wrist from his huge hand.

"I've never been this close to a real blue blood. I just wanted to see if it flowed just like regular red blood."

"You're silly," she laughed and enjoyed his responding grin, which eased so much of his aloofness and bathed his usually grim features with an interesting warmth.

"And you reek of silver spoons and blue-chip stock. That's some humble place to call home!" Some of the warmth faded. "I shouldn't have met you here." He started the car and moved into the traffic.

Carol let the remark go without comment.

"I saw you the other day, wearing a hard hat and orange vest and up to your knees in mud again. You were giving some poor soul the devil." He handled the big car effortlessly, driving with the traffic, not at all like Ethan, who tended to urge the other cars out of his way.

"Where was that, and how do you know I was giving someone a difficult time?" There had been so many terrible moments during the past week she couldn't remember the incident.

"At a site near the lakefront. Those were my cement trucks you had lined up waiting for the correct reinforcement to be laid. I heard the gossip later, but anyone who saw the way you were waving that clipboard at the supplier could read your message loud and clear."

"I don't think he'll try that again. Those floors would have cracked within a year, but what really made me angry was that the difference in the price of the specifications and the trash they had laid wouldn't have put enough into their pockets to pay the insurance premiums on this car." She warmed to her subject. "Claud would have flattened that supervisor for not reporting the substitution."

Steve found her temper amusing. "Tough lady, huh?"

She grinned, too. "When I have to be."

Steve nosed the long car into the parking lot adjacent to one of the city's more luxurious restaurants. "I thought we would start by having a drink in a lounge with a view."

The restaurant was located on the top floor of a skyscraper, and the ground-level mist produced glimmering halos around the lights far below. Steve seated her next to the floor-to-ceiling window, and though she had been there many times before, she enjoyed picking out familiar landmarks with him. He kept her supplied with fresh glasses of planter's punch, a fruity drink laced with light rum, but he had only one glass of lemon soda. She controlled her curiosity for a long time, but after the second drink her reticence gave way.

"Don't you ever take a drink, Steve?" she asked quietly as she wiped the beads of moisture from her glass with her index finger.

He turned away from the view of the communities across the river to let his glance slide over her hair, her face, then down to the rounded thrust of her breast. "Would you believe me if I told you that you are far more intoxicating," he answered in husky undertones. The scarred hand reached out, and he slid a finger into the hollow just above her collarbone to hook the delicate chain.

She felt the golden kiss slowly rising from the cleft between her breasts. "No," she protested. His intimate gesture surprised her.

"No, you don't believe me, or no, I mustn't do what I'm doing now?" He had the golden nugget in the palm of his hand.

"No to both, Steve." She tried to slip the object from his hand, but he held it firmly.

"A Greenlaw lode and talisman?" He lifted the shining ornament higher, dangling it before her chin.

She could only nod in reply as her original feeling of foreboding about this strange man filled her again.

"And how deep does the vein run?" He held her eyes.

She made the effort and managed to reply, "It's a very rich vein, and it runs deep." This time he dropped his eyes to the nugget, then he slipped it back into the bodice of her dress.

"Lucky Greenlaw," he muttered as he took a sip of his colorless soda.

"Lucky Carol," she retorted.

"And unlucky Steve." He signaled the waitress for the check, then turned to her again. "I have no intentions of trying to seduce you. I never trespass on another man's territory." He grinned at her, and immediately the earlier light mood was restored. She believed him, so when he asked her to go to another restaurant for dinner, she agreed.

"But do you think we can get in anywhere without reservations?" she asked.

His answering laugh resounded around them. "Miss Charbonnet, just as that blue blood of yours opens many doors closed to lesser mortals, my blue checkbook can perform its own share of miracles."

And Carol thought his checkbook would get a nice airing paying the bills they ran up in the elegant night spots they patronized that evening. He was right about the power of his money. More than one door locked to others had opened for them.

At midnight, amid the cacophony of blasting horns and the sentimental "Auld Lang Syne," he did not take advantage of tradition. The light brush of his mouth against hers was only perfunctory. At the grateful look on her face, he smiled a lopsided grin and repeated, "Lucky Greenlaw," before turning to join the others in the traditional New Year's song.

CAROL AWOKE early the next morning. While she was having her coffee, she glanced over her things-to-do list and saw that it was down to a manageable level.

She felt that her life was in order except for one important part of it—Ethan. She had received only that one call, and he had been away for more than a week. She brought the golden kiss to her mouth, sliding it absently across her lip. He had promised to be back by now. Why hadn't he called? How much effort did it take to call an eleven-digit number and say, "I love you," or "I'm delayed," or "I'm not sure," or... "I'll never be back...."

It was the possibility of the last that frightened her the most. What if he wasn't coming back? But surely he would return, Carol chided herself. Only a few blocks away was his apartment filled with personal belongings, and his expensive car was still parked at the airport.

That was ironic. Carol had once left behind an

apartment full of personal belongings, and he had made short work of that. Then Carol forced herself to get dressed and get to work.

At the office she wandered aimlessly through the empty suites. It was still a mystery how he had managed to get rid of her apartment, and why he had taken it upon himself to do so. She no longer believed he had personally collected and folded her clothes, gathered the intimate things from her drawers and shelves to place them in the wooden crates and trunks. Professional movers had done that. Still, how had he gained admission to the building? And why had he been so adamant in seeing that her return to New Orleans was permanent?

Carol wandered into Ethan's untenanted office. Noting that the closet door was ajar, she automatically pushed at it, but a safety vest prevented the latch from catching. Reaching down she picked up the electric orange garment to rehang on the rod. It was as she straightened the vest and bent the ends of the wire hanger to prevent its falling again that she saw a vaguely familiar hard hat on the shelf. Beside the well-known yellow one with the Guerard logo sat an acid green hat with one word: Landers. There was something about the name, something deep in her memory, but she couldn't bring it to the surface.

With a shrug she closed the door. She didn't have the energy to cope with another problem.

The weather had finally cleared, so today they could begin compensating for delayed work. There were too many jobs that couldn't be performed in the rain, but now all the sites were active, and she needed to check the progress. Thankfully everyone was back on the job, and she didn't have to tie herself to the Bordelon project so much.

The rest of the day found her visiting about the scattered sites. She was kept occupied with verifying specifications, smoothing labor disputes and running the office, which left her little time to renew her early-morning reflections.

Nor did she reflect much on Eva's behavior that of late had been so out of character. First Eva had startled Carol by agreeing to attend the company party. Another oddity was Eva's physical presence around the house. Ever since New Year's Eve, she was at home more than Carol could remember since they were teenagers. She was up early—a thing unheard of in the Guerard household—and being extremely helpful. She met the mailman at the door, sorted the mail, answered the phone, accepted and delivered messages. She stayed with Nan at night, insisting that Carol take walks or visit with friends, cooing in Nan's presence how Carol needed to get out more. That was the only clue Nan required to pick up the cause. These were the things Carol noticed but had no energy left to ponder.

Nor did she have the energy or time to shop for a new outfit for the office soiree that was only two days away and for something to wear to the Vili Ball. Regardless of her own feelings for Eva, Carol felt she had to put in an appearance at the ball. It was inexcusable to miss a ball in which a family member reigned.

Luckily Patti had returned to the city. One phone call to her and Carol's wardrobe problem was solved.

Patti would send several gowns to the house, and Carol could make her choice without taking time from the firm she could ill afford to take.

With that issue solved, Carol thrust the thought of the dreaded office party to the back of her mind and concentrated on keeping up with the most pressing issues of the business, issues that seemed to multiply unchecked. She felt she was using the last of her reserves of strength. She was especially aware that she had little more to give when she visited Claud the afternoon of the office party.

The minute she walked into Claud's room, she could feel death near; she needed no visible signs. How much time did he have? A few hours? A day? She knew it couldn't be much over a week. Why was she going home to dress herself in fine feathers so that she might stand around with business associates, when her grandfather lay dying? Had she stooped to the theatrical morality of "the show must go on"?

A coldness crept over her as she took steps nearer to the shell of a man, and her heart beat with painful anxiety. She could feel the thudding pulse in her wrists, her ankles and, chokingly, in her throat. She lessened the depths of her breaths to lighten the pressure in her throat. This wasn't really her grandfather, she thought. It didn't even look like Claud. So why did it matter where she spent her evenings? The pulses increased. When this form on the bed stopped breathing, it would have no resemblance to her grandfather at all. The real Claud had left a long time ago. And she shouldn't have run away. Guerards didn't run.

Carol shook her head. She tried to breathe deeply and slowly, telling herself that she couldn't give in to the despair. She had to take care of the family; she couldn't give in.

HER NEXT THOUGHT registered the pain in her neck as she fought the restraining hand that forced her head between her knees. "Let me up," she demanded of the body above the two black shoes and the navy pants as she pushed at the hand.

That hand belonged to Dr. Frahm. "As soon as the injection starts working, you can sit up." Though the tone was gruff, the pressure did ease, and after a few minutes he let her lean back against the chair in which she now sat.

Carol eyed the syringe he still held in his other hand. "It's just a little something to relax you—like a glass of sweetened wine except quicker."

He stood monitoring her for a few minutes, checking her pulse and the reaction of her pupils to a little light he flashed across her eyes.

"Stand up now," he directed, and when he saw she had her balance and reflexes back, he handed her briefcase and coat to her and pointed her toward the elevators.

"Go home and get in bed. You're absolutely exhausted. If I need you, I'll call you!" And with that he showed her down the hall.

BECAUSE OF HER COLLAPSE at the hospital and the lateness Carol paid scant attention to Eva, who met her at the door. "The Lincoln won't start. I had Judson try jumping it from his truck. But nothing happened, so it must be more than a dead battery."

"Eva, there was nothing wrong with the car last night." Carol placed her briefcase on the hall table and rubbed her eyes with the tips of her fingers. "Did you use it today?" Carol didn't want to face yet another problem. She was late, and she was getting a headache.

"No," Eva responded wide-eyed. "I spent the whole day here with *tante*."

Carol raised an eyebrow at that answer, but her head hurt, and she couldn't handle the argument that would follow if she disputed Eva's word. It was easier to let things go. "Then, Eva, we'll go in your car." Carol tried to walk around Eva, but Eva blocked the stairs.

"I loaned my car to René." Again Eva's answer didn't ring true to Carol, but as her headache intensified, she was beyond caring.

"Then you'll just have to call a cab because I certainly don't have time to play car mechanic tonight," Carol directed flatly as she finally managed to push by Eva and climb the stairs.

"Oh, we don't have to take a cab. I called Mr. Randle. He'll pick us up." Eva was following close on Carol's heels. "It was probably the most presumptuous thing I've ever done after all the horrible things I said about him," she gushed breathily, "but I have come to realize that the expression 'paid his debt to society' probably applies to us most of all since we *are* society. Sometimes Tante Nan's old-fashioned views make me forget that things have changed."

Carol's head was pounding. She didn't know if the scene in Claud's hospital room or a reaction to the injection had caused it, but she just wished Eva would shut up even if it meant she had to walk to the affair.

She just had to get through this evening. Tomorrow she would rest. One step at a time...she would take things one step at a time.

The first step was to escape Eva. Finally she reached the silence of her room, fighting the pain in her head that was nearly blinding her.

She eyed the four gowns lying across the bed, a pale apricot of layered chiffon, a black silk slip of ultra sophistication, a bronze satin shirtwaist—and then *the dress*. Carol couldn't imagine Patti thinking this dress suitable. Intuitively she knew it had been included by accident.

It was theatrical—like nothing she would ever wear. A flesh-colored garment relieved only by the strategically located appliqués of shimmering gold, it covered only the necessities, and it didn't do that very well.

Even as she criticized the ostentation of the design, she slipped into the dress. It left her front bare to the navel and a slit up the skirt almost met that of the bodice. What little of her body it clad seemed naked because of the way it molded her form.

She eyed her reflection in the mirror. It was a wicked costume, too wicked for the sweet golden confection hanging between her barely covered breasts. Slowly she lifted Ethan's token—no, she couldn't. She dropped it back over her heart.

Downstairs it was Nan who almost brought her to her senses, who almost convinced her that flaunting convention was no way to shield her own tender emotions.

"Surely you're not going out of this house dressed like...like...." Nan left the sentence unfinished when she couldn't find the word to describe Carol's outfit, which in her eyes was first and foremost scandalous, if not immoral. "It's...."

Carol supplied a choice for her aunt. "Decadent, shocking, unladylike, indecent."

Carol and Nan were oblivious to Eva's fluttering around the foyer, and neither was aware that she had opened the front door to admit Steve until he moved across the entry to hold out his hand and lead Carol down the last three steps. "I would suggest bold, stunning, modern. I think you'll be like a shot of whiskey the morning after, eye-opening but welcome."

Another wave of pain broke behind her eyes. Steve tightened his grip on her hand, his eyes never leaving her face. "Are you all right?"

Then the pain left her, and only a slight feeling of disorientation remained. Maybe that was why she paid little attention to Eva, who was dressed in a demure little gown of blue that would never raise an eyebrow among the most straight laced of the dowager wives or the pulse rate of one of their husbands.

Under normal conditions she would have suspected something when Eva forgot her handbag and dashed back into the house, only to return with a garbled message about receiving a phone call and a committeeman coming directly over to the house, and stolen crowns and other things Carol couldn't keep straight.

She should have insisted they wait for Eva. She should have, but it was too much trouble for her head, which chose that moment to throb again.

CHAPTER THIRTEEN

IT WOULD FOREVER REMAIN A MYSTERY how Eva got to the hotel before Carol and Steve, but she did. She had planned and plotted, schemed and slaved too long to miss the culminating act of her carefully choreographed drama.

As Carol and Steve walked down the thickly carpeted hallway leading to the suite, the sounds of music and talking filtered toward them. At her prompting, the staff had reported early to give them time to relax and to assure a full quota present, should any invited guests arrive early.

She caught a quick glimpse of herself in one of the hall mirrors. She wondered what Claud's reaction would have been to her costume and could almost hear him as if it were he who walked beside her.

She licked her lips, which seemed unusually dry. It was probably nerves. Stopping at the last mirror before the double doors of the suite, she spoke to Steve. "I guess after what you had to face, you find my reaction to a mere accusation childish." The glittering image blurred in the mirror so that she had to shake her head to focus her eyes. Again she wondered what had been in Dr. Frahm's injection.

Steve leaned against the wall with one shoulder, his

hands thrust into his pockets. "I never find reaction to an injustice childish." He watched her lazily, enjoying her feminine act of applying a fresh coat of lip color. But a modicum of concern drew a line between his brows at the sight of her flushed face and a strange glassiness in her eyes.

"Aren't you going to blot those soft lips for her, Randle?" Carol's hand froze at the brittle voice cutting through the sounds of the music.

Steve didn't move from his relaxed position, and only a muscle working in his jaw alerted Carol to the tension in him as he answered, "That's your job, Ethan."

Carol turned to face the questioner. He was back, and all she wanted was to fling herself into his arms, to raise her mouth to his, but there was no welcome in his face or his threatening posture. He seemed barely in control of himself.

"Ethan?" It was all she could manage.

"Oh, yes, Ethan..." he mimicked from a sneering mouth that she didn't recognize. "Ethan," he repeated harshly, coldly. "Dumb old Ethan, who has returned to find a rat has led his little mouse astray."

That brought Steve away from the wall, and he said warningly, "That's enough, Greenlaw. I don't know what you think she's done, but she doesn't deserve that."

They faced each other like opponents ready to wage war.

"What the hell do you know about what she does or doesn't deserve?" The rapier sharpness of his remark sliced into her. And there was no doubt about what Steve's reaction would have been had not a fat stomach thrust its way between the two men.

"Greenlaw, my boy, glad to see you back in town. Not that I've got any complaints about dealing with this pretty associate of yours. I must say, her face is a lot more welcome than your scowling puss...ha-ha."

It was Mr. Bordelon, jolly, intrusive, blustering and welcome Mr. Bordelon. He slapped Ethan on the back with one arm, encircled Carol's shoulder with the other and led them through the doors that Ethan had left open.

"Here's your equally pretty cousin, Miss Charbonnet. Now, Greenlaw, if you could get them both out in the field, you'd have every construction gang in the city lined up outside your hiring offices offering to work for free."

Having separated Ethan and Carol from Steve, Mr. Bordelon joined Eva to allow the entrance of the steady stream of invited guests who followed in his wake. Steve had wordlessly slipped in with the first group and now eyed Carol warily from across the room, a glass of what she knew would be lemon soda in his hand.

At the first break in the flow, Ethan motioned to a waiter. "Bring me a Scotch straight...the good kind."

"It's all good, sir." The white-coated man drew himself up proudly.

Nevertheless, he did not return the large bill Ethan stuffed in his pocket, and the drink he subsequently poured did not come from the store of bottles behind the portable bar.

At the waiter's return, Ethan lifted the glass from the tray, took a sip, then nodded in approval. Carol wondered if he intended to get drunk in the receiving line. "What are you trying to do?" she hissed while at the same time smiling to Mrs. Hurst, who kept eyeing the flash of thigh peeking through the slit in the sparkling gown.

"It's damn well not the same thing you're trying to prove by wearing that dress. Every man here and half the women are trying to guess what you're wearing under it." His eyes flashed molten steel. "And you should get rid of that gaudy necklace. It's in poor taste almost as much as that dress."

"Go to hell." She fought her hurt with anger.

"I'm there already, Miss Charbonnet. I'm there already." He held up the now empty glass to the knowing waiter. "I think it's just about time to circulate."

"Just make sure you circulate in a different direction from the one I take." She didn't know how much more of him in this attitude she could take.

"No need to worry, little mouse." Once more he held a glass filled generously with a pale amber liquid. He lifted the glass in a mock salute. "To a beautiful illusion," he taunted, before draining half the contents. He looked down at his drink, swirling the contents around the edges.

"It's you I should drown for what you have done. Not myself." With that he placed the half-full glass on the tray of a passing waiter and left her standing alone as he steadily made his way toward a particularly boisterous enclave whose center was dressed in a proper little gown of ice blue.

Carol made it through the next hour and a half on sheer reflex. She kept quiet at the right times, spoke at the right times and called everyone by the correct name. Not once had she given thought to the incident of two years past. A new pain nullified the old.

A section of her brain continued to register the presence of Ethan with the blue-skirted specter by his side. He had become one of the "good old boys," flattering wives and humoring the men—except for one.

When Carol thought her skull had shattered like the glaze of improperly fired pottery, that one was there, a steadying hand beneath her elbow. "Hold on, Carol. I'll get you out of here," Steve promised.

Sweat beaded her upper lip and forehead. "I think I'm going to be sick."

"Not here you won't." The pain in her head was matched by the pain in her arm where the powerful grip held her upright. By now her eyes couldn't focus beyond either of those pains.

"Damn it! I said hold on." All she was aware of was being forcefully shoved through doors and the smell of disinfectants particular to public rest rooms before the contents of her stomach refused to be quelled any longer.

When the last of the shudders left her body, so did some of the ache in her head. At least her sense could function. "What's that?" Steve still held her draped over his strong arm over a toilet.

He glanced toward the direction he indicated with the tilt of her head. "A building expert like you ought to recognize a urinal."

"The men's room?" she asked in wonder.

A sheepish grin softened those features she had more than once thought so harsh. "There wasn't time to flip a coin. Besides I don't know my way around the women's room as well."

She moved to a basin, splashed cold water over her face and rinsed her mouth. He handed her a paper towel.

"I think I'll check if the coast is clear. I know I got you in here without your being seen. Now if we can just get out the same way."

It was clear, and they took a secret exit.

In the privacy of his car she finally relaxed.

"Feel like a bite to eat?" He stopped the car at the exit to the street and waited for her answer.

"No, I don't think so." Even if she felt hunger, she would chance nothing in her stomach.

"I do a pretty good steak if it's just that you don't want to go out." Easing his foot from the brake, he allowed the car to inch forward. "Are you sure?"

"Positive." She leaned against the plush headrest and released a long pent-up sigh as the big car merged into the traffic.

"Do you want to talk about it?" he questioned gently.

"I honestly don't know what happened tonight. First he was out of town, and then he was there with blood in his eye. I just don't know."

"Well, I damn well do!" His anger permeated every word. "He thinks that you and I...." He didn't finish because she completed the sentence for herself.

"... are sleeping together," she contributed bitterly.

"Sleeping together," he parroted hotly. "My God, whatever blame I bear for tonight's fiasco is the same that any man who has ever laid eyes on you could share. Sure, I like the vibrations you send out, but so does any half-awake man. I damn well would like to 'sleep' with you, but so would a thousand others." He made a scornful sound. "If Ethan thinks he can punish you every time a man finds you sexually attractive, he needs a team of psychiatrists."

For a while they rode in silence, each concerned with his own thoughts. When Steve spoke again, his anger was gone. "Has tonight changed your feelings for him in any way?" He pulled onto the driveway, stopped the car and turned to her, waiting for her answer.

"I'm sorry." It was all Carol could say.

"Don't be. I just thought it might give your ego a little boost to know that Ethan can be replaced with a snap of your fingers, and you can have me anytime you want to snap." His tone was teasing. "So now you know I'm interested, and I know it does no good, but that's okay, too. Self-denial benefits the soul." He grinned a surprisingly boyish smile before straightening to face the steering wheel.

This time his words were ominous. "I hate to sound like the voice of doom, but Greenlaw isn't going to let this rest with just his asinine behavior tonight."

"Can he hurt your business?" she questioned as she watched the moonlight filtering through the live oak tree cast lacy shadows on the hood of the polished car.

His short was derisive. "He wouldn't even be stupid enough to try. It's you he'll go after."

"But why?" To her, pain and hate were private things that you shut away until you were better. You never tried to spread their evils around.

"You have done one thing that he won't be able to take. You shattered his masculine ego into a million pieces in front of all his business associates and a few friends. The whole town thought he had you in his bed. Tonight he himself foolishly showed them better, but through his eyes you're the one who shouted the news from the rooftops."

"I don't understand. You were the only person who knew there was anything between us and only because I told you."

"You little baby!" His teeth flashed whitely in the moonlight as he laughed at her. "Claud Guerard sold you to him at the price of one faltering but salvageable construction firm. If it was a secret, it was the worst-kept secret in the modern South."

Her reaction was violent as she vainly tried to slap the sarcastic sneer from his hard face. "You are lying."

Wrenching the door open, she almost made it into the house when he caught her. She struggled against his massive frame, screaming accusations at him the whole time, but he held her effortlessly.

"Listen. Listen, damn you," he shouted as she clawed and kicked at him. After one well-aimed blow against his shin, his hold tightened painfully, and his voice came rasping like a steel file.

"I've smashed more faces than I can count, but I

have never, I repeat, *never* hit a woman. But if you don't stand still and listen, you can be the first when I knock some sense into you!"

He meant it, and she knew he meant it. As she stilled her struggles, he cautiously softened his hold, not yet trusting her to remain calm. When he felt she had control, he slowly released her and slid his hands into his pockets, but she knew they could be cruelly biting into her within seconds.

"You're going to have some very colorful bruises in the morning." Then he scoffed at his own words. "That's a trivial thing to say under the circumstances, but you scared the hell out of me. I almost flattened you."

She didn't try hiding her feelings for him. "Let me go inside. I just want to get you out of my sight."

"I know that. I also know that you will spend a long time in thought. I want to add something else for you to ponder. I *am* your friend, and baby, you'll be needing a friend. When I call in a day or so, don't let what I said about my fantasies stand in the way of that friendship. Do you understand what I'm saying to you?"

"Yes. Can I go now?"

"Now, who's a liar? You don't understand anything. But the idea is planted. You know where I can be reached if you decide you need me. Good night."

She had slammed the lead-glass door before he had pulled out of the driveway. He had lied. It was all some horrible gossip spread throughout a city that thrived on slander and innuendo. It was served up on the sidewalks with coffee and *beignets*, over cocktails, and with the towels in the ladies' rooms. Claud wouldn't have, couldn't have done such a thing. Never....

Her swirling denials slowed...stopped....

Don't tempt me to tell you what gave me the right...everything has its price, even you...don't think you have forever...my right was established without your permission...my right...you do what Claud wants...my right! MY RIGHT....

There was no one awake to hear the chilling sound of a heart breaking.

THE FIRST THING Carol did the next morning was strip the house of all holiday touches. She wanted no reminders of that time spent loving Ethan. She had this weekend in which to recover, and she was determined to.

For the first time in unnumbered generations, the tree ornaments were not lovingly packed away but dumped unceremoniously into the big boxes. The Christmas season had officially ended two days ago, and the season of Mardi Gras had begun. It was past time to clear the house. It would be a new season for Carol, too, a season learning not to love...anyone.

Late that afternoon she placed a call to Steve. It wasn't the call he had expected, but he had anticipated a different reaction.

"Send two men over here. I have a few chores I can't do alone." There was no please, no thank-you.

And he matched her bluntness. "Is that all?" At her one word answer, he hung up. But two men arrived within the hour, and under her direction they took the tree outside and chopped it into small pieces, returned those pieces to the den and stood idly by in wide-eyed confusion as she fed the sections of the tree into the roaring fireplace.

That left only one thing more. A kiss, a golden kiss. She removed it from her neck where it had hung like a golden albatross. At first impulse she threw it in the trash can where it stayed less than a minute. Removing a silver-framed picture from above her bed, she draped the jewelry there to serve as an eternal reminder of her folly.

Next she visited the hospital. It was the time when she usually went, but time was the only unchanged element in that visit. She was now more dead inside than Claud.

"So you got proper management for your company, and the price was me! Well, you were wrong the second time, grandfather. I didn't take the kickbacks, and I don't always do your bidding. By this time next week I'll have that Yankee out of there and on his way to Philadelphia where he should have stayed." There was no passion in her voice, on her face or in her heart.

MONDAY MORNING she was at the Poydras Street building waiting. As the employees began drifting in, they showed their wariness of her, for many had witnessed part of the scene Friday night. To each she extended an emotionless greeting, which they gingerly returned.

When Ethan arrived, he found her standing in the window as he had done two months earlier. "What are you doing here?"

"I've come to watch you clear out." She turned to face him, her arms folded beneath her breasts.

He examined her from narrowed eyes as he took a wooden-tipped cigar from a package in his breast pocket, placed it between his lips and applied a flame from a slim lighter. Thrusting his hands into his dark trouser pockets, he silently studied her for a few minutes.

His perusal gave her time to note the changes in him. There were more than a few, and none was enhancing.

He clamped the cigar between his teeth and spoke around it. "Don't you think the eviction notice is mine to deliver? I think I'll be the one to watch you clear out, Miss Charbonnet."

"I want this finished as soon as possible. I do not wish to haggle over money. Name your price." She was as cold eyed as he.

"No sooner than I." He opened the briefcase and removed a folder. "Double, Miss Charbonnet. Will that take care of it?"

"I don't care as long as this relationship is severed. Just how much did Claud pay you?" If it took every cent she had and all she could borrow, she would get him out.

He gave a cold humorless laugh. "Claud pay me?" He named an exorbitant figure. "That's how much I paid for seven-eighths of this firm. But to get you the hell away from here, I'll gladly give you twice what the last eighth is worth."

She thought there were no more shocks for her. Ethan Greenlaw had just proved her wrong again.

"I don't believe you," she whispered as she sank into the desk chair.

"Unlike others, I don't lie." He had found the object of his search. "I've had the papers drawn up. All they lack is your asking price and our signatures. If you haven't changed your mind about the money, we can get this over and done with now."

She propped her elbows on the desk she had grown up thinking would someday become hers and dropped her face into her hands. "No...."

"Come on, Miss Charbonnet. As soon as the workmen get here, Guerard Construction will cease to be. By five o'clock those doors out there will read Landers Construction. Big brother and I finally resolved our difficulties. You're now sitting in the office of a subsidiary of Landers Construction of Philadelphia, branch offices New York, Chicago and New Orleans."

"You bastard...you absolute bastard." She was rising to her feet, her face a mask of hatred. "You will never convince me this is what Claud expected."

"What do you care? Steve Randle will buy you any company you want and let you play construction worker until your heart, assuming you have a heart, is content. Any company, that is, except this one. Now sign the paper. Or do you want more money?"

"You can have it, Mr. Greenlaw." She snatched the paper from his hand before he knew her intent. "I give it to you—gratis."

"I don't want it that way."

"Too bad. Because that's the way it is." Pulling the door open, she called in a steady voice, "Mrs.

McLin, Mr. Walters, would you please step into Mr. Greenlaw's office for a minute." Mrs. McLin and the bookkeeper were there almost before she had finished her request. Carol didn't doubt that more than one set of ears had been straining to catch snatches of their conversation.

"You are now witnessing my signature to a document that places my shares in the company that you know as Guerard Construction into the possession of Mr. Greenlaw."

Not waiting for their response, she boldly signed her name and straightened.

"Carol...." There was an odd familiarity about the way he pronounced her name.

"Go to hell, Judas!"

AFTER STORMING OUT of Ethan's office, she sought Steve. It took her nearly an hour, but she finally located him deep within the warehouse district. There was no pretty receptionist, no plush pile carpet, only a hum and throb of efficiency and industry.

"Give me a job," she demanded after briefly outlining her morning.

"Here?" Steve eyes her cautiously.

"Why not here?" Surely he wasn't to let her down, too.

"Did you come in a car?" He reached for the casual leather blazer that draped over his chair.

"I've got Claud's Lincoln." With her answer he steered her toward the door.

"Hold down the fort while I'm out, Sugarman." The extremely young male typist never looked up from his copy.

At the question in her eyes, Steve volunteered, "He's got a mind as sharp as the switchblade he used to carve up the man who raped his sister." He held his hand out for the keys.

"Oh...." She ventured another glance at the office door as Steve adjusted the position of the seat to accommodate his extra-tall frame.

"I distinctly remember telling you what kind of people I employ. I don't think you quite fit the bill."

"I had forgotten. Where are we going?"

"To lunch." Over a quiet lunch he worked at convincing her not to rush into anything. "Have you taken a good look at yourself?"

"What's wrong with the way I look?" She reached for the mirrored compact in her purse.

Reaching across the table to close the disklike case before she could raise it, he shook his head. "I'm not talking about a smudge on your cheek. In November when Greenlaw first brought you to me, you were no more beautiful than you are at this moment, but you looked better, if that makes any sense. Those circles under your eyes, that slight paleness to your cheeks, that drawn pinch just around that desirable mouth were not there." He allowed his glance to wander over her shoulders. "And those faultlessly tailored blouses didn't hang like they do now."

Self-consciously she tugged at her blouse. "I don't sleep very well."

"Why should you? Totally discounting your emotional involvement with Greenlaw, you have enough problems going to drive a lesser person stark raving mad." He stirred the steaming coffee a waiter had placed before him. "Will you take some advice from a friend?" He stressed the last word. "Don't do anything for a while. Sleep late in the mornings, sip tea in the afternoon with your aunt, audit a history course at the university, accept invitations to every Carnival ball in town. You don't need a job. You need a rest."

It made sense in a way. There was still Claud to think about, worry over and pray for. There was still Nan's painful and reclusive existence to overcome. There was still Eva's role to analyze. She could see a distinct irony in his suggestion. She could chuck her involvement in the construction business and take life easy.

Misreading her sardonic grimace, he leaned forward. "If it's money, we can deal with that."

"Would a lady who gives away stock in a rising construction firm be likely to need money?" She sarcastically dismissed his suggestion. "No, I think you described earlier what I need most, a far less stressful existence."

With the exception of auditing the history course, he had accurately sketched the program of her life for the following weeks. She rode the streetcar uptown to Audubon Park and walked beneath the spreading oaks. She rode downtown and browsed the antique shops of Royal Street. On sunny mornings she took the sedan to the lakefront and sat on the seawall, absorbing the warming rays.

At night she joined Patti's crowd at the night spots and smart supper clubs. Twice Steve took her to more sedate evenings of dinner and dancing. Once he took her to the Theater of the Performing Arts for the symphony.

As they left the theater, Steve surveyed the rows and rows of cars packed into every available space, then moved his eyes across the filled car parks to the Municipal Auditorium. "Do you have an escort for tomorrow's ball?"

"I'm not sure that I want to go," she answered as they moved toward his car.

"I've never been to a Mardi Gras ball; I've never cared to go, but someone slipped up and sent me an invitation. Since it is the ball in which your cousin will reign as a maid, would you go with me?"

They were approaching the intersection of Canal and Carondelet. Perhaps if a jaunty sports car had not cut so closely in front of them in a barely successful attempt at beating the traffic light, she might have given a different answer.

"Why not. I just hope you don't find it too boring."

CAROL HAD SEEN little of Eva since the infamous night. She knew Eva had played a part in her pain; she just didn't know how decisive a part. In the end it didn't matter to her now that she knew Ethan's motives in procuring the firm. She didn't consciously avoid Eva and knew full well that Eva wouldn't waste the energy avoiding her. It was just that her role as Carnival royalty kept her busy.

Nan did not try hiding her disappointment in not being able to observe a Guerard in the social limelight. Her only consolation was in Carol's attending.

Amid admonishments to both her and Steve to remember everything, she urged them out. They were not to be late and miss one minute.

After a committeeman checked their invitations, Carol led the way upstairs. Although the gymlike atmosphere of the auditorium had changed downstairs, in the balconies it was the same structure that housed ice shows, plays, boxing matches and a circus now and then. It was the auditorium floor that had been transformed into a fantasy world. Gone were the stage and the seats, to leave only a few boxes at the rear and sides, and a curtain hiding the fantasy world of a Mardi Gras ball.

"Who are those ladies sitting in the boxes?" Steve whispered to her.

"Most of this season's debutantes, some socially prominent women, sweethearts and wives of the krewe. They're the ones who have call outs," she explained.

"Call outs?"

"They received a card with their invitations and will be called out by the masked krewe members to dance."

Steve eyed the predominantly female audience around them. Carol whispered another explanation. "The requirement of formal dress is just another excuse for the men to avoid this kind of thing." She eyed the hand-tailored detailing of his tuxedo. Even to an unknowing eye, it was obviously made especially for him, and he wore it with the casualness of a man used to such. "Renting a set of formal clothes in which to watch other people having a good time is too great a sacrifice for some of the men."

He studied his surroundings intently. "Are the balls standard?"

"For the most part, all the balls are the same. During some there is general dancing instead of call outs. The Krewe of Bacchus sells tickets, and instead of a krewe member serving as king, it's a celebrity—Bob Hope, Al Hirt, Jim Nabors. The Krewe of Rex, with the exception of the captain and a couple of lieutenants, doesn't mask.

"Usually a ball begins with the entrance of last year's court. Then the costumed and masked krewe members come onto the dance floor. This is followed by a pantomime welcome by the krewe captain. The curtains open, and we see the tableau, the theme of tonight's ball expressed in elaborate stage design and exotic props that can include real fires, forests, circus tents, a complete kingdom.

"After the audience's reaction has quieted, the dukes enter, and then the maids, followed by the king and finally the queen. When all the royalty is out, the entertainment begins. The costumed krewe performs a series of skits to develop the theme. Their costumes reflect the scene they enact. For example, if the tableau suggests American holidays, one part of the show might be the Fourth of July, and the maskers might dress like firecrackers or American flags. Others might be Pilgrims for Thanksgiving or Santas for Christmas.

"One of the most sensational balls had a theme of 'The Loves of Men,' and each scene represented something a man loves—his home, science, food, money, wine. And the themes are the best-kept secrets in America. I'm very anxious to see what tonight will bring."

"What follows the entertainment?" asked Steve.

"The grand march of the royalty, the presentation of important guests to the king, a parade of the maskers and then the call outs, which last until midnight. Our role is like that of peasants looking down on the fun. We have to stay up here and watch. We cannot actively participate."

The lights began to dim, and for a while reality was suspended as the bejeweled spectacle unfolded before them. The theme of stories from childhood was not a particularly original selection, but its execution left nothing to be desired as scene after scene unfolded before the enthralled audience. "Little Red Riding Hood" followed by "Call of the Wild" and "Black Beauty" were completely presented in stylized glitter and grandness, all in the Mardi Gras tradition.

The gowns and trains and jewels of the court rivaled those of any imperial palace in splendor if not in cost. As the dukes and their maids were presented in the grand march, Eva fulfilled her role as one born to it, her posture regal, her curtsy to each section hinted at a royal touch of condescension with the slight sideways tilt of her head. It was an effect that others could never attain even after weeks of practice.

Carol and Steve sat silently amid the "aah's" of the audience around them. Though nothing tonight was new to Carol, there was that inexplicable sense of wonder in the spectacular event.

During the king's toasts, Steve whispered in her ear, "Why aren't you down there? You'd make a far prettier maid than most of them."

"I had my turn. It was enough," she answered.

He turned his head to the ruckus below. "Whatever is going on now?"

She smiled at his reaction. "The floor committee is calling out the names of the ladies with whom the maskers are to dance. Hence the name 'call out.'"

Steve watched the discordant procedure, only to look at Carol unbelievingly when after the first group of dancers had moved around the floor briefly, it all began again.

"Well, Mr. Randle, what do you think of your first Carnival ball? Would you like to be king for a night? I think you'd look particularly fetching in a blond pageboy wig," she teased him lightly.

"For me to wear panty hose and silver high-heeled pumps, there would have to be greater inducement than the glory of sitting on a papier-mâché throne for a couple of hours."

"His moment of glory isn't over just yet. At midnight the royalty will leave to reassemble somewhere very exclusive, and they'll manage to entertain themselves very well until dawn. The masks come off, and sometimes a lot of inhibitions are shed, as well."

"Any man dressed the way some of these are couldn't have that many inhibitions to start with," he commented.

Her ensuing laughter at his remark was severed by the announcement of her name. She felt the tensing of the man beside her as Ethan Greenlaw spoke.

"I think you had better come with me." She had no need to ask, but the question came involuntarily to her lips.

"Claud?"

"I'll take you home, Carol," Steve offered as he rose to drape her wrap around her shoulders and assisted her to her feet.

"You probably won't be able to get your car out. Many of the spectators are leaving now that the call outs have begun, and there's a small jam at the exits. My car is double-parked at the entrance." His posture shifted tiredly. "If you want to get to Miss Nan anytime soon, Carol, I'll take you now." His eyes then slid to Steve. "If you don't care how long it takes, wait with Randle. But make up your mind because the good graces of that cop won't last forever."

Steve gave her arm a reassuring squeeze. "You can call me later. Right now you need to get home."

He continued to grasp her arm as they followed Ethan to the entrance where the familiar green car stood, a door open as if Ethan had exited in a great hurry. He slipped his lean frame into that door and had the engine revving as Steve walked her to the passenger side, planted a tender kiss on her cheek and assisted her in.

The car screeched out of the portico, hurling Carol violently against the door.

"Can't he keep his damn hands off you even at a time like this?" Ethan's acid tone ate the air.

"He was doing nothing wrong. He was just trying to comfort me." She reached for the seat belt as he rammed the car into a particularly narrow opening in the traffic.

"I suppose you describe all those evenings you spent together while I was in Philadelphia trying to carve out a life for us just his attempt to comfort you." When the driver ahead refused to yield the lane, he brought the powerful car within inches of his back bumper and flashed his headlights onto high beam, muttering shocking obscenities under his breath before he finally had his way.

"I'd like to comfort you," he muttered to himself as he slammed the car abusively into a lower gear. "I'd comfort you until you hadn't an untouched place on your body, a breath in your lungs or an idea in your mind that you didn't belong to me."

Had it not been for her securing her seat belt, his next action would have hurled her through the windshield as he stood on the brakes.

"Damn you to hell! I can't even think because of you!" He reached for the shift and threw the car into reverse, then backed into a service way. "I forgot about Eva. We'll have to go back and face all that traffic around the auditorium."

Unthinkingly she placed a restraining hand on his arm. "No, she...."

"Take your hand off me." The frosty tone of his clipped words stopped the rest of her sentence. By the light of a security lamp, she could see a matching coldness in his face as he stared straight ahead and waited for her to remove her touch.

With exaggerated deliberateness Carol lifted her hand and placed it in her lap. The movement broke the brittle moment, and Ethan expelled an audible breath. He cut the engine and placed both hands on the steering wheel. He still did not look at her, but his voice came huskily from deep within his chest. "Why, Carol? For God's sake, why? I loved you. Heaven help us both, but I loved you to utter distraction."

Past tense. He had loved her. She clicked open the little beaded handbag, found a tissue and blotted at palms suddenly gone damp. The action gave her time to manage the timbre of her own voice. When she spoke, it was to finish the words she had begun when he had reacted so coldly to her innocent touch.

"I was going to say before my touch contaminated you that there is nothing to be gained by bringing Eva from the ball. It won't do Claud any good and will only dampen the spirits of the entire krewe since Claud was a member of that same group for such a long time. Besides, by now the members of the court have probably gone on to supper, and it will be very difficult to discover where."

She placed the soiled tissue in the bag and snapped it shut and in the same voice addressed his accusations.

"I want one thing in the open, whether you believe me or not. Frankly I'm past caring if you do or if you don't. It is the truth that I saw Steve Randle twice during your absence. Lonely, he took lonely me out on New Year's Eve. We had drinks, dinner, and danced. At midnight he kissed me with the same fervor you would kiss *tante* on a similar occasion. The second time was when he gave me a lift to *your* public-relations party. You were a witness to the ultimate outcome of that evening. There was no other intimate contact either night, nor has there been since then. In the name of the love that you profess to have once had for me, don't you ever, *ever* openly accuse or covertly insinuate that anything more has occurred between Steve and me."

He snorted derisively. "What about—"

"Don't say anything more, or I will get out of this car right here and now. I cannot take any more from you tonight."

He watched her briefly while she stared ahead, then he started the car once more and delivered her to the house in a far safer manner.

CHAPTER FOURTEEN

THE REST OF THAT NIGHT and the following morning was a horror tale for Carol. Its recurring motif was the black-ribboned wreath of white chrysanthemums that hung at the gates. She had not acted on Dr. Frahm's advice, and the details swamped her.

René was no help. He scoffed at her panic and suggested she end her problems by scheduling a jazz funeral with a horse-drawn wagon and the Olympia Brass Band. She was so near the breaking point by then that she didn't register Ethan's presence until his dark-skinned hand held out a snifter of brandy to her.

"Here, drink this." His steady eyes watched her until she had taken the first sip, then he turned to her cousin.

"I think you had better get the hell out of here and not come back until you have confirmation that I have decided not to smash in your face." He spoke dispassionately, but his tone was deadly.

"You can't talk to me like that. This is my home, too," René whispered.

"I can and I did. As to the other, just don't count on it." Even Carol raised her head at his last words.

"What do you mean?" René took a stumbling step forward.

"You are taking a chance hanging around here this long after I told you to leave." The menace in Ethan's voice matched the attitude of his stance.

René decided not to pursue his question further but gulped down the last of his bourbon and effected a very awkward exit.

She had to ask. "The house, too, Ethan? Was it part of the package? Is the house yours, too?"

"The house is not mine." He came to stand over her. "Put your feet up on the sofa and close your eyes for a few minutes. If you should fall asleep, I'll wake you in a short while, and we'll discuss what has to be done." He took the glass from her unresisting fingers and waited until she obeyed.

Soon his voice could be heard from the kitchen. She couldn't distinguish the words, but she recognized the tone. He was giving orders.

He didn't need to wake her, after all. When she opened her eyes, he sat in the reclining chair, the footrest up to hold one outstretched leg, while on the raised knee was a note pad on which he was scrawling boldly.

She watched him for an unguarded time, then closed her eyes again just as there came a discreet knock at the door. That was a first. The doors to the family room were never closed. Then she felt the cushions give and a hand on her shoulder. "Wake up, Carol." Ethan sat against her hip while a strange man placed a coffee service and sandwiches on the table.

Carol gave Ethan a questioning look. "Randle sent Thomas to help. Now sit up and have some coffee."

Thomas spoke in well-modulated tones. "Will there be anything else?" Steve had trained him well.

"No, thank you, Thomas," Ethan replied as he extended a hand to her, but she had slept on her arm, and it was full of needles. When she tried shaking it to get the blood back into proper circulation, Ethan took it between his hands to massage it firmly. Her eyes locked with his, and that firm massage became a gentle caress.

Then he was reaching for a cup of coffee. When he looked back at her, there was a matching hunger in his face. "Not now...later." Then he handed her a cup before taking his own and returning to the recliner.

"Eat a sandwich, at least a half, and there's soup in the kitchen if you want some."

She shook her head and bit into the thin ham sandwich. "Aren't you having any?" she asked.

"I ate a huge breakfast at Randle's. I don't think I'm ready for anything yet." He picked up the note pad without commenting on her obvious surprise.

"There's a work detail at the cemetery making any necessary repairs to the crypt. They will put a fresh coat of white on it, too." She hadn't even thought of the condition of the family mausoleum. New Orleans buried its dead above the ground in little houses, a tradition held over from the days before pumps lowered the water level so that coffins no longer floated in watery graves. As a result, the old cemeteries looked like miniature cities.

He ripped off a sheet from the pad, crossed the room and handed it to her. "Here's a list of people who have stated their willingness to serve as pallbearers. The right column would actually serve, the left list would be honorary. Miss Nan has left the decision to you. Check off eight from each list, and Mrs. McLin will call them." He gave her time to study the men who ranged from the socially elite to the bricklayers from the firm. Her final list held names from both ends of the social ladder.

Next, he set about soliciting answers to the other heartrending questions in such a methodical manner that the pain was bearable, but she still felt drained when it was over.

"Go freshen up, and then you should sit with Miss Nan for a while. She's the most vulnerable one right now. I'll call this in to the press, and then I've a few things to attend to."

"Where's Eva?" She had just realized that she hadn't seen Eva since the ball.

"Don't worry about Eva. You take care of yourself and Miss Nan. Eva is around, but she won't be coming near you." That same menacing threat that René had aroused in him reappeared in his eyes and in his voice. "If you can't reach me, call Randle." He gave her hand a little squeeze.

She sat in the semidarkened room for the greater part of the afternoon, listening to the sad reminiscences that Nan's grief poured forth. She could hear the muffled chimes now and then but didn't concern herself with the comings and goings in any part of the house other than that one room.

In the late afternoon she accepted a call from Steve. After she had assured him that they needed nothing, and that she was coping emotionally, he moved to a topic that had been in the back of her mind most of the day.

"Carol, I can't explain anything to you right now, so don't ask. Just listen for a while. In all our conversations about Ethan, not once have you said that you have stopped loving him." He paused for her to attempt a denial.

"As soon as all this is over, he'll probably ask you to talk. When he does, you must listen, regardless of what you feel now. You owe it to yourself, to him, and even to Claud to sit down and listen." At her nervous sound of protest he overrode her words.

"Just give the man a chance. Then if you want his face smashed in, call me."

He had been too logical. She couldn't fight his logic with emotionalism. She would give Ethan his chance, but not just because Steve asked it of her. She wanted a chance, also.

There was no keeping Nan from the Requiem Mass, though it meant she would have to be carried in to the ceremony. With René hovering on the fringe, Steve settled Nan and Eva into the first big black limousine. With Ethan's help, Carol would manage the three distant cousins in the following car.

She had just returned from fetching a forgotten rosary for one of the elderly ladies to find Ethan standing in the foyer holding a familiar garment. She began to balk, but he physically forced her arms into the sleeves of the hated fur.

"Claud knew you didn't sell your honor or his. And I think I can prove it to you after this is over.

Right now you just do as I say and wear this coat as a gesture to Claud. I can't think of a more appropriate time for you to show the world that you two had it straight."

He pulled the soft warmness more closely around her and smiled approvingly as she resignedly slipped her hands into the pockets. Then a frown marred her features, for this wasn't her coat. It looked just like hers, but there was a difference in the set of the pockets.

"Where did you find this coat?" To his puzzlement she began peeling it off, and there in the facing was the monogram E.M.G.—Eva Marie Guerard.

She held the damning initials up for his perusal. "I got this from the closet over there." He indicated the row of closets just across from the stairs, then glanced toward the relatives who sat in the second car that waited with its engine running.

"We don't have time to deal with this now," he muttered as he took the coat from her and draped it over the banister before taking the stairs two at a time. As quickly he returned with a coat about whose ownership neither of them had doubts.

IN THE ANCIENT CEMETERY Ethan held her back as the others began their return to the business of the living. "Steve will be at the house as long as he's needed. Right now you need to make your peace with Claud."

She looked at the crypt gleaming brightly in the rays of the afternoon sun. It was a well-built little house, a structure for its builder to be proud of, the kind of building Claud would have built. She traced her fingers over the slate roof, a good thick slate, not the expensive paper-thin product on the market now or the even worse imitation. She walked around the structure slowly. A good building stood the test of time, just like a good relationship, she thought as she glanced at Ethan, who had walked away to read inscriptions on neighboring monuments to allow her this privacy. But she knew he kept aware of her every movement.

She knelt on the paving stone, heedless of the fur that cushioned her knees. When she raised her eyes again, he stood beside her, a hand extended to help her to her feet.

"The limousine is back for us," he spoke softly.

But the long black car didn't take them to the family home. Instead it deposited them in front of a modern apartment complex several blocks nearer downtown. At the question in her face, he explained. "You've made your peace with Claud. Now you and I have to make peace with each other. I think it will be easier here."

He ushered her into a room of generous proportions that was comfortably furnished in masculine boldness. Taking her coat, he indicated she should sit on the big sofa of brown-and-cream plaid.

She did not take the seat he had suggested but wandered around the room, touching the things that were his, seeing the view of St. Charles the way that he saw it every morning and afternoon.

He watched for a while, then turned to a cabinet and poured drinks for them both. The silence between them became unbearable for her.

"How is the work on the Taalot bid progressing?" It would be a safe topic until they worked out some of the awkwardness between them.

"It's finished and submitted. We should be hearing something within the next six weeks." He held his drink untouched as he watched her move restlessly about the room.

"What do you think your chances are?" She knew she was killing time, and he knew she was killing time, but it seemed necessary to them both.

"As good, if not better, than any other. I submitted the best bid possible. If another company saw something I didn't...." He dismissed the subject with an air of unimportance she had not thought possible. He had been obsessed with the Taalot contract. He had worked like a slave for it, and now he shrugged off the awarding of the contract as if it were a simple single-family dwelling.

"I want you back, Carol." She whirled to face him, her face full of questions. "Under whatever conditions it takes. If it's just as part of the firm, then I'll settle for that to begin with."

"No." How could she return to the offices to be reminded daily of the deal between him and Claud.

"You didn't have to think about it, did you? Just no and that's it." His features betrayed nothing as he stood assessing her, measuring the finality of her word. He took a swallow from the glass, then moved to the desk that sat in front of a long window. From the top drawer he took a thick envelope and two boxes, and aligned them on the polished desk top.

"I wonder how different our lives would be right now if you had told me that the voice on these tapes belonged to Eva?" He indicated the larger of the boxes.

She grimaced at the remembered script of those tapes, and he caught at her pain. "We both deserved better families. Being a third son in the Greenlaw family with all that Landers money at stake is possibly worse than being a Guerard without the Guerard name." His hands raked through his hair.

"When I bought the company, Claud was to help me finance the Taalot bid until more of my family business came into my control, and I could use my inherited assets as I saw fit. Until that time everything is under the control of Clifford." He sneered his eldest brother's name.

"Clifford enjoys power almost as much as he enjoys money, and the way my grandfather Landers set up his will, Clifford had both for a few more years. You can imagine how a person like me reacts to being told what to do at every move."

And she could well imagine, but she allowed him to continue without comment.

"The constant battle between us was killing our mother, so I left to make my way independent of the family. With some money and the prospect of a great deal more, the agreement between Claud and me was perfect. He would carry me until I built up the firm to carry itself, or until I could use my third of the Landers assets to sponsor its growth. We didn't take into consideration anything like his illness." His recital came washing through the room.

"You know I exhausted every financial lead, but big brother was always right in front of me, using that power to slam doors just before I got there. He knew in time I would have to come to him. And I did. But not as meekly as he had anticipated. The only thing I really lost to him was the name. I kept everything else I wanted, but it was a costly battle in every other respect. Do you have any idea what was happening to me in Philadelphia?" He searched her face.

She could only look at him longingly as the memory of her feelings for him surfaced against her will. "I don't suppose it was any help when you called and found me out of my mind." She had settled in the seat he had indicated when they first came in, but he was still standing.

"You can't imagine how close I came to giving it all to Clifford and flying back to you that very same night. He had it all worked out to his advantage, and I made the choice to stay and fight him." His voice lowered. "I should have come back to you."

He slumped at the desk and propped his forehead onto his palms. "I owe you an apology for that scene at the Hyatt. Although I can never justify my attitude toward you that night, maybe you won't think so badly of me if you know what led to that moment."

He flicked an accusing hand toward the box of tapes. "Eva imitates your voice very well under any circumstances, but even better when the listener is at the point of total exhaustion and scared to death that he is losing you." He lifted his head to look at her. "The call that finally found you at the Quarter apartment wasn't the only one I made to you. I called every night...and each was intercepted by a very evil but totally convincing Eva."

His words were like a constricting band around Carol's heart, squeezing out all hope that she and Eva might one day salvage their relationship. Now she knew Eva's hatred for her was far greater than she had ever dreamed.

"When Eva took your calls, you had just left with Steve Randle. When she pretended to be you, the voice was so cold, so annoyed with my attention, and you were either dressing to go out or on your way out with...."

She supplied the words, "Steve Randle."

"How can that much vileness be in a body that looks so much like you? How can that kind of accident happen? How could God place such a bitch behind such a beautiful face?" For a moment she thought he would hurl the tapes across the room. Then he seemed to compress his emotions, and he reached for the envelope.

"There are so many things I should have done differently, and this is probably another." His words were bitter as he weighed the envelope. "I don't know what's in here, but now I can guess. It was in Claud's desk, and I had planned to give it to you the first time I saw you, but then you were so sure Claud would recover that I feared you would think I was burying him prematurely. I wouldn't subject you to whatever is in here and chance your attitude toward me." Again the bitterness welled to the surface. "I didn't need to worry about that, did I? I managed very well on my own."

He rose to hand her the envelope, and she instantly recognized the flamboyant penmanship. She was torn between Ethan's mood and the longing to rip open the letter.

Ethan balanced the second package on his palm, then set it back in the desk drawer. "I'll leave you alone with the letter while I fix us something to eat. You probably skipped lunch." He picked up his drink from the desk and topped it with more liquor, not bothering to temper it with ice or water. Then he left her alone.

She looked for a long time at her name flowing across the envelope in penmanship so uncharacteristic of an engineer who usually did everything in precise block lettering. In the background she could hear Ethan's movements about the kitchen as a drawer banged shut, followed by the rattle of utensils.

She eased her thumbnail beneath the loosely sealed flap. First she read the long letter hastily, then started over. It was not her grandfather who spoke to her, surely not. Claud had never been this humble apologetic man.

He began before the day that had changed Carol's world. He began with his first suspicions that within the company there was a confidence breach, and how he had begun the process of eliminating suspects, a list on which Carol's name had never appeared, not even when the man accused her and played the damning tapes. Instead, it was those tapes that identified the true culprit to him, as it had to Carol. And as the memory of predinner conversations between him and Carol were recalled, so were the pointed questions of Eva. He remembered how at first he had been startled at Eva's interest in the company and then pleased. He had thought Eva was developing an interest in the firm, that there might be a place for her there. But with the accusation and the details of the dishonorable transaction, Claud had seen the purpose behind Eva's attention. It was the knowledge that his own blood had betrayed them both that had made him lash out at everyone, including Carol who had been present during the acuteness of his pain.

He explained his purpose in staying away from the house. He had been waiting in the office for a confession, and in that week, he *had* confessions, confessions from people who had no possible access to the information divulged to the competition, confessions from the men of the company who had heard the rumors and wanted to comfort Claud and who wanted to protect Carol. And the architect came, willing to sacrifice his reputation to save Carol's. But still Claud had waited, waited for one more person to come to him. And when he finally acknowledged that Eva would never make her confession, it had been too late. Carol had gone. Each word was permeated with his sense of guilt, his loss, his loneliness for her.

He went on to explain why he had not made restitution to Carol in her absence, why he had not proclaimed her innocence to the city. To do that would require an equally public announcement of Eva's role, and that would have destroyed not just Eva, but Nan. His primary concern was Nan, but neither could he deny the claim of Eva. Guilty as she was, he couldn't close the only dimension in which she functioned. And he had allowed the continued sacrifice of Carol, though he had not meant it to be all-inclusive.

He had thought she would return, and he could make it all come right again. He concluded with words of love, the message she had been too long without.

Carol refolded the pages, but when she went to replace them, there was another thin sheet clinging to the insides of the heavy envelope. It was a kind of codicil dated much later. After she had read that carefully, she replaced everything and rose from the sofa.

In the doorway of the small dining room she stood to watch Ethan as he placed the silver in neat alignment. He had removed his coat and tie, and she smiled at the mark of concentration between his eyes as he performed the domestic chore. When he sensed her presence, he looked up to raise a questioning brow.

"He knew. He had always known." Her composure faded a little. "I should have believed in him and stayed here. I should not have gone off half-demented but listened to my heart."

He picked up his drink from the buffet and emptied its contents in a gulp. "It's a fault we're both guilty of," he stated flatly as he surveyed the table. "Everything is ready and sitting in the microwave. Something Gracie had sent over. All I have to do is turn it on, but it's still early yet. Let's have another drink." As he moved toward her and the room she had just left, a memory came of another apartment and another meal to which Gracie had made a contribution.

In the living room he poured himself a refill after Carol had refused another. She had never known

Ethan to drink so much, and from her seat in the corner of the sofa she kept a wary eye on him as he moved restlessly around the room. First he picked up a cigar, then put it back only to pick it up again.

She broke into his pacing pattern. "It's my turn to apologize. I did you an injustice, too." He looked at her with doubt, moving once more to the row of bottles. "Ethan...." The amount of alcohol he was consuming was alarming her. He saw and understood her concern.

"Come sit here," she indicated the other end of the sofa. He lounged down beside her to sit staring at the lighted end of the cigar.

"You don't owe me anything. I should have let you know from the beginning where I stood with the firm," he ground out before setting his teeth into the wooden tip of his cigar.

"Yes, Ethan, I do. I know now that there was nothing untoward in the deal. Claud explained that, too. He knew Eva and René had been seeking a market for their shares. And he was tired, perhaps because he wasn't well." She paused to pray that he hadn't given in because she had abandoned him.

"He sold the firm to you because he wanted to know and trust whoever gained control of something to which he had given so much of his life. I should never have said those things in your office. Claud wanted me completely free of any ties to Guerard Construction so that I could make whatever choice I wanted in life, unhampered by family responsibility. He was setting me free to be whatever I want—engineer, playgirl." Her voice tapered off as she added, "wife, mother." She swallowed the lump in her throat and continued. "He never intended me to have the firm. I know that now."

He eyed her closely. "Then the settlement with my brother doesn't bother you anymore?" At her negative nod he rose to move toward the liquor stock but turned back toward the desk again. The late afternoon sun spilled across the desk top to send a gold reflection to his face that did not hide the ashen hue.

"And will you be happy without the firm? Can you settle for a husband and children?" This time her heart did stop as he came to stand over her as he qualified, "Our children?"

"I could."

"Then what in God's name is holding us back. Why are you fighting us?" He reached down to haul her to her feet.

She met his penetrating glare with a matching look. "You want the truth?"

This time it was he who answered with a nod.

"I don't know how long it will take me to overcome the hurt of you and Claud trading me as if I were an open-market commodity. I don't know how to adjust to your having bought me and Claud having sold me. How do I accept being an economic good to the two men that I love?"

"What in hell are you talking about?" It was the old demanding Ethan thrust against her. "What do you mean Claud and I traded you?" It was like a scene repeated as his hands bit into her shoulders. Then he was dragging her across the room, kicking open the door to a bedroom, his bedroom. A slanting ray of sun speared the few inches between them. When he moved closer to her, the ray fell across his firm mouth but left his eyes in shadow so that the pupils enlarged to leave only a thin ring of mist gray. It created a desperate wildness in his face.

Then he turned her away from his hungry look. She reached up to push back a strand of hair that had slipped from the neat coil she had styled to match the severe dress of mourning black. That hand trembled as she took in the gigantic collage before her. "Why?" It was the only word she could manage as she took one step nearer. The wall in his bedroom rivaled the one in the den of the old house, but this one portrayed only one subject—Carol. And she was repeated over and over in all the poses from her office collection, in pictures that had been in Claud's office, in shots that she had forgotten about, and in candid pictures that she knew must have been taken since her return. She turned to face him, her question repeated in her eyes.

His answer came thickly. "This is where it began. I have loved you since the first time I saw this picture." He turned her again, this time to see an enlarged black-and-white press shot of her. In the pose she stood with her head thrown back to stare skyward at the progress of a steel skeleton rising tall in the background, and under her arm were rolls of blueprints, and on her head the hard hat bearing the Guerard logo.

"It has always been you, and with every detail Claud shared with me I loved you more, and he knew it, so he was generous. The rumor that he gave you to me probably comes from the last words he spoke before he slipped into his coma. You know that he was at a site when he was stricken, and that his workers were all around him. He said that I was to take care of his girls and he named Miss Nan, Eva and you. That's why I was with Eva so much—I was taking care of her, advising her about her finances, trying to direct her away from some of the shallow crowd that she favors. That's why I took her out." He paused to rest his cheek on her head.

"And maybe sometimes I would kiss her while I pretended she was you. But it was never more than a kiss, and the pretense was only a second, for she was never you and couldn't ever take your place."

He pulled her back against him and held her pressed against him. She knew he fought his need to do more than hold her.

"When Claud said in front of all those construction workers that the company was mine, and that you belonged to me, they were right in their belief that I paid for you, too. I have, but only with my love."

He turned her to face him and said it again. "I love you." There was no triumph in the moment, yet he reached to remove the pins that held her hair in restraint, to release the shimmering strands to cascade about her shoulders. He moved his hands into the tresses, separating them with his fingers. "If money would make you mine when my love has failed, there would be no price too high to pay. I'm begging, Carol." His voice broke, and he didn't try to hide it. "I'm going quietly out of my mind. You must say something... anything. I can't...."

"Yes." That one word was all she could say, and she repeated, "Yes." There was no reservation in that yes. It was the yes he had waited for, the one that said there was nothing held back. The time was right, and he knew what that little word meant.

He did not ask her to explain or to clarify. He had only one question. "Will it make us crazy if we sleep in the sunlight?"

"I'm willing to take the chance," she answered. "Are you?"

His reply was to lead her away from her repeated image to the king-size bed, where he folded back the covers. Then he turned back to her and reached for the row of crêpe-covered buttons that began at her shoulder and marched diagonally across her breast to her hip and down the side of the skirt.

She stopped him after he opened the first. Placing a stilling hand over his, she spoke. "No."

There was a flash of puzzlement in his eyes, but as she continued the process begun by him and each button released exposed more of her silken flesh, his look warmed as he silently watched her undress for him.

Even when she stood naked before him, he didn't question. It wasn't until he had laid her on the cream-colored sheets, and he had joined her to lie in the warm sun stripes cast through the shutters that he asked, "Why didn't you want me to undress you?"

By then his hands were on her. He couldn't stop them as he was compelled to touch her in quest of the secret places, to touch her experimentally in search of the nerve endings that would unleash all the power of her woman ways.

HEART'S AWAKENING

Through the tantalizing pleasure of his assessing hands she answered. "Later I may not know how to do the things you need. I may hesitate when you think I shouldn't. I thought my undressing for you might restate that I am holding nothing back, that I am yours, and that I have come to you freely."

His voice was as gentle as the stroking hands. "Are you afraid?"

She smilingly shook her head, unable to speak as he revealed one of those magic places and brought her in a breathless arch against him. As he moved on in his preliminary measurement of her sensuality, she relaxed against the pillows.

"Are you?" she asked of him.

The hands stilled, the kisses across her shoulders and breast stopped. "Yes."

"Why?"

"Because of the hurt I might bring to you."

She searched his face carefully and knew he spoke the truth. "I'm not afraid of your hurting me. Don't you think I know what to expect from our making love?"

He lay his head against her breast. "Oh, my love, my fear has nothing to do with what pain there might be if we make love. That pain is only once and then never again. It's a fear rooted in all the past pain I've cost you. I'm afraid to trust our future."

"If?" She rose on her elbow to nudge him off her and onto his back. Deliberately, provocatively she measured her body against his, feeling the abrasive quality of the hair mat of his chest against her sensitized breasts.

"If?" she questioned to the hissing intake of his breath as she imitated his earlier seeking ways.

"If...." The third repeating of the conditional word was vocalized into his mouth as he moved against her tender torment of him. His anxiety for their future together was erased by the long hard kiss that effectively camouflaged his effortless maneuvering of her beneath him.

Now he no longer had to hunt the magic places. He knew them, and he unerringly brought his touch to them, his moist kisses and the tantalizing teasing flick of his tongue, urging her, driving her, forcing her upward into a shared realm where they would physically express the spiritual love they held for one another.

"I love you. Oh God, how I love you," she managed through the exquisiteness of their erotic passion. He took her to the quivering edge, an edge so narrow that to stay there brought shadowed pain. When he knew it was time to make the commitment either to the pain or to the pleasure, he brought his mouth back to hers, and she could taste him and taste herself blended on his lips and tongue. The wonder of that elusive flavor was the last semirational thought she had before the blinding power of her own fulfillment, his fulfillment burst inside her, coursing, crashing, raging through her in pulsating high tidal surges that forced out the low moan of satiety and the unqualified final everlasting commitment to this man—interpreted and recorded in a shared triumph of climactic completeness.

The sheen of their love-slicked bodies shimmered in the sunlight. She reached up a tired hand to smooth back the dark hair from his damp brow. The afterglow was too fragile, too tender, too perfect to risk the intrusion of words. He kissed the palm of that hand, the rosy tip of each breast and the corner of her tender mouth. Then he rolled to his back, bringing her with him neatly tucked against his side. He held her close, and they slept in the fading western light—man and woman together.

IT WAS THE CLICKING of the wooden rings along the drapery rod that wakened her, that and the expanse of empty bed. There was a spill of light that illuminated Ethan as he adjusted the draperies across the shuttered windows. When he turned to her and saw that she watched him, there was an instant and overwhelming softening to his features.

"I've scattered rice and taken the double precaution of placing the broom behind the door. The moon is rising, but I've closed the draperies just in time. So we don't need to fear either the *cauchemar* or going crazy in the moonlight," he teased as he resettled beside her to kiss her so lovingly that it brought a wash of tears to her eyes. She squeezed her lids tightly, not wanting him to misunderstand. He had been frightened of hurting her, and she carried that same responsibility for him.

It was the slide of smooth gold across her breast that brought her eyes open. Then Ethan dangled the contents of the second smaller box he had left unopened earlier. It was a small golden kiss adorning the key chain she had given him for Christmas. Now it bore a single key, a key she recognized when he placed it in her hand.

"You asked yesterday if the house belonged to me. It hasn't for a while now." Her eyes moved from the golden confection to his face, and he read her question.

"I bought it the same time I bought *most* of the company. Claud's ultimate plan was for him and Nan to retire to the bayou country. He thought it might help stabilize Eva if she had to face the world on her own. He had been leasing the house from me until he had everything settled. It was part of the package until you in your temper foolishly gave your share of the firm away. That was when I transferred the title to your name, to pay for the share. I knew that in your given frame of mind, you would never accept money."

"What about Eva? Does she know?" The habit of picking up after her family, of being concerned, was too ingrained.

"She does." A brief bitterness colored his face. "I gave that distinctly nasty job to Steve Randle a few minutes ago when I called to check on Miss Nan. I thought he owed it to me since he was probably the one who repeated that tale to you."

"Ethan, you won't hold that against him, will you?" There was so much that was so vulnerable beneath Steve's iceberg calmness that she didn't want him being hurt because of something done and past.

He saw the concern in her eyes, but he did not misinterpret it. He knew they would never have that doubt between them. They had proclaimed their right to one another in a pledge that would be repeated over and over in their future together.

"No, when he told Eva that she and her damn coat have to be out of there within a week, he paid his debt to me." He smoothed the crease of concern from between her brows with a caressing thumb. "Carol, she had to go if we're to live there. Miss Nan can remain, but we will not risk Eva's influence over our children. They have to grow up like you, not like her."

"Children? Ethan...."

"I know. We may be needing the nursery a little too soon." He took the key from her unresisting hold and placed it on the bedside table as he added in a husky voice, "And if we haven't already begun our family, there is a very likely possibility we may yet before this night is over."

CAROL BROUGHT the snappy little car to an abrupt halt in front of the steel skeleton of the Taalot building that was rising skyward a foot an hour, in excess of two floors each week. She was late, and Ethan would be furious.

She made her way to the portable building that housed the on-site offices for Landers Construction, returning the greetings of the workers. At the metal building she had the supervisor page Ethan, who was at the top of the structure.

"He says for you to come topside," Mark relayed Ethan's instructions.

"No, you tell him that he has to come down here." She noted the puzzlement of Mark at her demand made of a man who issued commands, not received them.

She sat for a while on a high stool while she waited for Ethan. Through the window she saw Steve talking with one of his operators. She left her perch to join him. They spoke closely, and soon his operator was scurrying away. And across the construction rubble that was always strewn around an active site no matter how frequently the big trucks hauled it away, she saw Ethan striding angrily toward her.

Across the space he expressed his impatience with her, almost running over Steve's operator who was arranging a ladder beneath the big sign that announced the essentials of the building towering out of the earth.

"Carol, what's the matter with you? You of all people know I don't have time to waste running up and down this building at your whims." He stood with his arms akimbo in amazement as she skirted him and began to climb the ladder secured against the sign.

"What are you doing? Get down from there. There are a hundred things I need you to do." He eyed the small group of workers who were beginning to gather around the strange scene.

"Get someone else to do them. I quit," she called down from her perch, where she was calmly marking through the title that followed her name.

"What are you talking about?" He looked at Steve, who only shrugged his shoulders and grinned even more broadly.

"You have to hire a new structural engineer. I told you, I quit." She leaned back to admire her artwork.

Ethan eyed her skeptically. "You might as well

have quit yesterday for all the help you've been today. Where have you been?"

"Out," she replied flippantly, deliberately prolonging her disruption of Ethan's calmness. She knew she had him at a raging pitch now, but he was determined not to yank her from the ladder and create an even greater scene in front of the ever growing crowd of men.

"Out where?" The words came through clenched teeth.

"Out getting a new job," she grinned down at him, deepening the little dimple in her chin.

"Oh," his body tensed. "What kind of job?"

"Something I've never done before, but something I've been looking into for quite a while. I had just about given up on ever getting this particular job, but all of a sudden when I least expected it, I qualified." She moved on the ladder to expose a small portion of the sign that had once read "Machinery supplied by Randle Equipment." She had neatly crossed out the first word and written about it in heavy black letters *parrain*.

A cheer went up from the local workmen, and several reached over to slap Ethan on the back with hearty congratulatory thumps. At the look of utter confusion on his face, Carol relented in her taunting of him.

"Oh, Yankee boy, when are you ever going to learn the language?" She spoke softly as she came down the ladder. He had been watching her, but then his eyes lifted to the sign. His title and Carol's title had both been neatly crossed out and replaced with words in a language he did speak. At first he stood in total disbelief while the import of the lettered message soaked in, and then his grin broke widely, and Carol's bubbling laughter was no longer singular.

As Ethan pulled his wife into his arms to hold her in a protectively joyous embrace, neither heard the movements of the workers back to their assigned tasks, all at the urging of the *parrain* who was already planning a very active role as godfather to Ethan and Carol's first child.

What readers say about SUPERROMANCE

"Bravo! Your SUPERROMANCE [is]...super!"
R.V.,* Montgomery, Illinois

"I am impatiently awaiting the next SUPERROMANCE."
J.D., Sandusky, Ohio

"Delightful...great."
C.B., Fort Wayne, Indiana

"Terrific love stories. Just keep them coming!"
M.G., Toronto, Ontario

*Names available on request.

FREE!
THIS GREAT SUPERROMANCE

SUPERROMANCE

LOVE BEYOND DESIRE

RACHEL PALMER

EXCITING OFFER FROM WORLDWIDE

Yours FREE, with a home subscription to
SUPERROMANCE™

Now you never have to miss reading the newest **SUPERROMANCES**... because they'll be delivered right to your door.

Start with your **FREE** LOVE BEYOND DESIRE. You'll be enthralled by this powerful love story... from the moment Robin meets the dark, handsome Carlos and finds herself involved in the jealousies, bitterness and secret passions of the Lopez family. Where her own forbidden love threatens to shatter her life.

Your **FREE** LOVE BEYOND DESIRE is only the beginning. A subscription to **SUPERROMANCE** lets you look forward to a long love affair. Month after month, you'll receive four love stories of heroic dimension. Novels that will involve you in spellbinding intrigue, forbidden love and fiery passions.

You'll begin this series of sensuous, exciting contemporary novels... written by some of the top romance novelists of the day... with four every month.

And this big value... each novel, almost 400 pages of compelling reading... is yours for only $2.50 a book. Hours of entertainment every month for so little. Far less than a first-run movie or pay-TV. Newly published novels, with beautifully illustrated covers, filled with page after page of delicious escape into a world of romantic love... delivered right to your home.

Begin a long love aff[air] with
SUPERROMANCE.
Accept LOVE BEYOND DESIRE, **FREE**.

Complete and mail the coupon below, today!

FREE! Mail to: SUPERROMANCE

In the U.S.
1440 South Priest Drive
Tempe, AZ 85281

In Canada
649 Ontario St.
Stratford, Ontario N5A 6W2

YES, please send me FREE and without any obligation, my **SUPERROMANCE** novel, LOVE BEYOND DESIRE. If you do not hear from me after I have examined my FREE book, please send me the 4 new **SUPERROMANCE** books every month as soon as they come off the press. I understand that I will be billed only $2.50 for each book (total $10.00). There are no shipping and handling or any other hidden charges. There is no minimum number of books that I have to purchase. In fact, I may cancel this arrangement at any time. LOVE BEYOND DESIRE is mine to keep as a FREE gift, even if I do not buy any additional books.

NAME _____ (Please Print)

ADDRESS _____ APT. NO.

CITY _____

STATE/PROV. _____ ZIP/POSTAL CODE _____

SIGNATURE (If under 18, parent or guardian must sign.)

This offer is limited to one order per household and not valid to present subscribers. Prices subject to change without notice. Offer expires
Offer expires February 28, 1983

PR20